P9-BBU-621

On the Edge of the Woods

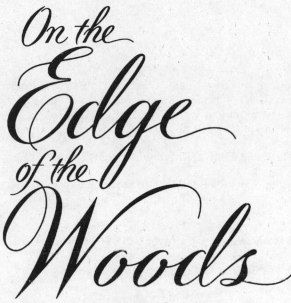

On the Edge of the Woods

A GOTHIC NOVEL

DIANE TYRREL

BERKLEY SENSATION, NEW YORK

This is a work of fiction. Names, characters, places, and incidents either are the product of the author's imagination or are used fictitiously, and any resemblance to actual persons, living or dead, business establishments, events, or locales is entirely coincidental.

ON THE EDGE OF THE WOODS: A GOTHIC NOVEL

A Berkley Sensation Book / published by arrangement with
the author

Copyright © 2004 by Diane Partie Tyrrel.
Excerpt from *Dead to the World* copyright © 2004 by Charlaine Harris Schulz.
Cover design by George Long.
Interior text design by Julie Rogers.

All rights reserved.
This book, or parts thereof, may not be reproduced in any form without permission. The scanning, uploading, and distribution of this book via the Internet or via any other means without the permission of the publisher is illegal and punishable by law. Please purchase only authorized electronic editions, and do not participate in or encourage electronic piracy of copyrighted materials.
Your support of the author's rights is appreciated.
For information address: The Berkley Publishing Group,
a division of Penguin Group (USA) Inc.,
375 Hudson Street, New York, New York 10014.

ISBN: 0-7394-3995-2

BERKLEY SENSATION™
Berkley Sensation Books are published by The Berkley Publishing Group,
a division of Penguin Group (USA) Inc.,
375 Hudson Street, New York, New York 10014.
BERKLEY SENSATION and the "B" design
are trademarks belonging to Penguin Group (USA) Inc.

PRINTED IN THE UNITED STATES OF AMERICA

Brand's Journal

October 22, 1993

Continued the survey today, without Ralph. Saw a woman on the Shapiro property, down in the woods, standing with her hands in the pockets of her jacket, her face tilted up, staring up at the tops of the trees, her long black hair curling and tangled down her back. Striking. I fumbled for the transit and caught her in my sight. I felt like a voyeur. She turned her face to me, black-Irish complexion, that creamy, slightly flushed pure skin, dark brows — her eyes were the thing I can't put out of my mind. Blazing, alert.

She nodded in greeting and I felt like she had turned me to stone.

January 13

The Shapiro house has been sold. They put the "sold" sign up on the property today. I want to punch a hole in the wall.

January 21

Met my new neighbor today, the one who scooped me on the Shapiro property. She's the woman I saw there in the woods several months ago. Tess brought her in for lunch. I was torn between an unreasonable resentment and an overwhelming interest in her. I wanted to be with her, but I kept saying horrible things to her. I don't think she likes me much.

Chapter One

IN THE STRANGE bed in the mountain lodge, I woke from a dream. It had the emotional quality of an oracle, deep significance, like a premonition of falling in love. Later that morning, when I saw the house for the first time, I thought I knew what the dream had meant.

"Now this one is *really* special. Just wait till you *see* it."

Uh-oh. I sneaked Russ a look of alarm over the front seat of Iona's big Buick.

We passed between two stone pillars which marked the entrance of the private drive off the main road. I gazed out my window in awe as we entered an avenue of immense trees, incense cedar and sugar pine, great straight trunks thrusting straight up through the shadowy canopy of green into the sky. The trees gave way to a meadow where the drive ended in a leisurely circle. Down in a cleft of the meadow stood a stout white house with a little garden in the front, a fence of pickets surrounding it like an untidy ribbon on a package. There was a curious animation about the place—I could imagine fairies and elves making their homes in the garden and woods around the house.

"Is that it?" Russ, who was sitting in the back seat, sounded severely disappointed.

"No, no, no—that's the neighbor's place," Iona assured him. "A much smaller property."

"It seems familiar to me," I said.

"Does it?"

"But it couldn't be. I've never been here before."

"Déjà vu," said Iona portentously.

"It's not the sort of house you would mistake for another," said Russ. "It's rather an odd-looking thing, isn't it?"

"It's a little white barn," I said. "I like the dormer windows. But where is the house we've come to see?"

"Just wait till you see how close it is," Iona said. "You won't believe how secluded it feels."

"So the two houses share a driveway?" My brother Russ was a contractor, and he had that critical eye, which was why I had asked him to accompany me on a property-hunting expedition in the Sierra. Now I wondered if that had been such a great idea—he couldn't find a thing right with any of the houses we had seen.

"The two houses share the access," said Iona in her breezy Realtor's voice. "It's actually a county road, which is lucky, because they maintain the road in the winter. But otherwise it's a completely private drive."

We drove to the end of the meadow and turned off into a parking area designated by a log lying between the gravel and the woods. Parked in front of the white house was a rusty old International, a big pickup truck, and a tiny yellow sports car. If that was the neighbor's house, where was the house we had come to see? There was no real estate sign. All I could see were trees.

We climbed out of the car, stretching our bodies and breathing deeply of the cold sharp air, so clean and intoxicating, layered with the spice of pine and cedar, the sweetly decaying soil, and the winds blowing down from the high Sierra.

"Damn, it's *quiet* here," said Russ.

"Yes, isn't it peaceful?" Iona hesitated, took a deep breath. "Now, this one is just the craziest thing you've ever seen. Folks around here still call it *The Apple Ranch*—you'll see the remnants of the orchards in the back—it was once quite a large estate. The house is really not in the best condition, but maybe you could do something with it, Stacy. At such a low price, I do think it will move quickly, once the papers are in order, and that should only be a matter of days—"

"The papers—?" said Russ.

"The lady who owns the place is very old, and recently she had to go into a nursing home," Iona explained. "And there's been some delay with the paperwork, so actually the property hasn't even been listed yet. You're lucky to be seeing it before anyone else."

We passed through an arch of tangled berry bushes and ivy and into a clearing where the house came into view. Though it was half hidden in its cloak of woods, I could see it was large, almost a mansion, a turn-of-the century rural manor house that had been expanded and renovated through the years, incorporating a variety of styles that somehow managed to complement one another— white clapboard siding, fat Ionic columns, gingerbread gables, quaint dormer windows, and a wide wraparound porch. All around the house, the overgrown woods leaned in. A giant black oak twisted up from the ground near the entry, arching over the front corner of the house. All the growth tangled around the house made me think of it as a shy wild girl hiding beneath her unkempt hair.

The house had been magnificent once, and still was, but as we came nearer it seemed to sag with neglect. Where the paint could be seen it was chipped and graying, and the old shutters hung limp from the windows, banging softly in the breeze. Aggressive arms of wild rose and blackberry twisted around the balusters and corbels, hung from the gutters, and all but covered an old stone fountain in the front yard. Feathery limbs of weedy young cedar trees crowded the house and sprouted from what had once been a lawn.

"It looks haunted," Russ whispered to me as we mounted the steps to the front door.

The porch was partially screened, breezy, and wide, but I

wondered if the rotted, springy boards beneath my feet would give way when we walked on them. An old porch swing stood in the corner near a couple of wicker chairs, their once white painted surfaces now peeling and gray, like the paint on the house. I walked down to the end of the porch and leaned over the railing until I could see, through the tangle of trees, the white house across the meadow, the steep gray roof with its little dormers and chimneys. I had thought it large when first I'd seen it, but now, when compared to this house, it seemed modest.

Iona unlocked the door, struggling to get it open, and for a moment it stuck. Russ stepped up beside her and wedged his boot against the threshold. There was a brief contest, and the door groaned open.

"Don't think it wants us to come in," Russ said, and when Iona wasn't looking, he made a face at me.

We wandered into the house like we were entering a cave, crouching a little as if expecting bats to rise flapping out of the shadows. It was cold, dark, dank, and musty, and the air reeked of something foul—a thick, nauseating odor of something decayed, long neglected, ill, or dead. The faded gray wallpaper was peeling and miserable. The floor creaked beneath us. But the entry hall was spacious and formal, and a generous staircase with a carved oak banister curved gracefully up to the second-floor gallery. Large double doors trimmed with wide moldings led off to rooms on either side of the entry hall, and beyond the staircase on the ground floor the hall extended to accommodate more doors opening to other rooms.

"Oh . . . this must have been something once," I said quietly, trying not to betray the strange exhilaration that had risen inside me. This house could be made beautiful again, I thought.

But Russ looked doubtful. It was an impressive-looking old house, sure, but we could actually feel the floor swaying as we walked on it. I wondered if there was anything left of the foundation—and I wondered what was wrong with the place, besides the obvious. My mind was busy, calculating and skeptical, but I was still laden with the deep emotional sensuality left over from my dream. Practical considerations seemed to be calling from a distance.

Iona led us through the arched doorway on the left side of the entry hall into a large room with tall windows, lavish moldings, exquisitely beautiful light fixtures, and coved ceilings of crumbling plaster.

"The front parlor!" declared Iona, with a gesture of ironic graciousness. The room was jammed with furniture, cardboard boxes, piles of books, papers, dead potted plants, old gardening catalogs and medicine bottles. Everything was coated thick with dust. The dark avocado-green shag carpet was littered with scraps of paper, dried apple cores and orange peels, empty TV dinner boxes, and old receipts. Despite the high ceilings and large windows, the room was gloomy.

I went to the window and tried to move the heavy gray drapes aside. I wanted to get a sense of how the light might enter the room. But the drapes had been nailed tight to the corners of the window frame—and all the windows were similarly barricaded. It was strange.

Iona reached up to help me pry the drapery away from the window and suddenly the wood trim gave way and the whole thing came down on us, plastic drapes, hardware and all. Not a good sign. I glanced at Russ, who shook his head regretfully. We couldn't help laughing. Iona was embarrassed.

"Now I'll be sued," she said.

Sunlight came in feebly through the waxy smudged glass, dusty with the lace of velvety old spider webs, dotted with the remains of dead flies. The room was hardly brighter with the drapery off, but I could see the window was well proportioned and glazed with its original wavy glass.

"Possibilities?" Iona suggested brightly.

We wandered through the house, alternately awed and appalled. Everywhere was trash and clutter; in the hallways, spilling out of closets, piled in corners—clothing and dishes, stacks of paper, old catalogues, books and magazines. In one room there was a torn-up bird, gray feathers scattered over the ubiquitous avocado-green carpet, wall to wall. And the heavy dank smell permeated everything in the house.

We climbed the staircase to the second floor. I was nervous, dubious about the structural integrity of the place, but the treads were firm and the banister seemed solid.

The place was strange, but I was excited. Beneath the dust and garbage were spacious rooms with high ceilings and elegant detailing. The house was large and of grand proportions—much more of a project than I had imagined taking on. It needed a lot of work. It was way beyond what I had envisioned.

"Possibilities," I said, reaching out with the word. I watched Russ carefully, waiting to see if he would laugh. The place, admittedly, was a mess. But he had on his poker face.

"It's being sold as is," said Iona.

"I can't imagine why," Russ murmured.

"The owner will carry financing. She'll have to. No bank would loan on the place. It's got great potential—but it's definitely a fixer-upper, isn't it?"

Which is what I wanted. I glanced at Russ. "What do you think?" I mouthed at him when Iona turned her head.

Russ was looking the place over with his critical eye. His expression was grim.

I thought, well, that's it. Undoubtedly, the place will have to be condemned. Already I felt regret for what might have been.

But perhaps it would be a relief to discover my plans were absurd. Maybe I would go home to San Francisco completely disenchanted with my dream of buying a house in the mountains. Maybe when I got home, there would be a message on my machine, and his voice would startle me with its warm familiarity: *Stacy, it's been too long. I need to see you—*

Ah, Justin. There you are.

His voice invaded my thoughts less and less frequently these days, but still he came to mind, insistent, so strong at times, I had trouble resisting him.

"Stacy, come look at this." Russ waved to me from a

doorway on the second floor. "This bathroom looks like it was added. It's old, but it's later than the original construction. Look at this door detail. This kind of stuff cracks me up. They didn't even bother *trying* to match the trim here."

"Put this in *Architectural Digest*," I said, tapping the countertop, which was covered with plastic shelf paper, yellow with brown butterflies. "What was underneath that contact paper must have been *really* bad if this was considered an improvement."

"You're just too darned fussy, girl." Russ fluffed the hair on the top of my head. "Wow." He stopped, frozen. "Will you look at that? An honest-to-God cast iron claw-foot bathtub. Ooh, baby."

"There's another one in the bath down the hall," I told him. "And look, all the doors have these beautiful glass doorknobs."

"Which probably don't work very well."

The house was large enough to get lost in. Various additions and "improvements" had turned the rear of the building into a labyrinth of stairways, halls, closets, and curious rooms all jumbled together and strange, but somehow it retained a curious charm, like a child's building-block castle. There were some peculiar details here and there, like the contact-paper countertop, but we found interesting little windows in the stairwell, beautiful cabinetry and woodwork throughout the house, and whimsical oddities in the architecture that showed a graceful, if eccentric, hand in design. Russ and I explored the place, cracking jokes when Iona wasn't near enough to hear us. Russ enjoyed riffing on the construction flaws in any building he happened to visit, and this old house provided plenty of material for comedy.

"Come look at this," Iona called. We were all up on the second floor. "This bedroom is just grand, isn't it?"

"Just *grand*." Russ mouthed Iona's words, affecting a foppish pose. I gave him a slug on the arm as I passed him going through the doorway into the bedroom.

The room *was* grand. Or it had been, once. There was a lovely, ragged old four-poster bed with finials carved to look like pine cones. A neoclassical writing desk stood on its four

straight legs in the curved bay window, one of the few windows in the house not fixed with dark coverings. Through
the branches of the big black oak I could see the strange
white house in the meadow, its three dormer windows set
into its wide gray roof, giving it the look of a face gazing
back at me.

"This must have been *her* room, I suppose," said Iona.

I turned away from the window and looked over the room
again. Against the far wall stood a heavy dresser with a
smoky mirror, its drawers open and spilling out old clothing
and papers. I crossed the room slowly, feeling the creak of
the floorboards beneath my feet, drawn to the mirror. I felt
compelled to see if I had changed since I had come into this
house. I felt as if I had.

My eyes, flashing back at me in the mirror, *were* larger
and darker than usual, somehow balancing a brow that often
seemed too fierce. There was an expression of unnatural
glowing about my eyes, as if I had ingested amphetamines.
Dark tangled curls set off an unfamiliar face, like a frame
around a pale cameo, glowing indistinct and ghostly in the
old silvered glass. The gothic wildness of my image in the
mirror was so different from how I usually pictured myself—businesslike, neat, professional—that I was startled
and actually wondered for a moment if it *was* me.

"*Boo.*"

I let out a yelp and jumped, bumping into the large warm
male body.

Russ. His handsome sunburned face appeared suddenly
next to mine in the mirror.

"Kinda jumpy, aren't ya?" he grinned.

I shoved him away. "Don't *do* that to me, Russ," I
snapped at him.

"Come on, Narcissus," he said, pulling me away from my
own reflection, linking his arm through mine. "There's lots
more to see in this fun house."

Downstairs, at the far end of the house, we found a paneled library with a stone fireplace, floor-to-ceiling book-
cases of mellow aged cherry, exquisite handcrafted
cabinetry, a marble fireplace and, beneath the piles of junk

and layers of grime, a floor of black and white marble tile set in a classic pattern of large and small diamonds. Arched windows topped two sets of double French doors leading out to a stone terrace. It was a wonderful space, marred only by a large green-painted plywood closet, which had been constructed in the corner of the room with no thought to styling nor quality of building materials. *Pity*, I thought, the green closet spoiled the look of the room. But it could be removed. Russ would say: "We *have* the technology."

But *did* we have the technology? Or rather, did I have the money, not to mention the heart—you'd need a strong one—to make this place right again?

"Think about it, Stacy—the golf course, swimming pool, weight room, private decks overlooking the bay, gardeners once a week . . ." Justin's voice invaded my thoughts again, but this time it was memory, rather than fantasy. He had wanted us to buy a house in an exclusive gated community we had been invited to join. We had come awfully close—visiting the model homes together on several occasions, talking to real estate agents, checking out financing. But somehow it had never happened. Justin grew angry with me, accusing me of "dropping the ball" with the loan people, with the paperwork—and after all, he was right. I didn't make it happen. I thought wistfully of the clean, easy life we might have led, the two of us, with the pool, the weight room, the gardeners. I had been tempted, but repelled, too. I told myself that was natural. Fear of change, and all that. But increasingly Justin was impatient. He wanted to live with me, he said. But I found myself becoming bitter toward him, that he would press for this move without offering or asking for any sort of commitment on a deeper level. Oh, sometimes he talked about marriage and having kids, but only in the most lighthearted, even cynical, way. Like it was something *other* people did, people who weren't that bright.

Certainly if I bought this property, this old apple ranch, any opportunity for buying into that gated community with Justin would be effectively finished. The very idea of sinking money into this white elephant was just the sort of folly that would tax Justin's sensibilities. But to me it was a thrilling prospect, full of potential. I could do something with this place, I thought.

I opened one of the French doors and drank in the air, such a contrast to the air in the house, delicious, fragrant, touched with the chill of late October. The terrace stepped down to a ragged lawn surrounded by the forest. I descended the stone staircase, following a pathway overgrown with blackberry, in places so thick and thorny the vines had taken over the path so that it was completely obscured and impassable. I had hoped to inspect the exterior of the house, but I couldn't get a good look at it for the tangle of vine and trees. The house was so large and rambling and the woods so thick against it, I couldn't walk all the way around the building. There appeared to be no vantage point from which to see the entire structure as a whole. I found it frustrating, yet intriguing. It was a mystery house, impenetrable. Sleeping Beauty's castle.

I wandered back across the old lawn, past the fountain, through a small wooden gate, and down another stone stairway, and the house disappeared from view. At the bottom of the steps I found a secluded stone patio ringed with immense trees. I stood in the center of the ring of trees, truly awed. Sugar pine, incense cedar, black oak and alder, an occasional slender fir—the trees surrounded me like the walls of a great shimmering cathedral. The pines were so tall I couldn't see the tops of them, and I had to tilt my head back all the way just to try.

The trees seemed to look down upon me speculatively. I had the uncanny impression *they* were deciding whether *I* was suitable for them, not the other way around.

The patio was hidden beneath a carpet of dead leaves and the blackberry bushes, which had taken over completely, sending their long runners across the stone. Down the slope from the patio ran a narrow creek, and beyond the creek, the land began to rise into the woods. There was nothing of civilization to be seen here, no roads, no power lines, no buildings. I felt giddy with the beauty of it. This place was different. It wasn't like anything else Iona had shown me, or like any place I had ever been before. A piece of real estate

like this in the Bay Area would be worth a fortune. Even
here in the mountains it would be worth a lot. I knew this
place was out of my league.

But these woods were enchanted. Who knew what magic
could be worked here? I lifted my face up to the sky once
again, offering a spontaneous prayer of desire. I felt ecstatic,
like a pagan priestess, drawing down the vast, agitated stillness of the woods.

There was a soft shimmer of sound on the wind, a bright
flash of motion through the trees. I heard the snap of a twig,
a rustle of leaves. I looked up and there he was, standing on
the hill just past the stream, motionless and half-hidden behind a screen of young cedars. He was about my age, nearly
thirty or a little older, hair and skin the color of dark bright
autumn, burnished gold. He was staring at me with an expression of arrogance, Conan the Barbarian dressed like a
lumberjack, in his faded jeans and work boots, blue and
white plaid flannel shirt rolled up to show his strong hard
forearms, his muscular thighs spread for balance. There was
a potent stillness in his body, a physical stillness that was
present even when he was in motion, which made me think
of a Tai Chi master I had seen in Golden Gate Park. A look
of perplexity and suspicion passed over his rugged, comely
face, like a wild animal encountering an intruder, territorial,
dignified. I wanted to turn away but I couldn't stop looking
at him.

Don't look into the sun, you may be blinded—

An orange tripod stood on the hill past the stream and
strips of orange plastic fluttered from the trunks of several
of the trees on the slope. He finished tying one off and
walked back to the transit. He peered through the lens in my
direction. I had thought his hair was short, but when he
turned his head I saw it was tied back off his face, falling
just down to the base of his neck.

"Ah, there you are." The deep, masculine voice boomed
out into the woods.

I turned to see Russ descending the stone steps to the
patio, taking the steps two at a time with his big boyish
stride.

I looked back to catch a glimpse of the stranger, and our eyes met again, a split-second of connection that had me shifting my stance, to catch my balance. But then he moved into the woods, slipping into the camouflage of the trees like a wolf.

I felt a proprietary jealousy mixed with a strange excitement. *Who is he?* And why is he surveying on *my* property?

And I realized I had made my decision. *This is the one I want.*

Chapter Two

IT WAS A jolt to come home to the city after being in the mountains. Life there was running on a different frequency. My apartment seemed small, slick, banal. I longed for the old house like a lover.

Monday evening, I called Russ. We debated the merits of all the different properties we had seen.

Finally I said: "So what do you think of that big white house, Russ? I can't stop thinking about it. All that gorgeous land. Those trees!"

"It's a great piece of property, all right, Stacy."

I had been prepared for an argument. His positive, if cautious, tone surprised me and I blurted out my fears. "But the *house* . . . ? Is it completely gone? Would it take my entire savings and every spare second of my life from now through eternity to renovate it?"

"Short answer? Yes, it would. Would it be worth it? Look, Stacy. I don't really know," Russ admitted. "My guess is it will need at least a new foundation, and probably a new roof. And a bunch of stuff in between. But there's no way to tell the full extent of the work needed until we get in and open it up."

"Yeah . . ." That was it. It was a gamble.

"You know, the land alone, even without the structure, would be worth the price they're asking. You could always doze the house."

"But that house, if it could be saved . . . it would be magnificent."

"I think it's a hell of a deal, Stacy," he said. "Listen to my advice. What you do now is, you buy the place, raze the house, subdivide the land, turn it into a bunch of condos or luxury vacation houses or whatever, and sell 'em off for a ridiculous profit. Hell, I'll invest in the project myself. We can call it *Addison Court*."

"Yeah. We'll become *millionaires*."

"Multimillionaires!"

"Yeah, thanks, but no thanks. I can't imagine filling up that property with buildings. It would be sacrilegious."

"Suit yourself," he said, and I could hear the shrug in his voice over the phone. "I suppose you expect me to give you a cut-rate deal on renovation."

"I was hoping you'd do it for free."

"Yeah, *right*. But listen to me—buy it. Let me doze it for you, rezone, subdivide, throw up a bunch of new structures—"

"Oh, Russ. You just don't understand."

"You're right, Stacy, I don't understand you. You could design yourself a beautiful, new, *modern* house, and probably do it a hell of a lot cheaper than fixing up that old heap, but you want to live in Tara."

"Tara?" I was momentarily confused. "Oh, *Tara*, like the big white house in *Gone with the Wind*. No, it isn't Tara . . . it's the House of the Seven Gables. Or Wuthering Heights . . . well, let's hope it's none of those. But it *is* a romantic house, isn't it?"

"That's your problem, Stacy. You're too much of a romantic."

"Maybe."

"Which leads me to my next point." He faltered a moment, which immediately put me on alert. Russ was never one to pull any punches.

"Which is—?" I prodded him.

"Stacy, are you sure you want to take on this place, so far from the city? So far from . . ." He actually hesitated to say the name. ". . . Justin?"

"Justin!" I could feel myself blushing and I was glad he couldn't see me through the phone line. "What do *you* care, Russ? You don't even like Justin."

"Well, *you* seem to like him."

"Yeah . . . well, actually, I haven't been seeing much of Justin the last few months."

"I thought something was up. But you never say anything."

"Well, we sort of broke up."

"Sort of?"

"I don't know. We never actually *broke up*, you know. I mean, officially. We're just giving each other some breathing room. But anyway." I hoped I didn't have to explain it any more clearly than that. Russ, bless his heart, didn't want the gory details anyway.

"So—this plan to buy a place in the mountains—does this have anything to do with Justin?"

"You mean, like I am buying a house on the rebound or something?"

"Something. Or—would he be interested in such a project?"

"Russ, you know I've been talking about buying a place in the mountains for a long time, long before I met Justin, even. I think that was one of the problems between us—he's a dedicated city person and I have this dream of living a more rural life."

"But I thought you were going to consider this a weekend place, not like your *home*."

"Well, I really don't have a choice in that, do I? My job is in the city, and that job is what will pay for the place in the mountains."

"So why would Justin object to that? Don't all hot-shit sales executives aspire to owning a place in the country?"

"I don't know. But if Justin wanted a place in the country
he would want it for different reasons than I do."

"You mean, he would subdivide the land for profit?"

I laughed at that. "Probably. Maybe you and Justin ought
to get together. No, actually, I think Justin's idea of a place
in the country would be a condo at Tahoe. Russ, don't get
me wrong—I'm looking at this real estate purchase as a financial investment, and think it could be a good one. But
I'm interested in other kinds of investments, too. The life I
envision for myself is a life surrounded by open space, and
trees—"

"Little Stacys running around wild and free," he teased.

"Sure, eventually. I'd like to raise my kids in the country,
and Justin—well, I'm not sure Justin even *wants* kids, to tell
you the truth."

"So you're really not seeing him anymore?"

"Russ, you don't even *like* Justin!"

"I just want you to be happy."

"Don't give me that crap."

"No, really."

"All right. I *am* happy. Yes, it has been hard about Justin.
As a matter of fact, I have been taking great pains to avoid
him lately because I don't even trust my own good sense.
But the longer we're apart, the easier it gets. I think I'm getting clear on what I want."

"And you want that house."

"Yes," I said. "That's the one I want." And for some reason, at that moment a vision came into my mind, the striking image of the man I had seen in the woods, the faded
denim on his muscular thighs, the turn of his neck, the dark
gold of his hair and his sunburned skin.

That's the one I want.

"SO THAT'S IT. You've just up and decided to do this
thing." Justin leaned back in his seat, drummed on the table-
top with his fingertips, glanced up and down the length and
breadth of the café as if impatient for a waiter. He wouldn't
look me in the eye.

I waited. I didn't say anything.

His profile was exquisite: the classic aquiline nose, the jut of his chin, the strong, high forehead with its neat sweep of dark hair. How I had missed him.

Finally he turned his head and met my gaze. "Is that it? You're really going through with this?"

"Is there any reason I shouldn't?" I asked quietly. Not sarcastically. I really wanted to know.

He seemed impatient with the question. "No," he said. "I guess there isn't." He threw a twenty dollar bill on the table to cover our drinks and stalked out.

AT THE CREST of the Altamont Pass my breath caught with the beauty of the world stretched out before me. The air was so clear I could see snow on the peaks of the Sierra range across the Central Valley. Above me on the pastured hills above the freeway, the giant blades of the wind turbines turned in slow motion while cows grazed beneath them like tiny toys. It was late January and I was finally returning to the mountains for the final walk-through of the property before escrow closed.

I had waited a long time for this.

From the beginning Iona had assured me the owner was interested in my offer on the house, but there had been a holdup with the papers. Something about the old woman's poor health, family issues, and various other delays. Finally, after more than two months of wrangling and reams of paperwork, the house had gone into escrow. I emptied my savings and investment accounts, and took out a modest loan on the equity in my apartment, but the bulk of the financing was to be carried by the seller at an interest rate so reasonable I could hardly believe my good fortune. It seemed the owner of the old Apple Ranch liked the idea of a young woman with romantic ideals taking over the place, rather than a developer. Iona told me that a large development company out of Sacramento had made an attractive all-cash offer on the property, but the seller had chosen me.

When I signed my name to the papers I ran my finger

over the seller's handwriting, tracing the extravagant loops
of her signature.

Madelon M. Shapiro

I studied the shaky letters thoughtfully before putting the
bundle back into the Federal Express envelope. I loved
the house so much already, I couldn't help thinking about
the one who had lived in it before me. She must have loved
it too. The house and grounds were ill-kept, but maybe she
couldn't help that. After all, Iona had told me Mrs. Shapiro
had left the house to go into a nursing home. I wondered if
she had any regrets.

I stopped at a serve-yourself kiwi stand in the valley and
left money in a wooden box for a bag of the fuzzy brown
fruit. In the distance, the vague mountains seemed to be
formed from the sky, with their blue bulk and frosting of
clouds. Behind me, the warm engine of my Celica clicked
softly. I could see my breath on the air, though the sun was
shining bright.

I drove on through Escalon and Oakdale, where the hills
began and the highway left the Central Valley behind and
curved up toward the mountains, the phantom mountains,
vanishing as the languid oak hills rose before them.

A good road, a fast car, a new beginning. I turned up the
stereo and opened my window. Suddenly the mountains
came into view again, larger and closer now, startling with
their massive presence. I let out a whoop of joy, uninhibited
and glad in my solitude, though at the same time I felt a little wistful there was no one to share my excitement with.

The movers were just packing up the last of what they
were to take out of the house when I pulled into the parking
area at the end of the meadow. I was thrilled to see the
"sold" tag on the real estate sign which had been posted next
to the drive. Iona was standing there, talking to a petite
woman dressed in jeans and cowboy boots, a pink western
shirt with ruffles down the front, and a strand of large pearls.
Her auburn hair was pulled up in a bun with tendrils curling
down in front of her ears. She looked like a country singer
from the 1960s. As I parked my car, the stranger turned her
cheerful, square face toward me and my first thought was

that the rich reddish brown of her hair must surely be a wig—the aged quality of her skin was at odds with the lush thickness and color of her hair. She smiled at me and went back to supervising the movers, who were trying to get the doors shut on a moving van stuffed with furniture.

When she had a moment, Iona introduced us. "Stacy, this is Jean Maguire," she said. "Mrs. Shapiro's daughter. Jean's been taking care of the practical details for her mother."

"It's nice to meet you, Mrs. Maguire," I said.

"Call me Jean, please. Very pleased to make your acquaintance." She shook my hand warmly. "Iona said you were a beautiful young single girl and she was right."

"Thank you," I said, embarrassed.

"I'll go ahead and give you the keys, Stacy," Iona said. "Let me know if you want anything that's left, and I'll have the rest of it hauled away. Are you sure you got everything out that you want to keep, Jean?"

"I'm positive," said Jean. "There were only a few things I wanted anyway. I'll just be glad when I don't even have to think about this old place again."

"All right then," Iona said. "I guess that's it. Enjoy your house, Stacy. I'll let you wander around on your own. And if anyone bothers you, you tell them I said it was okay for you to be here."

"All right . . ." I was thrilled to have the keys in my hand at last. But something in her tone gave me pause. "Should I be expecting someone to bother me?"

"Well, no, but—" Iona pursed her lips, hesitant. "I don't mean to alarm you, Stacy. It's just that one of your new neighbors is . . ." She glanced at Jean uneasily. "I don't know quite how to put it. But it seems your neighbor didn't want anybody to buy the place." She waved a hand toward the house across the meadow and gave me a knowing look, which I found impossible to interpret. "I guess the young man wanted the place for himself. I hear he's been chasing people off. He creeps around the place like a spy—I call him the creeper," she laughed lightly. "I think he's harmless," she added hastily.

"He lives over there?" I said.

The house across the meadow was quiet, gleaming white in the thin January sunshine. We had a good view of it from the parking area. Though it was smaller than my house, it appeared to have been built around the same time and perhaps by the same builder. Though the two buildings didn't resemble one another in shape or roof line, the eclectic styling of the architecture was similar and both houses were finished with the same white painted wood siding, except that the paint on the neighbor's house was shiny and fresh and mine was gray and peeling. Well, I thought, *that* would soon be changing.

"Yes, and you know how people talk," Iona said. "I don't know how much of it is true. But it seems he befriended Mrs. Shapiro before she went into the retirement home. Tried to get chummy with her. Whether that was part of his plot, I don't know. But apparently he attempted to filch the property from the lady."

"That part is definitely true," said Jean.

"How would he do that?" I asked.

"He thought he could get her to sell the place to him for much less than it was worth. Offered her a ridiculously low sum of money to put the property in his name, or something. Trying to take advantage of the elderly—you know how that is."

Jean nodded. "Mother isn't so sharp mentally as she once was, unfortunately."

"So the Creeper must have figured she would be an easy target," Iona added.

"But she wasn't such an easy target," said Jean. "She had *me* to watch out for her."

"Yes," said Iona. "So, fortunately, your neighbor's little scheme never went anywhere."

So, *that's* my new neighbor, I thought. A swindler and a con artist. I was sorry to learn it. I had thought neighbors in the country would be—well, *neighborly*. Helpful, upstanding, selfless. So much for another shattered stereotype. I looked back at the house across the meadow as if this new neighbor of mine would appear at the door on cue.

"That's just one more reason I'll be happy to be finished

with this place," Jean said to me when Iona had walked out of earshot to talk with the movers. "Everything about it gives me the creeps, to tell you the truth. I know I shouldn't be saying this to you, Stacy, but I can't help it. I almost feel like I should warn you."

"Well, I've been warned," I said. "Or is there something else I should know about?"

"I'm sure you'll be fine," she said. "I'm just a superstitious old fool, so don't listen to me. I'll tell Mother I met you. She'll be so happy when I tell her how nice you are. She did love this old property, and she, for one, would have a fit if she heard me say anything bad about it."

I COULD SEE the high dormer windows through the trees from the front porch of my house, but the big black oak obscured the view. I kept thinking about what Iona and Jean had said about my new neighbor.

When they had gone I went into the house alone. The door had been standing open, so the foul smell was tempered with fresh air, and I was surprised to find the rooms even more gracious than I remembered—probably because much of the furniture had been removed. The place was still cluttered and filthy and I was aching to tear into it, but since I had to be back in the city that night I couldn't do much yet. Besides, technically, it wasn't even mine yet. So I poked around the place, which was still cluttered with the personal possessions of Madelon Shapiro, whose ghost I was just beginning to know. Odd to think of someone who is still alive as a ghost, but that's what it was like. I felt her all around me. I held her things in my hands. I walked on the floors she had walked for years.

I went from room to room, noticing with disappointment that much of the better furniture had been taken, but gratified to see what remained. I was amazed to find the grand upstairs bedroom almost intact—the lovely old four-poster bed was still there, too beat-up and awkward to make it worth moving, I supposed. The writing table had been left behind too, and so had the bureau with the mirror I thought of as the Enchanted Looking Glass.

I went back downstairs and knelt at the edge of the dingy green carpet near the door of the parlor. I was trying to pry up the corner of the carpet to see what was beneath it when I heard the voice. "Don't you just *love* avocado green? My grandmother's kitchen was done in exactly that shade."

I looked up to see a young woman in the entry hall, leaning against the frame of the open door. Her gauzy red hair was tied back but enough of it escaped to be lifted, witchy and glamorous, by the cold wind. She wore a dark flower-print dress with the heavy black combat boots so much in style that year, black tights, and black socks. She didn't look like she could be much over twenty, but her eyes held an expression of shrewd self-importance.

"Well, it could have been harvest gold," I said. "Or orange shag—I think it's from the same era." I got up and gave her my hand. "Hi, I'm Stacy."

She shook my hand with strength and a lingering, penetrating appraisal, letting go slowly, as if she was using the touch of our hands to divine information about me. "Yolanda," she said. "I'm your next-door neighbor."

"I didn't realize I had a next-door neighbor."

"Well, I'm behind you, actually, down past the creek."

"You don't live in that white house across the meadow, then?"

"No," she said. "Not there. I live in a little cabin by the church. I'm the caretaker down there."

"The church?"

"Didn't you know you have a church practically next door to you?" She seemed amused. She was hip, breezy, and young. I was as much surprised by the idea of her being a church caretaker as I was to learn of the church.

"All the buildings down on the other side of the creek are owned by the church," she said. "The chapel is through those trees there, just past my cabin. The road in is on the other side, so you don't get the traffic."

"There's a lot I don't know about my new neighborhood," I said. I thought about how impulsive this move had been. I had studied the market for months, and looked at dozens of properties, but I had known little about this one when I made my offer. I had wanted it so much, I had jumped at it impetuously.

"And the neighbors across the meadow," I said. "I take it *they* aren't church people?" I was eager for more information on Iona's "Creeper."

"Church people . . ." Yolanda hesitated, and I had the feeling she didn't appreciate me putting *her* in such a category. She shrugged with a defiant, careless little movement of her shoulders. "No, I wouldn't say they are necessarily *church people*. But they're a mixed bunch," she added dryly. "Actually, I *was* surprised Brand didn't snag this place for himself. He wanted this house with a *passion*."

"Brand . . ."

"Yeah, he lives over there." She nodded at the house across the meadow. "Brandon Vandevere. Everyone calls him Brand. He's had his eye on the Apple Ranch for a long time. I thought he'd end up with it for sure."

Iona's *Creeper*, I thought. So it was common knowledge.

"And the old lady liked him a lot. Or at least she *used* to. I thought she might leave the property to him in her will or something. But anyway, I guess she decided not to do that, since she sold it to you instead." Yolanda shrugged again. "So. You actually *bought* this old place."

"I can hardly believe it myself."

"Where is your husband today?"

"There is no husband. It's just me."

"Oh! I saw you here, once before, with . . . I thought—"

"If you saw me here with a man, it was my brother Russ," I said. "I dragged him around with me house hunting."

"Oh, I see. Well, cool." Her expression lightened perceptibly. "Another single lady in the neighborhood. We'll have to go out and get into trouble together."

"Sure," I said. "I get the impression this is a real party town."

She laughed, appreciating that. She was wandering around the room, touching things, picking out details with her penetrating attention. "Already, it seems different in here." She seemed to be talking to herself. She turned and looked at me directly. "You could actually make something of this place, couldn't you?" she said.

"I hope so. I mean to do it."

"Quite a task to take on, especially considering all the weird stuff that—" she stopped abruptly. "But it's a great old house. You're going to fix it all up?"

"That's the plan. What were you going to say?"

"Oh. It's just the stories you hear, you know." She gave her little shrug. "The things that go on. This house has sheltered so much unhappiness. I suppose most old houses have."

"I suppose," I replied, suddenly uneasy, passionately curious. Wanting to know and not wanting to know. "Did you know the owner well?"

"I knew her well enough. She loved this place—this old house, the orchards, the forest—she just got too old to take care of it all."

"It would be a lot to manage. I'm a bit overwhelmed myself."

"Yeah—a lot of us were surprised that you would take it on."

"Why?"

"You're young, single. A female. I know, sorry. But really, think about it. You're by yourself, right? It's a huge . . . undertaking. For one person, especially, it wouldn't matter what your sex was. But still, *she* was alone, too, right? And she was okay. Until the end. Maybe it'll work out for you." She stared at me meaningfully.

"Well, it *is* a large project," I agreed, disturbed by her innocent, yet somehow piercing, expression. Some question I couldn't quite formulate was nagging at me. "There's no arguing that it's going to be a lot of work. But I've worked on a number of projects similar in scope. I have a pretty good idea of what I might be getting into."

"I heard you're an architect."

"You *heard*?" I said wryly. "Well, you heard right."

"So, that's gotta help. You know what you're doing."

"Well, we'll see. I'm prepared for the worst, actually—

hoping for the best, but prepared for the worst. And my brother is a contractor. I got the house for a good price, and I can put some money into the renovation. So I feel pretty good about it." I felt like I was pleading a case, and wondered why I should feel the need to do that. Then suddenly I realized what was nagging at the edge of my thoughts.

"You asked about my husband," I said. "But you already knew I was single——"

She smiled with a confessional charm, as if abashed but pleased to have been caught in this petty duplicity. "Yeah, I'm sorry about that," she said. "This town is a notorious gossip mill. Everybody knows each other and everything *about* each other. I asked about your husband because I wanted to know if it was true about you being single."

"It's true, I am single," I said. "And you weren't the only one interested in my single female status. It's 1994. Would you believe I had trouble getting a loan as a single woman, even with a decent down payment and a good job? They kept asking for my husband's income. Anyway, it all worked out for the best, because I found this place, and the owner was willing to finance the deal."

"Yeah, it's strange . . ."

"What?"

"Well, I don't know . . ." Yolanda cocked her head, looked off into the distance, her rich red hair falling in frizzy curls over her shoulder. "I didn't expect the old lady to put it on the market like that." There was that shrug again, an affected, yet somehow charming gesture. She turned her slender white neck and looked at me intently. "She came here as a young woman, and now she's really old. I think it must have broken her heart to go. Or——who knows? Maybe she was ready to put it behind her."

"I wonder why her daughter didn't want to keep the place? I couldn't imagine letting it go out of the family, if I could help it. But she actually seemed happy to be rid of it."

"Well, you have to understand, Mrs. Shapiro's daughter isn't all that young herself. She lives in Modesto now, and she's had her own troubles. Her health isn't so good, and I don't think she has any money. *She* would never be able to handle this place!" Yolanda gave a disparaging laugh.

Jean Maguire had seemed healthy enough to me, but I didn't interrupt Yolanda.

"*Bonnie Jean Maguire.*" Yolanda said the name with a slight distaste. "She stayed here for several months before they took Mrs. Shapiro away. The first thing Bonnie Jean did when she came in was to cover up all the windows. She said the light hurt her eyes. I remember one afternoon I went over there to see if they needed any help. I knew things weren't going well with the old lady or she wouldn't have had her daughter staying there in the first place. Mrs. Shapiro couldn't get out of bed. I'll bet she would have liked those drapes opened, but Jean refused to do it, I bet. I offered to help clean up the house, which was getting pretty bad by that time. When Mrs. Shapiro was stronger, it never got so bad. Not that she was ever a clean freak or anything. But Jean said no, they were all right, they didn't need a thing. It was like she was scared I was going to infiltrate her domain. It was weird."

She was silent for a moment, thinking. "I guess some people are just real particular about their privacy." She seemed suddenly finished with the conversation, with me, and she went to the door. "Hey listen," she said. "If you need anything to help you get settled—blah-blah-blah, and all that, okay?"

"Okay," I said. "I'll remember that. Thanks."

"No, but really," Yolanda said. "I mean it. There's a trail right through the trees there. It goes right on down to my cabin." She looked me at me with satisfaction. Her voice had changed. Her tone was friendlier—gentle, almost. She had decided to approve of me. "Holler if you need anything."

"Well, thank you," I said. "That's right neighborly of you."

"People around these parts are neighborly," she said with a put-on Southern drawl. She lifted a brow and lowered her voice. "Sometimes a little *too* neighborly. Know what I mean?"

No, not really, I thought, wondering what she did mean. But I didn't say anything. She disturbed me a little.

She laughed to herself and waved at me, and went off. I heard her singing in the distance, her voice deep and bluesy. I closed the door after her, and then opened it again for the fresh air, feeling strange and silly. I remembered the carpet and went back to see if I could pry a bit of it up.

The carpet came up easily, along with its pad, and yes, there was a floor beneath it, a floor of wood, reddish gold with a deep patina of age. I was pretty sure it was cedar. I hoped it would be in decent shape, but I would have to wait and see.

I STAYED ONLY until the short winter day began to darken the house with shadows, as I had a meeting early the next morning in San Francisco. I couldn't spend the night in the house, and I wasn't sure I'd want to, it was so cold and strange and dark, and there was that awful stench. But I didn't want to leave, and I lingered as long as I could. I stopped by Iona's office and told her I'd keep what was left in the house and she needn't hire anyone to haul it away. I wanted to go through everything myself.

I drove back by the house on my way out of town just to look at it again. I got out of my car and walked up toward the porch, to stand there a moment, to feel the forest and savor the presence of the house. I heard a rustling in the tangle of vines near the old fountain and two wild-looking children appeared, half-hidden in the bushes, looking out at me like fairy people.

I heard one of them whisper loudly, the boy: "It's the lady who's going to live in the haunted house!"

The girl answered, "She must be a witch."

"A witch!"

"A witch! Witch—" The little girl began to chant the words, over and over.

"The haunted house, the haunted house," the boy joined in the chant.

"Witch! Witch! Witch—!"

I pretended not to be aware of them, at first. Their taunting went on a little longer, and died away. I spoke.

"As it happens, witches *like* it when the house they buy is haunted. It's what they look for, in a house." I said the words slowly and let my voice gather a theatrical passion. "It's perfect for me. Perfect. And now, come to find there are little *children* in the neighborhood—so I shan't go *hungry!*"

I ended with my best witch's cackle.

They screamed and tore off through the woods, shrieking with laughter.

I turned to my car and glanced up absently at the house across the meadow, startled to see a man watching me from one of the high dormer windows. His face was striking, even at this distance—his bone structure sculpted, his expression hostile. But it was just an impression, and I questioned it instantly, as the apparition vanished, and the window went dark.

I DAYDREAMED CONSTANTLY about the house. At night I dreamed of loan documents and title papers, endless phone calls with appraisers, bankers, brokers. At work, preparing a drawing for a client, I found myself doodling on a piece of tracing paper, sketching an elevation of the wide front porch with its tendrils of blackberry vine, or scribbling a plan view of the second floor, or working out the way the various angles of the roof intersected. When I was supposed to be working on a client's house my mind would be exploring the mysteries of my own. I drew lines, rectangles and triangles, balusters, pediments and columns, the interlocking geometry of a bay window, a roof, a wall. But I didn't have the proportions of the house right. I didn't know all its rambling corridors and add-on rooms. I pined for the house, yearned to put my hands on it, to understand it, to wander at leisure through the hallways and rooms, up one stairway and down another, to discover its secrets. I still didn't *know* it, not even in the most rudimentary sense. I couldn't quite piece it together. Not to scale, anyway. The scale of it was what I wanted to understand. The texture of it, the colors and the buried smells of it. What would it be like when I had discovered the source of the stench and scrubbed the place clean? What lay beneath the rotted carpeting in the front parlor? How would the library look after I tore out the painted closet? What color was the kitchen? White with cheery yellow trim. Or was it cheery blue trim? *Can't remember. Can't believe I can't remember.* All I remembered was that it was a little too cheery. But I had been inside the house only twice. And the house had so many rooms. I should have taken notes. I had meant to. I couldn't remember which walls were paneled and which were painted. The room up in the northwest corner, that could be fixed up as a guest room—Russ liked that room. And the upstairs room with the bay window overlooking the meadow, the grand bedroom. Mrs. Shapiro's bedroom. My bedroom. I would work on that room first. Or the library, the beautiful lofty library—tear out that green-painted plywood closet contraption in there, clear the cabinets and bookshelves, set up a drawing board, a computer . . . and there I would have my studio.

The house was so *big*. There was even more square footage than I had realized and that meant more work, more expense, more space! Lovely space.

What had I gotten myself into?

I thought about my conversation with Yolanda. According to her, the neighborhood was already talking about me—a "single female," taking on a project like this. Great, now I couldn't fail without betraying the sisterhood.

And there was my other new neighbor, the one called Brand, the one who had tried to take possession of the property himself but couldn't quite manage it. He was no doubt hoping I would fail. I hadn't met him yet, but it seemed to me I already understood his character. I wanted to meet him. I disliked him sight unseen, but I was curious about him. We were natural adversaries because we both wanted the same thing. And only one of us could have it.

Sight unseen . . .

What about the face I had seen in the window?

What about the man in the woods?

Not for the first time, the image appeared to me again, the memory startling and vivid, how he had stood on the slope in the forest, motionless, haughty, his legs braced apart, long hair tied back and curling down the back of his neck. The strong bones of his arms, the architectural planes of his face catching the slanted October sunlight. Triangular eyes narrowed like those of a predator, surveying the land, the land he thought should be *his*.

Get back to work, I said to myself.

Chapter Three

THE NEXT WEEKEND I drove to the mountains to formally claim my new house. I parked in my driveway just off the meadow, and jumped out of my car and breathed in the scent of the air. I felt like I could get drunk off that air. It was still early in the morning. I had left San Francisco before daylight, I had been so eager to get there. I opened up the house, which in contrast to the woods, smelled ghastly, and I let it air out a bit while I walked the property.

I unloaded my car of cleaning supplies, mop, broom, and a big pile of rags, and I got to work in the kitchen, scrubbing down the floors and cabinets. It was a large bright farm kitchen with a wonderful old porcelain stove and drainboard, quaint cabinetry, and a pair of double-hung windows over the sink looking out over the apple orchard. I was finishing up the kitchen around eleven, just as my brother Russ pulled in with Rags, his half-grown German Shepherd puppy, riding shotgun in his pickup truck.

After a cold beer, I persuaded Russ to go under the house and take a look at the foundation, which he did, reluctantly, though he would have preferred to drink another beer first. My brother emerged from beneath the house to report that, though a few supports had fallen, causing the floors to sag and sway, the foundation, though not up to the code of the day, was actually in pretty good shape.

I was thrilled, and relieved. It seemed a good omen.

Russ drove into town to get some supplies, leaving Rags with me. She was high-strung and undisciplined, lunging about and chewing on everything. I reminded myself she was just a puppy, trying not to get too exasperated with her. I was surprised when Russ had turned up with a dog. He never seemed to want to tie himself down too much. But he'd always loved dogs—and she was a good dog, just young.

Around noon she gave me the slip and ran off into the woods.

I set off after her, swearing. I could hear barking in the distance, but after a short hike I discovered the barking was that of another dog in a fenced yard on the other side of the church property. It was a lovely winter's day, bright and brisk, and it was good to get out for a walk, but as time went on and I didn't find her, I began to worry I might have really lost my brother's dog.

Eventually I returned, without Rags, and passing by the white house across the meadow I noticed a man and a woman standing in the garden. A smell of something cooking came from within the house, savory and roasty with garlic and herbs.

"Have you seen a dog? A German Shepherd?" I called out. "She's just a pup—she's wearing her leash."

They shook their heads. The man came to the edge of the garden, craning his neck, looking through the trees to the west as if I might have overlooked a clue there. He seemed interested in conversing with me, so I walked closer.

"Watch out for the plants along the fence, Saul, don't step on them." The woman came up beside him, pointing at the small bushes he had almost trampled.

Saul was probably several years older than me, tall, with smooth, freshly cut dark hair. The idea that he might have just squashed the woman's plants seemed to amuse him. He made a show of pretending to stomp them further.

"I just transplanted them," she said to me, ignoring him. "Trying to replace the Scotch broom. It isn't native, you know, and it takes over everything. So, you lost your dog."

"My brother's dog, actually."

"Oh, that's not good." She had a kind, curious face. She was older than the man and dressed less stylishly—big brown sweater, stained trousers, dirty white sneakers, no makeup. She wore her faded blond hair clipped at the top of her head like she had pinned it up absent-mindedly on her way out to the garden. In contrast, he was meticulously groomed, perfect creases in his casual slacks, shirt collar showing over the V-neck of his color-coordinated sweater, tasseled loafers. Not like a local, I thought—but then, how many of the locals did I know, anyway?

"You're our new neighbor, aren't you?" the woman said.

"The new neighbor, yes," I said, pleased at that. "Stacy Addison."

"Well, it's good to meet you, Stacy," she said. She slipped off one of the leather gloves she was wearing, and we shook hands. She had a cool, strong grip. "It's been so long since that beautiful old house was cared for! I'm Tess, and this is Saul—" The man who had nearly trampled her plants smiled at me stepped forward to take my hand.

"Delighted," he murmured. "A beautiful woman for a beautiful house." He dropped the plant-trampling clownishness and looked up at me with his head lowered slightly as if he were about to kiss my hand. His eyes were deep blue and richly lashed, direct, and intense. He reminded me a little of Justin. I felt a thrill of response to his obvious charm, and withdrew my hand self-consciously.

I looked away from him, distracted. Another man had appeared at the gate next to the house. He was the one I had seen in the woods the day I discovered my house. The one with predator eyes, sly and triangular, like that of a wolf, or falcon. Now those eyes squinted in the sunlight as he looked across the garden at me. Looking into his eyes I had a strange and sharp sense of recognition—of course I had seen him before, but it was more than that. I felt I *knew* him. But I was immediately skeptical of such a romantic notion. I had never met him before in my life.

"Come here, Brand." Tess waved him over. "This is our new neighbor, and she's lost a dog. German—" she turned to me— "Shepherd, right?"

"Yes," I said. "She's just a pup. She's wearing her leash, and she's probably tangled up in the woods somewhere by now."

He came toward us but he did not join us. He stopped just beyond the row of careful plantings, bending for a moment to straighten a wooden stake tied with string. A forelock of dark gold fell over his brow.

So this is Brand, I thought.

There was the sound of barking in the distance.

"There you go," Brand said as he straightened up, and he nodded toward the barking.

"I walked over there," I said, "and I found a dog in a yard, but not the one I'm looking for."

"That sounds like a female German Shepherd," he said.

I was doubtful that he could actually distinguish the bark of a female German Shepherd from that of a male, or from another kind of dog, for that matter.

But then I heard a new bark mingling with the barking I had previously investigated, higher pitched, excited. Rags burst out of the woods, running along gaily with her leash trailing behind her.

Brand gave a low, sharp whistle. Rags broke her stride and trotted toward him, wagging her tail. He knelt and opened his hand to her, and she approached him warily, with her long, inquisitive nose extended. He held his hand for her so she could study his scent. When she was satisfied, she allowed him to massage her neck behind her ears.

I stepped on the leash and reached down to grab her collar. "Gotcha," I said.

Rags lunged at me and began licking my face with great enthusiasm.

"No, you don't," I said, pulling her collar. "No kisses right now."

I looked at Brand and we locked eyes for a moment as we crouched at the same level, close enough to touch. His irises were shockingly clear and colored like a river, blue and brown and green, reflecting the woods and sky. Mesmerizing eyes. I had to force myself to break off the connection. I stood up and told Rags to sit. I had to press her butt down to get her to obey me.

"Well, *good*," Tess said. She sounded relieved. "You won't have to tell your brother a story about dog thieves. Let's see. Introductions. Stacy, this is Brand, Brand Vandevere, this is Stacy, our new neighbor—"

I had to look at him again, but he barely glanced at me again. And yet I was startled by the turbulence of expression he turned on me, even in a glance.

"She's a good-looking dog." Saul grinned at me, leaning down to ruffle Rags's ears. Rags was startled by the sudden attention and she started away, but I held the leash tight. Brand backed off, hands stuffed into the pockets of his faded Levis.

"Come on, Rags," I said.

"Rags?" laughed Tess. "It that really her name?"

"Rags the raunchy runt."

"Oh, but she's so pretty," said Tess.

"She *is*," Saul said, not taking his gaze off me.

"Listen, Stacy," said Tess, "We were about to sit down to lunch. Brand is a great cook and he always makes too much—why don't you come in and join us? Bring Rags in, or put her in the yard. It's fenced in back by the garden shed. She can't hurt anything."

"I wouldn't want to test that notion," I said.

Brand threw me an expressionless look and went back through the gate toward the house.

"Please," she said. "Join us."

"Yes, do!" said Saul. "We insist."

"Well . . ." I hesitated, remembering Iona's warning about the Creeper. Maybe it wasn't a good idea to get too friendly with these people. But in spite of what I had heard—or maybe because of it—I was curious. I wanted to get to know my neighbors. And the smell coming from the house was quite appetizing. Russ had gone down to Sonora and wouldn't be back for awhile, and besides, he could fend for himself. But I wasn't sure the chef would appreciate it. He didn't seem to be very welcoming. There was definitely something hostile about Brand, though Creeper wouldn't have been the name I'd have given to him.

"Please?" said Tess.

"Are you sure it's all right with your, uh—husband?" I said. "The chef?"

"You mean Brand? Honey, he's my cousin, not my husband. He's my roommate, just like Saul, here. Housemate, if you prefer. But of course, you'd be doing us an honor. Brand loves to feed people. Just make a big fuss about his cooking," she added. "He'll be happy."

"No, don't make a fuss about his cooking," Saul said. "Please."

"Women are always proposing marriage to Brand after he cooks for them," said Tess. "Goes to his head."

"Really," I said. "He must be good."

"Come in and see for yourself," Tess said.

"This invitation is simply impossible to resist," I said. "And I promise I won't propose marriage to Brand after lunch."

"You can propose to *me* after lunch," Saul said. He moved close beside me, bumping into me, his face spread in a charming, boyish smile. His eyes were so blue I wondered if he wore contacts. "Tess isn't married to me, either, in case you're wondering."

"Don't let these menfolk scare you off, Stacy," Tess said as she turned toward the house. "Neither one of them is quite what they seem."

"Is that so?" Saul said. "And what do we 'seem'?"

She ignored him. "Come, Rags," she said, and she took the dog's leash. "You have to tell me what you have planned for the Apple Ranch, Stacy. It's such a mysterious old place, so full of history . . ."

When we came in, Brand got out wine glasses and a jug and poured each of us a glass of red wine.

"You can bring the pup in, if you want," he said to me.

"No, she's better outside, I think," I said. I was standing with Tess in the doorway between the kitchen and the dining room, which opened onto a lofty great room with a massive stone fireplace and raked windows on the opposite wall. Saul pulled out chairs for Tess and me from the kitchen table and we sat, drinking our wine, while Brand cooked. He had refused any offer of help, saying it was all handled, moving around the large kitchen in his big graceful body, silent and intent upon his work. He didn't look at me or speak to me again. But Saul and Tess kept up the small talk as we waited for the food to be served. Tess asked me about my house — my favorite subject. I told them about the wood floors I had found under the carpet and the carpenter ants I had discovered in the kitchen. Saul appeared to be keenly interested in anything I had to say, and yet the subject of the house seemed to hold little interest for him.

Brand did not join in the conversation; he didn't even seem to be listening — though I knew he was. He pronounced the meal ready and told us to help ourselves, and then he went out, saying he had something to do upstairs.

"Aren't you going to eat?" Tess called after him.

"Yeah, later."

"What's the matter with him?" asked Saul.

"Oh, he's just shy," Tess said.

"He's not shy," said Saul.

"You're right," said Tess. "He's acting strangely. Maybe I should go see what's going on."

"Leave him alone," said Saul. "If he wants to be moody, that's his business."

"I'm just going to change my dirty sweater," she said, and went out.

"She's gotta go after him," Saul said, and there was real affection in his voice for her. "She's such a mother hen."

Saul and I ladled bowls of a fragrant stew from a large pot on the stove. We sat at the round oak table in the sunny kitchen with windows overlooking the woods and the garden below. On the table there was a basket of corn muffins, a crock of sweet whipped butter, and a big pewter pepper grinder.

Through the windows I could see across the meadow, and my house was just visible through the trees. It was strange and interesting to me, to be looking at my own property from this perspective.

"Admiring your house?" Saul asked slyly. His eyes, intense and blue, were fixed on me, watching me with interest.

"As a matter of fact, I was," I confessed. "And I have been admiring *your* house too." I was curious about what the situation here was. Did they all rent? From the evident care lavished on the house and grounds, I guessed not. Which one of them was the homeowner? Tess? Brand?

"Yeah? You like it?" Saul smiled with such pride I guessed it must be him. "Well, thank you. It's humble, but it's home."

"How long have you owned the place?" I asked him.

"I've been here almost long enough to be bored. But not quite."

"I like it a lot," I replied, without need to exaggerate. I did like the house, very much. Inside it was airy and light, and yet solidly built with high, open beam ceilings of golden cedar. The furnishings were rustic and spare but elegant and comfortable. On the plain white walls photographs of various sizes were displayed, unusual compositions in simple frames—black and white studies, striking candid portraits, and color studies of nature: awesome granite faces, a singular mountain peak, clusters of leaves caught at the edge of a river.

"Did you do the work yourself?" I asked.

"The work?"

"The custom cabinetry . . . that handrail, those stairs. The windows and the mantel over the fireplace. This is all fine craftsmanship."

Saul leaned back in his chair with the grace of a jaded sophisticate. "I let the experts do the work," he said. "I'm an investment banker, not a carpenter. I just try to stay out of their way."

"And who is the photographer? These prints are good."

He seemed pleased that I'd noticed. "Oh, you know how

it is," he replied modestly, with a laugh, waving his hand. "You travel around, you end up with things . . ."

"Quite a *lot* of travel, from the look of it. Isn't that the Nepal Himalaya? No other mountains look quite like those—"

He grinned. "You're not impressed with that sort of thing, are you?"

"Well, yes, I am," I replied. "I'm also impressed with how you've tamed the blackberry bushes around this place. Mine are threatening to take over complctely."

"Tess takes care of the gardens for me," Saul said, watching her as she came into the room.

She didn't say what had come of following Brand, and I wasn't about to ask. Saul didn't ask either. I leaned back in my chair, stretching in the warmth of the winter sun streaming through the windows. I felt more at home in this house than I had expected to feel.

"She tames them with gentleness," Saul said.

"What?" asked Tess.

"The blackberry bushes."

"Gentleness!" Tess scoffed. "They respond only to cruelty. You're not having a problem with blackberry bushes, are you, Stacy?" she asked with a laugh.

"Well, they've covered everything. It seems they haven't been trimmed for years and years."

"You'd be surprised how quickly they grow," Tess said. "Especially near water, and you've got that creek running through your place. They grow like Jack and the Beanstalk. But they grab at you, with their sharp thorns, like something from another story! Gentleness, ha. You've got to be brutal with them."

"You seem to know what you're talking about."

"I've lived amongst the blackberry vines for a long time," replied Tess. "We have an uneasy truce."

"Have you lived a long time here in the mountains?"

"Me, I escaped from the lowlands, well—" she stopped to think. "It's been awhile now. I hate to think how many years. Makes me feel old."

I looked at Saul. "What about you?" I asked.

Saul avoided my eye and looked at Tess, giving her a lazy half-smile.

"Saul's been here a while," Tess said. "But he doesn't stay anywhere too long, do you, Saul?"

"Papa was a rollin' stone," he said. "On the other hand, I kinda like it here. I got me a nice setup." He glanced around the room with satisfaction. "If I had a good reason to stay . . ." He was looking at me now.

"Now Brand, he's lived in the area since he was a boy," Tess said, hurriedly, it seemed.

Brand had just come into the kitchen. I had a clear view of him from where I was sitting. He went to the cabinet, opening one door and then another, looking for something. The line of him, from shoulder to hip, was graceful and long.

"I'm talking about you," called Tess.

"What?" Brand paused at the doorway, on his way out again.

"I was just telling Stacy you're a local boy."

"You were born here in the mountains?" I said, to make conversation.

I felt his gaze on me. "No," he said coolly. "But I do actually live here, now."

The animosity caught up with me and I hesitated to reply, uncertain as to his meaning.

He went on: "Then there are those who come up to the mountains on weekends and holidays, whenever it suits them, to get away from it all—to appreciate nature—then they run right back to the city where they belong."

He means me, I thought.

There was a moment of strained silence. Saul and Tess exchanged glances.

"Too bad some of us have to work for a living," I said.

"What do you do, Stacy?" Tess asked, diplomatic, attempting to steer the conversation in a new direction.

"I'm an architect with a firm in San Francisco," I said. I was grateful my voice stayed even. I refused to let this guy see he'd shaken me. *What a jerk.*

"Ah," said Tess. "I love San Francisco."

"Me too," I said. "But I have to admit when I'm in the mountains I dream of making my work here, somehow. I never want to leave."

"You could be an architect here," said Saul.

"Oh, now there's a possibility," said Tess. "Your own mountain architectural practice."

"Yeah, that'd be great." Saul was enthusiastic. "Have you ever thought about that?"

"Actually, there isn't a big demand for architects around here," said Brand. "We try to keep the building to a minimum." His voice dropped softly, but there was an edge to it. "Over the ridge you find a lot more fancy new houses and commercial projects going on, but around here people like it rustic. We don't *want* a lot of development."

"So you don't like architects who live in the city, and you don't want any architects living here," I said. "You just don't like architects?"

"I've got nothing against architects in general."

"Just the one who bought the house across the meadow."

"Strange house for an architect to pick," he replied smoothly. "Don't you archi-types usually want to build your own houses? Something with lots of glass and steel? Post-modern, right? Or is it *post*-post modernism nowadays?"

There was silence in the room. Saul and Tess looked at each other, openly astonished at Brand's attitude.

Something flared up in me — anger, indignation — but something else sparked too. Excitement, a sense of challenge. Beneath his apparent rancor, I sensed humor. Brand was making fun of me and that got to me the most.

"You know," I said, "I appreciate this area for the same reasons *you* do. For its wildness. And its history. I'll give you this: I haven't seen much new construction around here. But I *have* noticed a lot of remodeling going on. People fixing their places up. There's always a need for a good designer. Anywhere."

Brand looked at me, long and hard. "And I suppose *you* are a good designer."

"Yes," I said. "I am a good designer."

He laughed.

Tess sighed with something like relief. Suddenly the tension had lessened—a little. Brand drew a chair away from the table, flipped it around and sat in it backwards, his arms folded across the rail. "Well, what *are* your plans for that . . . house?" He said *house* as if it burnt him to say it. His expression was mournful. It occurred to me that he was afraid of what my reply might be.

We weren't as close as we had been for a moment out in the yard, but now I had the occasion to really look at him, and I could see how the triangular shape of his eyes was caused by the juncture of his wide forehead with the slant of his brow, and I could see the manner in which his eyes were set apart above his cheekbones, the slash of his long straight nose, the warm volume of his mouth and jaw. But it was the eyes that struck me most, the changing river quality of them, the color of them, the rippling expressions.

"I plan to clean it up, for one thing," I said.

"Is that all?" he asked.

"For now."

"No remodeling scheduled?" That was Tess. She picked up the wine and poured herself another glass.

"I want to live in it awhile," I said. "Get to know it."

Saul tilted his head, amused. "It's a house. What's to know?"

"Oh—" I was surprised at the question. "There are lots of things. How the light moves through the rooms at different times of day, through different seasons. How the space flows—or doesn't! What colors it wants, what kinds of furniture. A house has its own personality and character. Like a person. It takes time to really know it well."

Brand nodded with the barest smile. What was he was thinking? I wanted to find out.

Saul had taken the bottle from Tess and was about to pour more wine for me.

"Oh—no, thanks," I said, holding my fingers over the glass. "I won't be able to get any more work done on the house this afternoon if I do any more of that."

Brand got up from his chair, turned it, shoved it under the table, and went out of the room. I felt relieved to see him go, and disappointed, too. I had taken pleasure in sparring with him.

WE WENT OUT on the screened porch after the meal, which, admittedly, had been superb. I hadn't realized how hungry I was, and the food had been just right, simple country fare, but so expertly prepared it brought rapture to the senses. The stew, flavored with wine and herbs, deserved a more elegant title than stew. The corn muffins were huge, slightly crisp on their tops, moist inside but with a fine crumb. For dessert there was a cobbler, rich with plump purple berries in a tender pastry, served in blue crockery bowls with whipped cream spooned over it. Berries from the very vines we had been discussing earlier.

So—he *was* a good cook, despite the fact that he looked like a man more at home with an ax in his hand than a soup ladle. But I was careful to be cautious with my praise.

Tess made coffee and I carried it out to the porch on a white enameled tray. Brand was there, sitting at a small table, typing something into a notebook computer. I sat down with Tess on the porch swing and Saul leaned against the railing. The coffee was excellent, deep and dark and freshly ground.

"I see you have a view of my house," I said. "Just as I have of yours."

"Yes." Saul yawned. "It's better for me, since yours is the more spectacular house to view."

"But *your* house is charming!" I said to him.

Brand closed his computer abruptly and went inside, banging the screen door behind him.

I murmured to Tess, "He doesn't like me much, does he?"

She lit a cigarette. "Who? Brand? Oh, don't mind him. He's just jealous."

"Jealous—?"

"Jealous, that you got that house and he didn't. He's coveted that place for years. He wanted—"

A lonely howl went up from the side of the house.

"Oh dear," said Tess. "Your baby's crying."

Rags. Damn her timing—I was curious to hear what Tess had been about to say.

I set my mug down and went to see if the puppy was getting into trouble again. Her leash was all tangled, in typical dog fashion, around the tree where I had tied her up. I knelt to disentangle her.

I was surrounded by a mountain garden, lush, even though it was January. From here I could see a tiny house, not much more than a renovated gardening shed, but it had a lived-in look about it, and I wondered if this was Tess's domain, or perhaps Brand's. Ironic, I thought. I had assumed I didn't want anything to do with them after what Iona had told me. Now I was curious to know their stories.

I led Rags out to the front, and I called up to Tess on the porch. "I think I better get Ragsy home now," I said. "Thank you so much for the meal. And please thank the chef for me."

She came down the steps to see me off.

"Well, I hope you do well with that old place," she said with a sigh. There was a note of doubt in her voice. "It does seem a major project. Brand says the house needs quite a lot of work."

"So—he's not too happy I got the place, then?"

"You don't even know. I almost cried for him."

I wanted to hang back with Tess and hear more, but it was hard with Rags pulling on her leash, whining and trying to get away to chase some movement in the weeds. She was a pup, but already she was huge and strong, and a little obnoxious. Clearly, it was time to be off.

"But it's all for the best," Tess said. "Brand's got enough to do without taking on that place too. And besides, I think we're going to like having you as a neighbor, Stacy."

Saul was still leaning against the railing, fingering a toothpick, observing me with his direct blue gaze. He had the look of belonging somewhere else, with his careful dress that didn't quite fit in, here in this mountain meadow. It made him a sort of comrade. *I* didn't fit in here either. I sensed he was in accordance with Tess about me: They both approved of their new neighbor. But with him there was something else too and I thought I could guess what it was. I felt slightly flustered with his keen expression on me.

"We'll see you soon, Stacy," he said.

As I walked toward my house with Rags at my side, a convertible BMW swept into the meadow drive, the top down in spite of the cold winter air. The driver was a striking woman with tawny hair and an aristocratic face—haughty chin, arrow-tip nose, high delicate cheekbones, big wide eyes. Her arm rested lightly on the edge of the open window of the car, and the wind played with the cream-colored scarf she had twisted around her long, slender neck. She gazed at me through dark sunglasses, impassively, and nodded slightly when I waved to her. She parked the car in front of the house across the meadow, jumped out with a light dancer's movement and ran up the stairs. She pushed open the screen door without knocking, and didn't look back at me.

"*Hey*—" I heard the male voice greeting her—Brand's or Saul's, I wasn't sure which—the women's voices mingling, excited high-pitched conversation, laughter. It sounded like the greetings of old friends who had been parted for a long time.

I'll bet he's not trying to avoid *her*, I thought moodily, brooding on Brand, thinking of how cool he had acted toward me. And I was exasperated at myself, that I even cared.

Chapter Four

IRAN THE rest of the way to the house, Rags hopping along gaily beside me with little nipping jumps. Russ wasn't back yet, but Yolanda was sitting on the steps, waiting for me.

Rags dashed up to her on the end of the leash, wagging her body furiously as if they were old friends.

"Hey, Yolanda," I said. "Meet Rags."

"Hi, Rags," Yolanda said, running her hand over the dog's coat. "Oh, you're just a puppy, aren't you?"

"Rags, leave her alone."

"That's okay. I love dogs. And you're a sweetie, aren't you? Aren't you? Oh yes. Smoochie smoochie. So, hey, Stacy. I see you met our illustrious neighbors. And lucky you, the ice princess, too."

"Who?"

"Alana." She said the name with exaggeration on all the a's. "Blond? Gorgeous? Elegant? New rag-top Beemer?"

I sat down on the step next to her. "No, I didn't meet her. I think I just encountered her, though."

"She's been off in Europe or somewhere," Yolanda said.

"They expected her back two weeks ago. It seems her trip was *extended*." She said the word "extended," extending the word. "Alana knows how to find diversions," she said.

Apparently Yolanda was not fond of Alana.

"You want to know why I referred to her as the 'Ice Princess' but you're too nice to ask," she said. "So I will tell you. She gets off on tormenting him."

"Who?"

"And, he's got a mad crush on her."

Uneasily, I asked again: "Who?"

"Brand Vandevere. And just about every other man in town."

Figures. "Well, she is beautiful."

"Not as beautiful as you," Yolanda said passionately, "with your long dark curls and those mysterious, deep blue eyes of yours."

I smiled at her. The more I talked to her, the younger she seemed to me. I realized she was barely out of her teens. "Well, not to return a compliment," I said, "but I think *you* are beautiful, too, Yolanda, with your red hair and your green tiger eyes—I bet every man in town is in love with *you*."

"But I scare off my suitors. It doesn't matter. At least I never tease them. Well—not in *that* way."

"Does *she* live there, too?" I nodded at the house across the meadow.

"Alana? Not formally. But you wouldn't know it, the way she carries on. One big happy family."

No, I thought, *there was some tension there.* I had thought it was something to do with me, but maybe that was my own conceit.

"So how *are* they all related?" I asked. "I'm confused. Brand and Tess are cousins, right?"

"Right. Saul is related to Tess in some obscure way. He's her brother-in-law's stepbrother, or something like that."

"Tess and Saul were very welcoming to me," I said.

"But not Brand?"

"He let me know architects aren't welcome in this neck of the woods."

Yolanda laughed. "That's right, you're an architect,

aren't you. Well, Brand's a local, you know. He's jealous of anybody who wants to come from the city and develop this place. Not that you're planning to do that, but still. He's suspicious of anyone new; he thinks he's an old-timer, and I guess compared to you, or me, he is."

"Wonder how long it takes to be accepted around here."

"I wouldn't know. I haven't been around all that long myself. But then, some of us never belong anywhere. The old lady told me that."

"The old lady?"

"The old lady who lived in your house. Mrs. Shapiro."

"Do you miss her?"

"Well, she kept to herself, for the most part. I used see her on her walks to town, in her red coat, carrying her little packages. But toward the end, she stayed in more. After her daughter came to look after her, we hardly saw the old lady at all. Her daughter didn't like her walking to town, then after the old lady fell and hurt her hip, she couldn't go anywhere. Mrs. Shapiro's daughter was sort of . . ."

"Protective?"

"Yeah, I guess."

I had the feeling Yolanda would have chosen a different word.

"She said she wanted her mother out of the house. Wanted to put her into an old folk's home, but her mother didn't want to go. Bonnie Jean, the daughter, she said her mom was losing it a little, there at the end, you know, like mentally? I never saw that, but then, like I said, I didn't have that much contact with the old lady. She was always sort of an eccentric, a hermit, living all alone in that big house, constantly fiddling with it, like it was the Winchester Mystery House or something."

"It's true," I said. "Some of the additions to the house make no sense to me. Stairways you don't need, odd rooms, corridors that seem to take you around in circles . . . that's something I find very intriguing about the house. I guess I'm an eccentric myself, like her, living alone in this big old place."

"And you seem like such a normal, sensible person," Yolanda teased. "Hey, didn't that Winchester lady keep building onto her house because she was told in a séance that it was the only way to elude death?"

"Yeah, something like that. She thought she could trick the grim reaper with false doors and stairs leading nowhere."

"So will you continue to build onto your house, Mrs. Winchester?"

"I don't have as much faith in building as all that," I said. "In fact, there are a few walls I would like to tear *out* of this house."

"Better be careful. You don't know what spirits you may be disturbing."

I laughed, but Yolanda looked at me solemnly.

"You might be opening Pandora's box," she said.

"That's true of any remodeling project. I guess I'll take my chances."

"I will visualize white light around you, for protection."

"Well, I'll take any help I can get," I replied lightly.

Yolanda wandered away and I was glad when big, practical Russ came back from town in his rattling old pickup truck, and the house was suddenly noisy with his stomping boots and the happy barking of a dog.

RUSS WENT UNDER the house to make some repairs to the foundation. I finished cleaning the kitchen and moved into the front parlor where I began to clear the stuff out of the room so we could take out the carpet.

When Russ came up from under the house and the room was empty, we started yanking up the corners of the avocado green carpet in the front parlor. The rotten carpet and pad came up easily, revealing, beneath a thick layer of dust, a plank floor. Soon I was sneezing from the dust, and large chunks of carpet lay in heaps on the emerging rows of wood. Some of the flooring around the bay window appeared to be rotted, but most of it looked pretty good. Tack strip ran around the perimeter of the room, a narrow bed of nails. I would deal with that later; for now I just wanted the rotten carpet out of the house. Russ used his knife to cut the carpet into pieces we could lift and haul out.

"I think we'll notice a real difference in the smell of this house with that carpet out," he said. "You can smell that odor awful strong in the carpet."

Russ, who had not dined on gourmet lunch fare like his sister, was getting hungry. He went down to the village to get a pizza, and I moved on into the dining room, tearing and cutting at the awful green carpet. The room was gloomy, shadowed in the late winter afternoon. I lifted the section by the east window and uncovered the letters, scrawled in red paint across the floor boards: *Edicius*.

I pulled the carpet pad away from the word, which took up a four-by-six square foot space on the plank floor. Graffiti, right in my own dining room! And I thought I was coming to the mountains to get away from graffiti. I started laughing.

I SHOWED IT to Russ when he got back with the pizza.

"Oh, that's nice," he said. "What does that say? Etiquette?"

Russ never had been much of a reader.

"Edi-que-us? Edge-i-see-us?" We tried several different pronunciations.

"I wonder what it means," I said.

"Do you think it means something?"

"It must have been significant to whoever wrote it."

"Nah. It's just scribbling," said Russ. "A gang tag."

"Russ, you have no imagination," I said.

"You have too much imagination, Stacy."

"I just wonder what it means."

"There is a message here," said Russ. "Guess what?"

"What?"

"I got a bake-your-own-pizza." He showed me the pizza. It was cold, wrapped in plastic, unmelted shredded cheese sliding off to one side of the disk.

"You brought home raw pizza."

"It was a take and bake. They don't cook it for you. But I'm so hungry I could eat it raw."

"Shall we see if the oven works?"

RAGS CROUCHED NEARBY, nose quivering.

"Well, the oven works."

"Yup."

Russ groaned. "I can't do any more work. I'm too full."

"What are you talking about?" I teased him. "I've been doing all the work."

"Hey, speaking of work, I met your new neighbor today."

"Who?"

"Forget her name. Cute redhead."

"Ah, that must be Yolanda."

"That's it. Yolanda. She recognized me as your brother, though I don't know how. Claimed she was psychic."

"She saw us together the day we came to look at the property."

"So she's not psychic after all, the little liar."

"Where did you meet her?"

"She works at the pizza place."

She works at the pizza parlor? She told me she's a church caretaker."

"You're kidding."

"No. But maybe she was lying about that, too."

"No reason a church caretaker couldn't be moonlighting as a pizza parlor girl."

"No reason."

"She's a caretaker at a church, hmmm? They don't make them like they used to, do they?"

"How did they used to make them?"

"I don't know, but not like that."

"I hope you're not hitting on my new neighbor already, Russ."

"Me?" Russ acted amazed. "That's not my style."

"Now who's the liar?" I said drolly. Russ had a policy of asking out every attractive woman he ever encountered. He was shot down quite frequently, but sometimes his strategy actually worked for him. He certainly dated a lot of different women.

"You're right, Stacy. I have already hit on her. In fact, we're getting married immediately."

"Marriage, huh? That's out of character for you."

"I've changed."

"Seriously, what did you think of her?" I prodded. I was torn between liking Yolanda and finding her rather strange, and I wanted to know his opinion.

"Oh—" He was stuffing pizza wrappings into a large black trash bag. "Well, she's a fine looking girl."

"She's too young for you," I pointed out.

"Yes, she is."

"So she turned you down."

"Actually, I didn't ask her out."

"You didn't?" I was surprised. Russ, always on the lookout for a new female prospect, wouldn't be deterred by the fact that they lived so far apart. In fact, he might look on that as an advantage. Yolanda was a little young for him, and a bit odd, but he wouldn't let that discourage him. She was beautiful, and he wasn't picky. He'd date anyone once. But he didn't mention her again.

RUSS WAS PLANNING to return to the Bay Area that evening, and he seemed preoccupied and anxious to get going home.

"Shall I take some of this trash with me?" he asked.

"You've already got enough to fill a Dumpster."

"Yes, I guess I'll let you take a few bags of my trash. Oh, Russ, do you have to go back now? Couldn't you stay longer? One more day? No more work, we'll just relax."

"Nope. Gotta get back."

"But why?"

"Things to do," he said, mysteriously. I didn't press him. I was actually looking forward to being alone in my house.

"Well, you've done a lot around here, Russ. I hate to admit it, but I'm indebted to you."

"I will think of some way you can repay me."

"I'm sure you will."

"So," he said. "Anything else you want me to do before I get going?"

"Yes, there is one thing . . ." I thought about my earlier conversation with Yolanda. But I was determined, spirits or no spirits. "I want that ugly green plywood closet yanked out of the library."

"Demolition," he said. "My specialty."

THAT NIGHT I had trouble sleeping. Russ was gone and I was alone in the big house. The heater in the grand bedroom was working well and I should have been cozy in the linens and blankets I had brought from home, but I felt a chill. I lit the lamp next to the bed, got up and went to the closet, where I had noticed blankets were stored. When I pulled a quilt off the top shelf, several envelopes fell to the floor. As I knelt to pick them up I saw they were brittle, yellowed with age. Letters from long ago, addressed to Madelon Shapiro, the old woman who had owned the house before me. For a moment I hesitated. This was personal correspondence, and I had no business poking into it. But what if something in the letters shed light on the history of the house? Curiosity won over conscience, and I took the letters to bed with me along with the quilt.

Inside the first envelope was a handwritten note on plain paper. The postmark was dated some thirty years earlier.

Dear Maddy,
Our hearts are heavy for you. If there is anything we can do, please let us know. He was a wonderful young man. May God comfort you in your sorrow.

James and Winifred Adams

Another envelope, postmarked around the same time. Inside was a greeting card decorated with painted violets. A message of sympathy, in rhyming verse. The note was penned in elegant script: *Dearest Madelon, so terribly sorry.*

And finished with: *Our prayers are with you, my dear. Love, Evelyn.* Or it might have been *Elaine.*

The third and last envelope held a single sheet of white lined paper with a few lines scribbled in odd, sharp, left-leaning handwriting:

who hears the screams in this house of your dreams?
now his heart bleeds as cold as your soul
now he belongs to me

This was signed with a scrawling letter "L." The plain white business-sized envelope was addressed to Madelon Shapiro in the same vigorous, jagged, left-leaning handwriting. The postmark was illegible. There was no return address.

If the three pieces of correspondence were related, the poetry—if you could call it that—was an eerie accompaniment to the sincere expressions of sympathy for a loss of a loved one. I read them again, trying to find meaning in the strange words. A feeling of uneasiness came over me. What had I got myself into here, buying this house, poking around in someone else's past, disturbing old ghosts? I wasn't particularly superstitious, but I knew there was a power in the collected energy of a place, an energy that could affect the well-being of its inhabitants. I tried to shut out the worries, but now, on top of my concerns for building problems, strange neighbors, and money issues, I was brooding over less tangible fears. It was no wonder, really, I thought. Being alone at night for the first time in this strange old house—anyone would be prone to such fancies.

It was a long time before I finally slept.

WITH THE MORNING light I was up and full of energy, my unsettled feelings of the night forgotten. By noon I had finished mucking out the guest room, so that I would have a place for Russ to sleep if I could ever talk him into coming back; I had trimmed the blackberry bushes from the fountain the front of the house, and I was on to the room that really interested me: the library.

It was one of my favorite rooms in the house. Facing the rear of the property, it was sunnier than the front of the house, with tall arch-topped French doors opening to the south-western light filtering through the woods. I loved the huge marble fireplace, the marble tile floor and the mellow old cherry paneling, and now that the monstrous green painted plywood closet in the corner was gone, the proportions of the room were restored and it was lovely. I opened the doors leading out to the stone terrace to let the clean air flow in and wash through the room. I brought a lamp in from the parlor, set it on an old box and began to sort out the books and papers that littered the room.

Books jammed the generous shelves two or three deep. Books on gardening, nature, poetry, history, and language; hundreds of novels, from Tolstoy to Sidney Sheldon, dozens of magazines on various subjects, some dating back ten or twenty years, some much more recent. For hours I sat on the floor, going through the books, looking at each title, setting some aside to give away, some to keep. I stacked the magazines to sort through later.

Glancing up from my work, I gave a start and nearly dropped the book I was holding when I saw a face staring in at me through one of the French doors. The face grinned broadly and I recognized Saul. He came around through the open doorway, a tall, elegant figure, and made a gesture as if he were tipping his hat, though he wasn't wearing a hat. He wore a blue wool sweater that set off his blue eyes, brown corduroy trousers, and brown loafers. I could smell him, a clean aftershave zing, and beside him I felt dusty and disheveled.

"I tried the front door but no one answered," he explained. "Holy Cow—" He was astonished at the mountain of books I had created. "Why does anyone need so many books?"

"Can you believe it? The owner left all these books behind."

"I believe you're pleased about that." He seemed to be laughing at me.

"Yes, I'm pleased. Why? Don't you like books?"

"Books are all right. I read a book now and then. But I'm not a book fanatic like Tess. She acts like every book any hack churns out is divinely inspired scripture. Or Brand. He's got a lot more books than he needs. I guess since he's a writer you could say he contributes to the problem."

"He's a writer? What does he write?"

"Oh, about nature, mostly. Adventure travel. Mountain climbing. How to do it in the wilderness, stuff like that."

"He writes for magazines?"

"Yeah, pretty much. He wrote for some film documentary called *Mountain Extremes*, or *Extreme Mountains*, I can't remember which it was. I'm really not into that whole John Muir thing myself. You got to put more sex and violence into a movie for my taste. I'm only kidding. Yeah, I like what you're doing to the place."

"I had my brother rip out an old plywood closet that was in the corner, there."

"Definitely an improvement. It's looking real good. The house is looking good."

"It will be a long time before it looks as good as your house."

"Oh . . ." He smiled, pleased at the compliment. "I don't know about that."

"Do you—would you like something to drink?" I asked hesitantly, hoping there was something in the fridge in case he said yes.

"No, I can't stay," he said. "But I wanted to invite you to a party we're having at my house next Saturday night. Strictly casual, you know."

"Well, sure, that sounds good. I'm going back to the Bay Area tonight, but I'll be back next weekend. What's the occasion?"

"No occasion. But if you need an excuse to party, I'll be glad to think of one."

"No excuse necessary." I stood up to see him out, groaning at the ache in my back and legs. I had been sitting on the floor too long. "This house is going to kill me," I said, stretching.

"Yes, we are all a little worried about you," he said at the doorway. "This old house could be hazardous to your health." There was a funny tenderness in his voice. He lingered a moment, looking into my eyes with a dreamy expression. "See you next Saturday, okay?"

He disappeared around the corner of the house and I stood motionless for a moment, staring off into the empty woods.

Back in the house I pulled on a sweatshirt and went outside for a walk. Amazing, I thought—the mountain air continued to startle me with its purity and fragrance. Such a contrast to the dark musty corners of that old house!

I walked along the trail behind the house and found the little church, with its white painted façade, and what I thought must be Yolanda's cabin. There was no smoke coming out of the stone chimney, and the small windows set into the log walls of the cabin were dark. I continued along the path and came across a makeshift fort in the woods, old planks nailed between the trunks of several trees. The forest was strangely silent.

Suddenly the two children I had encountered before burst out of the fort, shouting: "It's the witch! Run from the witch!"

I cackled obligingly, which seemed to give them enormous delight, and they ran away with their laughter into the thick of the woods.

"It's been some time since we've had a witch in this forest," said a deep, playful voice.

I turned, startled, to see a man on the trail, walking toward me with a potent athlete's stride. He was tall, and fair, and as he approached I saw his temples were well into their graying, though his face was the sort that would remain young for years.

"Hello!" he said. "Charming children, aren't they?"

"Are they yours?" I asked.

"No!" He looked surprised at the question. "I was not so blessed." The lines around his pale blue eyes creased when he smiled, and there was such a vigor and vitality about the man, I was instantly taken with him.

He held out his hand and we shook. "I'm Father Daniel," he said.

"Oh, from the church—" I tried not to appear surprised. With his easy manner, his casual slacks and polo shirt the same icy blue as his eyes, I would never have taken him for a priest. But what did I know of priests? Only my own stereotypes. I had been raised Unitarian, and seldom even attended church.

"And *you*," he said, "Must be the new lady of the manor."

"Stacy Addison."

He took my hand and shook it vigorously.

"Stacy," he repeated slowly, and I had the feeling he had already known my name. "Well, don't mind the brats. They're all right, really."

"No," I said. "I like them. Though it will be necessary to fatten them up a bit before they're of any use to me."

"And I thought modern witches were finished with all that business of eating children and such."

"Well, sure, most of us are into lighter eating nowadays, but you gotta give the public what they want, you know? Keep up appearances and all that."

"Yes, it's the same with the priesthood."

We laughed together, and I suddenly felt lighter. I had grown moody working alone in the house. We came to a fork in the path and hesitated, for we were about to go off in different directions. He dropped the teasing suddenly and touched my arm.

"It's good to meet you, Stacy," he said sincerely. "And good luck with that old place."

"Thanks," I murmured. "Everyone seems to think I'll need it."

"What, luck?" he asked. "Well . . ." He gazed up the slope toward my house, which was just visible through the trees. "I daresay it'll take something more than luck to put that place right. But a little luck never hurts either, does it?"

He gave me a wink and set off briskly down the path toward Yolanda's cabin and the church. I felt exhilarated with the energy he had left behind, but also a little dazed and unfocused. Was I being paranoid? Or was everybody I met trying to warn me of something?

Better be careful. You don't know what spirits you may be disturbing.

We are all a little worried about you.

It'll take something more than luck to put that place right . . .

Did they know something I didn't know? Maybe the house *was* haunted and nobody wanted to tell me. Nobody but the kids.

I WORKED MY way through the library, sorting, cleaning, hauling out bag after bag of trash and stuff to give away. Most of the shelves were neatly organized now, and I had come to the section of cabinets on the wall around the fireplace. I opened a door and found several dusty old boxes shoved deep inside the lower cabinets.

One of the boxes was filled with old maps, one with Christmas ornaments, and one with what appeared to be decades of personal correspondence, letters, cards, notes, journals. I felt a guilty elation. Wasn't this just the sort of thing you wanted to find in an old house? Perhaps there would be clues to the history of the house, when it was built, information about the people who had lived here. I wanted immediately to start reading through the papers but there was so much more to do, just to be able walk around in the room. Going through the papers would have to be a later project. Still, I couldn't resist a peek. I pulled out a letter at random and read:

. . . it is your selfishness that has led us to this. I am suffering, the children are suffering, and you yourself are suffering, all because your desire to avoid your responsibilities outweighs your sense of honor . . ."

Well! I wasn't prepared for *that*. I put the letter back and shoved the boxes back into the cabinet. The uneasiness I had felt earlier came over me again. It would seem the ghosts who haunt old houses leave their sign in various ways.

It was a relief to be going home to the Bay Area that evening. I told myself I was just tired and overwhelmed with the scope of the project to which I had committed myself, but I could not rid myself of the apprehension. It was a feeling of vague disturbance, like the sensation of being watched. After two days in my new house, much had been accomplished, but it was only a beginning. No wonder I was feeling a little off balance. I just needed to get away from it, get a little perspective.

I packed my car and locked up the house. As I drove slowly out of the meadow I looked up and saw Brand on the hill, his hair burnished with gold, like a crown or a halo, where it was touched by the light of the sun setting low in the woods. I could feel him watching me as I drove away.

MY CITY APARTMENT felt clean, comfortable and small after the big house in the mountains. I was glad to be home with all my favorite things—my comfortable furniture, my books, my paintings, my computer, my bed. And yet, already I was yearning for the mountains—for the house, because I had fallen in love with it, passionately, and for the mountains themselves, the vast distances between the rugged peaks, the maternal folds of the valleys, the absurdly large trees. I craved the scent of the air, with its taste of snow from the higher elevations, the dusky incense richness of the forest floor, the inky blue of the skies.

On Tuesday I passed my neighbor, Mr. Jacobs, on the sidewalk outside our apartment building. I didn't know many of my neighbors well, but I had been friends with Mr. Jacobs since the day I had moved into my apartment. He had lived in the unit above mine for sixty years.

"Did you enjoy your vacation in the mountains, my dear?" he asked with his dramatic voice, a slight scowl on his handsome, deeply lined face. I knew he disapproved of me living alone, and the mountain house was even more isolated than my apartment. "You were gone longer than you said you'd be gone. I missed your singing," he added.

"Don't get on my case today, Mr. Jacobs," I said sternly. "I was *not* gone longer than I said. And don't embarrass me about my singing." He had told me that he enjoyed hearing the sound of my voice floating up by his window on the second floor, which only made me feel too self-conscious to sing.

"Stacy, Stacy. The sound of a neighbor singing brings good luck."

"That's one thing about my house in the country. The neighbors are just far enough away to be spared."

"No, then it's a pity no one can hear you there. Your singing is a pleasure to my ears. Though I have to admit my hearing is not what it used to be."

"That could explain why you don't mind my singing."

"Stacy." He shook his head scoldingly, but he couldn't help laughing. "Oh, I wanted to tell you how much I enjoyed meeting your mother the other day," he said.

I thought I had heard him incorrectly. "Meeting—who?" I asked.

"Your mother. She stopped by to see you—I saw her at your door—and I told her you had gone to the mountains for the weekend, and she said, 'Oh, yes, *that's* right, how silly of me.'"

I stared at him dumbly.

"My dear. What's wrong? What have I said?"

"My mother—this woman said she was my mother?"

"Yes, I'm sure she did. Why? Is that strange?"

"Yes, it is strange. My mother is dead, Mr. Jacobs."

"Oh—I see! Yes, I think I knew that, didn't I? I'm so sorry! I must have misunderstood."

"Well, what did she look like, this mother of mine?"

"Well, I don't remember the particulars. She was a good-looking woman, though she didn't look like you. Her hair was brown, I think. Not as dark as yours. She was wearing a scarf over it. Paisley, I think. There wasn't a big resemblance. That I remember. I think her hair was brown."

That wasn't much to go on. "And she said she was my mother?"

"You know my hearing is bad, my dear."

But he went away perplexed, and I knew he was certain the woman had said she was my mother.

Chapter Five

SATURDAY NIGHT I changed my clothes seven times in front of the old smoky mirror, trying on everything I had brought in my small suitcase. I finally chose a pair of good-fitting black jeans and a dark blue cable-knit sweater the color of my eyes. I pulled on my boots and my white parka and went out into the night, feeling nervous, excited, and a little apprehensive.

Yolanda stood in the moonlight against the darkness at the edge of the meadow, her fine red hair blown by the wind, sharp chin raised, hands tucked into the pockets of a navy pea coat.

"Hi, you!" I called to her.

"Nice night for a party," she said.

"Yeah. You coming?"

She didn't answer, except perhaps with a shrug, and I walked toward her.

"Coming to the party?" I asked, thinking she hadn't heard me.

She turned and smiled blankly as if she was looking

through me, at something beyond me. "Oh, I'll be there—in
spirit," she replied.

"You're not coming?" I said, perplexed.

"Not this time. But you have fun."

"Well, all right, then. I'll see you later."

I made my way across the meadow and up the steps of
the stout white house. I glanced back before I knocked on
the door, but she was already gone.

"STACY!" SAUL OPENED the door as if he had been waiting
behind it, a glass of wine in his hand, a faint scent of cologne
lingering on his neck. I smelled it when he leaned forward
and kissed me off to the side of my lips, friendly, with just a
touch of sensual lingering. Inside the house the air was
warm and fragrant with rosemary and garlic and a hint of
woodsmoke. It was dark but for the light of dozens of candles burning in small glass jars, on tables, on the win-
dowsills. Someone was playing a guitar, the rich tones of the
strings a fine accompaniment to the sounds of laughter and
conversation.

There was a comfort and sensuality in the atmosphere of
the house that appealed to me. It was casual, and yet to
everything was a thoughtful simplicity, a touch of beauty, an
attention to detail. I walked slowly down the short entry
hall, my eyes drawn to the beauty of the photographs on the
walls. At the doorway to the kitchen I nearly collided with
Brand.

"Hello," I said.

"Ah, it's you," he said. "So you came back."

"I think you would have preferred that I didn't."

"I wonder what makes you think you know my prefer-
ences."

Saul stepped between us. "Why don't you fetch the lady
something to drink?" he said to Brand.

Brand was looking at me. "Anything she wants."

"White wine, please," I said.

"He'll bring it to you," Saul said. He seemed eager to get
me away from Brand. He steered me into the large main

room, where the architecture had the uplifting effect of the woods surrounding the house. Massive beams supported the lofty ceilings of rough-hewn cedar, and tall raked windows on either side of the stone fireplace opened up the far wall to the forest. Outside, the trees were lit with a golden glow against the darkness.

"Here she is!" Tess called out gaily. "Stacy, come sit." She was lounging on a caramel leather sofa, wearing an African print caftan in colors of gray and rust and gold. Her gray-blond hair was brushed smooth to her shoulders and dramatic drops of amber hung from her ears. On the hearth sat the guitarist, a young man with long hair so blond it was almost white.

"I was just telling Callie and Ralph about you, Stacy," Tess said. "Everybody, this is our new neighbor, Stacy. The musician is Jeff, and this is Callie and Ralph—they own the mountaineering shop in town. I've been wanting you to meet them, Stacy, because they're always talking about re-modeling their house. Maybe you can help them."

Ralph was a huge florid man who radiated humor and confidence. The woman beside him, Callie, was small and dark with a pointed chin, pointed nose, and black eyes sharp behind oversized glasses.

"We've been wanting to remodel our kitchen," said Ralph. "But we don't know where to begin."

"We can't agree on anything," said Callie.

"Oh, we agree on some things," Ralph said. "It's just that she wants to knock down all the walls, and *I* think that's a surefire—"

"See?" Callie broke in. "He doesn't even agree that we don't agree."

"I understand remodeling a house is a frequent precipita-tor of divorce," said Ralph.

"It can definitely be stressful," I said. "But it can bring you closer, too. Like having a baby."

"Uh, maybe we should do the remodel." Callie shud-dered.

"And then we can have the baby," said Ralph.

"We'll talk about *that* later," Callie said, threatening him with her fist. "Anyway, it's rude to seek medical advice from a doctor at a party, so I suppose it's probably rude to ask for architectural advice from an architect at a party."

"I don't mind," I said. "I like talking shop. What's your house like?"

"Well, it's sort of a funky old cabin," said Callie. "It's old and it's falling apart. But when I saw it, I *had* to have it, you know? I knew I belonged there. It was like it was a person . . . love at first sight."

"I know the feeling," I said.

"Wish I felt that way about a *man*." Callie threw a teasing smile at her husband.

"I've never fallen in love with a house," said Tess. "Not one I could have, anyway. But that's the story of my life with men, too."

Brand had come in to the room and was standing nearby, listening to our conversation. He had my wineglass in his hand but Saul intercepted it and brought it to me himself.

"I'd really like to open the space between our kitchen and the dining room," Callie said. The kitchen is really boxy and all closed in and I want it to be a little more up-to-date, more open to the rest of the house. Ralph is afraid I'd be meddling with the character of the place."

"Well, it's an old house. And I hate it when you knock out a wall and it's really obvious you've hacked the place up, you know. I think it looks hokey."

"It doesn't *have* to look hokey," I said. "If it's done right. Is it a bearing wall?"

"Yeah, pretty sure it is."

"So it's impossible," said Callie.

"Not much is *impossible*," I said. "There are usually ways to get what you want."

"Sure, if you've got the money," Ralph said.

"Exactly," I said. "If you've got the money you can do just about anything you like."

"The money is there, if we'd just get off our butts and re-finance," said Callie. "We've been talking about doing this for years and we can't seem to make it happen."

"All right, Miss Architect," said Ralph. "Just how would

you solve the problem we were just discussing? If money
were no object?"

"Well," I said, "If there is enough space above the ceiling, the header could be reinstalled flush to the ceiling."

Callie looked blank.

Ralph nodded thoughtfully. "You mean, hide the support
above the ceiling. Yes, that might work."

"And it really shouldn't cost that much more," I said, "if
it's feasible at all."

Ralph turned to Brand and asked his opinion. "What do
you think, Vandevere?"

"She's the expert," Brand replied, nodding at me.

"I would defer to the experts myself," I said. "I'm not a
builder, or an engineer. An architect is part of a team."

"Okay, so the architect is a like the team captain, right?"
said Callie.

"That's what we need to get started," added Ralph. "A
captain."

"Stacy," Callie said, clasping her hands as if in prayer,
"would you like the job?"

"Well," I said, "someone once told me you haven't got
much use for architects around these parts."

"We'll find a use for you," Saul said.

Tess winked at me. Brand remained inscrutable.

He looks good tonight, I thought. But then he always
looked good to me. He was wearing a twill jacket over his
Levis, a white button down shirt opened at the throat, buck-
skin cowboy boots, and a woven leather belt with a plain silver buckle. His hair was pulled back like it had been the first
time I'd seen him, exposing his strong bones, the breadth of
his brow.

"Well, we hadn't planned on using an architect," said
Callie. "But it seems we can't make anything happen on our
own."

Ralph said, "I thought an architect would just tell us to
raze the place and start new."

"Well, I haven't seen it yet, but—"

"I hear you've already done wonders to your place,
Stacy," said Tess.

"She's already torn the place up!" said Saul. "Pulled down walls. I've seen it with my own eyes!"

Brand was standing right next to me now, and I could literally see the clench of his jaw as Saul spoke these words.

"I just tore out an old closet someone had cobbled in," I said.

"Are you talking about that plywood thing by the fireplace in the library?" Brand asked me in a low voice.

"Yes." I looked at him, surprised that he knew what I was talking about, and defiant. "It had to go."

"I agree." His voice was so soft I nearly missed his comment. "I always wanted to tear that thing out myself."

He moved off and disappeared into the kitchen. I let out a great sigh, and stared off across the room at a pair of small oil paintings on the far wall, wilderness worlds created with spare shapes and bright energetic splashes of color. I hadn't realized Brand's presence had created such tension inside me. I found myself looking for his approval, and at the same time, I was eager to defy him. Why was I investing such emotion in his opinion? I felt irritated with myself.

Someone came into the entry hall amidst great fanfare— there was a howl of laughter and a chorus of enthusiastic greetings. A windswept woman in a white silk scarf made an impressive entrance into the living room. Caramel colored chin length hair, elegant, sophisticated, understated style, perfect slim figure. The woman I had seen driving the BMW.

"Alana—hello!" sang out Tess, who stood to greet her. "Welcome. Oh, you've cut your hair. It's so chic." The newcomer made her way smoothly across the room and accepted the embrace as if bestowing an honor upon Tess. She was a blond on blond beauty, wearing beige khakis, white safari shirt, camel jacket, sheepskin boots, and the white scarf. The rich coloring of her skin was striking enough to pull it off.

"So Alana, you made it back from darkest Africa," said Ralph, jovial.

"It was Thailand, actually," Alana said, drawing a strand of tawny hair away from her face. She was all smoothness,

I thought: smooth voice, smooth hair, and smooth skin, if you touched it.

"How was it?" asked Callie.

"Great," said Alana, with a tossed-away expression in her voice. Jeff, the blond guitarist, was staring at her.

"Buying treasures for your shop?" Callie asked politely.

"Mmm." Alana nodded, but only slightly, just with the tip of her chin, as if she couldn't be bothered to provide an answer. "Which reminds me—" She drew a small wrapped package out of her jacket. "I've got a little something for Brand's birthday."

Brand's birthday?

"He's in the kitchen, I think," said Tess.

Alana slipped away from the group with an apologetic smile—*sorry to be taking myself away from you so soon*—and glided away toward the kitchen. There were more exclamations of greeting at her appearance, and I heard Brand's voice among the others. I wondered what she had brought him. Would he be pleased with it, whatever it was? What sort of gifts did he give her?

Saul sat next to me.

"So it's Brand's birthday," I said to him. "You told me there was no occasion."

"Saul, I told you to tell her it was a birthday party," said Tess.

"Don't worry, he doesn't want any presents," said Saul.

"I wouldn't have given him one anyway," I said. "But you should have told me."

"No," Saul insisted. "It was better you didn't know. You would have fretted about it."

Tess went to help Brand in the kitchen. Saul and I sat together, talking easily about nothing much. He was breezy, quick-witted and admiring, making no secret of his attraction for me, though I suspected he was rather easily attracted. And he wasn't the only one. The house seemed to be filled with rugged, good-looking men. A dimpled, familiar-looking fellow ignored Saul's scowling, sat between us on the sofa, and introduced himself as Thaddeus Knight.

"That's not your real name, is it?" I said.

"Actually, no, not entirely." He took my wine from me and kissed my hand, then he drained the glass with a lusty groan.

"Thad, what the hell are you doing?" That was Jeff, the guitarist. His fingers never faltered on the strings.

"I drinketh from the lady's cup," Thaddeus said. "I was tempted; I could help it not."

"Thad, you have no self-discipline," Callie said.

"I think his problem stems from lack of self-esteem," said Ralph.

"He needs to get in touch with his feelings," Callie added.

"He's codependent," said Jeff.

"I'm trying to be codependent but no one will be codependent with me," Thaddeus sighed.

Tess leaned into me and said: "These guys are Brand's mountaineering buddies. They've been friends for thousands of years."

"They sound like therapists," I said.

Jeff began to play the guitar with a wilder, more abandoned aspect.

"Flamenco!" shouted Thad, and he mimed playing castanets.

"I've seen you somewhere before," I said to Thad, when he had calmed down a little.

"Honey, I've heard that line before."

"Sorry, but it's true. You look really familiar."

"I know. Do you ever watch the soaps?"

"Soap operas? You mean on TV?"

"I was Horatio on *The Young and the Restless*."

"Sorry. I never watch soap operas."

"I did a dog food commercial."

"That's it. That's where I've seen you. Mighty Dog."

"I played the handsome young dog owner who throws the stick into the lake."

"I really believed you in the part."

There was a big refectory table heaped with food in the dining room, plenty to drink, and good company. Besides Brand's friends, there were people from the county office where Tess worked, a friendly, jokey bunch. I tried to talk to Alana several times throughout the evening, but she never seemed interested in keeping a conversation going with me. Invariably she would turn away or speak to someone else. Once she excused herself to get another glass of wine, and once she said, "I'd better go see if we ought to put out more cheese," as if she were the hostess. But everyone else went out of their way to make me feel welcome, and even Brand, though he hardly said a word to me, made sure my glass was never empty.

I observed Alana and Brand, perplexed. I couldn't figure out how they fit together. They seemed more than friends, yet not quite a couple.

Later the party became smaller and more intimate. Most of the guests had gone home, but a couple of Brand's friends had traveled long distance and were spending the night. We sat jammed together around the kitchen table, Saul and Tess, Ralph with his arm slung over Callie's shoulder, Jeff the white-blond musician, Thad of the dimpled smile, Brand and Alana, next to each other but not touching. A colony of bottles and glasses in various stages of emptiness gathered before us on the table.

Brand's mountaineering friends were talking about climbs they had done, arguing about whether this or that one was really a "five or a five-seven," or even a "six." They were rating the difficulty of particular routes by number. The language was unfamiliar to me, and I was fascinated.

"Do you climb, Stacy?" Callie asked me.

"No," I shook my head. "I'm way too much of a coward."

"Maybe you just need the right partner," Thad suggested. "I'll take you rock climbing some time. You wouldn't be afraid with me."

"Be afraid!" cried Ralph. "Be very afraid."

"Maybe she's smarter than that, anyway," said Saul. "It's never made a lot of sense to me, pulling yourself up a mountain with ropes and pulleys."

"It's not like that," said Jeff disdainfully, and he tossed back a length of that amazing white hair. "Or it shouldn't be.

I don't use the equipment for direct aid. I only use it for protection."

"Not all climbers are as pure as *you* are, Jeff," said Thad.

"No, but they strive to be," replied Jeff.

"Sure," said Ralph, "the goal ought to be to leave the rock as clean as you find it. Get up the route on your own, without aid. But sometimes, purity isn't necessarily appropriate to the situation. Like if you're checking out a new route—"

"But there's not so much of that happening anymore, is there?" said Brand.

"It's the nineties, man." Thad shook his head sadly.

Ralph grew excited. "When we all started out, that was the thing. Everybody wanted to bag those first ascents. Nowadays it's more like, how elegantly can you perform the climb?"

Brand agreed. "The planet is shrinking. That's the way of it. Still, it must be said . . . there's nothing like being the first on a route." His voice softened and trailed away, and he seemed to be remembering one of those first ascents.

Alana tapped the bottom of her Beck's on the table. She had the look of someone waiting for an amateur recital to be finished.

"I sell the equipment for a living," Ralph went on, oblivious. "So it might sound kind of ironic for me to say this, but I think you can get too much into the gadget part of it, all the latest equipment, the technology. What is really righteous is when you can just get back into the bare essentials kind of balance climbing. Go lighter, take less stuff with you, get closer to the rock. Still, in the big mountains, you have to make concessions to your philosophies, just to be there."

"The smaller expeditions are nice." Brand's voice was wistful. "Even in the big mountains."

"Yeah, but Everest is getting crowded, Brand," Ralph said emphatically. "If you want to bag the mother, you gotta wait in line. That's just the way it is."

"I guess."

"You gotta do it, man. Hell. You know it's this lifelong dream of yours."

"It's *your* lifelong dream, Ralph," said his wife.

"Brand and me, we dreamed that dream together."

"Brand has bigger dreams now," said Callie. "Don't you, Brand?"

"Oh yeah?" said Ralph before Brand could answer. "I tell you what. Brand is going back to Everest."

Callie gave her head a shake. "Maybe. Or maybe he's past all that." She put up a hand in front of Brand's face, like a traffic cop, to stop him from speaking. "Brand summited K2, you know, and it was once thought that K2 might be even higher than Everest."

"Nah," Ralph scoffed at that. "Everest is the big prize. It always was, and it always will be."

"You're just after some kind of vicarious thrill, since you can't do it yourself, Ralph," Callie said.

"There is that," Ralph admitted.

"Ralph's got this thing with his heart and I told him if he goes to that altitude again, I will leave him."

"But I just have this feeling in my gut," said Ralph. "Brand is going back, and by God, he—"

"Ralph, calm down," said Callie.

I realized this must be an old argument.

"I'll go to Everest," Brand said. "If I get the assignment."

"Oh, man." Ralph was distressed. "I recall a time you would have hocked your mother's silver to get a chance at the Goddess Mother of the World. Now it's *If I get the assignment*—"

Brand laughed.

"He'll get it," Tess said, matter of fact. "And he'll go. If it's right for him to go."

"I'll go if they pay me to go," Brand said.

"You're becoming a mercenary, Vandevere." Ralph said it with disgust.

"Well, you would certainly have to pay *me* just to get anywhere near a mountain like that," said Saul.

"Brand has no choice," Thad announced with an air of proclamation. "He must go back . . ."

"He came *so* close," said Tess.

"Twenty-eight thousand, five hundred feet!" Jeff spoke

with portentous drama. "Banished from the mountain by the demon winds."

"Ralph was Brand's partner on that expedition," Callie explained for my benefit.

"We could practically taste the summit." Ralph moaned. "We were both strong as oxen, but there was another strong team. We drew lots and came in second, so the expedition leader and his girlfriend went first. We had to retreat when the monsoon practically blew the first summit team off the mountain."

Ralph grinned at Alana, nudged her with his elbow. "You know we practically had to tie Brand down and haul him off the mountain in shackles, he was so determined to climb that mother. But it was just too risky."

"Yes," she said dryly. "I've heard the story."

"But what's the point of it all?" said Saul. "Besides giving you guys these giant egos? And please don't give me that 'because it's there' bullshit."

"It's a spiritual thing," said Ralph. "You take on one of the big peaks—Makalu, K2, Annapurna, Everest—if you get through that experience, you're going to come home with your head screwed on a little differently."

"Yeah," Jeff said. "Climbing in the Himalayas doesn't give you an ego, it takes it away. It makes you humble. If you're *not* humble when you attempt those mountains, you suffer. The less humble you are, the more you suffer."

"You must have found yourself in continual, hideous pain, Jeffro," Thad commented.

"Shove it, Wifford."

"Maybe that's why climbing is such a high," said Saul. "It feels so good when you stop."

"I, personally, am not into suffering," said Thaddeus Knight, the dimpled dark cherub, and to look at him you believed it was true. He would have looked right sitting in the captain's chair on a yacht in the warm Caribbean. "I stay away from extremes. Look at Denali—Mount McKinley. I think the people who attempt *that* one are insane. If the weather was ever decent, it would be a pretty mellow excursion, but there you're facing blizzards and constant death conditions. I've never seen the charm in climbing ice."

"You're a puss, Thad." Jeff shook his white-blond head. "Ice climbing is awesome."

"It all seems so perilous," I said.

"Climbing is actually quite safe, if you know what you're doing," said Callie.

"In the Sierra, sure," said Ralph. "But the Himalayas, different story."

"And nobody knows what they're doing all the time," said Brand. "If you're really living on the edge, there may come a time when you just have to wing it."

"That's true of life in general," said Tess. "Not just for climbing."

"Except for Jeff," Thad said. "He always knows exactly what he's doing. Never a slip."

"For once, Thaddeus, you're probably right," Jeff deadpanned.

"Well," said Brand, "I would rather be roped up with Jeff Planter than just about anybody else in the world, not mentioning a couple other people in this room. But I never say never. That's what *I* got from the big mountains."

"Our bud Dan McKnight died in a crevasse fall on K2," Jeff said, looking at me. "And he was the best climber I knew."

"The expedition to the seventh ring of hell," Ralph said. "The mountains were so gorgeous that day, it was unreal."

"And then, there was the avalanche," Alana put in. Her voice was tired, as if she knew exactly what was coming next.

Ralph ignored Alana's tone. He wanted to tell it. "The three of us—Brand, Jeff, and me," he said, "We were coming down the mountain after summiting that big bastard. We were roped together when it happened. I thought for sure we were gonna die together."

"The avalanche really changed something in me," Brand said. "Here I am, in the middle of this churning thing, this avalanche—I'm hurtling down into nothingness, I'm going to be buried alive and I have about thirty seconds left to live—and suddenly, it was like, *hey*, I have thirty seconds remaining to me, so I'd better make them the most complete thirty seconds I have ever experienced. And then I found out I was going to live and there wasn't just thirty seconds left to me but thousands, maybe millions of seconds, and it just seemed like such a gift. And I could never *not* feel that way again. Even when we were burying Dan at the base of the mountain, I kept thinking, *Wow.* It's all like—a *gift.* Even that, the horror, the joy—all of it. A gift."

"The present is a present," Callie said.

"The weird thing is," Ralph went on, "we all survived the avalanche. We were blown away, literally, but we made it out okay. All three of us, together. Then we were walking down to camp for the night and Dan fell. He never saw the crevasse. He was roped, and we got him out, but it didn't matter. Hit his head on the ice, and he was gone."

Alana stretched, looking bored. "I'm going to get going," she yawned. "Walk me to my car, Brand?"

I felt irritated with her for breaking the rhythm of the conversation, especially when the guys were speaking of something so personal. She had been quiet, not really joining in the conversation. Maybe she didn't like not being the center of attention. Maybe she hadn't been around when these adventures had taken place and she felt like an outsider. I understood how that felt.

"You're not exactly strangers to each other, the lot of you," I said when Brand and Alana had gone out.

Ralph stretched, throwing his massive arms into the air, settling them down comfortably around Callie's shoulders. "Oh, yeah. Well, Brand and me, we go back. Knew each other as kids. Hooked up with Thaddeus at the university . . . he introduced us to Jeff, and Callie—"

"Jeff and Thad have known each other since they were *babies*," Callie said.

"Have they always been so polite and nice to each other?" I asked her, as if they weren't sitting right there.

"Oh, that gets worse every year," she laughed. "We try to ignore them."

"We aren't easily ignored," Thad warned.

"Anyway," said Callie, "We should apologize for all this bragging about past exploits, that's all it is. I know Alana gets irritated with all the climbing talk."

"Well," said Tess, "You've got some entertaining stories."

"Yeah, but some of them we've heard before," said Saul.

The door banged shut again. Brand came back into the room and slid into the booth, glancing at me from across the table.

"What's going on, bud?" Jeff said, jabbing Brand with an elbow. "We didn't expect to see you back so soon."

Brand ignored him, took a swig of his beer. But I could see they were all wondering about it.

"Well," I said. "It's about time for me to be going too." I got up from my chair and brought my wineglass to the sink.

"Stacy," said Tess, "I'm so glad you came tonight."

"I'm glad you came tonight, too," said Saul.

"Me too!" shouted Thad.

"I'd have to agree with Thad on this one," said Jeff. "Damn."

Callie and Ralph dutifully added their concurrence.

I waited a beat, then said, "Well, Brand, that leaves only you. Happy birthday anyway."

Everyone laughed, and Brand rose and followed me as I walked to the door.

I turned just before I went out, and he was looking at me, seemed about to say something, when Saul appeared and stepped between us.

"I'll walk you home, Stacy," he said, taking my arm.

Brand's expression changed. He moved away.

I allowed Saul to show me out.

SAUL WALKED ME home, and when we arrived at my door he asked me out for the next Saturday. There was an antique fair and flea market every weekend at the bottom of the mountain and he wanted me to go with him.

I hesitated. I hadn't gone out with anyone since Justin. I still felt like I was his girlfriend. Which was stupid. Buying the house in the mountains had been a huge statement of intent, and he had done nothing to change that course.

"You *are* coming back up next week? . . ." Saul said.

"Yes, if the weather holds. I'm not coming up in a storm."

"Good, I'll pick you up at eight Saturday morning. Right after breakfast. You gotta get there early to get the best stuff, right?"

"All right," I said. "But make it nine."

We stood awkwardly by my porch, and I looked up at the high dormer window of the house across the meadow. A man stood motionless, dark against the glow of the room behind him. He seemed to be looking down at Saul and me.

"Is that Brand?" I asked.

Saul turned and followed my gaze. "Probably. Those are his rooms up there on the top floor."

Saul waved lazily, but the figure in the window had moved away.

Chapter Six

TUESDAY MORNING I was in my office in San Francisco working on a stairway detail for a client's new house when Janine, my manic boss, came in, blustery and panting, flinging off her jacket and purse, dropping her briefcase on the floor with a heavy thump.

"So, did the building department give you an audition?" I asked, glancing up from the computer screen.

"I jumped through a few hoops," she answered. "We have to ask for a variance."

"For that setback? But there's an existing structure!" I was dismayed, though not really surprised.

"We're redoing too large a percentage of it. They're counting it as new."

"I was afraid of that."

"The Garcias won't be pleased," she said matter-of-factly. "And Stacy, that reminds me."

"What?"

"Carlos Garcia told me he had a rather strange phone call a couple days ago. He said someone called him and spoke about *you*. Asked questions about you, actually."

"What kind of questions?"

She shrugged. "Something about money, about how much he's paying for your services, or something. And he said you should be watched carefully, because you're a junkie, or some damn thing."

"What—?" I stared at her, incredulous.

"I know, I told him it had to be a crank call."

"That's weird."

"Well, don't worry about it. You get the messages?"

"No."

I stared out the large window which looked out over the city toward the glimmer of the bay beyond. Who would have done such a thing? Just some crank caller, obviously. Carlos must have misunderstood it being about *me*. But I knew Carlos was a practical man. He wouldn't have even mentioned it to Janine unless he was sure, and that bothered me.

Janine punched on her answering machine and sat down with her pad and pen.

She took the number of a prospective client and doodled when Mrs. Elliot's voice came on, rambling, as usual, about her various worries. Would the cabinets be delivered on time? Was the new lighting plan adequate? Did the contractor really know what he was doing? Mrs. Elliot's kitchen was being remodeled and it was very traumatic for her. There was a message from Janine's daughter and one from Bob at the building department—Janine had left her reading glasses there.

"Oh, damn," she said. "I knew I'd forgotten something."

There was a loud buzz on the machine, like feedback into a microphone. Then came the voice, impenetrable, indistinguishable, male or female? I couldn't tell.

"This message is for the employer of Stacy Addison. You should be aware she will be leaving you soon."

There was a click, then a dial tone. The machine stopped, and the tape rewound.

Janine snorted. "What was *that* about?"

A chill of apprehension rippled up my spine and raised the goosebumps on my arms. I shook my head.

"Weird. You're not planning to leave me soon, are you, Stacy?"

"No!" I replied, with a guilty conscience, thinking about my fantasy of starting my own business in the mountains. But that was just a daydream. I hadn't even mentioned the idea to Russ, because he would think I was crazy.

"Well, you know this city is full of wackos," Janine said reassuringly, but I could see she was puzzled too.

The phone incident stayed with me all day, a thin layer of worry coloring all my thoughts. I went home a little early and went straight to the answering machine, expecting something awful. But there were no messages at all.

"ABBY, I'M SO glad to see you."

"Me too. I've *missed* you, Stace."

We hugged each other so hard it hurt. It had been a long time since I'd seen my best friend. We had known each other since high school, and she owned one of the apartments in my building, but several months earlier she had moved down near Monterey to be with her boyfriend.

"Well, I can't stay long," she cried breathlessly. "I've come to make arrangements—I'm selling my apartment!"

"You're *selling* it! Are you serious?"

"We're getting married, Stacy."

"You—oh my God. Congratulations! Oh, *Abby!*" I grabbed her again. I think we were both screaming at this point.

She showed off her ring.

"That diamond is *huge*," I said. We screamed again. "Why didn't you *call* me?"

"I wanted to surprise you. You're not mad that I'm selling?"

"Of course I'm mad. I'm furious. I'm jealous—of that beach house you're marrying."

"Stacy!" She punched me. "You know I'd marry Eddie even if he had nothing."

"Without the beach house, without the diamonds?"

"Certainly. Do you really think I'd marry for money?

Well, maybe you know me. But, no. He's a sweet, sweet man. I'm completely smitten."

"Yes, he's nice. I approve of him."

"And Stacy . . ."

"What?"

"I want you to be my maid of honor. Will you?"

"Of course I will be your maid of honor, you idiot!" We screamed some more, but I was beginning to get hoarse. "When? *When?*"

"June, obviously!"

"*Ob*viously. Oh my God. I can't believe one of us is finally getting married."

"And I will make sure you catch my bouquet."

"Uh—thanks."

"So . . ."

"What?"

"So how is *your* love life? Don't tell me you're still in limbo."

I shrugged. "I have a date Saturday. But who cares about that? You're getting *married*—"

"Stacy! With whom do you have a date?"

"Why do you sound so amazed?" I asked, offended.

"Stacy, you haven't dated anyone in months. Not since Justin."

"You've got a point there."

"So who is he?"

"My neighbor. In the mountains. He's an investment banker, which should please you."

"The one you told me about, that pirate guy who tried to steal your house from the old lady who owned it?"

"No, no, not that one," I said with a smile. I liked the image of Brand as a pirate. "Though I *have* met him . . ."

"So, what's he like?"

"Well, he's . . . wild. He reminds me of a wild animal, like a wolf, or an eagle. Fierce, but elegant, somehow. He's sort of quiet, though he speaks well. He scares me sometimes, when I think of him coveting my house like that, and he seems to resent me, but—"

"No, I don't mean *him,* I mean the one you're going *out* with."

"Oh . . ." Somehow I wasn't interested in discussing Saul. I wanted to talk about Brand. But why? He was nothing to me.

Abby laughed at my distracted expression. "What's this? I think *you* are the one who is smitten. He's really turned your head, hasn't he? Where's he taking you?"

She was talking about Saul.

"We're going to an antique fair and flea market."

"The flea market." She grimaced. "Sounds like a *cheap* date to me."

"I happen to enjoy flea markets. You can find things you would never find anyplace else—"

"Sure, fine. I just think it's a bad precedent to set, for a first date."

"Where did Eddie take you on your first date?"

"Monte Carlo."

"Oh yeah, I forgot about that."

She smiled, very smug.

"Fuck you," I said.

PROMPTLY AT NINE on Saturday morning, Saul appeared at my door. He had on chinos and a pink polo shirt, and carried a black motorcycle jacket slung over one shoulder. I was reluctant to leave the house, there was so much I wanted to get done. I had arrived late the night before, so I hadn't had a chance to work much on the place. It was satisfying to find it untouched and silent, just the way I'd left it. In the morning the sun filled the windows, which were bare since I had pulled off all the old draperies.

"You're punctual," I said.

"When I have a compelling reason to be," Saul replied.

We drove off together in a sporty little roadster which was marvelous on the curving mountain roads. The forest was green with patches of snow here and there; during the week a small storm had passed through but when the sun returned the snow had melted. Winter in our little village,

3,500 feet in elevation, was much more forgiving than it was at the higher mountain elevations. The Sonora pass, at almost 10,000 feet, was closed from the first snowfall until spring. As we drove down from the pines and cedars into the rolling oak hills above Sonora, winter disappeared altogether.

"Great car," I said. "But what is it?"

"It's an Austin Healy Sprite," he said with a touch of satisfied pride. "Completely restored. An oldie but goodie."

In the pleasure of the drive, the bright low-slung sunshine, and the morning bustle of the flea market, I forgot my reluctance to leave my projects. I found several items for the house, including an old mantel clock, a small Persian rug, and a copper tea kettle. We bought hot dogs and sat on the grass to eat.

"So tell me, Saul. What does an investment banker actually do? And how did you end up in a little village in the Sierra, rather than, say, Wall Street or someplace?"

"Answer to question number one: as little as possible. Answer to question number two: when you are very successful at what you do, you can do it anywhere. And when you are very *very* successful, you can retire quite comfortably."

He must have been very *very* successful, I thought, to have retired at such a young age. He was a bit older than I'd first thought him, but he still couldn't be older than his late thirties.

"Well, I'm surprised to see *you* here, Saul," said a woman's voice from behind us.

We turned to see Yolanda squatting on a quilt a few feet away. She was wearing shorts with tights underneath, and sunglasses. Her white silk blouse was tied at her slender waist.

"Hello, Yo-landa." Saul drawled her name.

"Hi, Stacy," she nodded at me. "So you're into treasure hunting too?"

"Yeah, look at this stuff she found," said Saul. "It's good stuff."

"I didn't think you went for the previously owned, Saul," Yolanda said.

"Well, I admit it," he replied. "I like new things. I was always a sucker for a new car. Even though they depreciate by the thousands as soon as you drive them off the lot. Love the way they smell."

"But the Austin Healy Sprite —" I said.

"I make exceptions for classics, of course."

"I like beautiful old things," I said. "If they're a little old and battered, so much the better."

"In that case there is someone I want to set you up with," Yolanda joked.

"She's already got a date," said Saul.

We finished lunch and the three of us wandered together through the flea market, until Yolanda left us abruptly, saying she had to meet someone.

Saul drove home slowly. He seemed tired.

"So, you and Yolanda are old friends," I commented.

"Oh, we dated for a little while," he replied. "Nothing serious. She's not my type."

"For some reason I thought she was coming to your party last Saturday. But I guess not."

He shrugged. "Alana doesn't like her."

"And what Alana says goes around your place, huh?"

"Alana doesn't have to *say* anything. But yes. Mostly."

"Aren't you as fond of Alana as everyone else seems to be?"

"Well . . ." he smiled to himself. "Let's just say that not *everyone* buys into her act."

"Her act?"

"Oh . . ." He snapped himself out of his pensive mood, deliberately, as if afraid he might say something he would later regret. "Alana's all right," he went on. "She's just insecure."

"Insecure?" I pondered this. That wasn't the impression she made on me. But then, maybe that was why she was cool toward me. Maybe she was just shy. "So, you are a student of human nature, Saul," I said.

He pulled the rearview mirror down for a moment to look

at himself as he drove, and said earnestly: "Yes, I like to think so. I'll tell you about my theories sometime."

"So Alana and Brand are . . ." I hesitated, wondering how to put it.

"Alana and Brand *are,* yes!" He laughed. "Or at least that is how Brand would like it to be. Alana has other ideas, I think."

"He likes her more than she likes him?"

"I think she likes him fine. She just likes to have her cake and eat it too, if you know what I mean."

"Does he mind?"

"Of course he minds. Brand is very traditional in some ways. He wants the house with the white picket fence and a princess in a tower to rescue."

"And she's the princess."

"Yeah, though she won't let him rescue her. But she lets him wine and dine her a lot!" He laughed, and I stared out at the oaks with their twisted trunks growing along the side of the highway. Occasionally the distant peaks of the Sierra could be glimpsed through a dip in the hills. On the high ridges, there was snow.

"Is Alana jealous of Yolanda, then?" I asked

"I don't know. Maybe. I think she just doesn't like her."

"Yolanda is so outrageous and funny and direct—"

"Maybe that's what Alana doesn't like about her. Alana doesn't really appreciate anyone who might possibly up-stage her in front of Brand. She probably doesn't like you for the same reason. Isn't it obvious? You're beautiful in a weird way—"

"A weird way!"

"Yes, unusual. What's wrong with that? You're sexy. You're smart and you make good money at an interesting job. And you've got the house. Brand always wanted that house."

"So I've heard."

"Yeah?" He peered at me through dark sunglasses. "What have you heard?"

"Just that. He wanted the house."

"I think you heard something else."

"I heard that he tried to do a deal with the old lady—tried to get her to sell the property to him for way below market value."

"You know about that?" His voice was wary.

"Is it true, then?"

He shrugged. "You can't blame a guy for trying, I guess."

"I guess."

"No law against making a lowball offer on a piece of real estate."

"No, there isn't."

"Still, he shouldn't have tried to take advantage of someone, just because she's old and senile, you know?"

So it was true, what I'd heard about Brand. He was Iona's Creeper. I was unreasonably disappointed. I realized I had hoped it was just an ugly rumor. Now why should that be? I didn't even like the guy. This just proved I had a good reason not to like him.

"So who told you about this?" asked Saul.

"The real estate agent who handled the sale of the house."

"Iona, right?"

"Right. You know her?"

"Sure, she's a great old gal."

"Yeah."

"Word gets around, it would seem." Saul sounded sad. "I just hope Tess doesn't get wind of it. She feels responsible for him, you know. She's bailed him out before, same sort of deal."

"Same sort of deal?"

"Yeah. Another scam, you know. That one went a bit further, further out on the limb legally, if you know what I mean. An old woman down in Phoenix. Multimillionaire. Authorities caught on, busted him. They did some plea bargain thing, Tess paid out a bunch of money and took him in when he didn't have a place to go. He's her cousin, and she wants to do well for him, but he just uses her, I think. She's always trying to reform him, but I just don't think he's ever going to change. It would break her heart if she found out about this latest stunt of his."

"Well, I wouldn't tell her. But maybe she should be told, for her own sake."

"She *does* know. And yet, she doesn't want to know. Understand what I mean?"

"Yeah. I understand."

"And I certainly wouldn't mention any of this to Brand, if I were you. Not if you want to stay healthy."

"Sounds like a warning."

"Well . . . he's already a tad upset that you got the house and he didn't. I know he wouldn't be pleased if it got out, what he tried with the old lady. No telling what he'd do if . . . but *anyway*. I wouldn't worry about it."

"Well, what *would* he do?"

Saul hesitated, then shrugged. "I don't know. Brand has a violent nature, which he tries to keep hidden. It's just better left alone."

"Why do you let him live in your house?" I asked.

"It's because of Tess. I do it for her. If it was up to me, he'd be out on his ass. She's trying to reform him. Maybe she'll succeed, who knows? Anyway, don't let what I've told you make you think any less of us. Brand's really not a bad guy, you know."

Just greedy and unscrupulous, I thought.

We pulled into the parking area next to the house and Saul flipped off the engine just before the car came to a halt. I wanted to get home but he insisted I come up with him, if only for a moment, because Tess wanted to say hello.

I did want to see Tess—and I wanted to see Brand, too. I was drawn to him, and I wondered why, knowing the kind of man he was. I wanted to prove to myself he had no power over me.

Alana was sitting in the dining area, studying a sheaf of blueprints spread out on the big refectory table. Brand was bent over her, his arm on the back of her chair, a pencil in his hand. He straightened up when we came in and nodded a stiff greeting.

"Hey," said Saul. "You guys are back early. I didn't see your car, Alana."

"I didn't drive it," she replied coolly. She looked away from us and returned her attention to the plans.

I thought: No, she isn't shy; she *is* cold.

"Where is Tess?" I asked.

"Tess has a weaving class every Saturday afternoon," Alana answered without looking up.

I was feeling more and more uncomfortable. Why did Saul bring me here to see Tess if she wasn't going to be here? If Alana knew about the weaving class, surely he did too.

"Oh, *that's* right," Saul said. "I forgot about weaving class. Well—how about a drink, Stacy?"

Alana and Brand flickered a look at each other, one of those secret expressions that pass between intimates when pitiful and obnoxious people are near. I wanted to slink away but I thought leaving abruptly would be worse than pretending I felt at ease and accepting the drink. So I took a bottle of mineral water and sat down with Saul on the sofa by the fireplace. Surreptitiously I gazed at the couple working at the table, curious to know what the plans were for but too shy to ask.

Saul didn't seem the slightest bit interested in them or their plans. He chattered on about something or other and I found myself growing irritated with him, wishing he would be quiet so I could hear what Brand and Alana were talking about.

I was almost finished with my drink, relieved that I would soon be able to go home. Brand's voice cut through Saul's monologue and I heard the words: "Let's ask Stacy. She's the architect."

My guard went up. Was that a grudging respect in his voice? Or was it sarcasm?

"Ask Stacy what?" Saul asked with a frown.

"How wide does an interior door in a retail shop have to be?"

"Three feet, for wheelchair access," I said. "With a three-foot turning radius after the door swing. But I don't know local codes yet."

Alana cocked her head at Brand. "See?" she said. "I told you so."

I stood up and made for the door. "I better get going. I have a lot I want to get done this afternoon."

"Good-bye," said Alana gravely. Brand folded his arms and nodded.

"I'll walk you—" Saul started to rise.

"Please, no need. Thanks for everything—" I pulled the door shut behind me before he could say any more, and ran down the steps.

I checked my mailbox before I went into the house, and was surprised to find there was actually something in there. It was a letter in a plain white envelope, postmarked San Francisco, sender unidentified. I opened the folded lined paper and read the words:

Go back to the city where you belong

I looked over my shoulder, feeling suddenly spooked. I read the words again, and again. I didn't recognize the handwriting, though something about it seemed familiar to me. Finally I crumbled up the paper and tossed it in the woodpile. I didn't even want it in my house.

"SO YOU HAVEN'T said a word about this hot date of yours."

It was late Sunday night and I was in bed in my apartment in San Francisco, talking to Abby on the telephone. We had been on the line nearly an hour, as I told her about the progress I was making on the old house, and she talked about her wedding plans. The local trash hauler had taken several loads of junk away for me and the house was clean. Though badly in need of paint, the rooms were bright, all the heavy plastic drapes were gone, the old carpet was out, and the house had a new, more subtle perfume, like campfires and cedar trees. My thoughts were on windows, scraping layers of old paint, repairing sashes, polishing the old wavy glass until it sparkled. But Abby wasn't very interested in talk of house repairs.

I had also told her about the prank calls and the threatening letter.

"Hey, I wouldn't worry about it, Ace," she said. "It's probably those two kids you told me about. You know, the ones who taunt you and call you a witch."

"You're probably right. You're probably right!" I was hugely relieved to have this explanation. Even if it didn't make a whole lot of sense. "But they're just little kids. How would they have information on my clients?" I asked. "They've called my clients, and my boss."

"Maybe they snooped into your address book or something. Do you ever bring it with you to your house in the mountains? Leave it in your car, unlocked or something?"

"I do, yes. The numbers are in my planner. I guess that's a possibility."

"So how was it?"

"How was what?"

"Your date, you idiot."

"My date . . ." My date with Saul. Already it seemed so long ago.

"I want details," she insisted.

"Abby, have you ever been attracted to someone you know is just no good for you?"

"Sure, lots of times. You know I've always gone for bad boys, the ones who drive too fast, smoke cigarettes and drink too much, swear too much, and don't like to wear ties."

"No, I'm talking more like, bad character. Someone who would deliberately harm a weaker person."

"Oh. That's a different kind of no good. Are we talking about the investment banker?"

"No. That's the thing. Here's this guy Saul, who seems to have everything. The charm, the good looks, the money, the property, the nice car. He seems like a perfectly nice guy, he's not gay, he's interested in me, and—nothing. There's no spark there. But his roommate, on the other hand—I dream about him. Not that he's interested in me anyway. But even if he was, from everything I've heard about him, he's just bad news."

"Well, Stacy, sounds like maybe you should give Saul a chance. Maybe the spark will ignite."

"Maybe."

"You know, I think you're still hung up on Justin. That's why you're fixating on the ones who don't make sense for you, and rejecting the ones who do."

I thought about that. It was true, I had been thinking of Justin more often lately, what with the first flush of house infatuation dying down. Reality had set in and the bridges I had burned lay in charred ruins behind me. Thinking about what might have been with Justin was an occasional pastime for me, especially at night when I was lying in bed alone, thinking about property taxes and trips to the dump and the cost of refinishing floors and repairing dry rot.

"Anyway, whoever this other one is, this roommate, re-member someone who would harm a weaker person would harm you, Stacy. I say, leave him in the ten-foot-pole de-partment. You don't need that kind of energy in your life."

This was good advice, and strong advice, coming from Abby, who normally encouraged me to go for it, whatever it was, just for the experience. But she was right, I thought. Even wild girls like Abby draw the line somewhere.

Chapter Seven

T HE NEXT WEEKEND serious snow finally came to the
mountains. It had been a dry year and we were low
enough in elevation that the snow was infrequent, and
a treat. The world looked very different dressed in white.

The circular drive was plowed, but the parking area for
my car was not. I parked my car on the drive, but the road-
way was narrow and I couldn't leave it there long. I got out
the plastic snow shovel I had picked up at the drugstore and
was just attempting to clear a place for my car when Brand
and Tess appeared, advancing across the meadow with
shovels over their shoulders, marching through the drifts.
When they reached my parking area they began shoveling
without a word, and they were so much more efficient than
me that I was thoroughly embarrassed. Though Tess was
small, she was experienced and strong. But Brand swept
past both of us like a machine.

Each shovelful of snow was, to me, surprisingly heavy.
Another reminder of my naïveté when it came to mountain
life. After awhile I began to feel it in my back.

"You can't leave your car on the drive or the plow won't

come through," Tess told me. "We've got a snowblower but it's on the blink. Luckily this isn't too deep."

Not too deep? For this California beach girl, it seemed like a glacier.

She and I stopped for a break, but Brand kept on. I could see the muscles of his back working beneath the soft cotton of his chambray shirt. He hadn't even bothered to put on a jacket. His body tapered gracefully from broad shoulders down to the tail of his shirt, the long line of him continuing into Levis and Sorrel boots, his well-muscled legs braced apart enough so that his body was well-balanced and flexed as he plunged his shovel into the snow and lifted it aside, again and again. His face was taut with concentration, yet there was a looseness about his mouth and in his limbs. His breath came stronger as he worked, powerful and rhythmic, and the color rose beneath his skin as his muscles relaxed and contracted relentlessly.

I thought to myself: *He must look like this when he's making love . . .*

He glanced up and caught me staring at him, and the rhythm of his shoveling faltered. "Get back to work, Stacy," he said with mock authority. With the back of his hand he brushed a strand of hair off his damp brow and began to dig again.

I picked up my shovel, a cheap plastic florescent pooper-scooper. It was an embarrassing little thing, next to Brand's more serious-looking aluminum shovel.

"Don't step on the walkway until it's shoveled or you'll pack the snow down and make it harder to shovel up," he told me. "Hold your shovel like this and you won't wear out so fast."

Finally, relief: The driveway was sufficiently cleared and Brand instructed me to pull my car in.

Inside my car it was cozy and small and I was suddenly alone, thinking about how arrogant he was, bossing me around, taking over the shoveling of my driveway like he owned the place. I grew agitated, the more I thought about it.

Well, I had never lived in the snow so of course I was ignorant. I was glad they had taken it upon themselves to educate me—and to help me.

I parked the car.

"Well—I can't believe that's done!" I was still panting. "I would have been out here all day shoveling. Thank you."

"It's a lot for one person," Tess said. "With the three of us, it's nothing. Or should I say, with Brand, it's nothing! He makes it look easy."

I was beginning to get my breath back, but I felt it escape me again when I looked at him. He was leaning against the trunk of a large cedar, his hand on the handle of the shovel, his shoulders relaxed, his hair slightly damp and swept back away from the bones of his cheeks. The line of his body sloped so that his loins thrust forward.

He seemed unaware of the effect he had on me. He was getting his own breath back—he had just done three times the work I had done, in a quarter of the time. He was staring down at the ground.

"The woods look all magical, covered with snow," I said.

"Yes," Tess agreed. "It's pretty. But it is a pain."

Brand leaned forward and rested his weight on the shovel. He looked up at Tess as if to say, *ready?*

"Well, we'd better get going," she said.

"I'd ask you in, but it's going to be awfully cold inside until I heat up the place," I said.

"That's right," said Tess. "So you go in and turn on your heat and then come over to our place for some hot coffee. Or maybe after all that exercise you'd like something cold."

"Yeah, a beer sounds good," said Brand. He flashed me a smile.

"Sound good to you, Stacy?" asked Tess.

"Well, yes," I said, drawing in a deep, slow breath. "It does. I'll be over in a few minutes."

"COME SKIING WITH us this weekend, Stacy." Tess pulled two fat, beautiful loaves of home-baked bread from the oven. "You ski, don't you?"

Brand was kneeling on the floor, fixing a piece of trim

that had come off the refrigerator door. He didn't look up, so I couldn't see his expression.

"We're going tomorrow," she went on. "Brand and Alana, and Brand's friend Thaddeus—you met him at the party, do you remember—?"

"Oh, please, don't tempt me, Tess. There is so much I want to get done on my house this weekend."

"New powder," Tess said coaxingly. "It's why we live here, right?" She used an opener to pop the cap off a bottle of Heineken and handed it to me.

"Alpine or Nordic?" I asked.

"Oh, it's got to be downhill," she said. "I need that lift. Brand does Nordic and alpine, and he snowboards, too—but then, he's a crazy man. He has helicopters fly him into remote canyons so he can ski off sheer cliffs like James Bond. He'll do anything. And then he gets paid to write about it."

Brand sat back on his haunches. I could see him pulling a face beneath a fall of amber hair. "The stupider the thing I do, the more they pay me," he said.

"Don't worry," said Tess. "We're not planning on making any money tomorrow. Pleasure only. Go ahead and have a seat in the living room, Stacy, and I'll bring in some of this bread."

I went into the living room and found a comfortable chair. I sat down and felt the stillness, admired the beauty and simplicity of the house. Everywhere was evidence of custom handiwork—in the moldings, the wide base and trim, the windows and doors, the hardware, the furniture. Near the sofa was a Japanese sea chest, piled with books: Galen Rowell's *Mountain Light, The Joy of Cooking, Autobiography of a Yogi, Publishers Weekly.*

Tess came into the room with plate piled high with thick slices of buttered bread.

"Try it," she said.

I took some of the bread on a napkin. "Oh, yeah," I said. "It's still warm." The bread was soft and fragrant of yeast and melting with real butter. "Fantastic," I murmured. "You're a goddess."

"I know I am. But to tell you the truth, all I did was take it out of the oven. Brand made it."

Saul appeared at the door of the living room in his bathrobe, looking dazed, as if he'd just woken up. He flopped down in a chair across the room and stared at me a moment. "Hello, Stacy," he said.

Brand walked into the room with a beer. He ignored Saul, and Saul ignored him.

"Did you get it?" Tess asked Brand.

"Yeah. It's fixed."

"He's so useful," she said to me brightly. "I'm sure I'm becoming codependent on him."

Brand sat next to Tess on the sofa, letting her teasing slide right off him.

"Let's go out to dinner tonight, Stacy," Saul said suddenly. "Oh—I can't tonight, there's something I have to do—how about tomorrow? Lunch?"

I looked from Tess to Brand. She was looking at me with an odd expression; Brand was staring out the window.

I thought of Abby's advice. *Give Saul a chance. Forget about Brand.* I glanced at Saul, sitting dully on the sofa, then I looked back at Brand, who seemed to glow for me, and I could not do it.

"I think I'm going skiing with Tess tomorrow," I said.

Saul shrugged. "Suit yourself then," he said. He pushed himself up out of his chair and retreated down the hall.

Chapter Eight

OUR SKIS JAMMED the racks on the top of Thad's black Mercedes. I sat in the front with Thaddeus; Brand, Tess, and Alana sat in the back. Our voices filled the car with raucous singing. Thad's voice was the loudest. It wasn't a particularly melodic voice but it was expressive and uninhibited. He insisted that everyone sing, even Brand, who obliged grudgingly and proved to have a pleasant voice, gravelly and deep. Alana begged off, claiming not to know the words of any of the songs, and Thad finally gave up pressing her, satisfied by the efforts of the rest of us.

We drove deep into the mountains, the snow banks next to the road rising higher as we climbed in elevation. The road was a river curving between the dirty white walls of a sheer canyon, and from the tops of the canyon walls the smooth snow fields sloped up, steep, glistening in the sun, dotted with Christmas fir standing fattened and white, their branches weighed down heavily with the cold snow.

When we reached the ski area, Thad dropped us off with our gear and drove off to find a parking place. Tess went to rent skis, and I went with Brand and Alana to buy the lift tickets. Walking slightly behind them, I carried my skis, acutely conscious of my status as an outsider, not sure if I was truly welcome with them, torn between wanting to tag along and the impulse to flee. Brand and Alana laughed freely together, and they spoke in a casual shorthand, so it was easy to see they had been familiar with one another a long time. They looked like a couple, or a brother and sister, both of them so striking, with their almost matching hair lifted back by the light wind, hers tawny, his bronzed gold, their smiles flashing white against tanned skin when they smiled at each other.

The five of us met in the locker room and went out to the lifts together. The sunlight inflamed the snow, and everyone wore sunglasses. On the triple chair lift to the top of our first run, I sat in between Tess and Thad, who valiantly continued the singing. Behind us, Brand and Alana rode alone. I felt nervous, forcing myself to stop swinging the skis hanging heavy off my boots. Getting off the lift the first time always scared me, and now, with Alana and Brand coming off right behind us, I was afraid I would wipe out directly in front of them.

I felt my skis touch the snow bank, fought the urge to lurch forward, and allowed the edge of the chair to push me away. Down the steep little hill I went without mishap. I stopped neatly at the edge of the ridge next to Thaddeus and Tess. We looped our pole straps over our wrists and paid homage to the mountains.

"Magnificent!" cried Thad.

"It's perfect," Tess crowed. "A sunny day, brand new powder—"

"And *fine* company," Thad bowed. "—*Ladies.*"

Brand and Alana skied down to join us in perfect form. Alana wore a ski suit with color-coordinated mittens and hat in black and turquoise. As usual, she looked great and was dressed in perfect taste. Apparently, she could also ski well. Why couldn't she be stuck on the bunny slope doing the snowplow?

We all started tentatively down the mountain together. It

was my first time skiing that season, and I hung back a little with Thad and Tess, who were cautious skiers. Brand and Alana swooshed ahead, slender and elegant in aesthetic partnership.

"I've got to get my sea legs!" Tess called out to me. She was a bit wobbly. Thad was a pretty good skier, but he disliked any loss of control, so he took it easy.

It was a good first run. The fresh powder was glazecoated with a thin rime of ice, but it was only nine-thirty in the morning.

Brand and Alana waited for us at the foot of the mountain.

"Let's do that one again, shall we?" Alana suggested. "It's a perfect little warm up."

Tess threw me a comical look; I knew she had found the run to be rather challenging.

I felt the competitive edge. Obviously, Alana felt confident in her superior athletic abilities against the rest of us. I was aware of a desire to challenge her. I warned myself to be cool, lest I make a fool of myself.

In fact, our level of skill was similar enough that we naturally tended to end up at the end of a run about the same time. We began to lap Thad and Tess, and finally lost them altogether. I suspected Alana was a bit put out to find I could keep up with her—she would have liked to have seen *me* stuck on the bunny slope, too. It was obvious Brand could have left us both in the dust—or powder, rather—he skied effortlessly. He was on another level of skill altogether. But he stayed with us. So Brand, Alana, and I were a natural threesome, though I knew Alana wasn't keen on having me along. I let myself lose them, or let them lose me, I couldn't say which it was.

In the middle of the afternoon I went into the high lodge near the top of the mountain, ordered a cup of hot mulled wine and sat down next to the fireplace. I was staring out the window, watching the skiers blur past, when Brand came into the lodge.

He appeared next to me, large and clomping in his ski boots, breathless, hot and damp, an exhilarated expression shining off the bones of his face. He slid into the chair across from me and set a beer down on the little table next to my wine.

"You disappeared," he said.

I took a slow sip of hot wine. "I guess I just couldn't keep up with you."

"I think you can keep up with me."

I felt the flush of the wine in my blood. "Where is Alana?" I asked.

"Oh, down at the lower lodge, probably. The thing she likes best about skiing is sitting in the lodge by the fire, having a drink, reading Ann Tyler."

He spoke of Alana with familiarity, like a husband of a wife. I looked out the window at the slope, watched the skiers come down the mountain.

"The lodge is definitely one of the great pleasures of the sport," I said, raising my cup.

I couldn't not look at him for long. He was studying the map I had spread out on the table. He pointed to a particularly scary looking multiple black diamond run and asked me, "Have you skied that one yet?"

"I don't think so . . ." I leaned over the map and shook my head. "No. It looks long. It looks *hard . . .*"

"It's fun. You could do it."

I glanced up at him quizzically.

He said, "With me you would not be afraid."

I laughed, knowing he was doing a parody of Thad.

"I watched you, a bit," he said. "Until you disappeared. You could do it. Easily."

"Ah . . ."

"Let's do it."

I didn't respond. The alcohol had lent a languid lack of self-consciousness to my perceptions. I'd only had one cup of warm mulled wine, but it was potent, and I was susceptible. For once I didn't feel so taut in his presence.

"Let's do it," he repeated. He leaned forward, resting his arms on the little table, keenly awaiting my reply as if it was a response to a dare.

"You could do it," he said.

"I know I could do it!" I said, haughty. "Easily? I don't think so. But I could do it."

"Well, then? . . ."

"The question might be, would I actually have *fun* doing it? I'm probably skilled enough to get down any run on this mountain. But I'm not skilled enough to *enjoy* them all. And if you don't enjoy it, what's the point?"

"With me, you would enjoy it. Come . . ."

I hooted at his arrogance, and he grinned broadly. I shook my head in mock disgust; but there was no doubt in my mind that I would go with him. I would go anywhere he asked me to go.

And that disturbed me. So I pretended I wasn't going to do it.

I FELT A surge of adrenaline as we skied out to catch the chair together for the first time. We got into place and waited—the seat bumped against us and we settled down, swung out, and up, and in moments we were high over the snowfields, sailing silently, alone with each other for the very first time.

I was aware of the silence between us. I made no attempt at small talk and neither did he. The contradictory things I had heard about him came into my thoughts. Though he smoothed it over very well, there was a weakness—perhaps even violence—in this man, I thought. And I was beginning to realize there was a weakness in me, too, because I didn't give a damn.

You're in danger, here, Stacy.

Look, I told myself. I can enjoy his company without falling in love with him or something.

I glanced at him furtively, suddenly insecure. He seemed to have grown moody—he stared off over the tops of the trees. Maybe he had decided this wasn't such a good idea after all.

It was a long lift, and so much time had passed that I began to feel like a spell had been cast over us and it was impossible to speak.

We were nearly at the top of the mountain when we both suddenly began to talk at the same time. We both broke off at once, laughing.

"Go ahead," he said, and he looked at me with a curious expression in his clear river-water eyes. "What were you going to say?"

"I can't remember."

I WILL NEVER forget that afternoon, which remains to this day one of the most exhilarating of my life. Simply gazing at Brand brought up the greed in me. And when we touched—accidentally—the greed roared, ravenous. Never had a man ever stirred me so on such a purely physical level. It was a heady, pleasurable state, akin to drunkenness. I questioned whether I was drunk; a cup of warm wine at high altitude, I scolded myself, was apparently too much. As the afternoon went on I was less and less able to blame my intoxication upon wine. My blood was spiced by something far more subtle, elemental, and powerful.

I was glad to be sublimating it by tearing down the mountain with him at my heels. Only flying could be better than this, I thought, or making love with him.

He skied like a kid, with no thought of form or style, but his utter lack of awkwardness on the skis gave him a rugged grace, elegant and completely male. He was dressed in old Levis and a black Goretex windbreaker. He wore no hat; the wind curved his hair like a gold wing away from the strong bones of his face. He is so beautiful, I thought, and something pierced through me like pain.

We reached the bottom of the mountain and got back in line for the lift. A young woman who was sitting with the lift operator took our photograph with an expensive-looking camera. "I couldn't resist," she said. "You two look so gorgeous together—the contrast of your hair—the dark and the gold. Here." She ran up to Brand with a pen and a scrap of paper. "Give me your address and I'll send you the photo."

He did as she requested, and she gave him a big smile and went back to sit with the lift operator.

"Think she'll send us the picture?" Brand asked me.

"I think she just wanted to get your address," I said slyly, and to my surprise and delight, he blushed.

We went up the lift again, and this time we were more abandoned, chattering about the run we had done together, watching the skiers and snowboarders below, amused by this one, humbled by another. I was intrigued by the snowboarding, which was a relatively new phenomenon in those days, and rapidly gaining popularity. Brand told me he thought eventually more people would be snowboarding than skiing. "It's a whole different feel," he said. "It's really fun. You should try it."

"I'll be happy to make it down that run on two skis," I said.

When we got off the lift, Brand motioned to another chair which was going up still higher, to the most supreme run on the mountain, the route which would take you down along a spectacular trail, a long leisurely run of perfect skiing, *if* you could make it down the first few hundred feet of incredibly steep, terrifying moguls—the most difficult terrain on the mountain.

"Ready?" he asked.

Without answering, I pushed away and led him down to the second chair lift. There was no waiting, and in what seemed to be choreographed symmetry we moved into position and let the big swing swoop us up.

"Here, let me have those." He surprised me by taking my poles. He put them together with his, and stashed them out of the way on his side of the chair.

"My dad always did that for us," he said. "When he took us on the lifts, my sister and me, when we were kids."

I felt naked without my poles, and touched—it seemed an oddly chivalrous gesture. "And you carry on the tradition," I said.

"I've never done it before." He blushed again.

As we gained elevation, the air grew colder. Fewer and fewer skiers or snowboarders went by below us. There was no sound but the creaking of the chairs and the little bump of the cables running over the supports.

"Cold?" He asked softly.

I nodded vigorously.

He reached inside his jacket and for a second I thought he was going to bring out a flask, but instead he withdrew a soft gray cashmere scarf, which I hadn't even noticed him wearing, untangled it from around his neck, and he turned to me, very businesslike, and looped it around my neck, and around again. His hands brushed against my face softly as he did it.

"There," he said.

"But now you will be cold."

He made a face like, *give me a break—*

I felt ridiculously happy. He eased a little closer to me, for warmth, of course. It was like flying slowly to the top of the world, with Brand beside me, the mountains below us, all around us, rippling away over the curve of the planet, mountains and sky, all white and blue and vast. I didn't want it to end, though my body was so charged with feeling it was almost painful. Just before we reached the top he pulled out my poles and handed them back to me.

Off the lift, we stood silently together for awhile, taking in the view. From a little rise we could see valleys spreading below us on either side of the mountain.

"This is incredible." I stretched my poles toward the infinite panorama, rapt. I turned to Brand. "But then, maybe you're not so impressed, after those mountains you've seen in your travels."

He shook his head, and a length of his hair was picked up by the wind and refracted into a dozen shades of color. "The Sierra is my first love," he said. "These are the mountains I always return to." And then he did something odd, for that moment, because the tendency was to stare out into the immensity of the world below—he turned his gaze on me. I looked away, but he continued to stare at me, hard, until I looked back at him, questioningly. He didn't say anything, but he held eye contact for three, four seconds—it was far too long, and very unsettling. I felt breathless.

We haven't even begun the run yet, I thought, and I'm gasping for breath—

As if the view finally proved too compelling after all, he

broke his gaze away from me and looked out over the countless ridges layering the horizon.

"Well . . ." I hesitated, now regretting my earlier cockier
attitude about my abilities. Blame it on the hot mulled wine.
"Now I must see if I can get down from here."

"You'll get down just fine. I'll help you."

"If I don't lose you first." I laid my palm straight, like a
blade along the wind, cutting a gesture down the mountain
toward the hidden folds where the trees clustered and the
trail ducked into the shadows. *Woosh.*

"You won't lose me," he said. "Because I won't lose *you*.
Look, here's the way—"

His assured manner was proffered matter-of-factly, with
a charming arrogance. He was like a young nobleman. I was
intrigued and perplexed by the image. Aristocratic. Noblesse
oblige. In spite of a sort of roughness—a shaggy, undomes-
ticated wildness—he brought to mind the master who
would kneel to serve the servant, with no sense of the dis-
tinction. His contradictions charmed and bewildered me.

I skied beside him along the ridge, overwhelmed by the
look of the mountain. The cliff actually dipped inward for a
short distance before falling off almost vertically a hundred
feet down to thick humps of huge, impossibly steep moguls.

"I am out of my depth here, Brand," I said. I stopped and
leaned over the edge.

"Come with me, Stacy." He reached out and laid his mit-
tened hand on my arm, and I felt the contact, the weight of
his touch, and an impression of warmth.

He dropped his hand away. Yet I could still feel the contact there on my arm through my parka and my wool sweater
and my thermal undershirt, an imprint like a warm footprint
in sand.

"You go first," I commanded.

He leapt easily off the ridge, flew straight down like a
bird of prey dropping through the sky. With a graceful arc of
his skis, he demonstrated the best place to carve a switch-
back in the vertical face of the mountain. Then another, then
another. He worked his turns in concert with the slope and
came to land modestly on the top of a large mogul. He

looked up at me and raised a pole. I took a deep breath and plunged after him, immediately thrust into intense concentration and physical fight, just to remain semi-upright, my legs straining desperately to pull my skis around and prevent my body from hurtling straight down the mountain. I came to an inelegant halt near him, gasping with terror.

"I am going to die on this mountain," I cried.

"You looked *good*," he said, with an incredulous expression, as if he truly couldn't understand my attitude.

So down we went, first Brand, carving the way, and then me, trying to stay in his path. Sometimes I would pass him and curve around to a place further down and he would follow, stopping below me, where he would look up, waiting for me to come down. Sometimes we stopped side by side. I had to admit I was doing all right, thanks to Brand's patient coaching. When you ski with someone who's better than you, you tend to lose the other skier, and then you're on your own about getting to the bottom of the run. But Brand stayed with me. He watched me, called out suggestions, offered encouragement. Or he left me alone, and was simply there, nearby. He was patient. He didn't seem to be in any hurry to be down the mountain.

At last we finished the vertical sheet of moguls and discovered an immense, luscious bowl where the powder was so smooth it looked as though no one else had come through there all winter. We picked up some speed and relaxed and just played for awhile, zig-zagging along together, laughing and whooping and hopping over little jumps on the straightaway where the bowl emptied into the woods and the trail crossed over into another small valley.

It was there on the cut-through that I lost control suddenly and went down. All the way down the moguls I hadn't fallen once, and here on this easy section I was tripped on a chunk of icy snow. Brand came from behind, and suddenly he was beside me, leaning over me, reaching a hand out—

I pulled my skis under me, praying hard that I would get right up without falling again, and I accepted his hand. I was aware of the sensation of our bones folding together like an exchanged glance, somewhere beneath the padding of our gloves, and our eyes suddenly clasped like hands, warm and full of sensation, yet clothed, padded, protected. Then I was up, brushing away the snow, and we were off again.

After that, we hardly spoke. We skied silently the rest of the way down the mountain. He didn't stop again, and really there was no need to stop anymore, but I was disappointed. I had enjoyed our short comradely stops along the way.

We reached the lodge around four-thirty. Long beams of gold from the kneeling sun shot through the branches of the pines on the ridge and glowed brilliant off the glass windows of the buildings. Shadows were long and the air was growing chilly. The ski patrol was heading up the mountain and some of the lifts still ran with the chairs empty. Skiers streamed down the mountain into the lodge, bending over to snap their boots out of their bindings, piling equipment onto the carpeted counters at the rental booth. People gathered at the tables on the patio above, calling out for each other, loading cars, buying drinks and snacks at the snack shop, swapping tall tales.

Brand was out of his bindings before me. He threw his skis over his shoulder and tromped into the locker room without looking back. I was embittered by his sudden diffidence. I followed along behind him with my equipment, and I remembered I was wearing his scarf.

Tess looked happy and exhausted, sitting on a bench next to the lockers, surrounded by piles of sweaters, hats, soda cans and sunscreen, goggles, and a half-eaten bag of potato chips. She was stuffing things into her duffel bag.

Thad and Alana came in through the other door. "We've returned the rental equipment," Thad announced.

"Good, thank you," sighed Tess. "Oh, how I want a hot bath."

"What a perfect day," Thad said, stretching and groaning. "Except I lost you, Stacy. I can see I'm going to have to hustle a bit more than I'm used to, if I want to keep up with you."

"I'm not all that hard to keep up with," I teased him. "You're just slow. Hey, I thought you mountaineering guys were all hot-dog skiers."

"Not me. But then, I like warm rock. I've never been a real cold-friendly person."

"Well, on a day like today you don't need to be," Tess said. "It wasn't quite spring skiing, but oh, those wide blue skies!"

"So where have you been, Brand?" Alana asked, hands on hips. Her voice was pitched to be cheerful, but her expression was edgy. I was about to pull his scarf off from around my neck and return it to him, but I decided it might be best to wait.

"Just came off the top," he replied, busy with his locker.

"Oh—!" Thad nodded knowingly, his mouth a smirk. "I know what that means. Blood alley."

No one was impressed, because it was Brand, but they rolled their eyes.

"I knew he'd go do that run," said Alana, throwing up her hands in resignation. "Even though he said he was going to take it easy today."

"Brand's got a death wish," said Thad.

"Well, anyone else doing it would have to have a death wish. It's a walk in the park for Brand," said Tess.

I was about to say I had done the run too, and brag a little, but I looked from Brand to Alana, sensed the tension there, and decided not to mention it. Brand didn't say anything either.

Thad turned to me and said, "You know which run they're talking about?"

"Yeah," I said. "I think I do."

"That run is a good place to lure unsuspecting people one would like to rid oneself of."

"Really. I'll have to remember that."

During the long ride home I sat again in the front next to Thad. We were too tired to sing, though Thad amused us with anecdotes about his day at the ski resort—he had great skills as an entertainer, if not as a skier. Brand was quiet and didn't speak at all.

Genesis played on the radio. *I will follow you, will you follow me?* Thad made another joking reference to the perils of dangerous ski terrain, luring unsuspecting enemies to their death, and I turned my head to look back at Brand. Tess was dozing in the corner, and Alana's head was resting on Brand's shoulder. He returned my glance hard and I looked away.

I gazed out the window toward the west, where the trees stood in darkness against the orange blaze at the edge of the world. Slowly the light went out of the sky.

Chapter Nine

ONE NIGHT SEVERAL weeks after the ski trip I came home from work late with take-out Chinese, threw my coat and bag down, opened the window for some cool bay air and hit the button on the answering machine. There was a "just called to say hi" message from Abby, which made me laugh as she went on and on about the trouble she was having with various aspects of her wedding plans, her mother's involvement in particular. There was a vague message from Russ, canceling yet another shop-for-plumbing-fixtures-and-pizza date we had planned, with no explanation.

"You're getting to be rather flaky lately, big brother!" I said to the machine, disappointed.

And then there was a click, heavy breathing, low laughter. A voice, low and inhuman, maybe even electronically generated. Unintelligible in meaning, then the words, clearer now: *"You are finished—"* more garble, and then odd, slow-motion laughter.

I began to shiver from a sudden wind in through the window. Just another crank call, I told myself, but it's funny how they can affect you. I went to the window and closed it, locked the front door.

Just another crank caller.

I couldn't ignore this any longer. I could perceive a pattern when it hit me over the head. The phone calls, to my house, my boss, my clients. The weird letter I'd received, warning me to go back to the city where I belonged.

So it was time to do something about it.

But what?

I sat down with my chopsticks and took a few bites of chicken and rice but the savory richness seemed to lay heavy in my stomach. I closed up the little white containers and went to bed early that night.

"WE'RE HAVING A few friends in to dinner tonight, Stacy. Will you come?"

Tess's hands were thrust into the pockets of a new jacket. The color of it, a rich, royal blue, was good for her faded blond looks. It brightened her. It was good to see Tess again. Already the ski trip seemed so long ago.

She refused my invitation to come in.

"I've got to get back to the house," she said. "I'm making centerpieces. It's my birthday," she leaned toward me and whispered it confessionally. "No presents, please. I don't believe in them."

She went off, trudging across the smooth frosted forest floor. I was elated.

I'll see him tonight.

I knew I was becoming stupid about Brand. He could walk across the meadow any time I happened to be in residence if he had any desire to be with me. I didn't see him doing it. He wasn't interested. He had a girlfriend. Saul, on the other hand, had been dropping by to see me so often he was becoming a pest, until I put an end to it, letting him know (subtly and tactfully, I hoped) he was wasting his time.

I went upstairs and bathed. The lamp on my bureau burned as I dressed and brushed my hair. I peered into the mirror, studying my face intensely. Brand will be there tonight, I thought. Brand will be there.

I finished dressing and walked across the meadow.

The small table in the hall glistened with the light of a dozen candles; more were placed around the great room: on the window sills, on the old pine sideboard, on the big oak table in the dining area where the china and crystal were set and waiting. The effect of it all was beautiful and other-worldly. Tess was putting the finishing touches on an arrangement of fir boughs and pine cones on the dining table. Brand was doing something in the kitchen. I was alone with Saul and Alana, sitting on the sofa near the fireplace.

Saul poured wine for Alana and me and we raised our glasses a bit awkwardly. Saul's manner was frosty whenever he had anything to do with me lately. In contrast, he was deferential and flirtatious with Alana, though she carried off her usual impassive chill, perpetually smooth. She made no attempt to keep conversation with me, and since Saul was virtually ignoring me, this left us rather strained. Fortunately Tess soon finished her arrangement, joined us, and took up a glass. She was comfortable with everybody, and her chatter easily filled in the awkward spaces. She treated Saul like a younger brother, indulgently, with a rather anxious affection.

"So, how old are you today, anyway, Tessie?" asked Saul.

"Past the age where I tell," she replied.

"Oh, come on," he urged her. "Don't be like that."

She stood. "I'd better go see if Brand needs any help with dinner!"

"Uh oh!" Saul put on a guilty expression, and we all got up and followed Tess into the kitchen where a huge lasagna rested on the counter. Brand was pulling a long foil-wrapped loaf of French bread out of the oven, and the aroma of hot fresh bread and garlic filled the kitchen. A green salad filled a huge glass bowl and Tess began to toss it with a great flourish, sprinkling it with a vinaigrette stirred up in a glass measuring cup.

"Can I help?" I asked.

"Nope," Brand replied. "It's all taken care of." His tone was cold, and he turned his back to me abruptly and kneeled to get a platter out of a lower cabinet.

I felt slighted and embarrassed, a knot stiffening between my heart and my throat, and I took a step away from him, resisting the impulse to turn and walk away. There came, then, a drum-riff knock at the front door. Tess bounded into the hall and returned with a man who was large and bearish and handsome, his steel-gray hair braided long down his back. He was wearing a suit and he carried something in a paper bag.

"Everybody, this is Tom Wheeler. Tom—" Tess named the rest of us for him.

"Howdy," said Tom.

"Now that we all know each other—" said Tess, "What about a drink?"

"I brought some wine," Tom said. "But if you have a beer, I'd rather have that."

Alana edged up beside me and said to me in a low voice, "That's Tess's new squeeze." She raised one of her perfectly arched brows and smirked. Actually, she had a beautiful smile. She stepped up and took the salad bowl from Brand, who did not object to her assistance. They began to carry the food into the dining area.

I wondered what Alana's comment meant, for it clearly held more than information—there was a judgment there of some sort. Maybe she didn't think much of Tom. Or perhaps she wanted to make it known to me that she was on the inside track with these people, and I wasn't.

The meal was so good it was not necessary to speak, for which I was grateful. I savored the food and listened to the talk, watching the changing expressions of the faces around the table, studying the relationships. Tess and Brand were cousins, housemates, and friends; they teased each other and argued about trivial things, like how much garlic to put on the French bread and whether to rinse the pasta, as well as larger issues, like the occupation of Tibet and how to keep a worm hole open long enough to travel into a parallel universe. Alana was deferential to Tess, and Tess was careful with Alana. Saul was obviously attracted to Alana, his earlier comments about her "insecurity" notwithstanding, and she met his cocky ardor with just enough tolerance to keep his attentions going. Brand and Saul didn't seem to like each other, but they didn't interact much—perhaps they even avoided each other. It was hard to tell. The relationship between Brand and Alana intrigued me most.

I remembered the day Saul had brought me up to the house after the flea market, how they had huddled at the table by the big window, studying and discussing the plans, whispering together. They had seemed so intent upon their task. Or perhaps their intensity was generated by something other than the blueprints they studied. Alana often glanced at Brand, as if to measure his reaction to a comment somebody had made. He paid her no undue attention, but he talked to her, and joked with her, which was more than he was doing with me tonight. In fact he seemed to be pointedly indifferent toward me. I was bewildered.

I felt a flash of anger toward him, and was determined not to respond to his mood, but what could I do? My first reaction was to be cool, to ignore him back, but I felt manipulated, and exasperated with myself for even considering such a tactic. I could come on strong, with either hostility or humor, or a bit of both—but whatever I did it seemed to be in response to him. I was determined to deal with him on my own terms. But I felt stung by his coldness tonight. I thought we'd gone beyond that.

I was attracted to him, that was undeniable, but I wasn't even sure I liked him. I tried to analyze my feelings. I told myself it had to be a purely physical attraction. But the sheer power of it knocked me off balance. I tried to determine what it was in him that made me catch my breath whenever he appeared, what it was in him that resonated viscerally through my body, the words he spoke to me echoing in my mind long after he was gone from me. He was only a man. A stranger, really, about whom I knew nothing. Nothing but the fact that he could cook and he could ski, and that he was the kind of person who would try to manipulate a disabled elderly woman for his own gain.

The spirits had warmed all of us and conversation was no longer halting. The dinner table grew lively. A heated exchange arose between Alana and Tom. Both owned businesses in town, and they disagreed on a recently passed ordinance restricting neon signs for advertising. Tom thought it was nobody's business if he flashed neon in the windows of his liquor store. Alana felt the architectural review policy was lenient enough.

"We need to keep the look of the town intact," she said. "Charming and rustic. Neon just doesn't fit in with that."

"But that's just unfair," he said.

"Why is it unfair?" Alana asked. "If no one is allowed to have neon signs, there is no discrimination. Everybody's on the same playing field."

"I've got a *liquor* store here! You put *neon* signs in the window of a liquor store. That's what people look for, when they look for a liquor store. Hey, I pay my taxes. I don't want the government telling me what I can hang in my own damn windows."

"When I renovated my shop, I had to comply with the rules," Alana said. "I would have liked to put in larger front windows. But I wasn't allowed to change the vintage façade of the storefront."

"And that doesn't bother you? Them telling you what you can and can't do, with your own building?"

"No. I mean, I think it's important that we preserve the historic character of our town. That has value in itself, to me, as a retailer. I'm glad they're strict about it." She flashed a look at Brand, looking for his approval, no doubt.

"They can really get you with that historic preservation stuff," Saul said. "Stacy, you better be careful. Don't ever let that house of yours get declared a historic landmark if you want to keep control over it."

"It's a fine line, isn't it?" Brand said. "Between private property and the need to take care of what would be destroyed if a few individuals had their way."

Tess said, "Yes, if some concerned people hadn't stepped in, we would have lost the old Frost building, and that would have been really shortsighted and tragic."

"Okay. But some of the preservation laws are ridiculous," said Tom.

"Well, that's true," I said. "Some of them are. And some of the most well-intentioned measures have backfired. But I'd rather err on the side of preservation, of wildlife habitat, old growth forests, historic architecture—"

"It's about being respectful of the planet," Brand said, "and all the beings who inhabit it, human beings, animals, plants, minerals."

Yes, I thought. That was just what I had wanted to say. I felt a glow of accord between us. A thrill of pride in it. I was as hungry for his approval as Alana was.

"Minerals aren't beings," said Saul.

"An old Navajo woman I know would argue that point," said Brand. "Mary Begay says everything that is, is alive."

"She must have a strange definition of life."

"Spirit lives in all things," I said. "Even old houses. And we humans need our habitat protected too. From ourselves."

"So that's what you're doing, with that old house, Stacy," said Tess. "Restoring human habitat."

"Or will she tear it down and build something new?" Alana asked, all sly innocence.

My eye snagged suddenly on Brand—for the first time that evening he was really looking at me. Staring. And then he broke away, passing the basket of bread to Tess. I tried to fathom the meaning in his expression. Some powerful emotion was roused in him—I could see it in his expression when he turned that look on me, though I sensed he tried to hide it. Was it bitterness he felt toward me for having taken what he thought should have been his?

"If the house burned down, you would have to start over," Saul said ominously.

"Oh, Saul!" Tess reprimanded him.

"What? Well, she *would*."

We went to sit by the fire after dinner. I sank into the soft leather sofa, feeling languid and sensual, glad that I didn't have to drive home. I must have had more wine than I'd realized.

"You look enchanting by candlelight, Stacy," Saul said, slumping into the place next to me on the sofa.

"That's the first thing you've said to me all evening," I answered. "Or should I say, the first nice thing. Or are you implying that I look good only by candlelight?"

"Not at all. But I accept your rebuke. If I have been aloof, it is only to protect my tender feelings. You have been avoiding my company. I am very vulnerable."

"I don't believe that," I said with a laugh.

"That's because I maintain my defenses with you."

"What about Alana? You didn't appear to be defending yourself against her with much vigor earlier this evening. And yet she doesn't seem to encourage your advances—are you not vulnerable to such a woman? She is very beautiful."

"Am I that transparent?" He put on an expression of mock astonishment. "Or could it be *you* are jealous?"

"I *am* jealous of her," I said. "She's got something I haven't."

"And what that might that be?" he asked, genuinely curious.

Brand.

"Blond hair," I said.

"Mmm. Well, never mind," he said, moving over to allow Tess to sit beside him. "Your hair suits you."

"It does, Stacy," Tess agreed. "It is dark and wild and romantic, just like you are."

"Who is wild and romantic?" Tom came over to join us. Brand and Alana followed with coffee.

"Stacy is," Tess said. "Why else would she have bought the old Shapiro place?"

"Well, it is rather wild," I agreed. "Romantic? Maybe . . . or maybe just foolhardy."

"Nonsense," said Tom, accepting a cup of coffee from Alana. "That place is worth a fortune. And I know what you paid for it. You got a great deal. The house could be demolished, the lot subdivided and with a couple of new structures thrown up, the whole thing could bring in big money."

"So I've been told."

"But is *that* what she's doing with it?" Alana asked. Her eyes were bright. "Is it? Tell us, Stacy."

"Yes, Stacy. Do tell," said Saul.

Brand didn't say anything, but I could see he wanted to know, too. I felt suddenly uncomfortable. They were all looking at me, each with a different expression. It was peculiar.

"What *do* you plan to do?" Tom prodded. "You're not actually going to try to *restore* that old place?"

"Well . . ." I hesitated. " 'Restoration,' in building terms, means you're bringing an historic structure back to its original state. Most buildings intended for people to live in aren't restored, they're renovated."

"So, which are you doing, restoration or renovation?" asked Alana.

Saul grinned through his teeth. "Or demolition?"

"Some of each," I said. "Some of the additions have become part of the house's character, and I probably wouldn't change them, even though technically they're not original, nor are they in keeping with the original style of the house."

"So you aren't going to tear it down?" said Tom.

"Stacy loves that house," said Tess. "She'd never tear it down."

"Ah—" said Tom. "So she *is* wild and romantic."

"Maybe," I said. "And yet, you know, the house is in surprisingly good shape. Some of the foundation needs more repair, but mainly just around the front porch. There is some rot, but not as much as I feared. The place was actually well maintained up until quite recently. There are a lot of weird old construction details, but someone has been working on it—someone who knew what they were doing. It was just hard to see it, under all that clutter and grime, but somebody took care of that house—"

"Well, I'll tell you who—" Tess began, but Brand interrupted her.

"That old woman loved that house," he said. "She took good care of it as long as she was able." He seemed impatient to end this topic of conversation, and he changed the subject so deftly nobody seemed to notice. It was becoming increasingly obvious to me that the house was a definite sore spot with him. It wasn't something I had imagined.

Later, Tom brought it up again. He told me that if I ever did think seriously of subdividing, he knew people who could help me and might possibly invest in the project. Brand stood listening nearby, obviously interested.

"You know, you'd stand to make quite a profit, I'd say, if you did go that route," said Tom.

"My brother tells me the same thing," I said.

Brand turned away and he didn't come near me for the rest of the evening. It seemed that losing the house to me was so offensive to him he that just wanted to avoid the subject—and me—altogether.

I WAS WALKING along the trail between the church property and mine one afternoon when I saw Father Daniel striding through the woods, purposefully off the trail, coming straight toward me as if he would intercept me.

"Stacy," he called. "I've been wanting to talk with you."

We fell in step together beneath the trees.

"This is the weather for walking, isn't it?" he sighed.

"How are you?" I asked politely. We saw each other frequently, in the village, on our walks, but we didn't know each other well.

"Oh—well, I'm all right," he said. "I'm a little tired. The thing is—I was thinking about this idea I've had for a long time. Tell me, you're an architect, aren't you? Do you do your own rendering?"

The question surprised me. "Well, yes I do some drawing, some watercolor painting—"

"Perfect. I'm asking because I've been wanting to commission a painting, of a building—the chapel, actually, and I thought perhaps you—?"

"You want me to do a painting of the chapel?"

"Yes, that's what I'd like."

"Well, sure, I might be able to do that."

"I had a feeling you might."

"I could show you some stuff I've done, see if you like it."

"It's such a beautiful old building, I'd like a remembrance of it."

"You're not leaving us, are you?" I asked.

"I hope not, but there are no certainties in life," he smiled.

"Well, I'll tell you what. I'll do some watercolor sketches of the chapel, and if you like one, you can have it."

"I will purchase it from you," he replied, formally.

"It will be good to have a reason to paint again. I've been putting all my creative energies into the house."

"Already it looks so different," he said. "Less oppressed, somehow."

"Yes, I think that's true. The chi is flowing again, as Yolanda would say."

"The chi? Ah—yes, the life force."

"And yet, I don't know. It seems there are still certain spots where it seems stuck."

"In the house?"

"In the house, in my life—I don't know where to begin, sometimes."

"Lao Tzu said, 'A journey of a thousand miles begins with a single step.'"

"Sometimes when you see a thousand steps in front of you it's hard to tell which one to take first."

"So you don't move," he nodded.

"I think I will sand the dining room floor."

"That's a move!"

"A huge, painful, dirty one. But it has to be done. I want to get the graffiti off the floor."

"Graffiti?"

"Bright red paint, about so big—painted right on the floor boards."

"Oh—you found it beneath the . . . carpet?"

"Yes. Very charming."

"Right!" He seemed oddly disturbed, suddenly, as if the blood had drained out of him. He held his head in his hands and rubbed his temples.

"Are you okay?" I asked him.

"Yes, yes, it's just my blood sugar. I just suddenly felt a little light-headed. I'm hypoglycemic, I think. If I don't eat six times a day, I'm a wreck."

"Can I get you something?"

"No, no, I've got a sandwich on my desk. Listen, I really want to see your paintings, and have you do one for me."

"It would be my pleasure," I said. "Why don't you let me make you lunch?" I felt concerned about him.

"Thank you, but if I don't eat the sandwich Yolanda made me she won't speak to me for days."

I went back to the house, inspired with nervous energy. There was something strange about that encounter with Father Daniel. It seemed odd that he hadn't asked what it was I had found painted on the floor. I know *I* would have asked. It was as if the very mention of it had caused him to become ill. But I shoved those thoughts aside and decided I would take that first step, stop procrastinating and start a new project. I made a few calls to get estimates for floor finishing, and then I went to town to pick up watercolor supplies. When I returned to the house, there was a message for me, pinned to my door. Callie and Ralph wanted me to come take a look at their house sometime during the weekend, if I had the time.

RALPH AND CALLIE showed me around their place and explained their ideas for renovation. They wanted the kitchen enlarged, and they had thoughts about a second story master bedroom addition. I did some quick sketches of various elevations, floor plans, and roof lines, giving them an idea of what their house could look like, how an addition could blend into the existing structure, and they seemed excited about the prospects. We had a natural, easy rapport and my sense was that they would be good clients to work with.

We were sitting in their living room talking when Brand's name came up. It seemed I couldn't get away from the specter of *him.*

"I like lots of wood and tile and glass," Callie was saying. She slid her glasses off her sharp little nose and polished the lenses with the bottom of her shirt. "Elegant, yet rustic. Simplicity, but with comfort." She waved her glasses for emphasis. "You know, like the barn."

"The barn?"

"You know, *The Barn.* Brand's place. I just love the interior. All that wood, and yet it's light and bright too. Simple, yet classy."

The barn . . . *The Barn.* Of course. It *did* resemble nothing so much as a quaint old barn with a porch and dormers added.

"Oh," I said, "You mean Saul's house?"

"Saul's house—?" They said it in unison, incredulous, and cracked up laughing.

"I thought the house belonged to Saul."

"Hell, no." Ralph shook his big bear head as if resisting a gnat. "Brand owns that house."

"Oh . . . but—"

"Brand rents out the cottage to Tess and he lets Saul stay there, but it's *his* house," said Callie. "Tess and Brand are cousins, and Saul is Tess's brother-in-law—her sister's husband's brother, something like that. Saul sponges off Tess because she's so sweet and giving, and Brand puts up with it for her sake, even though he can't stand Saul, thinks he's just using Tess."

"Brand's the one being used," Ralph said gruffly.

"I'm confused. I thought the house belonged to Saul. What about the photography—?"

"The what?"

"The photographs hanging on the walls all through the house. Aren't they Saul's?"

"No," scoffed Ralph. "That's Brand's work. Some of the paintings were done by Brand's sister, but he does the photography. You know he's traveled a lot for his work. He's been doing that stuff for years."

"I see . . ." Actually, it made more sense. The more I knew of Saul, the less I cared for his sensibilities. And the one whose touch was on that house had an eye for exquisite

things. A discerning sensuality. The combination of rugged-
ness and beauty. Brand.

But why would I attribute such qualities to Brand? He
was no better than Saul, for all I knew. Worse, for what I did
know.

"Why?" Ralph was suspicious. "What did Saul tell you?"

"Oh—nothing. I probably just misunderstood." I
couldn't remember if Saul ever actually claimed to own the
place. I was beginning to wonder what else I had misunderstood. "Well, is it true, as I have heard, that Brand tried to
get my house for himself?"

"Oh, yeah," said Callie. "Everyone knows that. He
wanted to murder you when he found out you'd bought it. *I*
was surprised. I had thought the old lady might just be-
queath him the place, or at least give him first shot at buying it. I think he was hoping for it."

I hitched my breath in. "But why? He already has that
one—"

"Which is why he wanted yours. Are you aware that the
two properties used to be part of one estate? You bought
the main house—Brand's house is actually what used to be
the old barn."

So he had wanted to restore the estate to its former
glory—? An interesting idea. But he didn't have enough
money to swing it, so he tried to influence the owner into
giving him the property at a fraction of its worth.

"Anyway—" Callie said. "What were we talking about?"

"Yes, enough gossiping about the neighbors," laughed
Ralph. "The point is—we like what Brand has done to that
old barn, and we'd like a bit of that flavor in this old place.
Can it be done?"

"Yes," I nodded. I was already seeing it. Rustic, charming. Cheery and bright, cozy and elegant. "Certainly it can
be done."

MY BOSS CALLED me into her office on Monday, and from
the hands-folded-on-her-desk seriousness of her expression,
I knew something was up.

"Stacy, I really regret having to do this," she said, "But I'm pulling you from the Miller project."

I was stunned. I knew my work was good, and getting better all the time—the Miller project one of my best.

"Okay . . ." I said slowly.

"It's those crank calls—"

"The Millers? I didn't know *they* had received the calls too! I thought it was only the Garcias."

"No, it isn't. And the Millers want you to know they don't blame you, but they won't put up with it. They say they'll keep working with us as long as you're not involved, and see how it goes. I don't have to remind you they are very important clients and we need to do whatever it takes to make them happy."

"Of course," I said woodenly. "I understand."

"Have you called the police?"

"Yes, I called the police," I said. "They were very sympathetic . . . what can they do? It's so sporadic. Whoever it is calls different people—me almost never. It's almost impossible to trace something like that. It's just some nut, and he'll stop when he gets bored of it. That's what they said."

"Yes," she sighed. "I hope so." She softened at my troubled silence. "Look, Stacy. Maybe we should inform the police again. I mean, when it's beginning to be a real problem . . ."

Yes, I thought, when it gets to the point where you're taken off a job because of harassment, it *is* a problem.

I called again and talked to a rather harried-sounding police officer, who listened politely and yet somehow impatiently, and assured me the matter was "being looked into."

Chapter Ten

I T WAS LATE February when I was finally able to take a few days off and come up to the mountains again. I walked through the house, pleased at the progress. The estimates had come in on the floors, but the work had yet to be done — there was still a deadly row of tack strip around the edge of the walls, and for the umpteenth time I just barely missed stepping on it. I decided I must pull it up immediately.

I went to my tool box and took out what looked to be the appropriate tools with which to tackle the problem — a wedge and a hammer. I got down on my knees and began to chip away at the tack strip, feeling like a caveman trying to write on a stone tablet, except I was trying to avoid the tablet. It wasn't working well. The tack strip splintered but the nails held fast — when they weren't jabbing into my hand. I sighed with exasperation, sitting cross-legged on the floor, already exhausted.

There was a soft knock at the front door. "Come *in*," I barked crossly.

Through the wide arched doorway between the parlor and the entry hall, I could see the front door opening, slow and tentative. I was startled to see Brand's face in the crack of the door. He came in hesitantly. He saw me sitting on the floor, he saw the tackstrip and the tools, and he saw my frustration.

"You're doing that wrong," he said.

"Really. Would you like to take over?"

"Have you got a shovel?"

"What—?"

"Just a minute." He was gone.

I sat on the floor, motionless, feeling dazed. When Brand returned, he was carrying a small flat shovel.

"What's that for?"

"Just a minute."

"What are you doing?" I demanded.

He slammed the edge of the shovel hard against the edge of the tack strip along the floor. I let out a yelp of alarm. I couldn't believe it. I feared for my house. But a section of the tack strip had come up, nice and neat in one piece. It was no fluke—he did it again. And again. He kept up a rhythm like that all the way down the wall, and the entire tackstrip came rolling up loose like a quilled snake. In only a few places did it stick, and there he loosened it easily with my hammer. In less than four minutes, the entire wall of tack strip lay on the floor, with very little impact upon the floor boards or the baseboard.

"You try it," he said, and offered me the shovel.

"I'll scratch the wood floor," I said, though I had scratched it more with my technique than he had with his. I began jamming the shovel against the wall and found it to be sort of fun and surprisingly effective, though my efforts weren't quite as efficient as his. He coached me, like he had coached me down the ski run.

"So," I panted. "Where did you learn—to do that?"

"Where did I *learn* it—?" He frowned, thinking. "I don't know. I don't remember ever learning it. My dad was a carpenter. A builder—he did electrical, plumbing, masonry. He was always working on something, and making me work with him. I absorbed some of his knowledge, I guess. I made my living as a tradesman until I started making money as a writer. Writing is just a different kind of craft—and easier on the body in old age." He stopped abruptly, as if suddenly aware that he was beginning to reveal himself. "This room looks a lot better with that old carpet out," he said.

"Doesn't it?" I said, gratified. "I can't wait until the floors are refinished. I just got some estimates."

"What are you going to do with them?"

"Just have 'em sanded down a bit and match the original finish."

"What about the walls?"

"Well, I'm going to paint them."

"Better do that before the floors."

"Yeah, I know. You sound like my brother. It's just that I don't mind the walls, but the floors. They could be so beautiful."

"I brought you some firewood."

"You did?"

He caught me off guard with that one.

"Yeah, a friend of mine gave us some really nice seasoned oak. I noticed your pile looked a little sparse and I thought you could use some."

I was absurdly touched. "I've been hoping I could get through the winter without having to buy a big load of wood," I admitted. "And I was running out. Thank you."

"There's plenty on your property, you don't need to buy any—you know, some of the stuff you need to clear out anyway. We could buck up some of that stuff for you. But you'll want something tonight, there's a big storm coming in. Or are you driving back to the city tonight?"

"No . . . I was planning to leave tomorrow."

"You might not be leaving if you wait till tomorrow."

"I guess I'll take my chances." I followed him to the door.

We stood together on the porch. There was my newly stocked woodpile, under the shelter by the carport.

"Thank you, Brand," I said, embarrassed by the tone in my voice. "Thank you for the wood, and for the tack-strip-removal lesson."

"Sure, no problem. If you ever want help with construction stuff . . ." He hesitated, and his voice sounded very young and boyish, insecure. "I know your brother is a contractor, so you're probably all set, but—"

"Well, yes, he is a contractor, but he's avoiding me. I think I've gotten about as much out of him as I'm going to get for awhile. Besides, he thinks I should tear down this place, same as Tom does."

A look of shrewd curiosity crossed his face. "What do *you* think?"

"Sometimes I think they're right." I smiled.

He didn't say anything. He stared at me, his eyes fixed on me as if he was trying to catch me in a lie.

I felt nervous and searched for something else to say. "You've done a lot to *your* place. I would have liked to have seen the 'before.' "

"You can, if you want to," he said. "I've got pictures. If you're really interested."

"Of course I'm interested."

"That's right, because you're an architect." He smiled at me and I knew he was making reference to our earlier sparring.

"That's not the only reason I'm interested," I said pointedly. "I understand you're living in what is actually my barn."

He looked startled, caught my grin. "*Your* barn?" He squinted his eyes so that the long, light-filled triangles became dark slashes and he studied me, his mouth considering a smile. "What if I am living in your barn? What are you going to do about it?"

"The question is, what are *you* going to do about it? I'm going to need a place to put my cow."

"You don't have a cow."

"I may be getting one."

"Idle threats."

"I want to see those pictures."

"I don't know if I should show them to you after all," he said. He jumped off the porch and strode away, his thumbs hooked into the top of his jeans.

"Brand!" I yelled.

"What?" He stopped at the end of the drive, swung back to look at me.

"I want to see the pictures."

He appeared to be considering it. "We'll see," he yelled. "We'll see!" He turned and walked off through the woods. I went into the house, smiling at the sight of the tack strip laying in a spiky coil on the floor, touched by the gift of firewood he had brought me, trying to ignore the feelings of giddiness and excitement I felt whenever I happened to encounter him.

I HADN'T HEARD any other mention of a storm coming in, and I didn't think much about it until the middle of the night when I woke to the wind moaning and whipping the trees. I felt alone and isolated in the big old house, and at the same time, strangely comforted to know my neighbors were close, knowing, especially, that Brand was near. I felt confused. I mistrusted him less than I should, I thought, but there was something about him that inspired confidence and the feeling that I wasn't without support up here in the mountains. It was odd that I would think of him, out of all my other neighbors.

Brand could be rude. Cold. Secretive. But he had stocked my woodpile. And he had shoveled my parking area. And when we skied together, he had stayed with me all the way down the mountain . . . he took care of me.

Well, so what if he had accompanied me skiing? The next time I saw him he had turned the cold shoulder on me. We'd had some fun together, but that didn't make him a good guy, did it? What if he had done all that nice stuff for some ulterior motive? I forced myself to recognize certain truths. A con artist, by nature, must be able to inspire trust. And he was doing it, gradually winning me over.

And that began another round of interior argument.

He had warned me there was to be a storm tonight, which I had ignored, and now the winds pounded rain against the walls and rattled the old windows of the house—lonely, agitated spirits, moaning and crying through the night. I turned the switch on my bedside lamp and found the electricity was out.

I got up out of bed, feeling too restless to sleep. I slipped on my warm white terry cloth robe, belted it, and felt my way over to my writing table, where there were candles and matches in the top drawer. I lit a candle and carried it down to the library, shielding the flame with my hand.

I slid the boxes out of the cabinet by the fireplace, opened the dusty lid of the largest one and pulled out the first thing I touched. It was a letter dated some thirty years earlier, written in loopy handwriting on elaborate stationery, chatty and friendly, discussing someone's high school graduation.

Dearest Mother,

You won't believe who we saw there! Daddy couldn't believe it, either. Do you remember Louise Shaw? You would never have recognized her, she's gotten so fat! Grandma Shapiro was asking about you. Daddy told her you weren't planning on teaching at the college this fall, which I didn't even know about!

It was a long letter, and I ended up skimming most of it. The letter was signed, *With love, Jean.* Bonnie Jean, Mrs. Shapiro's daughter. I soon found there were a great number of letters from her. And there were letters from Mrs. Shapiro's son, too:

Dear Mother,

Hi, how are you? I am fine. I'm playing baseball and I was a member of the chess club but I dropped that. We went to Uncle Burt's ranch last weekend and we got to shoot cans off the fence with a real gun. We are all doing all right here, but I want you to come back, or at least come visit as soon as you can. And I hope you can come see one of my games. I play third base.

Love, Tim

I flipped through the letters, reading as I went, and I began to organize them by author and date, looking for some reference to the house, and I wasn't disappointed. There was correspondence with a man named Lawrence Patrick who had been the caretaker of the property for Madelon Shapiro before she had moved there permanently, more than forty years earlier. He wrote in detail about the maintenance of the house, construction projects and landscaping, down to the colors of certain flowers he had planted, all in response, apparently, to her exacting wishes. There were references to weather patterns, and notations of wildlife sighted. By that time the Apple Ranch was no longer a working farm, but the orchards still flourished. It seemed the property had once boasted magnificent, carefully cultivated gardens, which was almost hard to imagine, so wild was it now. I grew excited as I read, for now I could begin to understand the history of the house.

From the letters I learned that for years the family had commuted to the mountains for weekends and holidays. Madelon in particular was devoted to the estate. She was passionately involved with every aspect of the house and grounds, but the estate was her family's country home. She spent the greater part of her year in San Francisco with her husband and children, but her heart was in the mountains. And then came the change: Madelon Shapiro left the city, left her family, and moved into the house in the mountains. In none of the letters did I find a clue as to why she had done this. Only the result:

Madelon,
*   I am trying very hard to understand you. I am giving you another chance to come back to us. I love you and I despair of losing you. You don't realize what this is doing to the children and to me. We can start over, please.*

Dear Maddy,
*   I was very disturbed to hear the news. I find it difficult to believe you are happier in that old house in the mountains by yourself than you would be at home where you belong. I spoke to Mick the other day and he is very distraught.*

I am your mother and I only want what is best for you and the children.

I shivered, suddenly aware of the violence of the storm outside, moaning and thrashing against the walls.

Amazing what stories can take shape with so few words. I was fascinated at the emotional pain to be found in decades old correspondence—it seemed nothing in the box was dated more recently than twenty years earlier. I was repelled, too. I was becoming less certain I even *wanted* to know the history of the house.

Most of the correspondence was from Jean, the daughter, but unfortunately, there was little about the house in her letters, and they tended to be rather dull in spite of the efforts of the stationery, which was always tinted, always adorned with flowers and curling scrolls of decoration, and the handwriting, with all its loops and circles and exclamation points. I was certain they had once reeked of perfume, but now they just smelled musty. I put all of Jean's letters together in their flowered envelopes and snapped them together with a rubber band.

There were a number of letters in the handwriting of the author of the eerie poem I had found during an earlier exploration, jagged, exaggerated handwriting, leaning backward, usually starting off with the salutation, *My dear M,* and ending with the initial *L.* They were written on binder paper, mostly, and they were difficult to read, for the handwriting tended to bunch up against itself until it seemed to overlap. And the writing was so disjointed and monotonous I found little of interest in it. Still, whoever *L* was, he—or she—had a prominent position in the life of Mrs. Shapiro after the breakup of the family. I found no correspondence from *L* before that time.

Along with the letters, cards, and notes were newspaper clippings and various other items. I culled a pile of trash: a stained napkin, a crumbled religious tract, twenty-year-old bank statements and propane company receipts. But the things I kept surprised me. I had expected to save only some of the personal correspondence, keeping only what pertained to the property, but I found I was becoming involved in the personal drama of the woman who had once lived in my house. I began to search for clues about her as well as the house.

The journals I found proved to be rather disappointing, containing more in the way of laundry lists than personal revelation, trailing off after the first ten pages or so anyway.

In between the pages of one of the journals I found a note in the crabbed, backward handwriting that was always signed with the loopy letter *L*.

L was beginning to give me the creeps.

My dear M—
Why can't anyone believe it was a suicide? I loved him so much. The only thing I ever wanted for him was what was best.
I don't want him to be in heaven alone. But they won't even let me die. They only want to punish me.

This is too weird, I thought, as a convulsive shudder ran through my shoulders and down my back. I pulled my robe tighter around me. I tucked the note back into its envelope, put it in the pile I had made for the *L* letters, and shoved everything back into the box. I sat there for a moment in the candlelit darkness, hugging my arms around myself. I had a prickly feeling up my back and down my arms, like someone was watching me unseen from the dark corners of the room. I longed to be back in bed, hidden and warm.

I stood up, stretched out my back with a groan, belted my robe tighter and tried to shake off the creepiness that had come over me. The lack of electric light didn't help matters. I picked up the candle and walked toward the stairs.

All of a sudden an enormous shuddering boom rocked the house on its foundation. The floors, the walls, the ceilings—the whole house was shaking, rattling, groaning. Something had crashed into the house. A car or an airplane. Or an earthquake had rent the ground. I stumbled and almost fell to the floor with the impact of it. The candle went out with a sputter. The old structure reverberated like the plucked string of a mis-tuned bass.

I groped my way through the dark toward the front of the house. An unnatural pale light shone from the front parlor. I stood beneath the arched doorway, and only after a moment did I register what I was seeing. It was as if the fabric between waking reality and nightmare had suddenly torn, and the dark arms of hell had thrust their long limbs down through the rip, clawing right through the walls.

The big black oak tree had fallen into my house.

I SAW THE branches of the massive tree through a gaping wound in the ceiling and front wall of the house. A creaking and moaning came from the tree, and from the house itself, like the death cries of a huge animal. Already the debris was mingling on the floor with the rain that continued to pound on the roof and spill in through the hole. The tree groaned suddenly and shifted its weight, and at that moment I realized that the corner of the house upstairs where my bed stood must have borne the greatest impact of the fall. I had to consciously calm my breath so that I wouldn't hyperventilate.

I should have been dead, I kept thinking. *I should have been dead.*

I groped my way into the kitchen to see if the phones would work. Looking back I think how crazy I was then, that I should have gotten the hell out of there, but I wanted desperately to talk to Russ, though there was nothing he could do for me at the moment, being a hundred and fifty miles away in a storm! I knew that, of course, but I wanted to talk to him anyway.

I stood next to the counter in the kitchen, stubbornly trying to get a dial tone. Phone lines can work when the electricity doesn't, I argued. But the phone was dead, too.

I heard the sound of the front door opening. I thought it was the wind—then I heard the voices—I heard Tess calling my name. I put the phone down and ran out to the entry hall where she was standing.

She grabbed me, embraced me. "My God, Stacy. That *tree*—"

"Did you hear it—?"

Yes, my God. We were horrified—Brand just ran up the stairs to look for you—" She turned to stare at the amazing tree-filled hole which had opened the wall and ceiling to the night.

"You'd better get out of the house," I said, "I don't know if it's safe—I'll go get Brand."

"Okay," she agreed.

I dashed up the stairs, churning with adrenaline. I ran down the hall to the bedroom and through the door where I collided with Brand, who was in a similar pumped-up state.

"There you are! Thank God," he exclaimed, grasping me hard with a spontaneous protective embrace, like Tess— only he didn't feel like Tess. I felt his body against me, long and solid and hot, through my soft cotton robe. We came apart abruptly and I caught my breath to see how the tree had sprawled one enormous segment of its trunk across my bed, which lay shattered beneath it. Without thinking, I stepped closer, fascinated.

He grabbed my arm and pulled me out of the room. "Come on, you, let's get out of here." We ran downstairs and out to the porch, where Tess, Saul, Yolanda, and Father Daniel had all assembled to marvel at the damage done by the great fallen body of the old oak tree.

I SPENT THE night in Brand's house.

Tess brought a stack of blankets and a pillow into the den where I was to sleep. She lit a candle and set it on the table next to the sofa.

"You've got your flashlight, you know where the bathroom is . . . I'll get you a nightgown—?" I was still wearing nothing but my robe.

"No, that's okay," I said. "I'll sleep in your shirt." She had lent me clothes, shoes, and a jacket, because they didn't want me to go back into my house until it was safe again. "I'm all set. Thank you for everything."

"You sure you're all right, Stacy?" she asked with concern.

"She'll be fine," Saul said. He hung in the doorway like a bat, sidled in, looked around the room as if assessing its suitability for some dark purpose. Tess gave him a stern look, folded her arms. "Saul, you leave Stacy alone," she said.

"I will. If she wants me to." He smiled, his eyes gleaming.

Tess rolled her eyes and we exchanged a secret girl's smile.

"Goodnight," she said forcefully and waited for Saul to withdraw before she went out and shut the door behind her, leaving me alone in the cozy pine-paneled room.

I sat on the sofa and wondered if I would stay awake all night. My mind was stuck in rewind mode, playing back the crashing of the tree, over and over, hearing that explosion, the prolonged creaking and groaning, feeling the vibration still shaking my body. And, just as insistently, my mind played over the warmth and texture of Brand's voice, Brand's touch, the length of Brand's body against mine, in the doorway of my bedroom where we had come together so fleetingly.

How would I ever sleep?

I was less preoccupied with the thought of my wounded house than I was with the image of him, there in the darkness, looking for me, and the relief I'd heard in his voice when he had found me unharmed.

Now it was deep in the night, and I was in his house, and he was somewhere in the house too. I tried to imagine him in his rooms at the top of the house, pacing the floor, unable to sleep because he was as agitated as I was.

The sound of the storm had changed, grown quieter. Then it was silent. I looked out the window and saw the rain had turned to snow. I took off my robe and put on the shirt Tess had lent me, and then I blew out the candle. I slid between the blankets on the sofa and lay like that awhile. But I was used to sleeping naked, and I didn't see any reason I shouldn't sleep in the nude tonight. I sat up, opened the buttons down the front of the shirt and let it slide off my shoulders.

Here I am naked in Brand's house.

Sometimes such pointless thoughts go through your mind.

Tess had been the one to insist upon my staying there. "Stacy," she said, "You don't have any choice. You have to stay with us. You can't go back into your house tonight. She can't, can she, Brand?—" Brand had merely said, "Of course not."

She had provided me with plenty of soft blankets and the sofa was roomy and supportive. In spite of myself, I began to feel sleepy, and I was just dozing off when I heard a soft knocking on the door.

My eyes opened wide and my heart kicked up a hard pounding. I sat up a little, saw the door opening, a wedge of light widening slowly, interrupted by a shadow filling the doorway.

"Stacy . . . you're not awake, are you?" It was a whisper. Saul slowly crept into the room, letting the door swing almost shut behind him.

"What is it, Saul?"

"I thought you might be feeling a bit shaky." He came up to the bed and loomed over me, nothing of him visible in the darkness but the hulk of him. "I have something for you. Something for your nerves."

Now I wished I hadn't slipped beneath the sheets completely naked. I sat upright, pulling the blankets up to my chin. I felt vulnerable, unable to react. It was so dark.

"Are you . . . interested?"

"I'm fine, really," I said. "I was just about asleep."

"Well . . ." He hesitated. "What I have for you is guaranteed to make you feel all better." I felt him shift his weight against the sofa, leaning against the cushions so that I felt the tension of his body pulling against the blankets I clutched to my chest. I was alarmed; at any moment I thought he might lower himself down upon me. He was so close now I could smell the sweet sour scent of his aftershave.

"I'd really like to get some sleep, Saul," I said firmly, shrinking away from his touch.

"Yes, you will sleep soundly—I guarantee it," he murmured, and now I could feel both his hands on my shoulders, near my neck, as if he would give me a massage—or strangle me.

"Saul, get *out*," I said in a loud voice.

There was a flickering at the doorway and the sound of the door creaking, opening wide, bumping against the wall. Brand's unmistakable form appeared in the room behind Saul.

"Stacy?"

The flame of the candle he was holding danced its dark golden light on Brand's face. He looked as beautiful as an angel.

"I came to see if you had everything you . . . need?" His voice was soft, friendly, and he didn't seem to notice the awkwardness of Saul, who stood up straight and stepped away from me abruptly.

"Yes, I have everything I need," I said, my voice wavering a little. "I was just about to go to sleep . . ."

Brand stood there a moment, motionless, silent, and Saul fidgeted in the pause and said, "Well—goodnight, then." He went out, pushing past Brand without looking at him.

Brand and I occupied the small dark room without speaking for the barest of a moment, alone with the glowing of the candle between us, and the sigh I suddenly let escape was audible.

"I'm afraid I don't allow any hanky-panky between my guests," Brand said.

"Thank you," I said, half whispering, too shaken to return the jest.

"Don't mention it."

There was a silence between us, and then he murmured: "Good night, Stacy."

I wanted to say, *don't go* . . .

"Good night, Brand."

Good night.

Chapter Eleven

I WOKE WITH the first light, light-headed and heavy-eyed with lack of sleep. I tried to fall asleep again, but I just lay there and thought about where I was—*Brand's house*—and why I was there—*the old oak crashed into my house last night*—and how much I wanted to talk to Russ. I got up, wrapped my robe around me, and went down to the kitchen.

By the dim light of the open refrigerator door, I saw the tall dark shape of Brand's lean body in gray sweats, kneeling, searching for something on a lower shelf. He straightened up with a bag of coffee beans in his hand, caught sight of me and gave a start.

"The electricity is back," I said. I hadn't thought of it until I saw the light in the refrigerator.

"Hi—" His voice almost stuttered. "Want some coffee?"

"Are you kidding?"

He went to the counter next to the sink and opened the lid of the coffee grinder.

"Can I use your phone to call my brother collect?" I asked. "If it even works."

"Sure. It's in the hall. And don't call collect."

I went out into the hall, found the phone, and I heard the whine of the coffee grinder as it pulsated in the kitchen — once, twice, three times. I heard the dial tone click into place. I felt a crazy happiness when I heard the sleepy sound of Russ's voice, a hundred and fifty miles away, familiar and cross with his scratchy-throat, irritable bark. It was way too early to be calling my brother, under normal circumstances.

"Russ Addison. Can I *help* you—?"

I went back into the kitchen. Brand was looking through the cupboards, and the coffee was dripping into the pot, filling the brightening room with the dusky, delicious smell.

"My brother is coming," I said happily.

"Breakfast?" Brand asked shyly. "What do you like? Eggs, waffles? Pancakes—? Too much? Well, then, how about cornflakes. We have lots of cornflakes."

"Yes, I like cornflakes."

"Oh, look. *Two* opened boxes of cornflakes. I think these are the fresh ones." He brought the big yellow box to the table.

"Well, shouldn't we use the older cornflakes first?" I asked.

"No. Because the fresh ones taste better and are crispier. And if we use the old ones first, by the time we get to the newer ones, *they* will be stale. So you might as well use the unstale ones first."

I opened the refrigerator, frowned. "Do you propose to use the new milk first?"

"No. With milk you always use the older milk first." There was that smile again. Rare, bright, flashing.

We sat down together and had our cornflakes and coffee. Neither of us talked much, but there was a fine companionable silence between us, broken when Saul stumbled into the kitchen, bleary eyed, complaining of the sun which, he said, had streamed into his room and awakened him rudely.

THE SNOW WAS deep on the ground but the storm had gone quietly away. Electricity was restored throughout the village and the roads were plowed. Russ was coming. I called Janine and begged for a couple days off work. I had less to do these days without the Miller project anyway.

"I'm forever in your debt, my dearest beloved brother," I said when Russ arrived just before ten in the morning. I had run down to the parking area to meet him. "You must not have even stopped for breakfast!" I was impressed with his immediate response to my plight.

"You were already forever in my debt," he replied. "And no, I haven't had breakfast—my God, Stacy." He had caught sight of the tree.

"The structural damage isn't as bad as it looks," I said. "At least that's my initial diagnosis."

"Who put up the temporary supports, and the plastic?"

"The priest from the church next door helped me. Father Daniel. And my neighbor, Brand."

"They did good. Brand. That's the guy you went out with?"

"Uh, no—not him. Anyway, you'll meet them. So what do you think?"

"I think we have a big repair job to put together fast."

RUSS ASSEMBLED A crew of volunteers without even having to recruit—there was a rather touching interest in the project. The neighborhood men—Father Daniel, Tom, Ralph, Brand—became a crack military unit under Russ's command. It happened almost wordlessly, mysteriously. The women, Tess, Callie, Yolanda, and me, found ourselves at various tasks supporting the effort, but the actual job of lifting the tree in sections from the house and the subsequent repair of the building, this work the men took over as if they had received a calling.

Tess and Callie prepared food and drink for the workers while Yolanda and I stayed closer to the action. I wanted to make sure I had a handle on everything that was going on, because a job like this could be disorganized and dangerous. But Yolanda had an itch to get right into the work herself. At first she poked around, carrying away broken branches and debris, but she gradually edged her way in with the men and they started to include her as part of their crew. Pretty soon, I noticed, she was one of them, whereas Saul, who had started out helping the men, had wandered away.

I made runs to the hardware store and the lumberyard in Russ's big truck. I called the break when lunch arrived. I reveled in the energy of purpose, and I had no time to be horrified at the damage done to my house. I felt alive and grateful for the show of strength and kindness these people were offering. It was like an old time barn-raising, with plenty of shouting and joking, good food, coolers full of beer and soft drinks, rock and roll blaring from a radio someone had rigged up, and a hell of a lot of work getting done in the middle of it all. They cut the tree up and yanked the pieces out of the great gaping hole in my house.

WE HAD STOPPED for the day, and Russ and I were alone together in my kitchen, sitting at the table, Russ with a beer, me with a steaming cup of Earl Grey, both of us exhausted, feeling the dampening down of the exhilaration of crisis which had driven us since daybreak.

"We'll have that puppy nailed by tomorrow night," Russ said thoughtfully. "I mean, not the entire job, obviously, but the majority of that repair will be history. Know of any good plasterers around here?"

"It could have been worse, you know," I said. "That plaster needed work anyway, didn't it? I'm scared to see the materials tab for this one. But still. I'm just amazed at how it all came together."

"It was the manpower," he said. "It was awesome."

"People power," I said.

"I stand corrected. *People*—those girls pumping us with food and beer. And Yolanda was great. She should be a carpenter. I'd hire her."

"So that's what it takes to get you to notice? She's gotta be able to swing a hammer, huh?"

"Oh, I always noticed her. She's a cute girl. But I'll tell

you what, the one who really made it happen today was that guy—Van—"

"Vandevere? Brand?"

"Brand. Yeah."

"Yeah?" My heart quickened at the sound of his name.

"That other guy was useless. Saul? He's the one you dated, huh?"

"Come on, Russ, I went out with him *once*."

"He was a turkey. Fortunately, he didn't last long, or he would have seen to it that the whole goddamned roof collapsed. The other guys were good, too—that priest, and what's that other guy's name—?"

"Ralph . . . ?"

"Right. And that guy Tom was all right. But Brand—I wish I could hire him myself. He's smart, and he's a better craftsman than I am. He's not all that fast—but then he doesn't do it all the time, so hell. He was there when everyone else had given out. He's not that fast, but—hey! I wouldn't want to go up against him in a nailing race. The guy is good."

"Apparently Brand is good at many things," I said.

"Stacy, by the end of the day he was running the crew for me."

I listened, bemused, to hear Russ speak so glowingly of Brand. It wouldn't matter to Russ if Brand had climbed Mount Everest or won the Pulitzer Prize. This assessment of Brand's talent as a workman was Russ's highest praise and the thing he valued practically above all else. He rarely bestowed such compliments, and never lightly.

"You know," I said, "Brand is the one I told you about. The one who tried to finagle the property from the old woman who owned it—"

"Finagle? *Finagle?* What the hell is that? Vandevere doesn't strike me as a finagler, Stacy."

"I'm only telling you the facts."

"Really? Where'd you get your facts?"

"Well, I've heard from several sources—"

"Exactly. You don't know."

"I wish I didn't, Russ," I said sadly.

"I'm going to have to forbid them all to help tomorrow," he grumbled. "None of them would accept any pay."

"Not even Saul?"

"Well, he probably would have, but he disappeared, pretty much right off. We got lucky, I guess."

But in spite of our protests, which were admittedly feeble, they did come back the next day, all of them except Saul, and Tess, because she had to work. Being around Brand so much was making me crazy, giddy, and high.

His name went through my mind. His name went through my mind like the refrain of a song. A haunting sound. Since his name was a common word, I would hear his name in phrases having nothing to do with him, in conversation, on the radio; I would see it written on the page, in advertisements, and I would think of him. I said the word over and over to myself, the word that was his name. I felt the word in my mouth, and my tongue rolled over it and my mouth tasted it. His name. Brand.

On Sunday night we all had dinner together over at the barn before Russ headed home to the Bay Area. Everyone who had been involved with the project came, bringing a potluck dish to share, and many stories were told amidst great hilarity.

Around nine o'clock Russ had finally finished telling tall tales and he had gulped down enough of Tess's strong coffee so that he was ready to push out. I walked him out to his truck and I gave him an unusually affectionate hug goodbye.

"Thanks, Russ. I am so grateful for you. You saved the day."

"Yeah, well." He was embarrassed.

"I really needed you."

"Nah, you would have been all right. Brand would have taken care of you."

I loved hearing that, even as I protested. "No," I said. "I do need you." I kissed him on the nose, and sent him on his way.

I was tired and ready to go home, but I needed to go back

to the Barn and help clean up and get my casserole dish and a couple other things I had left there.

Inside the house it was quiet, with only the mystical music of Enya playing on the stereo. Father Daniel and Yolanda had already left, and Saul had gone off with Tom to get more beer. Callie and Ralph were talking quietly in the kitchen, doing the dishes. It didn't seem right to interrupt them just then. I walked down the hall to get my things from the den. The room I had lived in, for one night, in Brand's house. I went into the room and started to collect up my white bathrobe, my jacket. I heard the voices in the hallway outside the room.

". . . just can't believe you would say something like that!" It was Tess, more agitated than I had ever heard her before.

"Why do you find it so hard to believe?" That was Brand. They didn't seem to be trying to keep their voices down, and they were both apparently rather worked up about something.

"After what happened in Phoenix? You were very nearly arrested for assault, on top of everything else!"

"Well, thanks to you, I wasn't."

"I just want you to remember that. It could have gone very differently for you."

"Sometimes I wish it had."

"Don't talk like that, Brand."

"Anyway. What has that got to do with the situation here?"

"It's got everything to do with the situation here. Don't you understand?"

"Are you asking me if I learned my lesson?"

"That house belongs to Stacy now, and there's nothing anyone can do about that."

"I'm not so sure. There are other ways to get what you really want in this world."

"Brand, that's ridiculous."

"Oh, you think so? I don't think you've learned *your* lesson. Listen, Tess. There are all sorts of ways she could be eliminated from the scenario."

"What do you mean by that?"

"I mean, if you are willing to do whatever it takes to get what you want, it's fairly easy. If your adversary is dead, you win."

"Brand, you scare me when you talk like this."

"Well, take it as a warning, then, Tess."

"Brand, please . . ."

"I'm not going to just lie down and let it go like I did before. There's too much at stake here."

"I wouldn't characterize what you did in Phoenix as lying down and letting it go, Brand. You could have hurt an innocent person."

"I think you're missing the point."

There was a short silence. "No, I understand. I do." She sounded contrite, and in a quieter voice she said, "You know I'll help you anyway I can. Just be patient, please. That's all I'm asking."

"I'll wait a little longer, Tess. I'm a patient man. But I'm not backing down this time."

They continued on down the hall.

I was paralyzed.

Saul had told me of an incident in Phoenix. Brand had tried to scam a wealthy elderly woman, he said, and was only saved by Tess's intervention. I was sure this was what they had been talking about. And then they mentioned me. Brand's latest target? Was he so determined to have my house?

I got myself together with a few deep breaths, wondering what I should do. I could not reconcile the great show of support and friendship Brand and Tess had shown me with this strange overheard conversation. I was too disturbed to face them, so I wrote a note of thanks, gathered up my things, and slipped out without saying good-bye.

ONE EVENING I was sitting alone in my apartment in the city when the phone rang. I answered hesitantly, because I was scared that when I picked up the phone these days I would get nothing but a click or the old heavy breathing rou-

tine, or some weird garbled message. It didn't happen very
often, but it happened. Whoever was harassing me with
these calls was not terribly creative. But the call was Brand's
friend Thaddeus. He was planning to build a house in the
foothills, he said, and he was looking for an architect. Brand
had encouraged him to give me a call.

"Brand told you to call me?" My voice must have be-
trayed my surprise.

"Well, he said I should check you out. I know you're with
a firm there in San Francisco, but he said you might be taking clients up here in the hills. I've got a choice parcel of
land and I want to build a *palace,* you know, or at least a really awesome house. I'm going to be in the Bay Area at the
end of the week and I wondered if we could get together.
Maybe I could look at some work you've done. I'll tell you
about what I have in mind; we could have dinner."

"Sure, we could do that. I could probably meet you Friday afternoon."

"Sounds like a plan."

At first I was a little suspicious. Thad treated our time together more like a date than a business appointment. He arrived in his black Mercedes, wearing a long gray raincoat
over a stylish and expensive Italian suit, and he presented
me with one perfect red rose. I was proud of him when he
came into the office. Janine and Kate, our office manager,
both thought he was adorable, with his curly black hair and
his dimples, and it was obvious he had money, which instantly impressed them.

"Is it okay with your boss that we're doing this?" he
asked when we had left the office.

"Yes, I talked to her about it. Janine knows I have my
own projects. She's given me some referrals that she didn't
want to handle herself."

"Sounds fair," he said. "Just don't want to getcha in trouble." And he winked at me, and took my arm. I had a feeling that getting me in trouble was the least of his worries.

We drove down the Peninsula in Thad's black Mercedes.
Thad was smart and witty and wickedly flamboyant, and he
always displayed excellent taste, except for his jokes.

"Oh, I've got to turn this up. I love this song," he said, and blasted the stereo.

"You aren't going to make me sing this time, are you?" I asked.

The last time I rode in this car, I thought, Brand was sitting in the back seat.

"I should. Though you'd charge me extra for that, wouldn't you!"

"You can consider this afternoon a free consultation," I laughed. "But if I have to sing, yes, I'll charge you. And it won't be worth it!"

"I think it just might be worth it," he grinned. "So where are we going?"

"Burlingame. I thought I'd show you something I did myself. You know, not just the work I do for the company. This was my own client."

I had arranged it with the owners, who weren't home. We parked near the carport and I led him around back to the sliding door off the kitchen where there was a hidden key.

"Nice situation," Thad whistled, looking around, hands in his pockets, while I unlocked the door. The architecture was sleek and unadorned, yet it had a rich rustic quality that pleased me. It had turned out well. The materials were aging nicely; all the wood and stone and glass combined gracefully in the setting of eucalyptus and Monterey pine around the house. The stunning view of the bay didn't hurt, either. Inside, the rooms were large, well-situated to the view, full of light, wood, glass, and Italian stone.

"Yes. This is what I like." Thad went from room to room as if he owned the place. I found myself wishing it was Brand who was admiring my work, and I wondered if Thad would tell him about it.

I tried to shrug off those thoughts which, I was convinced, could only drive me mad.

We continued on down to Palo Alto to look at another place I had designed, and Thad seemed impressed. We talked about what he wanted to do; it sounded intriguing, and I thought we could probably work well together. When he mentioned the sort of budget he had in mind, I had to warn myself not to get too excited.

We drove back up to the city and had dinner together at an Italian restaurant in North Beach. I showed him my portfolio. Afterward, we took a walk down toward the bay.

"My hotel is right around the corner," he said. "How about it?"

"You mean——?" I laughed at his semi-serious expression, his bluntness.

"You know what I mean."

I shook my head, feeling like, *uh oh*. Thad was adorable but I felt little attraction for him.

"Look," I said. "You and me——I have a feeling we could really do something together. Are you serious about this building project?"

"Oh——" he looked surprised. "Oh, yeah, absolutely. Give me your contract. I want to go for it. I probably won't do anything until after taxes, you know, but yes. I'm very serious about it."

"Okay."

"But now. My hotel? . . ."

He was charmingly persistent.

"I'm sorry. You are a client. Or, at least, I hope you will be. I can't do that."

"Oh!" he scowled. "Well, what if I fire you? What then?"

"Fired already!" I exclaimed unhappily. "That was quick."

"All right, all right. Come, I'll take you home."

When we had parked in front of my apartment, he tried again. "Are you *sure*?" he cajoled. "You can invite me up."

"No. I'm sure."

"You're saying no because you are going to be my architect?"

I smiled.

"Well, good night then, Miss Stacy. And I won't kiss you goodnight. This time. Because I know you don't want me to. I also know it's not because we will be working together. You don't strike me as a woman who would let the professional-client relationship interfere with passion, if you were really interested."

"Oh, I see!" I laughed. "Don't think I could control myself, huh?"

"I'll be in touch," he said.

I WAS WORKING on the computer in my office in the city when the package came in the mail. It was small and square, nothing unusual, except that it was addressed directly to me, instead of to Avalon Architectural. I was alone in the office that morning, engrossed in a fireplace detail I had been working on. The package sat on my lap, and I opened it absentmindedly as I stared at the monitor, not paying attention to what was in my lap until I began to wonder, with the periphery of my brain, what this strange jumble of stuff could be. I broke my gaze away from the screen and stared down at the contents of the package. When it finally hit me what I was looking at, I was stunned.

Inside the box was a wide-mouthed ceramic urn containing the broken up pieces of an old architectural model of a house. It was one of my own models from school.

I turned the pieces of the model over in my hands, bewildered. What the hell was this?

It was one of the first projects I'd done that I was really proud of, and I had kept it for a long time. It was a house, designed along classic lines, simple, but elegant—or so I had thought when I designed it. I couldn't remember when last I'd seen it. I vaguely recalled storing it in a closet in my apartment, probably in a box with some other old school projects.

Who could have got hold of it? Had I done something with it, given it away, thrown it out? Why had it been sent back to me, all broken up like this? Who would do that?

The model hadn't just come apart in the natural way, at the joints, from the stress of age and neglect. It appeared that each individual piece had been deliberately snapped in two or three pieces. The broken bits were stuffed into the urn, a squat gray thing coated with a texture like concrete, set carefully in black tissue paper and packed in a box. The impression was one of broken bones in a funeral urn.

I turned the empty box over and shook it furiously, hoping a note would fall out, a clue of some kind, something to explain this bizarre thing, but there was nothing but the black tissue paper and the pieces of the model. I pushed aside some papers on my work table and laid out the pieces in a semblance of order, feeling mesmerized, under a spell of attack, as if someone was working voodoo upon me.

WHEN JANINE CAME into the office I showed her the broken model.

"That is creepy," she said. "It's like someone is trying to give you a warning, or something."

"A warning of *what*?" I cried.

"God knows." She picked up a piece of the model and held it up like it was radioactive.

"Maybe you should call the police."

I laughed humorlessly. "I *have* called the police," I said. "Last week. Again. They're looking into it. They advised me to change my phone number."

"Do you know, I heard there's this new thing they're coming out with where pretty soon you'll be able to just push a button on your phone and find out who just called you."

By the look on my face she could see I wasn't that excited by the news of this impending technology.

"They already have phone tracing capability. I guess I ought to press to have it done. But on which phone?"

"Well, maybe they could trace the package," she said. "I don't know. I don't know, but this is too weird. You have no idea what this is about? Who might not want you around? This all started around the time you bought that old white elephant in the mountains, didn't it?"

It had. Though I hated to put it together. I was silent.

"It's like someone doesn't want you there."

"Where?" I asked, but I knew. The house in the mountains, where more and more of my heart was hanging. But who would—? My voice trailed off, my heart pounded. Brand's face came into my mind's vision.

Someone doesn't want you there . . .

"The model was taken from my apartment, not the house in the mountains."

"All right—but by whom?" Janine wanted to know. "Who has access to your apartment? Who could have got in there and got it?"

"Well . . ." I said. "*You* could have."

"Right," she deadpanned. "You found me out."

"I've been taking too much time off, is that it? You want me to stay away from that house." I almost hoped she would admit she *had* done it, though of course I knew she hadn't.

"Are you sure you didn't have the model in your mountain house?" Janine suggested. "Could it have been taken from there?"

"No, that isn't possible . . ." but the moment I said it I knew I was wrong. There was a box of things I had brought up with me when I planned to see Callie and Ralph for our first meeting. They had asked me to bring some samples of my work and I had grabbed some old projects, because I planned to go through my portfolio, to get rid of some things and add others. The model might have been in that box; I couldn't remember.

So, whoever sent it to me might have found it in my house in the mountains. But I would have noticed if someone had broken into my house, taken things. Or would I? Someone with the right skills could have easily broken into that house without leaving a trace, what with all those old windows and doors.

Someone with the right skills. Brand, I thought. He could get in and out of the house easily, if he wanted to.

When I got home that evening, I punched on the answering machine.

"Hello," a voice came on, unfamiliar, feminine—a bit of a put-on Southern accent, I thought suspiciously, but then, I was just suspicious nowadays.

"We've heard of your troubles," the voice said without identifying itself. "We'd like to help. Isn't that big old house

rather a thorn in your side, anyway? Best to let it go—
cheap, if you have to—before it *burns to the ground.* With
you in it." The pleasant little voice ended with a hysterical
high-pitched whine, as if electronically manipulated.

I was stunned. I slammed down the phone. Feeling pan-
icked, cornered. I had changed my phone number last week
at the advice of the police officer I had talked to. The
Creeper had found me anyway.

I LEFT EARLY Friday afternoon and drove up to the mountains. I had a horrible fear I would arrive to find my house
vandalized or lying in charred ruins. I felt a little nervous
about going up there. Lately at night in the big house in the
mountains I had been feeling as if someone was in the house
with me. But then, I felt that way in the city, too. I glanced
into the back seat before getting into my car; I watched the
rearview mirror obsessively as I drove. I made odd slow little detours and other times I drove recklessly fast. I pulled
off the main road and drove a mile into the countryside and
parked, my car hidden in the lee of a gully. I desperately
cherished the solitude, knowing that no one in the world
knew where I was at that moment. But I knew it didn't matter. The Creeper knew where I was going.

I was being merciless on myself. The Creeper, of course,
was what my real estate agent had called the neighbor who
had attempted to con the property away from the old woman
who had owned my house. Brand. Brand wanted my house.
He wanted it when it was owned by Madelon Shapiro. He
wanted it still. But I never thought of Brand as the Creeper.
I forced myself to make the connection.

If at first you don't succeed, I thought. There are many
ways to eliminate someone who stands in the way of what
you want. Brand himself had said so.

What I had overheard between Brand and Tess had left
me reeling, and I hadn't yet recovered. An overheard frag-
ment of a conversation, that's all it was. I knew better than
to think I had necessarily drawn the correct conclusions
from what I had heard. Frankly, I could come to no conclu-

sions. There were all kinds of ways to interpret what I had heard. The contradictions were enough to eventually drive me mad, like Ingrid Bergman in *Gaslight*. Was it really possible that a woman could fall in love and place her trust in a man who was plotting evil against her? It seemed to be happening to me.

As I left the Central Valley behind and began the climb into the hills, the beauty of the land touched my soul the way it always did, and soon I forgot to fret so much. I grew excited about seeing my house. My orchards and meadows, my stream and forest. I laughed at myself. Owning a forest seemed a strange concept, and somehow wrong. Like owning a wolf.

This weekend I would see Callie and Ralph and show them the finished drawings for their addition. Yolanda might come over and amuse me with her caustic wit. Maybe we would sit on the porch of her little cottage, drinking tea, and maybe I would see Brand in the woods, hiking by in his big Sorrel boots, nodding a curt greeting. Or maybe I would look out my bedroom window in the late afternoon and see him standing on his porch looking out toward my house (or at the sunset), the last rays of light striking the edge of his face and shining on the gold in his hair.

I thought of what Janine had said when she had come into the office to find me staring at the shards of my architectural model.

It's like someone doesn't want you there.

Not Brand, I prayed. Please don't let it be Brand.

Chapter Twelve

THE HOUSE WAS silent and everything looked exactly
as I had left it. I walked through the rooms apprehen-
sively, peering into each cupboard and closet as if I
might find somebody crouched inside. But I didn't; not a
thing was out of place. I was struck anew with the beauty of
the old house, the wide and intricate moldings, the rich
patina on the old paneling, the details of the coving of the
plaster, the wainscoting and picture molding decorating the
walls, the graceful windows. After I had ritually assured myself the house was empty and safe, I began to relax and
laugh at my own spookiness. The feelings of delight and
gratitude I experienced each time I returned here were prov-
ing stronger than my fears.

I SAW HIM through the wavery old glass windows, standing
on the porch, and I heard his knock, soft and firm. My heart
went like a fist in my chest.
Someone doesn't want you there.
He's jealous that you got the house and he didn't.

Someone doesn't want you there.

The ominous voices crept back into my thoughts. But the worst of them was his voice, so offhandedly blunt.

There are all sorts of ways she could be eliminated from the scenario.

I mean, if you are willing to do whatever it takes to get what you want, it's fairly easy. If your adversary is dead, you win.

I opened the door and he was in front of me, close enough to reach out and strangle me. Or take me in his arms. I caught a glimpse of his scent, like the forest, woodsmoke and leather.

"Hi Stacy."

"Brand." My voice surprised me with its coolness.

"You look like you've just seen a ghost."

"Maybe I have."

"These old houses are full of them, I guess."

I studied him silently for a moment, unsure of what to reply, what to think, what to feel. With his clear river eyes set into the strong planes of his face, regarding me directly, guilelessly, it was difficult to cast him in the role of sinister villain. This was all the more horrifying. I could not trust my own perceptions, which was unusual and disconcerting to me.

I waited stiffly for him to explain his visit. I didn't invite him in.

"Sometimes," he said, "the thought of you living in this big old house by yourself . . ." He didn't finish and I thought maybe he never intended to finish, maybe never finished the thought before he spoke the words. Perhaps he was trying to fill in the silence I had allowed between us.

I said, "You think what I'm doing is . . ."

"What—?"

"I know some people think I'm strange."

"No," he said. "I don't."

"Sometimes it seems strange to me," I said.

"Mrs. Shapiro lived here for years, all alone," he said "But she seemed to fill the place with her own huge presence."

"I think about filling it with a family, someday," I said, and immediately I wished I hadn't. I expected him to laugh at me, but he just looked at me with that deer in the headlights look he sometimes got when we were talking about the house.

"But that's all in the distant future," I added hastily. "I'm starting to realize it's a lot more work than I even dreamed."

"I was hoping you would show me what you've been doing to the place," he said, hesitantly, shyly, as if he was afraid I might turn him down.

I almost did. I was startled, and wary. My suspicions rose and spiraled around me. Should I let him come in, alone with me? Was he a stalker, a psychopath? But that seemed absurd. At most, he was nothing more than a resentful neighbor. And if he resented me having the house, maybe it would help if he saw the good I was doing for it.

"Is this a bad time?" He seemed to be wondering if he had made a mistake.

"No—" I stood aside and held the door open. "No, it's not a bad time. Come in."

We went through the front parlor and I nodded toward the repair in the wall where the tree had come through, which was detectable to the trained eye only in that the new construction looked slightly smoother. "You remember this room, of course," I smiled wryly. "And you see I took your advice and I'm painting before I do the floor. Just the parlor and the dining room for now."

We went on into the dining room. "I'm having the floors refinished next week," I said with satisfaction.

He spotted the letters painted on the floor and scowled. "Edicius?"

"I found that under the carpet. Charming, isn't it?"

"What does it mean?"

"I have no idea."

"E-d-i-c-i-u-s." He studied the letters thoughtfully. "It's capitalized, like a name. Of course, it's also 'suicide' spelled backwards."

"Suicide? Oh—I never noticed that. Like in *The Shining*."

"Yeah."

"Remember that? Murder spelled backwards, right?"

"*Redrum. Redrum.*" Brand imitated the throaty little child's voice: "*Edicius, Edicius—*"

"That is *so* creepy." I hugged myself to smooth down the shivers. "The little kid alone in the vast old hotel, with his father slowly going mad . . ."

"He wasn't quite alone," Brand reminded me. "He had his mom. And he had the Shining."

"That's true . . ."

"*Edicius—*"

"Stop it!" I laughed. "That's just too creepy."

"All right. I'm sorry."

"Let's get out of here. This is my least favorite room in the house anyway. I don't know why."

We wandered through the house together and I pointed out the various changes that had been made, all the beautiful old wood floors revealed when moldy carpets were torn away, plywood removed from the fireplaces, the windows shorn of their gray plastic curtains, the plastic flowers and cheap laminated furniture and papers and junk all gone.

I was amazed to find he noticed many of the changes I had made before I pointed them out. He certainly knew the place well. His attitude was curious and touching. He walked through the rooms almost reverently, reaching down to lay his hands on the wood that had been hidden for years beneath green shag carpet, examining a window sash, speculating whether it was original to the house, or added in later construction. He reminded me of Russ. He was openly delighted with the change in the library, with the closet stripped away and the debris removed.

We went upstairs and I hesitated a moment before walking past him into my bedroom. He paused just in the doorway and stopped, as if there were some kind of invisible force field there. In this room the repair from the tree damage was obvious. I had decided not to do anything with the old wallpaper until I was ready to do all the walls in the room. We were momentarily silent, standing still, both of us knowing that we were both thinking about that night. Here

we had come together fleetingly in the darkness, furious
hearts pressed close, the great tree lying groaning across my
bed, Brand's arms around me tightly, protectively. Not like
someone who wished me dead and gone.

The bedstead lay against the wall now, in several pieces.
I had been sleeping on the mattress without the frame. We
both looked at it, and at each other.

You came to me that night.

"Russ says the bed can't be fixed," I said, and my voice
was a little husky. "But I can't bring myself to throw it out!"
We withdrew from the room quickly and went on.

He listened intently to everything I said as I explained
what had been done and what I intended to do for the house.
He said little, only asking questions now and then. "And
what will you do *here*? And what about this?"

Many times my answer was: "I don't know yet." And
since he evidently had ideas of his own, I asked him, "What
do *you* think?"

He seemed torn about how much of himself to reveal.
But he was easily coaxed to give his opinions on various aspects of the old house. I found we were in accord on many
points.

There were moments when I had the feeling he was on
the verge of saying something to me, something beyond the
technical talk of plaster and planking and plumbing fixtures;
but he would retreat and I wondered with bursting curiosity
what was going on beneath the surface of his mind. What
was he holding back? I wondered about it, impatient, intrigued.

"Will you keep the old glass windows?" he asked.

"Of course." I pretended to be offended, that he'd even
ask. I assured him I intended to keep all the old glass intact,
even if I had to replace the muntins and frames. He seemed
relieved to hear this, and he assured me he understood this
meant more time and money for repairs, but it was worth it
in the end. He was also pleased with my intentions to keep
the old doors and locksets, and as many other original details as possible. His anxiety on behalf of the house amused
me and warmed my heart. I thought of the mysterious pack-

age I had received with the broken house model in the urn, and the arson threats against the house. Sometimes it seemed as if my mysterious adversary directed his hatred against not only me, but the house itself. It seemed impossible that Brand would be capable of threatening the well-being of this house. It was obvious he loved it. Could it be he loved the house so much he would threaten its owner?

It seemed ridiculous.

When we were finished with the tour of the house, we went out on the terrace outside the library and sat on the low stone wall in the sun.

"Thad told me you showed him a couple houses you designed," Brand said. "He says you're a killer architect."

I blushed violently. I could feel my cheeks burning.

"I think it's really good, what you've done to this house," he said quietly, and I felt immensely gratified. Somehow his praise meant more to me than anyone else's.

"Well, it's a beginning," I said, wishing I could think of a more clever reply.

"I brought the pictures," he said shyly.

"Pictures? Oh—! Of your place? Let me see."

He stood up, drew them from his back pocket and handed them to me. They were warm from being next to his body. I slid the photos out of their envelope and he sat down again, right next to me, so he could explain them.

I felt flustered with his presence, so large and physical and *close*. I was aware of the tension of the worn fabric of his jeans stretched over the large muscles of his thighs. I was aware of the texture of the skin on his arms, smooth sun-browned skin over firm flesh, touched with scars, scattered with darkish hair.

He pointed to details in the photos and related them to things I had seen in his house. He brought me through the chronology of the barn renovation, and I was amazed at the transformation he had accomplished.

"It truly was a barn, wasn't it?" I murmured. "And yet . . . it's interesting how little you actually did change it, structurally . . ."

"Mrs. S wasn't very happy about it."

"Mrs. S?"

"Mrs. Shapiro, the lady who owned the house before you."

"So she didn't like what you did to the barn?"

He shrugged. "To her, it was drastic. She remembered it from when it was a real, working barn. When she was a little girl."

"But now it's such a comfortable, beautiful home."

"Well, she would have preferred everything to stay as it was, unless she was the one changing it . . ." his voice trailed off.

"What?" I asked softly.

"Well, she got mad at me, and disowned me, so I have no leave to talk about her anymore." He gave a little laugh. "Look," he added, handing me the next photo. "Here is where Tess has her garden now, and the cottage. It used to be a dilapidated chicken coop."

He was good at changing the subject. I would have loved to pursue the topic of the old lady and his relationship with her. How had he come into possession of the barn and the land around it? It had once been part of the estate she owned—had he managed to con her out of that property? Is that why she disowned him?

"Yes," I said absently. "Her garden is enchanted."

"Especially this time of year, on the verge of spring. There's an apple tree on the property that is fifty years old. You have a few that old, too . . . and the apples are still good."

"So it is true that our properties were once joined?"

"Sure. Not just our properties, but this whole tract. Even the chapel was part of the estate once."

"Was it a chapel then?"

"It was the family chapel, yes. When it was parceled out in 1920 the wine cellars and a few other buildings were sold with it, but the family kept the house and the surrounding farm."

"When I bought the place I was surprised there wasn't someone in the family who felt strongly enough about it to save it."

"There is very little left of that family."

"What was she like? Mrs. Shapiro. I feel like I know her

from—" I hesitated, wondering if I ought to tell him about the letters I had read. "From living in her home, going through her things."

"She was a great lady. I really loved her."

I regarded him quizzically. I could see he believed his own words. He had *cared* for the old woman. Was that why he felt justified in trying to wrest the property from her?

"She had it tough, though," he said.

"How so?"

"Oh, stuff with her family. A bitter ex-husband. Problems with her kids."

"Did you know them well?"

"No. Her family never lived here. I got to know her daughter, a little. She stayed at the house for a while, at the end."

"But you knew her mother well."

"Yes." He was silent.

He is holding something back, I thought again, uneasy.

"Were you upset when you didn't get the house?" I asked him suddenly.

"Yeah," he said. "I was upset."

He said the word "upset" as if it was an understatement. His simple, honest response caught me off guard.

"I would have done whatever it took to get this house," he said. "I'd always thought it would be mine someday." There was a strange soft vehemence in his voice.

I felt a thrill of fear pass through me.

He looked up at me and smiled sheepishly. "I was wrong about that, wasn't I? I was just so blown away when . . ." He heaved a great sigh. "Anyway. What's done is done."

I wanted to accept his philosophical outlook, to believe he had put his disappointment in the past. But something prickled at me, an intuition of uneasiness.

I can't allow myself to trust him.

But I did trust him. I felt an elemental safeness with him, like I felt with my father when I was a child, a naïve belief in his ability to protect me from bullies and bad guys.

We turned our heads at the same time toward the sound of rustling in the thicket mingled with suppressed giggling.

Brand glanced back at me and held a finger to his lips. He slipped off the stone wall where we were sitting and made his way with exaggerated stealth over to the edge of the patio, where he ducked behind the wall. At the same time I saw the red and blue colors of the jackets on the backs of a boy and a girl who were crouched in the bushes nearby, spying, evidently, and doing their best not to burst into laughter.

Brand ambushed them, and the kids ran out of the bushes screaming. He dashed after them, pelting them with pine cones. They ran around in circles, overcome with laughter, and then took off in different directions. Brand jogged back to me, grinning.

The girl called out to the boy, "It isn't the witch, Jason, it's Brand!"

"I know," said the boy.

They approached us cautiously.

"Bubble, bubble, toil and trouble," I sang out in my best wicked witch voice.

"Watch out for the witch, Brand," the girl called out.

"Who, *her*—?" Brand flashed his smile at me and looked back at them.

"Yes, yes, she's the witch!"

"I *knew* there was something unusual about her," Brand said.

"Beware! Get away before she casts a spell on you!"

"It's too late," Brand murmured.

Seeing that *he* wasn't worried about the witch, the boy came a little closer. The girl, deciding the game was finished, shrugged and followed him.

"You know this is a haunted house, don't you?" she said to me with defiant friendliness. "There was a murder here."

"Really?" I said mildly.

"Yes!" the boy puffed up with importance. "Didn't you know that?"

"No, I did not know that," I replied.

Seeing I didn't believe him, the boy turned to Brand and demanded he confirm what they had said.

"*Tell* her."

"Uh, yes—it's true," Brand said.

I was silent, wondering if it was still part of the game. Brand jumped the low stone wall and began to chase the kids around the patio, and then off into the woods around the creek. They screamed with happiness at the attention.

I watched him move, so easy in his body, crouched in play, bursting into a run, turning and twisting, doubling back—he was so lanky and long, so agile. His strong thighs in the jeans he wore, catch-your-breath sexy. His belly, flat as a sheer cliff, swept with dark hair, revealed when his Pendleton shirt came undone in the scramble. His beautiful broad shoulders and well-made, neat-muscled arms, flexed now as he let sail another pine cone.

We heard a shout. Tess's voice carried over the woods from the distance, and Brand abruptly stopped the play.

"That's a phone call I've been expecting," he said. He tossed the pine cones toward the kids, gave me a quick, shy grin and jogged off through the woods toward the barn.

The boy stood with his red jacket and short blond hair caught in a beam of sunlight, next to the girl, who was trying to poke him in the stomach with a stick. They looked up curiously at Brand as he suddenly turned and ran back to me to get his photographs.

I had them in my hand and was walking to meet him. He reached out to grab the envelope, looking down at it, glancing up at me through the hair falling over his brow.

"I guess you don't want those," he smiled.

"Bye, Brand! Bye, Brand!" The kids were vying to see who could say it the loudest.

"Good-bye, aliens," he called to them affectionately.

"Bye, Brand," I said.

He turned and we rested our eyes on each other, lingering.

"I'll see *you* later," he said to me.

THAT NIGHT I went out with Yolanda. We walked down to the village and hit every bar in town—both of them—and the coffee shop as well. We sat in a booth, and I kept looking up at the eyes of a stag whose head hung on the wall.

"Yolanda, what do you know about a murder in my house?"

She started. "What?" she gave an incredulous laugh.

"You know those kids who hang out in that fort above your cabin?"

"Oh yeah. Jason and Melissa." She seemed to know them well. "They're Tammy's kids, the organist. She practices the organ in the church on Tuesdays and on other days, too, and her kids run around wild in the woods."

"They told me there was a murder in my house. I couldn't tell if they were joking or not."

"Well, you know how kids are. They have great imaginative abilities, that's all."

"Yes, well, they think *I'm* a witch."

She cocked an eyebrow as if to say, *See what I mean?*

"But maybe that's not such a stretch," I added with a smile.

"I'd take it as a compliment."

"What about that Father Daniel?" I asked.

"What about him?"

"Well . . . I mean, he's a character, don't you think? He doesn't strike me as the priestly type. He intrigues me."

Yolanda's expression was almost prim. "Daniel is completely committed to his work."

I almost laughed at the look on her face.

"His work . . . you mean, being a priest, or—?"

"Yes, of course, being a priest. That is his work," she said.

"You call him 'Daniel,' " I pointed out curiously.

"That's his name." Her voice was peevish. Then she smiled, and explained: "We've known each other a long time. It's like, you know, when you're close to an uncle. Sometimes, you drop the 'uncle' and he's just . . . his name."

"I'm just curious. I'm not Catholic, and I was just wondering how it works."

"I'm not Catholic either." She started to speak again, then caught herself, laughed self-consciously, and looked up at me with her shrewd, streetwise expression. She seemed annoyed with me.

There is something between them, I thought. Something she's trying to cover up.

"Well . . . I'll tell you." Her voice had a quality of resignation now. "I came to see him—he was an old friend of the family. Father Daniel. After my mom died, when I was seventeen, I decided to look him up. He helped me screw my head on a little straighter than it was—I guess I was a little young to be on my own. I mentioned to him I was looking for a living situation, and he helped get me into my cabin, in exchange for doing work around the place."

"What about your dad?" I asked. "Wasn't he around?"

"My mom raised me alone," she replied. "My dad wasn't into commitment. I never knew him. So what about your family?"

"I had a very traditional upbringing," I said. "Mom, dad, brother, me, cat, dog. But my parents both died young."

"That's sad."

"I'm getting drunk," I said.

"Me too, a little."

WE CAME HOME and she ordered me to come in to her little cabin.

"I am going to read your cards," she declared.

"My cards?"

"Shut the door, shut the door. Come in and sit."

I obeyed, following her into the rustic, cozy little shelter. She stoked the fire in the wood stove, and we sat cross-legged on her bed, a mattress on the floor of her cabin covered with an Indian print bedspread. She lit candles and incense.

"Very atmospheric," I said.

She removed her tarot cards from a velvet pouch along with a silver bell that rang with a clear shimmering chime, and several small quartz crystals. She poured red wine into a big ceramic goblet for us to share. In the candlelight she looked beautiful and a little creepy as she turned the pack and let the cards fall out into her hand.

"I do a modification of the Celtic Cross spread," she told

me. "I use the interpretations of Eden Gray, then I go on my own intuition.

This meant nothing to me but I nodded anyway. "Does the Church frown upon this?" I asked.

"The tarot? I don't know. Probably. But of course, there is no 'the Church,' as if it was one single-brained entity. It's people. Individuals. We all come to the divine in our own way."

She shuffled the cards easily, matter-of-fact and calm, then she handed them to me and told me to shuffle them thoroughly.

"Now. Think of what you want from this reading."

"Something I want to know?"

"Or just something you want." She gave me a knowing look, almost a smile.

I want *Brand,* I thought. But I tried to put that out of my mind.

"All right," I said. "Should I tell you?"

"If you want."

"I've been wondering if I should move up here to the mountains and start my own business."

"Okay, let's get started." She took the cards from me and began to lay them facedown, one at a time, in rows of a particular design. In the center she put one card on top of another, then laid another on top of those, lengthwise, to form a cross.

"Are you ready?" she asked. She closed her eyes a moment, took a long deep breath, then lifted the bottom card in the center of the spread. She murmured, "This card is the significator. It represents you."

I read the lettering on the bottom of the card. "The Queen of Pentacles."

"A queen sits on her throne, surrounded by symbols of fruitfulness. See the rabbit in the corner?"

I hadn't; I was looking at the mountains behind the queen's throne. I stared at the card, transfixed. The drawing was simple, crude even, and yet, as I studied it, the scene evoked deep dreamy feelings in me. Probably because I was drunk.

Yolanda spoke. "She uses her talents well and she is blessed with abundance, and she will be generous with it. Intelligent, thoughtful, a creator on the physical plane." She looked up from the cards and fixed me with her sharp eyes. "But she doesn't trust someone she is close to . . . suspicion is draining away energy that ought to be used for other things."

That's true enough, I thought.

"This covers you," Yolanda said. She picked up the card on top of the first and put it down again, face up. "These are the influences surrounding the situation. The Knight of Cups. You see he's riding quietly upon his horse, wearing a winged helmet, which is a symbol of imagination. He is contemplative, not warlike; he bears his cup firmly as the horse prepares to cross the stream and approach the distant peaks."

"Mountain peaks," I murmured dreamily.

"He is a young man," she went on, "With light hair and hazel eyes, of high intelligence and romantic dreams. Love may come from him to the subject of the reading—that's you. This card may indicate advances, or an invitation; but propositions should be considered carefully— there may be fraud, trickery, rivalry . . ."

She turned over the only card in the spread which she had placed lengthwise, and laid it across the first card. "This crosses you."

"The Tower," I read, a little shocked at the image of bodies falling from a tall, cylindrical tower which stood on a crag, struck by lightning, bursting with flames.

But Yolanda was pointing to something else in the picture, yellow tears raining down from the sky. "These little droplets are the falling drops of light, the Hebrew 'Yods,' " she said. "They signify the descent of the life force from above into material existence. The lightning flash represents the power which is drawn from above, spiritual truth, which breaks down ignorance and false reasoning. But there is also indication of oppression . . . imprisonment."

"That's nice."

Yolanda ignored my sarcasm. She went through the cards

at a swift but leisurely pace, with simple, cryptic commentary. The Ten of Pentacles. The Seven of Swords. The pictures shimmered in the candlelight. Much of what she said was obvious, merely calling attention to the symbols, but in that simplicity was power. In spite of myself I was being drawn into this. It was affecting me.

"The Queen of Wands . . ." Yolanda hesitated. "There will be an influence in your life very soon, a woman most probably, older perhaps—she is interested in your welfare. She is associated with money, love, home . . . She brings a warning of opposition, jealousy, deceit or infidelity—"

Yolanda turned over a card picturing a knight on galloping horseback with sword outstretched, mountains receding in the distance. "Someone is about to rush headlong into your life," she said. "Perhaps you already know this person."

"Is this the same older woman?" I asked.

"Could be. But from the look of it, and the position of the card in the spread, I would say this person might hold some romantic interest for you. See how it relates to the Knight of Cups? I might be able to clarify that a bit in a moment . . . now, this row of cards over here on the left, this is something of my own, a variation on the traditional spread. This next card is what I call the soul mate card."

She turned the card over and laughed. "Well!"

"It's blank!"

"It certainly is," she said.

"So what does that mean?"

She didn't answer. "It happens sometimes. There is one blank card in the deck. It's the missing image. I guess you'll have to supply that image for yourself."

"No soul mate, huh?" I pouted.

"I wouldn't come to that conclusion," she said.

Later, I could remember bits of Yolanda's commentary mingled with scenes depicted on the cards like snatches of a dream: "Obstacles, deception may soon be uncovered . . . caution against dealings with rogues . . . vigilance, scrutiny, spying for good or evil. Possible inheritance. Unforeseen events—"

I listened, bemused. So much of what she was saying did seem to fit with my life, but I knew that was how it was with newspaper horoscopes and palm reading. It's all very vague and so it could speak to any one, at any time.

At last all the cards lay face up. Yolanda regarded me soberly.

"What?" I said.

"I have an odd feeling about this spread, Stacy," she said.

"What do you mean?"

"I think you should be careful."

"Why?"

"I just do. I think you're in some kind of danger."

"Danger!" I scoffed, but a walking on-my-grave shudder went through me. "What do you mean, danger?"

"I have a strong feeling about this, Stacy. You are in some sort of danger. It could be physical danger. Or it could be something in your soul."

"Well, which is it?"

"Maybe it's a combination of the two. Look, I'm not saying this to bum you out. I almost didn't say anything, but . . . I feel I had to. Forewarned is forearmed."

I was on the verge of telling Yolanda about all the weird things that had been happening in my life, but something stopped me.

She could see I was struggling with my thoughts. "There's nothing in those cards that you can't overcome if you stay pure and in tune with your path," she said.

"Thanks for the mysticism, Yolanda." I punched her shoulder gently, but she didn't smile.

"Just watch your back, girl," she said. "Okay?"

I hiked home on the trail that wound up the slope from Yolanda's cabin. It was about three in the morning, and the moon was nearly full above the shadowy trees. I came out of the woods behind my house and started up toward the back terrace. In the moonlight I saw something lying on the ground and I bent to pick it up. It was a small book. I thought it must have been one I left outside, but as I neared the house and came into the light of the lamps on the wall next to the French doors, I could see the book wasn't mine.

Inside, the house was quiet and smelled of the sweet lingering scent of cedar logs burned down in the fireplace. I sat down in the armchair by the hearth, switched on the light, reminded myself to breath. It was a small notebook I held in my hands and I knew it was Brand's. He must have dropped it when he was chasing the kids around earlier.

It was the journal of someone who really kept a journal. This particular volume had been started only recently, within the month. He wrote in it regularly, but he didn't write every day. Though it was a sort of diary, it was also his appointment book, his address book, his scribble pad. There were notes written in a confident, untidy hand. Phone numbers, scribbled appointments, outlines for writing projects, scraps of ideas for stories—stuff a writer might jot down in a notebook. He recorded something of his personal observations, but cryptically, in short bursts of what appeared to be a shorthand code. Hard to make out. Not every entry was dated, nor did he necessarily use the pages in chronological order.

What I did was wrong, but I make no apology. I turned the pages, one by one, seized with a delicious guilt, my curiosity completely engaged.

The photograph fell out into my lap. I picked it up gingerly by its edges and gasped. It was a picture of Brand and me. Together.

Yes, I remembered. The afternoon we had skied together. The young woman who had taken our picture—she had promised to send it.

I couldn't stop staring at the photograph.

Our heads were close, his hair striking and almost gold next to the darkness of mine. My sunglasses lifted my hair on top of my head like a Spanish mantilla. I looked young, startled, wistful; my face turned slightly toward the camera, as if about to question something. He was leaning toward me, looking at me through his dark shades, alert and loose, with that particular combination of big-male size and graceful leanness that made me so hungry to touch him.

It's the missing image, I thought. The photograph had been framed vertically, and it was odd how much it resembled one of Yolanda's tarot cards. The two of us in the foreground, and in the slightly blurred space behind us, something else not quite defined but implying movement, the distance of time, a line of trees, a vague cluster of buildings, the crest of a ridge.

At last I set the photograph aside and continued to flip through the notebook, alternating between a sense of sinful trespass and passionate discovery.

> *I got the interview with W——!!! Research. He's difficult, but worth the effort. Talk to Pete D.*
> *Remember seeds for Tess*
> *I'm green. Thought I was used to it all. Envy and indifference. Incredible. I threw her at T, as if she were mine to throw. Like a falcon flung off the arm of the falconer. Knowing she might not return. Trusting she will. Grateful and awestruck, when she does. (Will she?) She's wild, like that. And so so beautiful*

Wow, I thought. What was that about?

Most of the notebook was empty. I came across a few more loose papers stuck in the back, which turned out to be bills. Propane, electricity, water, telephone. Utilities. All made out to Brandon Vandevere.

I was keenly interested in all of it.

I shuffled through the bills, comparing them to my own. Propane, electricity, water. A hefty phone bill, calls all over the state, Maryland, Idaho, Arizona. Several calls to Pismo Beach and San Francisco. I stopped short and read the number again.

415 area code . . .

One phone number, repeatedly called, never more than a minute in duration.

It was my phone number.

It was the phone number of my apartment in the city. I had given the numbers to Tess—my old phone number, and then the new one—in case there was ever a problem with my house in the mountains when I was in San Francisco. But no one from the Barn had ever called me, that I could remember. None of them had ever left a message on my machine.

No. I would have remembered.

I tried to breathe deeply. My mind was running with the images, the weird messages left on my machine, the click and silence on the other end when I picked up the phone. The raspy, high pitched voice, threatening me . . .

No, I thought. *Not Brand.*

But it could just as easily have been Tess trying to call, I thought, or Saul. It could have been innocent enough. People don't always leave messages. I would ask them.

What would I ask them?

Hey, by the way, I've been going through Brand's journal and your personal papers and I studied your phone bills and I noticed you've been calling me. How come?

Right.

I stuffed the papers back into the journal.

I crossed the meadow to the Barn in the moonlight, stealthy and scared. I climbed the steps to the door of the screened porch, holding my breath. I slid the journal under the door and pushed it off to the side, hoping it would appear he had dropped it there. I didn't want him to know I had seen it, that I had looked through his personal belongings.

Slipping away from his house, I prayed the brilliant light of the moon wouldn't give me away. It was the middle of the night and everything was asleep and silent. Somebody would find the journal in the morning, I thought, and if Brand noticed the photograph was missing, he would just have to conclude it had fallen out of the book, which actually it had. I felt sinful, but compelled to keep the picture.

After all, I told myself, if there was some sinister meaning in the appearance of my phone number on Brand's phone bill, the least I could do was disarm the capture of my image, like those who guard themselves from photographers to protect their spirits.

But the real reason I kept the photograph was that I wanted to keep looking at it.

I felt saturated with the strange images, the scenes from the tarot, and the photograph, a captured moment, the instant in time when Brand and I had stood together in line for the ski lift. The soul mate card, Yolanda had said—that was the one that was missing.

And I had found it, right outside my door.

But Yolanda's warning came to me, melodramatic, and yet oddly affecting. Warning me. Pleading with me to watch my back. I was in some kind of danger.

There is a logical and innocent explanation for my phone number being on Brand's phone bill, I said to myself, desperate to believe he had nothing to do with the strange harassment I had been receiving. Behind those dark shades I knew those eyes that gazed at me, knew their mysterious, clear intensity. I couldn't believe Brand would want to harm me. I couldn't believe it.

Or wouldn't?

Chapter Thirteen

I WAS SITTING on the marble floor in the library next to a stack of Mrs. Shapiro's old magazines, sorting out those I wanted to give away. The cover of one magazine in particular caught my eye—a plane of granite crossing the page, a thin athletic woman clinging to it, the muscles in her neck stretched like rope.

On a hunch, I flipped the magazine to the masthead and saw the name: Brandon Vandevere, contributing editor.

I wandered over to the armchair, pushed off a pile of books, rearranged my lamp, and sat down to read the articles under Brand's byline. There was a piece on the ethics of mountain climbing hardware, a witty sidebar on how not to choose hiking boots, and a personal story about an expedition to Aconcagua.

I was impressed. Brand's writing was spare, thoughtful, friendly, and often strikingly perceptive. He had a knack for describing, with a few well chosen words, the deep emotions wilderness and physical exertion can arouse. He had a playful way with words, and he knew how to render both sides of a debate.

I went through the magazine, hoping to find more, then went on through the pile, culling from it anything connected to adventure or nature, and found several publications with contributions from Brand. It appeared the former owner of my house had collected such publications.

Inside one of the magazines I found a brochure for the Bethany Retirement Home near Sacramento. I recognized Mrs. Shapiro's handwriting, notations scribbled in the margins, numbers, and short comments.

The Bethany Retirement Home. That must be where the old woman had moved, after she left the old house.

And that gave me an idea.

SHE SAT IN a wheelchair in a sunny room overlooking a small meadow. She was very old, quite small, and a great vitality shone from her. She wore a long gown of purple satin, fastened at the neck with a large pale cameo. There was a rhinestone pin in the thin white braid that coiled around her head, and her frail spotted wrists bore the weight of numerous silver bracelets, blackened with age, some studded with large chunks of purple amethyst and garnets. She welcomed me and seemed to understand who I was.

"So. Stacy Addison, is it?" Mrs. Shapiro looked at me critically with small black eyes. "So far you have come, to visit an old woman! You are taking good care of my house, are you?"

After all the work I had done, and considering how run-down the house had been when I had bought it, I thought she was pretty nervy to ask if *I* was taking good care of it.

"I love the house," I said. "And the land. I feel very blessed to be there."

"Good. I was also—" she seemed hesitant to use the word—"Blessed. To have made my home there as long as I did."

I relaxed a little. I had come here on a whim, obviously. But when I found the brochure for the retirement home something had clicked in me and I knew I had to do it. Up until this moment I had been afraid I might be wasting my time.

We talked about the house, and I could sense her relief to find I was as passionate about it as she was.

"You remind me of myself when I was young," she said. "I was as pretty as you, once, but you're much more personable than I ever learned to be. I was a bit of a recluse, never liked people much. But I loved that old place . . . and I did have a fondness for one or two of the neighbors."

"One of your old neighbors, Brand Vandevere—" I was keen to inject his name into the conversation—"He speaks highly of you."

"Does he?" She looked at me sharply, and speculatively, I thought. But she couldn't know how much I desired to draw out her story of what happened with Brand.

"Is he well?"

"Yes. I think so."

"So what have you done with my house?"

"I—well, nothing, really. I—"

"I hope you cleaned the place up!" she rapped it out angrily. "I let it go the last few years, after I started having trouble with my hip. Those nurse hospice girls did their best. They kept the toilets and sinks spotless and the linens changed, but the rest of the place went to hell. That's what drove me crazy. That's why I finally let them take me. I saw the house was falling apart around me. It never used to be that way. My daughter helped, but she and I have our differences about what's to be done, you know!"

"I can see there was a lot of tender loving care given to that house for many years," I said. "And I hope to give it many more years of the same."

"So. You will be making changes, then?" she asked shrewdly.

"Well . . . nothing major, for a while at least. I had the closet torn out. The one in the library."

She looked thoughtful, turned her wheelchair a bit to stay in the patch of sunlight near the window. "I had that closet put in when my son moved in with me for a time, back in . . ." She fumbled for the date. It wasn't important but it made her angry not to remember. "Anyway. He was recovering from surgery, so I didn't want to put him upstairs. He's gone now," she added, her voice emotionless.

We sat together silently, listening to the sound of a trapped fly buzzing around the edges of the sliding glass door.

"I suppose it was about time that old closet came out," she said finally. "I always meant it to be temporary. Did it come out easily?"

"Yes. The paneling that was behind it is a different color than the rest now. But it's sort of interesting that way."

"I wish I could see it," she grumbled.

"I wish I could live there and never go back to my apartment in the city," I said. "It's a marvelous house."

"Yes. It's got a lot of character. All those odd rooms. I was never much into the interior decoration end of it but I was fascinated with the architecture of the place, and the history. When you live in a house that long, it becomes a part of you. I was a sculptor before I met my husband, and after we married, he made it difficult for me to do my art. He wanted me to spend my days dandling babies and having tea with the garden club ladies. But he didn't seem to mind if I played with our country home. He thought I was ordering curtains and planting flowers. But it was the architecture that interested me. Creating spaces. So the house was my sculpture. In the old days, I had a full-time handyman. I had lots of ideas. Some of them I carried out, and some of them I didn't. Some say I was obsessed with the old place. But obsession is a funny word. Now, young Brand Vandevere, he—"

She hesitated and I felt like my ears must have pricked up like a dog's ears do when they hear their own name.

She was clearly reluctant to finish what she had been about to say, and I wasn't sure I wanted her to finish it, either. Until now I had been able to cling to the possibility that Brand had been somehow maligned, by gossip or conjecture, and maybe what I'd heard about him wasn't true—

"What about Brand?" I urged softly.

"Oh, Brand . . ." she shook her head slightly. "I was hard on him. Too hard. Not that he didn't deserve it! He shouldn't have done what he did—it was *my* house, not his—" she broke off. "But I'd rather leave all that in the past. He often helped me, you know. Started when he was a teenager. He'd do odd jobs around the house. His father was a builder in town, and he used to come in and do some repairs for me, after I let old Mitchell go. Then later, it was the boy, Brand. After Jim Vandevere retired and moved to the coast, I relied on the boy exclusively. He would do anything I asked."

"*Anything?*"

She sensed my interest and her mind seemed to wander back to those days as she talked. "Well, I wasn't so unreasonable, I don't think. Yes, he'd do anything I asked of him. When he was about, that is. As he grew older he was gone more and more often. In the beginning, it was only the weekends. He tagged along with the older boys—they would go up into the high country and test themselves on the rock, you know. Hiking and climbing. He became rather involved with it.

"After a few years he grew impatient with the mountains here. He'd say to me: [and here she mimicked him] 'But Mrs. Shapiro, I *have* to go away. These California mountains are too perfect—beautiful warm granite you can climb like stairs! Where is the challenge in *that?*' And he'd go off to other places—Alaska, the Rockies, South America, Asia. After he graduated high school he began to go for weeks at a time, sometimes months. He came back just long enough to scrounge up enough carpentry work to pay for equipment and transportation so he could go back out into the wide world.

"He always showed me the photographs he made, and one day he let me read a bit of the journal he kept on his travels. The more I read of his writing, the more I saw the gift he had been given, that it was something quite aside from his remarkable physical talents, his strength and agility, his stamina. He had the ability to communicate his experience with his writing and his photography. I urged him to make something of it. I knew what I was talking about, of course. I worked as an editor and translator for many years. He ignored my suggestions at first, until I pointed out to him that developing his writing would enable him to participate in certain adventures from which he would be otherwise excluded. It was a means to an end. But then it became an end it itself."

"It seems he took your advice after all."

"I don't know how much I had to do with it. He took a few journalism courses at the university. But he dropped out of school when he was offered a place on an expedition to the Himalayas. He came back from the big mountains humbled, I think. On one expedition he lost one of his best friends—and it wouldn't be the last time. After that, I think, Brand changed. I thought he might even quit climbing. He didn't, but it was never the same. In recent years the art began to take precedence over the adventure. He didn't even notice it at first, but I did. The compulsion to seek danger began to lose its grip on him, and he became more and more interested in his photography and his writing. I suspected it was happening, though outwardly he was much the same.

"I realized something had changed in Brand when I happened to mention to him that I was thinking of selling off some of my property. I had received permission from the county to subdivide and sell the barn. I really didn't want to do it, but I couldn't think of any other way to keep the house. My health was on the decline, and so many of my resources had gone into family matters.

"'Well, Mrs. Shapiro,' he said to me, 'Maybe I will buy that old barn from you myself.' I thought he was joking. But he was dead serious. Apparently not all his earnings had gone into his travels! He made me an offer and I accepted it, though I could have got much more for the place."

Oh, God, I thought. There it is. And yet, as Saul once pointed out, there was nothing illegal about getting a good deal on a piece of property.

"When he bought the barn, it was as if he had discovered a new obsession," she went on. "It was a mess, it needed so much work. And then, to turn it into a home like that! He began to stay in town more. I never regretted selling to him, either—at least not until . . ."

Until—? But Mrs. Shapiro had stopped talking.

"What happened?" I asked. But I miscalculated. She

drew herself in like a hermit crab. I thought I would cry with frustration.

"As I said before, all that is behind, in the past where it belongs. Things didn't turn out the way I had planned, but perhaps that is as it should be. It's odd, but I have the feeling you are just the right person for that house, Stacy."

"I do too, Mrs. Shapiro—I hope that doesn't sound self-serving, but—"

"No. That is exactly how I felt myself, when I owned it. At least until the later years. I must say, I do have a few regrets. I told myself I would never have regrets, but I do . . ."

I didn't press her this time when her voice trailed off. She seemed to be growing tired.

"Mrs. Shapiro," I said, "You know there are some personal things of yours which were left in the house, and I was wondering . . ."

"I thought everything had been taken out."

"No. I've been going through things myself."

"Goodness, what a mess that must be."

"Well, the thing is, I was wondering if you wanted anything. There are a lot of old letters . . ."

"Just toss it all." She waved a bony, impatient hand.

"You don't think your daughter would want any of it?"

"I'm sure she has already taken anything she wanted. I'm sorry you were left with the mess, but please, just be done with it."

She seemed irritated and I didn't press it. She was apparently very strong-willed, and eccentric, as I had been told, but her mind seemed sharp. It wasn't until I was about to leave that she seemed to lose track of reality.

"You tell those folks from the organization they better mind their p's and q's," she said forcefully. "You understand?"

"Ma'am?"

"I like you, Stacy. But you can be replaced, anybody can be. I don't suppose they pay you anything much. So you tell them if I find out there's any disrespect being done to my house, they're not going to get their play-money! Not that I really have any say over it anymore. But tell them anyway. Will you?"

"Sure," I said gently. I stood up, disappointed, awkward with the discomfort I suddenly felt at her strange, meaningless words. It had seemed we had understood each other so well. Now I wondered. I held out my hand to her. "I'm glad to have met you, Mrs. Shapiro," I said.

She took my hand regally and appraised me with her cool gray eyes.

"A pleasure, Miss Addison," she replied. "Do come see me again, won't you? I've enjoyed our meeting so much."

I came away from Mrs. Shapiro with mixed feelings. I hadn't expected to like her so much. There was nothing sinister about the former owner of my house. She was a forthright, solid, and very real person. She was no longer a ghost to me. But I wasn't much closer to understanding what went on between her and Brand. Did he try to steal the old house from her? She said she had sold the barn property to him for less than it was worth. But she said she hadn't regretted that—*"at least not until . . ."* until what? Until he tried to take advantage of her a second time?

How I wished I knew the answer to that one.

YOSEMITE VALLEY WAS empty and quiet, still emerging from winter, and heartbreakingly beautiful. Thus far I had resisted Thad's repeated requests to take me out, but when he suggested a day trip to Yosemite, I finally gave in and said yes.

It took us about an hour and half in Thad's Mercedes from my house in the mountains to the valley floor. We parked at the general store and walked down to the visitor's center, where Thad went off in search of the men's room.

I wandered through the gallery, which was featuring one artist's paintings of Yosemite through the seasons. The paintings were accomplished with a graceful virtuosity, fluid and magical. Most of the canvasses were quite large. There were several in particular that completely captivated me. A painting of Stone Man Bridge; a study of the ubiquitous

Half Dome with an unusual composition; a simple stark peak in the high country, touched by the light of late afternoon.

A young woman dressed in plum colored overalls was there in the gallery talking to an older couple about one of the paintings. I was instantly drawn to her deep laughing voice, and her authoritative manner, and I thought she must work in the gallery. I came near, hands behind my back, studying the paintings, trying to eavesdrop on what she was saying about them, and she smiled at me.

"These paintings are incredible, aren't they?" I said.

The older woman motioned to me, indicating the woman in purple overalls with a delicate little pointing motion. "Stephanie here is the artist," she said.

"I'm impressed."

"I'm Stephanie Green," she said, extending her hand. "This is James, and this is Blanche—Thompson, isn't it?"

"Tom-lin-son," the man corrected. "But please—just Jim and Blanche."

I introduced myself.

"We were admiring her work and the young man at the desk told us the artist happened to be here this morning," the man said.

We talked about the paintings, moving about the gallery together, and then Blanche said it was time she and Jim stop procrastinating and get on with their walk.

"He wants to go look at that Indian village they have set up outside," Blanche said. "Would you like to join us?"

"Actually, I'm waiting for someone," Stephanie said. She glanced at her watch. "Though he should have been here by now."

I was beginning to wonder what happened to Thad.

"Well, come on, then, Blanchette," James laughed. "I'll take you on the Mi Wuk tour."

"I've already seen that village a hundred times," Blanche said, but she followed James. She waved good-bye to Stephanie and me. "We'll see you later, girls."

"Bye now, and thank you," called Stephanie. The old man blew her a kiss.

"Looks like you made a couple of new friends," I said.

"Yes, I'm partial to folks who appreciate my work. They bought one of my paintings."

"Which one?"

"Stone Man Bridge."

"Yeah, I like that one a lot. I like them all a lot."

"I just wonder what I'm going to tell my ex-husband. Technically, that one was his. I gave it to him for his birthday several years ago, when we were still married!" She grinned, a gleam of pirate teeth. "But paintings are like kids. You feel like you ought to have custody of your own. They're so hard to part with! Unless someone offers you enough cash, of course."

"That always helps," I said. "Your work *is* very good. I have clients who would probably like to take a look at it."

We exchanged cards, talked art and architecture, and the local hiking trails. I felt instantly simpatico with this woman. I loved her dark red-gold hair in its long thick braid, and her large green eyes in an expressive, vulpine face. I just wanted to stare at her, she was so interesting looking. She had a devilish sense of humor, too, which I liked.

She went to the counter to look at the guide books and I continued wandering through the little gallery. I was starting to think I should go look for Thad. I was just about back at the entrance again when I heard a very familiar voice.

"I'm real sorry, Steph."

I glanced around and found myself doing the classic double take, thinking I must be seeing a vision. A manifestation of my inner preoccupation, perhaps. Brand had just walked into the visitor center, a day pack slung over his shoulder. Stephanie turned and smiled wide at the sight of him.

"I had a blowout on one-twenty," he was saying to her. "Thought I was going to go over the cliff."

"My God, Brand," she exclaimed. "Are you okay?"

"Sure," he shrugged. He dropped the pack on the floor and they went into an embrace full of warmth and affection and the ease of intimacy. I had never seen him this way with another person, not even Alana. I thought I would faint or disappear.

He didn't take his arm from around her shoulder. "You're looking good, lady," he said.

"Hey Brandie," she blushed, kissing his cheek. "So are you."

Brandie—?

"So," he said, dropping his arm away from her at last. "Let's have a look at your stuff—then we'll hit the trail."

"Well, you've seen most of these paintings, I think."

My throat hurt and my heart beat too fast. I could not believe I was experiencing this. It was a cruel cosmic trick. It wasn't the first time I'd felt jealous where Brand was concerned, but I had thought Alana was my rival. Suddenly I wished that were the case. This woman, with her startling talent, her open friendliness and humor, her beauty, her sharp sweetness—she was someone worthy of a man like Brand Vandevere.

"Brandon!" Thad, coming through a door into the visitor's center, had just spotted Brand.

"Hey—"

"What the hell are *you* doing here?" There was an untidy meeting as people were introduced. "Thad, you remember Stephanie," said Brand.

"I sure do," Thad said. "But she's changed. She grew up." They shook hands and words were spoken I didn't quite catch. "Stacy's here, somewhere," Thad said. He glanced around for me. "Where is she?"

I couldn't pretend not to be there any longer. I walked over to join them.

"There you are, Stacy—look who else is here. What a coincidence." Thad took over the social niceties. "Have you met Stephanie? Steph, this is Stacy—"

"We've met!" said Stephanie, smiling at me.

"Yes, we've met," I said, trying to project calm. "I'm Stephanie's newest fan. So—" I looked at Brand. "You had a blow-out, huh?"

"Yeah—"

"That could be deadly on that road."

"It wasn't so bad. I just barely missed a flight off the cliff. The worst part was changing the tire on a blind curve."

"You all know each other?" Stephanie was amazed. "That *is* quite a coincidence."

"Some say there is no such thing as coincidence," Brand said. He was still looking at me.

"No such thing as coincidence?" Thad said. "That's all anything is! So—what brings you here?"

"Waterfalls," said Stephanie.

"Stephanie's got a show of her paintings there in the gallery, Thad," I said. "Go look at them. They're great."

"Oh, yes, *Stephanie the artist*," said Thad, remembering. I wondered how long they had all known each other. We went together back through the doorway into the gallery and Thad let out a low whistle when the paintings came into view.

"So, Stacy . . ." Stephanie sidled up to me and asked, curiously: "How is it you happen to know my big brother Brand?"

"Your brother—" I breathed, feeling like a big soft foot had stepped on my chest.

"We're neighbors," Brand said. He watched expressionlessly as Thad came up to me and slid a friendly arm around my waist.

"Hey, Thad said. "*That* one looks familiar." He nodded at one of the paintings—the shimmering rainbow of light dancing on the crown of a peak in the high country near Lake Tanaya.

"That one is my very favorite," I said.

"That one's mine," said Brand.

"Right!" Thad said. "I remember. You used to have it in the dining room. But I don't recall having seen it for awhile."

"I put it upstairs," Brand replied, "So I could look at it when I'm daydreaming while I'm supposed to be working. I sure will be glad when this show is over and I can have it back." He pulled on her braid.

"Well, you'd better watch her," I warned him. "She just might sell it."

"I just sold one that really belongs to Clyde," Stephanie admitted with a guilty grin.

Brand frowned. "That's not good."

"Don't worry, Brandie, I wouldn't do that to *you*. I mean—it's no big deal if Clyde gets mad at me, since he's always mad at me anyway. But I'd be a fool to get *you* mad at me."

"I can vouch for that," Thad said. "He doesn't get mad often, but when he does—"

"Oh, I *know*," Stephanie laughed.

"What?" Brand said innocently.

"Yeah, what?" I asked.

"He's quiet, like a big, easygoing panther," Stephanie said. "But when he pounces, watch out."

Brand did not like being the center of this banter. He headed for the doors.

I wondered about it. Someone had once told me Brand had a violent nature. I couldn't remember who—possibly Saul, in which case I wouldn't put much store by it, but then Saul had been right about other things. I was curious. Was Brand really a violent man? I thought of the heated conversation I had eavesdropped on between him and Tess. He had seemed angry then, and yet he remained cool and controlled. Like a cold-blooded killer discussing his plans.

We all went outside together. The air was sweet and cold and layered with the rushing wind sound of the waterfalls. Being in this place, with Stephanie and Thad and Brand, was for me a moment of nearly perfect pleasure. On such a day as this, the idea of Brand as a psychopathic killer seemed preposterous. Look at him, I thought, reaching down to pick up a pine cone, lobbing it at his sister. He was playful, and he was beautiful, and grounded, and he could be so sweet. But that fit the profile, didn't it? You never suspected the real dangerous ones.

"So whataya say?" Thad said. "You wanna do Yosemite Falls?"

"I do," Stephanie said. "Let's all do it."

"I'm game," Brand shrugged. "Stacy?"

"I'm with you," I said.

*   *   *

WE WERE SURPRISED to see James and Blanche on the trail ahead of us, slowly but steadily picking their way along. Blanche wore a camera around her neck, and James pointed out scenes for her to photograph.

"How'd you get up here so fast?" Stephanie exclaimed when we caught up to them.

"We decided not to do the Mi Wuk village," Blanche said.

"Blanche hates that village," said James.

Blanche stopped to take a photograph, and Stephanie told her that her brother Brand was a professional photographer.

"Is that right? Maybe you'll give me some pointers," Blanche said to Brand.

Since Brand and Thaddeus were climbers and Stephanie was no slouch, I expected they would soon leave the Tomlinsons far behind, and that I would have to hustle just to keep up with my group. But as we walked along the trail with the older folks, Brand got involved in a philosophical debate with Blanche on some point of wilderness conservation and he seemed perfectly content to hike at her pace.

Thad and Stephanie wandered along up the trail together, chatting about people they both used to know. I lingered behind with Blanche and her husband, listening to Brand and Blanche talk about F-stops and the quality of light.

The photo was finally finished, and we continued on. After a while Blanche and James stopped again, intent upon some unusual bird or bush, and Brand and I continued on without them. We were alone on the trail together.

"You were a quite the hit with Blanche," I said. "First your sister, then you."

"She reminds me a little of my Aunt Adele," he replied. "She died of cancer last year."

"Oh, I'm sorry. That's hard."

"Yeah. It is. I miss her."

"My dad died of cancer. But that was ten years ago."

"You were young."

"Yeah. And then my mom died about a year later in a car accident. I felt like an orphan—though I guess I wasn't, really, since I was grown up. Just barely.

"I think you become an orphan whenever you lose your parents. No matter how old you are. But I guess I can't weigh in on that yet, since I still have both my parents."

"Thank God I have Russ."

"Yeah, Russ is cool."

"He likes you, too. He says you're a good carpenter."

Brand threw back his head and laughed. "That's a compliment, coming from him."

"Damned right. His highest. I wonder what happened to Thad and Stephanie?"

"Who knows." He didn't seem concerned.

"Your sister is beautiful. I was enthralled with her before I even knew she was related to you."

"She's a good girl."

"Extremely talented, as well as beautiful. I guess Thad agrees, because he seems to have vanished with her."

"Does that bother you, Stacy? That they took off together?" He looked at me intently.

"Oh—!" I must have flushed. "No, not at all."

But wasn't I on a date, here, with Thad? That was what he was asking. Wasn't I supposed to be annoyed, that my date had gone off with another woman? Funny, I hadn't given it the slightest thought. I was too busy being right there with Brand.

We rounded a curve in the trail, and there they were, sitting on a fallen log, waiting for us to catch up. The air was filled with the mist and roar off the waterfall.

"*There* they are—" said Stephanie.

"You guys are slow," Thad said.

It seemed Thad had remembered his duty as my escort, and he fell firmly into step beside me, and touched my arm, subtly reaffirming our initial pairing, but the four of us stayed together until we parted in the late afternoon and Thad drove me home in his car. Thad's Mercedes was luxurious and comfortable, swift and agile on the curving mountain roads, and it had a fantastic sound system. And yet I yearned to be sitting beside Brand in his rusty old International.

Chapter Fourteen

WEEKS PASSED AND I was busy at work in the city, and busy working when I came to the mountains. Callie and Ralph's project was progressing nicely, the plans done and approved, a good local contractor found, the loan funded, and the addition was begun. I was amazed at how much faster projects moved through the building and planning departments in these rural areas, the mountain villages and the foothill towns, compared to what I was used to in the Bay Area. Fewer rules and regulations, less paperwork, less official oversight. I wasn't sure that was a good thing, but I enjoyed the benefits. Tax time was behind us and the warm weather brought referrals for several other projects in the area.

Thad called in May to say he wanted to break ground as soon as possible on his property in the foothills. We got together at his place in Sonora and he told me of his ideas and showed me some sketchy plans he had drawn for the site and some tear sheets of things he liked. There was the seed of a great house in that jumble of material, and in the verbal fantasies he was constantly weaving around me. I liked working with Thad, and I could see he liked working with me too. He had discerning, if flamboyant, taste, and he had the necessary courage as well as the financial means to plunge into a project of some magnitude.

As late spring slowly warmed into early summer, we went down to the site several times together. The view from Thad's lot was spectacular over the valleys to the west and afforded glimpses of the mountains rising behind the hills to the east. I took my time, because the property was large, with several possible building sites. I wanted to discover how the sun moved across the face of the land, how the wind blew through the trees. Thad was very observant and had spent several years coming to the site, getting to know the land, camping there sometimes, noting the seasonal changes, and he was able to communicate a sense of the place to me. There was a stream on the property and he told me that he and Brand had spent many afternoons there fishing with great success.

One morning I went down to Thad's property to meet with the surveyor when it happened that Brand was there too. I saw his International sitting next to Thad's Mercedes when I pulled into the dirt circle that would one day be the driveway. I felt my heart beating unnaturally strong, in my throat, it seemed.

I don't want to see *him!* I thought. Yes, I *do!* It seemed such a long time since I'd spoken to Brand. He had been here last week when I had come, but we had passed each other as I drove in and he drove out. We had nodded a prim greeting through the dust.

And he was here again today. I pulled the rearview mirror down to see what I looked like. Okay, I thought. The thought of him being here had heightened my color.

"Hi Jay." I walked up the slope toward the surveyor, trying not to look for *him.*

Thad appeared and greeted me with his usual ebullience. He kissed my cheek elegantly, side to side, like a European. "You are radiant today, Stacy," he said.

"And you are *always* radiant, Thad."

"Yes. I'll probably burn out young! Alas."

We talked with Jay, the surveyor, then Thad pulled me aside. "Look, my beautiful architect, come see what I have planned." He grabbed my hand and hauled me up to the top of the slope where the master suite would be one day.

He excitedly explained his new ideas, redrawing the plans in the air for the fiftieth time, and I listened patiently.

"Can you picture it, Stacy?" He was very dramatic, very physical, grabbing me, holding my hand, throwing his arm around me, flirting constantly. "Lying in the huge king-sized bed, looking out the wall of glass to the east, watching the sun rise—"

He held me close and dazzled me with his beautiful smile as if proposing that I lay there with him.

"You told me you are never awake at sunrise," I reminded him. "You said you wanted to lie in bed and watch the sun *set*."

"I want both. I want it *all!*"

And, I thought, you will probably get it. He had plenty of money to buy it all with, it seemed. He had been an actor on a soap opera for seven years and he'd invested his earnings wisely.

He was giving me another one of his ubiquitous hugs when I noticed Brand nearby.

"*There* you are, my friend!" Thad called out. "The very same man I have to thank for this wonderful architectural paragon. She's not only a fantastic designer, she's an excellent shrink!"

I wriggled out of Thad's grasp.

"I didn't realize architects spent so much time with their clients," Brand remarked dryly.

"Well, I'm paying her a lot," said Thad.

We all laughed, but there was a funny tension between the three of us.

Brand's *jealous,* I thought wonderingly.

I drove home slowly, saturated with an obstinate heaviness of body and spirit I could not quite understand. Brand had left shortly after I had arrived at Thad's, and I kept asking myself why. Why did he act so coolly with me, as if he wanted to avoid me? It could be that he just didn't like me, but I knew that wasn't it. We connected on some level that I think surprised both of us. But he seemed unwilling to do anything about it. Was it because of Alana? Was he really that committed to her? It seemed an odd, sporadic sort of relationship they had, but maybe he was hooked on her. Or maybe he just wasn't that interested in me.

One thing was for sure. I was hooked on *him*. It was just a good thing that he wasn't pushing it, because I was definitely vulnerable. And a lot of good it would do me, getting involved with him anyway. I was lucky that he didn't return my feelings. I didn't need to find myself with another attractive but unsuitable man, like Justin.

Justin. Funny, how seldom I thought of him lately.

I pulled into the drive later that afternoon and saw Brand's International parked outside the Barn. There was another car parked in the drive, one I didn't recognize. Yolanda was standing near my mailbox, talking with a petite older woman dressed in jeans and cowboy boots, a denim shirt with western embroidery, and long auburn hair teased up for fullness. I was struck with a sense of recognition, but for a moment it was nothing I could place.

Yolanda introduced us. "Stacy, you remember Jean Maguire," she said. "She's the daughter of the woman who owned your house."

"Oh, yes, hello!" I said. So that was why she looked so familiar. "We've met. Nice to see you again." I was about to say, "I've been reading your letters!" But I stopped short, feeling my face flush. I couldn't tell her I had been reading her letters. I felt strange, having read them, especially now that she was a real person again, standing in front of me, shaking my hand.

"I was in the area on business—" She spoke in a calm, deep voice somehow out of keeping with her diminutive, feminine appearance, and the loopy childishness of her handwriting and the chatty letters she wrote. "I'm trying to sell some other property my mother owns, farther up the mountain. And I just had to stop and see the house. I'll bet you've made a lot of improvements."

"Well, why don't you come in and take a look?" I said.

"Oh—would you mind? Could I?"

"Sure. If you don't mind seeing some changes. Come on in."

"I've got something in the oven," said Yolanda, "So see you all later." She hurried off toward her cottage. She seemed eager to get away.

Jean followed me into the house and let out a gasp of surprise.

"Oh my goodness, you've done *so much* to the place. It looks wonderful."

She followed me from room to room, making little exclamations of surprise and appreciation. She seemed especially interested in the library, commenting on the paneling and how intricately worked it was, though she didn't seem to notice the missing closet or how the wood changed color where it had been. I thought about the correspondence I had found, the boxes of letters and journals, and wondered if I ought to offer them to her. I hesitated; I felt oddly possessive of them—I still wanted to study them, but of course by rights they should go to her, if she wanted them.

"It's just astonishing, the transformation!" she exclaimed. "I know my mother would be very pleased."

"Do you really think so?"

"Well, she wouldn't like it that someone else was here, in *her* house, you know. But yes. I think she would be glad, in the end."

We were back in the front parlor.

"I never lived here, you know," she said. "Well, for a very short time just before mother went into the home. As a child, I lived in the apartment in the city with Mother and Papa. Later, after the divorce, he moved us out to the ranch in Stockton. I liked the ranch. I learned to ride, and shoot, and fish. I was always something of a tomboy. We got to visit Mother here in the mountains, sometimes. But there was always some reason for my brother Timmy and me to stay with Papa. I suppose I preferred life with Papa. But it was difficult for Timmy, I think. Oh, this brings back memories."

Jean laughed self-consciously. Her eyes had filled with tears. I knew people could get very emotional about houses and the memories they can evoke. Going back and visiting a house after you've left it can be cathartic. I thought of what Thaddeus had said. Architect-Shrink: that's me. I patted Jean on the shoulder, and she smiled up at me, gratefully, it seemed.

"I met your mother, you know," I said.

"Did you?" Her face was transformed with an expression of pleased surprise. "How extraordinary!"

"Yes, I went to see her. I just felt I was getting to know her through the house, and I wanted to meet her."

"Really! When was this?"

"About a week ago, I guess."

"Well, how nice for you both."

"It *was*, you know. I really liked her."

"Actually, she isn't so well these days . . ." Jean tapped her forehead meaningfully.

"She seemed perfectly fine—" I caught myself, thinking of the old woman's rambling words at the end of our visit. "Anyway, we had a nice visit and I think she was happy to know the house is being cared for."

"Yes, I'm sure she is. She's stubborn, but she is practical!"

We chatted a bit longer, and she turned down my offer of something to drink, saying she had to get going. We were walking toward the door when she stopped suddenly, her face filled with concern. "Oh, my goodness . . ." she murmured.

"What is it? What's wrong?"

"Well, it's just the oddest thing. I almost didn't even put it together, but . . . I happened to get a call last Wednesday from the director of the home where Mother lives. He told me Mother had had a visitor earlier in the week, a young woman . . . he didn't know her, said she was pleasant enough, but after the visit Mother worked herself into such a state they ended up having to sedate her. He said she was beside herself, fretting about her house, practically hysterical. A state of mind, apparently, brought about by her chat with this visitor."

"Me?" I was incredulous.

"Do you think?" Jean looked at me, wide-eyed. "She doesn't get many visitors."

I found it hard to believe. The woman I had visited that day had seemed well balanced—very old, to be sure, but not psychologically unstable—at least until the last part of our conversation. All that stuff about how I could be "replaced"—that *was* strange.

I was horrified to think I might have brought on some condition requiring restraint for her. And it was true, she had been quite spirited about the house.

"My God, I'm sorry if I was responsible for anything hurting your mother," I said.

"Oh, I know, I know you are—I'm sure you didn't have any idea something like that could happen. I'm afraid it's just that my mother is declining mentally—I don't think you're supposed to call it senility anymore, are you? But I'm afraid it's reality. Actually, I am relieved, because I am glad to know what brought on Mother's spell. It makes more sense now, at least. She was rather crazy over this house, even at her best."

She was crazy over the house. Something pricked at me; an uneasiness I couldn't articulate.

"I'm hoping soon to move her closer to me," Jean said. "It's such a long drive. I just can't do it anymore. When she's closer I can keep a better eye on her. With my diabetes—and now they think it might be lupus!—I just can't keep up my old pace. It's hard, because I used to be so active."

"Well, I hope everything will be all right with both of you."

"Thank you, dear. You're very sweet." Jean assured me that she did not blame me for disturbing her mother, and thanked me again for allowing her to look at the house.

I walked her out to her car.

"I know I don't even need to mention this," she said, "but I think it would be best if—that is to say, I know my mother, and—I'm sure she extended you an invitation to visit her again. I realize it's probably not even an issue, you're probably too busy anyway, but—"

"You don't think I should see her again."

"I don't think it would be a good idea," she replied, kindly, apologetic. "I think it would be best if she wasn't reminded about the old house."

I nodded, trying not to take it personally. Jean was just trying to care for her mother. I probably never would have visited Mrs. Shapiro again anyway.

She waved at me as she drove away and I thought to myself how different she was from her mother.

As I turned back toward the house, Brand emerged like a wild animal from the woods. For some reason, I was struck with the notion that he had been watching Jean and me as we talked and had only just now decided to show himself.

"Wasn't that Jean Maguire?" he asked, casually, walking over to me slowly, with studied disinterest. I was immediately suspicious.

"Yes. Why didn't you say hello?"

"Hello." He looked at me directly, gave me a brief smile. "What did she want?"

"Nothing, that I know of. She said she had some property she was trying to sell for her mother up the mountain, and just stopped by to look at her mom's old house."

"For old time's sake?"

"Sure, I guess. She said she likes what I've done for it."

"She's not very discriminating," he said.

"Well, thanks a lot!" I said with a laugh, nettled. "So what do you want?"

"I—" for a moment I thought he was trying to think of an excuse for being there. "Well, you know there's a street fair in the village next weekend."

He was asking me out! I felt a leap of joy, followed at once by anxiety, frustration. I didn't know I had wanted it so badly. Or maybe I did. Oh, why next weekend of all weekends!

"Have you heard about it?" he asked.

"Yes, Tess told me about it. Unfortunately I won't be coming up next weekend—my best friend is getting married in Monterey."

"Well, Monterey is a good place to be," he said, meeting

my news with disappointing equanimity. "I thought, if you were going to be here, there's a friend of mine you might be interested in meeting. He builds custom furniture—I think you'd like his stuff. I'll be out of town next weekend myself, but I thought I'd give you his card."

"Oh!" I said. "Well, thanks. I'd like to meet him."

"Maybe another time."

He seemed to have decided our meeting was finished, and he set off into the woods again.

So that's how it is, I thought, fuming. He wasn't even going to be here next weekend, but he wanted to set me up with one of his friends. That was just too nice of him.

MEETING JEAN AGAIN had sparked my interest in the correspondence I had collected from various drawers and boxes around the house. Now it was all organized according to date and authorship. Some of it I had read, but much of it I had not. In the evening I made myself a cup of Earl Grey and went into the library. I had a big worktable in there now, where I was able to spread things out. I had separated out everything in reference to the house and constructed a chronology of the estate. But it was the personal stuff I was interested in tonight.

I pulled out the letters.

But Jean's old letters, when I looked them over, proved to be as dull as I had remembered, which was why I hadn't delved into them too deeply before. They were long lists of day-to-day activities, mundane reiterations of minor injuries and illnesses and requests for money, pastel-tinted multiple-paged tomes stuffed into countless floral-decorated envelopes.

Jean's brother, Tim, on the other hand, wrote charming little notes, regretfully short, and unlike his sister, he was not a prolific writer. I began to wonder about Tim, for whose benefit the green closet in the library had been built.

He's gone now, his mother had said.

I was struck once again with a sense of trespass, reading these letters, and I made up my mind to send them to their rightful owner once and for all, or better yet, just get rid of them, burn them, maybe.

But I went on reading.

Folded inside of one of the decorated envelopes of Jean's correspondence, I discovered a plain white business-sized envelope addressed with the *L*-handwriting, as I called it. One of *L*'s letters had gotten mixed up with Jean's pile.

I plucked the letter out of its hiding place and opened it. It was one I hadn't seen before, hidden as it was.

My Dear M

> *If you think it can go on like this, think again. Do you think I will be left behind? I will destroy that house with you in it before I let that happen.*

L

And for a moment I was washed with a sense of confusion. For a moment I was sure the voice that rose from the lined paper with the backward, crabbed handwriting was the voice of the same entity who was harassing me. But this note was written and dated from another time. Years and years earlier. It had probably been tucked away in that dusty box since before I was born.

I thought I must be going mad. The familiarity was uncanny. The recognition threw me into confusion, chilled me with its strangeness. I was ignorant of the identity, but I knew the voice. For the first time I wondered if my enemy was something other than human. I thought of myself as open-minded, but the idea of supernatural entities manipulating objects and events on the earth-plane had never seemed very plausible to me. And if such entities existed, I liked to give them the benefit of the doubt, assuming they would be benevolent, helpful beings, like nature spirits and angels. *L* was neither benevolent nor helpful. *L* wanted me out of the old house, and had waiting for me *since before I was born.*

But that was ridiculous. This note was just one of many others sent to the former owner of my house. Not to me. *My dear M.* I checked out the envelope, and it was just like all the other envelopes sent by the mysterious *L*. Plain white, addressed to Madelon Shapiro, no return address. Postmarked San Francisco some thirty years earlier. And it would be rather far-fetched to believe that whoever was harassing me could have gone to so much trouble as to devise planting this note as some part of some plot to drive me mad. The paper was really old, the ink faded, the postmark convincing. Besides, the letter was written to *M*—Madelon. Not me. Maybe whoever was behind the persecution was after *her*, not me. Some confused spirit, haunting the one who came after . . .

I realized then that all this was really starting to get to me. I felt impatient with the police, who didn't seem to be doing anything. At the same time, I sympathized with them. They'd put a trace on the package I'd been sent and come up with nothing. This person did things so sporadically it was difficult to anticipate the pattern. I had tried to put it out of my mind, these strange incidents. The phone calls, the threatening note, the urn filled with my broken model, the real estate agent from Sonora who called and asked when he might set up an appointment to come look at my house, having heard it was for sale.

But the worst was to come.

ONE MONDAY MORNING I went into work to find my boss Janine sitting on my desk, legs crossed, arms folded across her chest, a funereal expression on her strong face.

"Am I late?"

"We've been getting more of those calls again, Stacy."

My stomach clenched like a fist.

"Oh, Janine, I don't know what to say."

"Well, Stacy, I know what I must say, though it pains me greatly."

It was with sincere regret that she let me go. Fired me, really—though I got severance pay, an excellent letter of reference and a very earnest apology. I went home in a daze, pushed the button on my message machine and slumped into my sofa.

There was a message from my brother, and then, *the voice.*

It was a woman's voice, disguised to sound like a man. Or was it a man's voice, disguised as a woman? It was distorted somehow. It sounded familiar, yet alien. There was an aggressiveness to the tone, a growing anger.

"Listen," the voice said. There was a pause, some breathing. "You're in the way, and I'm beginning to get impatient. Stay where you belong. This is your last warning." A few moments later the message ended with an abrupt click.

I heard my own breathing, fast and shaken. I got up, ran around the apartment, checked all the doors and windows, looked into every closet. Then I called my brother.

Chapter Fifteen

I DON'T KNOW what to make of it." He shook his head and tried to look less worried than he was. "But I can't believe she would *fire* you for this!"

"Well, it's become a real problem. What else could she do?"

"Who would want you to lose your job? Who would benefit from that?"

"Nobody. I don't know."

"What happens now that you've lost your job? You could lose your apartment if you couldn't pay the mortgage. That wouldn't help anybody, would it? If you defaulted on the house in the mountains, who stands to benefit? The bank?"

"No. The owner financed part of the deal. The rest I paid with cash. It all goes back to the owner."

"So if *she*—the owner—"

"No. I've met her, she's great. I can't believe she could orchestrate such a thing. She lives in a nursing home, for crying out loud."

"What does that have to do with it?"

"I don't know."

My mind played over the things I had heard her say,
heard her daughter say. *She was crazy over that house.* Just
how crazy?

"You really don't think it could be her?" asked Russ.

"Oh, why would it be her? She wanted someone to love
the place and take care of it like she did! She *likes* me."

"Then—maybe it's nothing to do with the house. You
haven't gone and aroused anyone's jealousy in carnal matters, have you little sister?"

"What?"

"Well, these threats have a certain jealous lover's tinge to
them, don't they? Or they could be construed as such. You
stealing somebody's man, Stacy?"

I pondered this. Tess had said to me offhandedly once:
"Brand stares at you all the time because he thinks you're so
beautiful." I thought of Alana. Would she be capable of seriously icing me? To keep me out of Brand's way, would she
sabotage my job, hoping I'd lose the house? Maybe Alana
was responsible for those phone calls on Brand's bill.
Maybe she was responsible for sending me the broken architectural model, the weird messages. It seemed like a lot
of trouble to go through, to discourage a rival, but maybe
that was it.

Well, if that was it, your plan backfired, I thought. Instead of keeping me out of my mountain house, it would put
me there for good. I would sell my apartment, use the money
for start-up capital and open my own business in the mountains, where it was feeling more and more like home to me
anyway.

Shyly, I told Russ of my ambitions. To my relief, he did
not scoff at me, but he was quiet.

"Am I utterly crazy? It's not easy to start a business *anywhere*, let alone a small, rural town."

"It's risky," Russ mused. "Who's to say this mysterious
enemy of yours won't follow you there? Sabotage your
clients there?"

"Who's to say he—or she—isn't already there?"

"Well, there's no guarantee," he admitted.

"Nope," I said. "There isn't. But so far, none of my clients up there has been hassled."

"There you go," he said, but he sounded dubious.

"Of course, I've only got a couple of clients," I pointed out grimly. "Its going to be sink or swim. I may well end up losing the house."

"No, you won't lose the house."

"Not without a fight, I won't."

MY NEIGHBOR IN the city Mr. Jacobs was having his apartment painted the weekend of Abby's wedding, so he planned to stay in my apartment while I was in Monterey. I was glad to have someone to keep an eye on the place for me. I guess I was getting paranoid. No, I reminded myself, paranoid means you're scared and you have no *reason* to fear persecution. I had an enemy.

I arrived at the cottage near the beach the afternoon before the wedding. Abby's mother and father were there, sitting on the little deck with its view of the sea, sipping the iced tea Abby had made for them, looking uncomfortable. Abby pulled me inside.

"They're driving me crazy!" she exclaimed.

"Who, your mom and dad?"

"Yes. Do you have any valium?"

"Abby!"

"I swear. Come in here, I want you to see my dress—"

She shut the door of the bedroom behind us and went to the closet. She lifted the plastic wrapped confection off its hook and brought it out into the room. She lifted the plastic and we admired the dress.

"Mother says I have no business wearing white. Can you believe it? I really want to wring her neck. And my father complains about everything—"

"Well, you're lucky to have parents at all, aren't you?"

"Oh sure," she laughed, flip. "You can afford to be sanctimonious—*your* parents are dead and out of the way."

She realized at once how that had sounded, and grabbed me tightly. "I'm so sorry, Stacy. That was awful of me.

You're right. I am glad they came. It was really important to us both, to have our families here for this. And Eddie's parents are coming down from San Jose tomorrow. Each with his or her respective spouse! Fortunately, it was an amicable divorce. His Aunt Florence is coming from L.A. and my cousin Mary is coming from Cleveland—and oh—guess who *else* is coming?" Her voice was teasing. She twirled around, holding the dress against her.

"Put it on, I want to see you in it."

"All right. I ought to get all the use out of it I can. You know, the cost-per-wear factor of wedding dresses makes them the single most expensive article of clothing you will ever buy."

"How much did this thing cost, anyway?"

"Like, a lot. So—*guess who's coming?*"

"I give up! Who?"

"Justin."

"*Oh!*"

"Ha ha!" she said. She pulled off her T-shirt and shorts and stepped into the gown. "Do me up, Ace."

"Wow. Abby, you look—"

I was dazzled with her. She was transformed by the dress. And my mind was full of Justin.

"Am I not dazzling?"

"Yes, that is just what I was thinking."

"And aren't you excited about seeing Justin?"

"I don't know what I feel about it."

"Liar—or have you found someone new?"

I shook my head, thinking of Brand, and felt myself blush. "No," I said.

"He can't wait to see you," she said slyly.

EDDIE WAS BANISHED to his best man's house for the night. He didn't understand why, but we assured him that was the way it had to be. Abby and I slept together in the big white iron bed which took up almost the entire bedroom. We lay side by side in the darkness, giggling like teenagers, talking about the past, which we always did when we ended up together for any duration. But what struck me this time was the talk of the future, and Abby's core of seriousness, all joking aside, about getting married. She really did love Eddie, and I already knew he adored her, and she was in awe of what she had found in him. She felt very calm and right about what she was doing, so at peace with it she actually fell asleep before I did.

To be lying in bed with another warm body curled beside me felt strange. It had been many months since I hadn't slept alone. As teenagers, Abby and I used to sleep together on overnighters, but it had been years since I'd shared a bed with her. Since I usually slept in the nude, I felt a little constricted in the T-shirt I was wearing, a little awkward in the unfamiliar bed. I thought about how it would feel to lay down with Brand in a bed like this one, sensual and supremely comfortable, with the sound of the ocean waves on the sand. With his body beside me I might feel a certain awkwardness, a shyness, at first.

From where I lay beneath the thick soft white down comforter, I could look out the sliding glass door to the redwood deck, and through the railing I could see the gleam of the moon off the ocean. When I finally slept, I dreamed of Brand, holding me in his arms, and there was no awkwardness, no shyness, and none of the suspicion or fear that made me ashamed of my own desire. There was only pure bliss, and in my dream I thought: *This is right.*

Abby awoke on the morning of her wedding day to the breakfast I had smuggled in to surprise her: fresh squeezed orange juice, her favorite blueberry muffins, and fresh flowers.

"Stacy, you devious darling!" she said when she came into the little kitchen with its tiny breakfast nook overlooking the ocean. "But of course I couldn't eat a thing—"

"You said last night you'd never sleep and you slept like a log."

"I *will* have a little juice, oh, isn't it pretty—those flowers! God, that reminds me—I hope that florist doesn't screw anything up."

"Don't *worry*," I said.

She ate two of the muffins and drank all the juice.

"Are you nervous?" I asked her.

"I just feel irritable. I guess I am nervous. Thank *God* Mom and Dad got a motel last night or I would have freaked. This place is too damn small anyway."

"This place is wonderful," I sighed. "I want a beach house just like this."

"Yes, I love it, actually. Listen, let's trade—some weekend you come stay here and we'll go stay in your place in the mountains. A romantic getaway."

"Sounds great. But romantic? Maybe for *you.*"

"Your sex life is suffering, isn't it? I could tell. Which is why I am so excited about getting you back together with Justin."

"Abby," I warned.

"He's been talking about you. A lot. Never mind. Anyway, who cares if it's romantic! How about just a plain old *unromantic* getaway?"

"Sure. I'm thinking about going to the AIA conference here in Monterey just after Christmas. Maybe we could do it then."

"Let's do."

"In fact, if you want, you could go stay at my place for your honeymoon and I'll go to Maui for you."

"I'll ask Eddie about it."

"Think you can talk him into it? You know how much your husband is looking forward to getting a good look at a volcano."

"My 'husband' . . ." she murmured. "Good God, yes, he will be my husband by then."

"He'll be your husband by three o'clock this afternoon."

"I think I'm in denial. Actually, the volcano I could do without. I have this hunch he is secretly planning to throw me into it when we get there. That this whole thing is a clever, complicated ruse designed to provide a sacrifice to Pele the volcano goddess."

"Don't worry, I think *she* only wants virgins."

"Right. Have my mother explain that one."

ABBY WAS MARRIED in a tiny white church on a hill above the sea.

I stood beside her in a simple gown of deep blue jersey, with a strapless, fitted bodice, very feminine and sexy. Abby had told me how lucky I was—"I picked out a nice dress for you, unlike *some* brides do for their unfortunate maids!" I had to admit she was right.

The music started to play and everybody stood up, and emotion burned in my throat and behind my eyes. I glanced across the crowd and suddenly I saw Justin. Wow. What a handsome man. How could I have ever compared him to Saul? He wore a stylish, expensive suit of dark chocolate brown. His dark hair was cut short in back and long over his forehead. There was that perfect strong chin which I remembered so well. The funny way his nose slanted, which you couldn't see in profile. His expansive, dynamic aura.

His eyes were fixed on me, and he was trying not to smile too broadly. I responded with the facial cast of the Mona Lisa and turned my head to focus my attention on the altar.

Justin, I thought.

But my feelings were grand, larger than the regard I had for him in particular. The pageantry of the wedding provided a framework that put Justin into a certain context I didn't quite understand. But I hadn't even spoken to him yet, and I wasn't sure what might happen between us.

The church was silent as the chords of the organ died away. I knelt and straightened Abby's train. I thought of Abby in the white PE clothes we wore in high school gym class, with their baggy shorts and shapeless snap button blouses. How different she looked today, so sleek and elegant in her pearl-trimmed satin wedding gown with its long, luscious train; and yet she was still white and golden, just the way I remembered her as a young girl.

"With this ring, I thee wed . . . " I felt a shiver run through me. It was my favorite line of the wedding ceremony. I was surprised Abby had used such a traditional version of it—though, of course, she had left out the part about obeying her new husband.

When I was little I had never understood the whole thing

about crying at weddings, when they were supposed to be such happy occasions, like birthday parties or Christmas. Until today no one I loved like I loved Abby had ever married in my presence. I was filled with so many different feelings—happiness and fear, wistfulness, envy, hope, sadness, deep joy, pride, and it seemed the chemical reaction of so many emotions produced the warm salt liquid of tears, swelling in the corners of my eyes, stinging and threatening to overflow.

I took a deep breath to maintain my composure.

Justin is here.

He and I had attended another wedding together a year earlier, the wedding of one of his colleagues. The incredible attention to detail lavished upon that wedding had been astonishing to me. It was quite the event, designed to set off the shell pink and gold beauty of the bride. Everything was dove gray or shell pink: the roses in her bouquet, the linen napkins, the matchbooks engraved in gold with the names of the bride and groom and the date of their wedding, the bridesmaids in shell pink and groomsmen in dove gray with pink rose boutonnieres. The mother of the bride wore pink and the mother of the groom wore pale gray. The end of each pew was decorated with pink roses tied with silver ribbon and the altar was set with pink roses. A horsedrawn carriage in pink and gray livery waited outside to transport the bride and groom to the reception hall.

It sounds overdone, and it was, but it worked.

Sitting next to Justin as the pink and gray bride and groom exchanged vows, I had felt proud of his sophistication, his ease in any social situation. I felt confident the dressy silk suit I wore flattered me, satisfied that it was well made and cut of good material, and projected the image of a successful, creative professional. Such things seemed important in this company. It was as if you were given the challenge to do your part in upholding the aesthetics of the production. I considered myself an artist, so I didn't mind—but ultimately I found it exhausting. As the bride approached the altar, Justin had leaned over and whispered in my ear: "When we do it, we'll do it just like this." And I had almost laughed out loud, feeling a warm thrill run through me, a thrill of delight mixed with panic. It was the first time he had ever mentioned marriage without mocking the idea. Or maybe he was still mocking the idea. I almost hoped he was.

The color-coordinated elegance and madness for detail had been carried into the reception. Waiters served champagne in glasses tied with pink ribbon, and seven different kinds of hors d'oeuvres; dinner was served on shell-pink and silver china, and for afterwards, there were baskets full of pink Jordan almonds and birdseed sachets wrapped in silver net. When the bride tossed her bouquet it fell into the hands of one of the girls dressed in pink and was promptly ripped away by another. Justin drove me home after the pink and gray reception, in a good mood, still humming a disco song the DJ had played—but the wedding had overwhelmed me.

"What's on your mind, Wildcat?" he asked solicitously.

"Oh," I said, "I just thinking about the wedding."

"That was something, wasn't it?"

"It was. And I was just thinking that if it were me . . . I think I'd prefer a simple wedding. Maybe outside, in the woods."

He laughed as if I had made a joke. "Barefoot?" he said, and laughed again. I guess I had intended it as a joke—the whole idea of marriage was a joke—but I was vaguely disturbed at the way he threw back his head and rolled his eyes, as if I had said something absurd. I realized then that the overdone, moneyed world we had inhabited all afternoon was the one to which he aspired. He wanted to live that perfectly color-coordinated life all the time. And I had no doubt he would, and would do it well. I just knew that wasn't for me. I think that was the beginning of the end for Justin and me.

In her own way, Abby had lavished the same care upon her wedding. Abby's tastes were simpler, and yet, all the elements were there, the flowers, the rings tied to the little satin pillow, the organist who played the wedding march, the groom who lifted her veil aside to kiss her after the minister had pronounced them husband and wife. Both brides had been given away by their fathers, and I thought about who would give me away if I married. It would be Russ, of course, since my father and mother were gone. I guessed that would be all right.

In contrast to the sedate procession we had made up to the altar, the parade away from it was raucous, excited, joyous. Abby was glowing like the quintessential blushing bride. Eddie looked stunned. Justin was grinning widely at me through the stirred-up crowd of people waiting to be released from the pews, and I recognized the look in his eyes. It was the way he had looked at me after that other wedding, the shell pink and dove gray wedding, when we had discussed the possibility of our own marriage.

I rode with Abby and Ed, and Ed's brother George, in a vintage Cadillac to the reception hall, a posh golfer's club next to the ocean with a nice springy hardwood floor for dancing.

"You're really married now, Abbs," I squeezed her.

"Yeah, now I can be a bitch." She frowned. "Where's that from?"

"*Love Story*," I said. "My mother's favorite book."

"My mother banned that book from our house."

The wedding party moved into formation at the door to receive the guests, one by one, an old-fashioned receiving line. The moment before I met Justin seemed to stretch elastically until I was tense and breathless with the thought of coming face-to-face with him.

I glanced at Abby, who was startlingly calm and gracious; she was even kind to her parents, who seemed to be in awe of their beautiful daughter and for once had little to say. Justin was coming closer down the line, and then he was shaking the hand of the girl next to me, another bridesmaid, complimenting her on the beauty and dignity she had brought to the ritual, charming her in that smooth, energetic way he had about him.

"Stacy Addison . . ."

Now the charm was turned on me. His eyes held so much promise, but I knew from experience that he turned that look on everyone he encountered, like a politician. Still, I knew he was sincere. He had a lot to give, and he was generous with it. He reached for my hands and I placed them in his automatically. He pressed his thumbs on my palms and handled my hands gently, trying to get some message across. He was glad to see me.

"You look dynamite, Wildcat," he said with soft-spoken, earnest conviction, and quickly kissed me on the mouth. I drew back a little, unbalanced by his vigor. He let go of my hand and moved down the line, letting a meaningful look trail behind. I felt excited and sexy, turning my attention immediately to the next person I was to greet.

Justin made his place beside me at one of the small round tables on the patio overlooking the water. He brought me melon wrapped in prosciutto and champagne. He escorted me to the banquet. After I danced with the best man, Justin steered me back to the dance floor, flung me lightly to the swing beat of a big band number, and caught me up in his arms.

It felt good to be with Justin again. He was fun, masculine, smart, and awfully good looking. He was a nice guy. And I had a feeling he had been rethinking our relationship during the months we had spent apart.

As the afternoon turned slowly into evening, all the old comfort returned. Like an old-time comedy dance team, we picked up on one another's cues, we clicked to one another's moves.

It was nearly dark when he took my arm and led me down to the beach.

"You know, Stacy, lately I've been thinking about you a lot," he said. "A *lot*."

"I thought about you a lot too, Justin."

"I think it's significant that we really never broke up, don't you? I mean, officially broke up. I think that shows the confusion we both felt about the situation."

"It was never stated that way," I said, hesitantly. I had made the same argument to myself. "We never used the words 'break up,' but it was pretty clear."

"No, it wasn't clear. I had the sense that it was more like a trial separation, really, than a breakup."

"Sometimes trial separation is a gentle way of saying breakup."

"Sometimes it is. And sometimes it isn't."

He reached for my hand suddenly and I thought with alarm that he was going to say something I wasn't ready to hear, or do something I wasn't ready for him to do, but he just kept walking up the beach, holding my hand, and I followed along. I felt so relieved he hadn't said anything more that I allowed him to continue holding my hand, though I didn't feel completely comfortable with it.

We watched the sun set over the water. I was feeling vindicated, and a little smug, which was understandable, I guess, because although our breakup, or trial separation— whatever you wanted to call it—had been a mutual thing, I was sure I took it harder, at least at first, than he did.

"The last time we talked," I said, "you walked out on me in a restaurant without saying good-bye."

"I was hurt, Stacy. When you bought that place in the mountains, I knew you were making a decision about me."

"You made a decision, too."

"I know that." He looked at me longingly. "I know what you wanted. What you needed from me. I knew it then, but—I was a fatheaded guy, full of pain."

I burst out laughing. He did a wonderful Cary Grant. Unfortunately, I had always found Cary Grant to be a bit over the top.

"Look, I'm trying to be serious here," he said. "Don't laugh."

I felt susceptible to him physically. It had been months since I had been held by a warm, loving man, and when he touched me, my body wanted to sink into the sensation of heat and sensuality. Justin was sensitive enough to understand my reticence—in fact it seemed to please him, as if it gave him a foil against which to play his seduction. He had brought me along slowly, with subtlety, throughout the afternoon and into the evening.

I recognized his tactics this time around, but even so, I was still embarrassingly receptive to them. He touched me lightly, consciously; he looked into my eyes as if he had never seen eyes like mine before; he listened to what I said with all of his being. He waited until I was under the influence of a pleasant champagne buzz, and the sun had set in the west, and we just happened to find ourselves sitting side by side in a picturesque cove of secluded, private sand dunes above the ocean. He brushed a lock of hair out of my eyes. He leaned forward with leisurely assuredness and began to kiss me. His eyes were closed. I ended it before he did. He opened his eyes and we looked at each other and went in for another kiss. The kiss was nice. It was nice to be kissed again. How long it had been! We kissed for awhile. I might have enjoyed just kissing like that for a long time.

But kissing wasn't enough for him and his body grew tired of waiting and he pushed me deftly back onto the sand. He pressed his weight against me and I felt the insistence of him snuggling my legs apart. I began to feel a little sick.

My body was aching for the physical release of sex, but my emotions stirred up my stomach and brought a feeling of nausea to my throat, and a rebellion in my mind. So strange how comfortable he had once felt to me, and now he was like a stranger, with a scent I didn't like.

I pushed him off me and stood up, shaking the sand from my dress.

"I can't do this, Justin," I said. "I'm sorry." I began to walk back to the club. He jumped to his feet and fell into stride next to me, not saying a thing. I think he was astounded. We got back just as the bride was about to throw the bouquet.

Abby yanked me aside and hissed: "Where have you *been,* Stacy? I've been holding off throwing it, but the natives are getting restless. I want *you* to catch it, okay? Did you go off with Justin?"

"Yeah."

"Well—?"

"He tried to seduce me in the sand dunes."

"He *tried—*?"

I shook my head and spread my hands to display the emptiness there. She went off, baffled, to gather up all the unmarried girls who had been hovering around, waiting. I joined the group, feeling self-conscious and silly. Abby gave us a lewd look, turned her back on us and threw her bouquet.

I tried, halfheartedly, to catch it. It was flying straight to-ward me (Abby was aiming) but the arms flew up to grab it like swords crossing above me, and without more conviction than I could muster at that moment, there was no chance in hell of me getting it.

"You didn't catch it," Abby said to me a little later, after she had changed into a white linen travel suit and was getting ready to leave on her honeymoon with Eddie. "You didn't even try. It would have been the perfect end of a perfect wedding if you had. I *know* you want to get married, Stacy."

"I don't want to get married just for the sake of getting married."

"You know that's not the point."

I was sorry to let her down. It was as if my catching the bouquet would have really capped off the day for her. Her lower lip poked out as she pretended to be the picture of disappointment.

I said, "Well, you know, Abbs, I just don't think it was meant to be. I just had this superstitious *certainty* that if I had caught that bouquet, I would have to marry *Justin.*"

She looked at me without reaction. "And that would have been so bad?"

"I just can't," I said.

Justin knew I was to go back to the beach house alone. After Abby and Ed went off in their whipped-creamed honeymoon car with dazed smiles and birdseed in their hair, he offered himself to me once again, as accompaniment to the night.

I shook my head.

He looked more puzzled than hurt. He gave a gallant shrug, and said softly, "I guess I blew it last summer, when I let you go."

He kissed me on the cheek and then he was gone.

In the darkness I sat alone on the deck, watching the waves roll up the beach. I tried to think of what it was in me that was now so certain I would never be with Justin again.

I hadn't stopped loving him, I hadn't even really stopped responding to him physically. But I didn't need him or want him anymore. All through the afternoon and evening with Justin, there had been someone else on my mind, constantly, just there beneath my consciousness, rising now and then on a wave of awareness. He was with me all the time, always on my mind. Did I need him? I didn't need something I couldn't have. But he was the one I wanted.

Chapter Sixteen

I GOT BACK to my apartment in San Francisco Sunday night to find Russ there, waiting for me. From the look on his face I knew immediately something was wrong. He told me Mr. Jacobs, my neighbor, had died suddenly the night before.

"He had a heart attack, apparently," Russ said, gently, his hand on my shoulder. He knew how fond I was of the old man. "He called nine-one-one for help, but by the time the paramedics got there, he was gone."

"He was in my apartment when it happened, wasn't he, Russ?" I said. I was astonished at the lack of tone in my own voice. I was almost grateful for the numbness of shock.

"Yes, he was. Stacy—"

"Russ, don't you see—"

"Yes, I know what you're going to say. But it was a heart attack, Stacy. It was a heart attack."

"Maybe he was poisoned or something, Russ. Maybe it was supposed to be me."

"Stacy, I talked to this detective, about the stuff that's been happening to you."

"And?"

"Well, they were cool. They listened. They nodded. They said, well, you know, this city is full of nuts."

"That's what my boss said, too. Before she fired me."

"They're going to do an autopsy, and they promised to look into the harassment connection. But Stacy, they didn't seem to think there was much to go on."

"We're talking possible murder, now, Russ. It's not just about crank calls anymore. We're talking murder."

I TOLD TESS about Mr. Jacobs's death, and the next day Brand came to see me, apparently to offer consolation, but I wouldn't talk about it with him. I didn't want to tell him about my fears that Mr. Jacobs's death was not an accident. I didn't want to admit it, but Brand himself was suspect, as far as I was concerned. I didn't know whether to be touched by his concern or suspicious of it. I could never seem to shake the image of him trying to take possession of my property. He must have been angry and frustrated to see his plans foiled. Motive for attempted murder? I had heard of lesser motives. With the strange things happening in my life, I found my thoughts doing some pretty crazy loops.

"I was just on my way out," I said. We were standing on the porch together. The earth had entered the state of profusion that was late spring and early summer. There was lively activity in the woods around us, the simmering of insects, birds rustling in thickets.

"Well," he said, not to be rushed. "I just wanted to say I was sorry about your neighbor. He was in your place, at the time—?"

"Yeah."

"Are you okay?"

I nodded, staring off into the woods. I had my big black work bag over my shoulder, and my jacket folded over my arm. My hair was pulled back tight and I had my professional-woman makeup on. He stood a few feet away from me, his arms folded, regarding me intently.

"Okay. I'll let you get going," he said. But instead of

going down the steps, he moved toward me, and he made a circle around me. One hand lightly on my arm, the other at the small of my back, he lowered his head and kissed me on the forehead. It was a swift kiss, but his lips lingered a moment. Then he was gone.

THE AUTOPSY SHOWED the cause of death to be a heart attack. After all, Mr. Jacobs was in his nineties. Nobody was surprised to find he had taken ill unexpectedly and passed on. It was just his time, everybody said.

But I felt full of grief and guilt, and I could not rid myself of the feeling that it had been murder and I had been the intended victim.

IT WAS SUMMER and instead of taking time off to work on the house as I'd planned, I was working longer hours than ever, trying to get my business off the ground. My apartment in San Francisco sold quickly for a good price, and from that came my start-up capital. I was keeping my overhead low, but the cost of doing business shocked me even though I expected to be shocked. For awhile, what was coming in wasn't as much as what was going out, and I struggled to live one day at a time and not indulge myself in worry. My clientele grew slowly but steadily, with referrals for drafting, interior design, and several architectural projects in the mountains and in the foothills, but my house languished. Practically nothing got done on it that summer.

I lived in the mountains full time now, but it seemed I saw my neighbors less than when I had been merely a visitor. Though I missed Brand particularly, I found myself avoiding him even while I longed to go to him. But I was keeping to myself more and more, working alone in my house. I no longer trusted anyone, really, except Abby and Russ.

I had begun to notice things missing. Not stolen. Moved. At first, I would pass it off to my own scattered brain. A book I had left in the parlor turned up in the kitchen. A towel I had hung in the bathroom would be discovered on the floor in the dining room. One day I found the carton of milk in the cupboard, and the teapot in the refrigerator. I knew I was supposed to think I was going mad. The thought did cross my mind.

Brand was the only one I knew who could slip in and out of the house without leaving a trace. He would be the one to know the window locks that didn't latch tight, or how one of the French doors opening to the terrace could be unlocked from the outside simply by pulling up hard on the knob. I forced myself to consider the possibility that he was some kind of revengeful sadist. *"I'll get her for this!"* he would say, playing out the scenario in my mind like an actor in a bad movie. *"She'll pay for taking that house from me!"* But it was absurd. I could not put such words into Brand's mouth.

He was many things imperfect, it was true. He could be sullen, cold, evasive, and sometimes rude. But he was not an imbalanced psychopath, out to do me harm.

Or so I most fervently prayed he wasn't.

MEETING BRAND'S SISTER Stephanie and seeing her paintings had inspired me in my attempts to start painting again myself, though I had no illusions I would ever be in her league. I completed several watercolor studies of the old chapel, and when I was satisfied with some of them, I brought them down to the church office to show Father Daniel.

"Oh, they're *marvelous*, Stacy." He seemed genuinely pleased. "You've really got some talent."

"When I was in school, I loved my art classes the most," I said. "I don't do enough of it anymore."

"Odd how you were able to make something inanimate look so fluid. So alive."

"I tend to think of buildings as animate. Living, breathing entities."

"With minds of their own—" His eyes shone bright.

"Yes. I've got a love-hate relationship with mine."

"Yolanda tells me you're living in the house full time

now." A worried look passed over his handsome tanned face. "Are you sure you're doing the right thing? Leaving your job, your place in the city?"

Leaving my job wasn't exactly my choice. I nearly said it aloud, then thought better of it. "Well, it is a risk," I said. "But I have to take that risk."

"Sometimes I think these old places should be burned to the ground," he said in a murmur, as if to himself.

"Why would you say that?" I asked, bewildered.

He glanced up, noticed my expression, and laughed. "Forgive me, Stacy. That was tactless. It's these old church buildings. They're so full of dry rot, we have trouble keeping one step ahead of the wrecking ball. Sometimes I wonder if it's worth it, with these old places. But that house of yours is a magnificent structure, and your fresh blood ought to bring that place to rights."

Fresh blood. It seemed an unsettling choice of words.

"All right," I said. "I want you to tell me the sordid history of my house. Everybody else seems to know it but me."

"Sordid—?"

"There's a story there that nobody seems to want to tell me. Murder, mayhem, it was once a brothel? What?"

"Well, let's see . . ." He was either reluctant to get into it, or he was thinking back. "They say your house is standing on the site of a tavern and trading post, dating from the late 1800s, I believe. It was nothing but a shack in those days. There was a livery stable attached, some corrals. For a time it was used as a stopover for travelers on their way over the Sonora Pass. According to local lore, a gold prospector and a Mi Wuk Indian chief shot themselves to death in a duel over a woman."

"In my house?"

"Well, in the building as it was then. That structure eventually burned down, and the Johnson family bought the property and built the first stage of the house as you know it today, as the story goes, right over the foundation of the original. That's about the extent of that story."

"Well, that's more colorful than sinister," I said, oddly relieved.

"I'd like to see you do a painting of that old house," Father Daniel said.

"Yes, I've done some sketches of it," I said. "But I'm not satisfied. The chapel was a natural, just a few simple shapes catching the light though the trees. The geometry of the house is more complex. I'm not sure how to compose the painting—I haven't been satisfied with anything I've done of it yet."

Yolanda came into the office. She stopped in surprise when she saw me, and the paintings.

"Oh, Stacy—hi." She set a stack of church programs on the desk. "Hey. Nice paintings. Oh, that's the chapel, isn't it?" She looked up from the paintings. "You didn't—" She glanced back at the painting, then to me. "Did *you* do these, Stacy?"

"Yes, I asked her to do them," Daniel answered for me. "I commissioned them."

"Wow. I'm impressed." Yolanda sighed. "I wish *I* had artistic talent."

"I think I'll take these two, and hang them over the desk," Father Daniel said.

"Good," Yolanda agreed. "I like this one." She was holding the one he had set aside.

"And she's doing more," Father Daniel said. "I'd like to see the others, when you're finished, Stacy."

"Well, we'll see how they come out," I said.

THE DUEL STORY was something out of a B-movie. A B-movie western. I'm sure at the time it was a great tragedy for those involved, but I had to laugh about it now, more than a hundred years later. And selling the paintings was a good omen, I told myself as I walked through the woods back to my house. I grasped at anything I could to feel more secure in the move I had made, the risks I had decided to take.

IT WAS THE Fourth of July and we were going up to the lake to picnic and watch the annual fireworks display over the water. I was standing by my mailbox, wearing khaki shorts and a white sleeveless blouse tied at the waist, gray socks, and hiking boots. I had my sweatshirt tied over my shoulders in case it got cold later. Tess's big beast of a truck rolled around the drive and seemed to have sprouted tentacles of waving arms. I pulled a letter out of the mailbox and stuffed it into my pocket, and then I ran to the truck, slinging my pack into the back like a hitchhiker. Brand was there, leaning against the back of the cab, his long legs sprawled out in the bed of the pickup.

"Howdy."

"Hey, Brand."

Saul, Alana, and Tess were sitting together in the big cab. Saul got out at Tess's prodding—or was it Alana's?—and offered me the inside.

"Oh, no, that's okay," I said. I had already jumped in and settled. I patted my pack to show I'd made myself at home.

So it was Brand and me in the back of the truck. We sat on an open sleeping bag, our legs stretched out, mine tanned and bare in my shorts, his long and lean in denim. We leaned against the back of the cab, the wind whipping up our hair as the truck turned onto the highway and picked up speed. I wondered how it was that I had managed to snag the place next to Brand—ordinarily Alana would have made sure she occupied that spot. I suspected he had volunteered to sit in the back and she had preferred the comfort of the cab. Probably didn't want her hair to get messed up.

Brand and I shouted at each other for a while in a vain attempt to chat. It was so noisy we didn't have to talk, but I was in a boisterous mood and didn't mind yelling some. After a while I took out the letter I had found in my mailbox and looked at the return address. I was surprised to see it was from Mrs. Shapiro. I sliced the envelope open with my finger. Brand politely looked out at the scenery.

Dear Miss Addison,

I was hoping you'd call or come see me again, but since you haven't, I shall have to be the one to reach out to you. I have more stories to share with you about my house. Or should I say "our house"? Anyway, do

*keep in touch. Your visit was the best diversion I've
had in some time.*

Sincerely, Madelon Shapiro

I slid the note back into the envelope and stuffed it into
my pocket. My mood had changed. Brand seemed to sense
it; he stopped joking around and left me alone. We settled
back in silence, watching the forest and sky moving past.

I felt troubled, thinking of Jean, Mrs. Shapiro's daughter.
I had all but promised her I'd stay away from her mother—
and what if I really had disturbed the old woman? I could be
responsible for her health, her mental state, or something.
And yet, I liked her a lot, and I did want to see her again. I
wanted to ask her questions about the house. I wanted to
hear her stories. I wanted to tell her what I was doing with
the house, or at least what I would be doing if I had the time
and money. I wanted to find out what really went on between her and Brand.

He tapped my arm, pointing out a family of deer camou-
flaged against the dry meadow next to the road. The touch
of his fingers on my bare arm sent a chord of shivers through
my body, tugging at my breath and making me gasp.

I am losing it, I thought. Whenever I thought I was putting him out of mind, there he was again and I had to start
all over, trying to get him out of it.

The truck swung around the arc of the mountain, gaining
elevation, the big tires gripping the highway at a tilt. I felt
the force of speed on matter, taking the curve, a primal
power pushing me hard against Brand. My tendency was to
stiffen, but I allowed my body to relax into his and enjoy the
warmth of him, the simmering current passing between us.

The road straightened out and we sat up a little, breathing
deeply. The truck hesitated as the highway ended. We
bumped over a cattle guard and turned onto a rutted twisting
narrow stretch of dirt road. Tess threw the truck into low
gear, and it ground its way up the hill.

"We're almost there," Brand said.

"Good," I replied. "This road is bad news." But really I

was enjoying the forced contact, the repeated jolt against his living body. He felt so large and solid, and at the same time so protoplasmic, fluid, and warm. Now and then he would reach out with instinctive protection to steady me when we hit a particularly nasty bump. I felt his hair feathering in the wind, caressing my face, tangling with my hair when we moved our heads close to talk. By the end of the ride we were pressed together, side by side, and more and more comfortable being that way. I wished the ride would never come to an end.

Tess's friend Tom was at the picnic area already, unloading some fishing gear and a cooler from the back of his jeep when we arrived. Everyone jumped out and started bringing supplies down to the lake shore.

When we got settled, Brand went off on a hike with Alana and Tom. Tom tried to persuade Tess to come with them, but she just laughed and waved him off.

"I'm going to hang out and get the barbecue ready," she said. "You go ahead."

They didn't ask me to come along. Of course, I could have simply joined them, but I felt inexplicably hurt. Just as they set off, Tom said, "How about you, Stacy, you comin'?" and I shook my head no.

Alana wore short shorts that showed off her long, slim model's legs. At her neat ankles, carefully rolled sports socks topped impeccable white running shoes. She had rolled up the sleeves of her little T-shirt, showing off her strong, slender arms. The men fell in with her long-legged, show-horse gait, one on either side of her—Tom, with his long gray braid, carrying his fishing pole like a banker with a briefcase, and big, lanky Brand, with his rolling, loose stride, holding his fishing pole like a knight with his lance.

Tess spread a checkered tablecloth over a picnic table while Saul set up some folding chairs and a chaise lounge.

"Are you going to get the charcoal ready, Saul?" she asked.

"Yeah, sure, but it's too early yet. I just want to try out this thing first." He stretched out on the chaise.

"He'll never do it," she said to me.

"I can do it," I said.

"I'm so glad you came with us today, Stacy!" Tess suddenly gave me a warm hug. It had been a while since I'd seen her. I had tended to keep to myself lately, I was so wary of everyone. But I couldn't help but like her. If anything, I thought she was the kind of person who would stand up for what was right, but I didn't believe her first loyalties were to me.

I cut up some tomatoes and cheese for hamburgers. We had brought the fixings in a blue cooler. Another cooler was full of iced soda and beer, and there was a big batch of fresh-baked fudge brownies. Saul never got up, so I poured out the charcoal, forming it into a pyramid on the bottom of the concrete barbecue pit.

"I'm sure there's plenty of time before we eat if you want to go for a swim or hike, Stacy," Tess said. "Thad should be here soon."

"Oh, good," I replied in a cheerful voice.

Saul and Tess settled down with sunscreen, sunglasses, and magazines. I went off by myself and hiked along the edge of a creek on a trail that veered away from the canyon and began to climb in elevation. The trail opened to a small meadow where butterflies dangled over the grasses like flowers from their stems. The intense beauty of the mountains, the vigorous exercise, and the fragrant high mountain air washed through me, body and soul.

A pair of hawks circled above the tops of the trees, their wings seemingly motionless, moved only by the whim of the wind. I wanted to be where the hawks were, and the winds, sighing in the tops of the pines. I wanted Brand. I wanted him despite the warnings of my fearful mind. Being with him again this afternoon, touching him, intensified the feelings I tried so hard to ignore, both the longing and the suspicion.

I wanted to live in the moment, without thought of what might come next. But I was too racked with desire to find any peace in the moment, whenever the moment did not move toward touching Brand. Perversely, I craved the torment in my body. It was an exquisite pain I did not want to relinquish. A sickness I didn't want healed. A disaster I didn't want to escape.

When I was a kid I discovered, like most kids do I guess, that I could pass my finger through a candle's flame. I remember courting the heat, moving deeper into the drop of fire, wondering how slowly I could travel through its dancing heart without getting burned.

"Look, I can put my finger through the fire," I boasted to Russ one night when our mother had lit candles on the dining room table.

"Anyone can do *that*," replied my brother, unimpressed. "Try holding your finger directly above the flame." And he was right, of course, passing through the fire was much easier than lingering just above it. That was what I felt like now. I felt like I was dangerously close to the tip of the flame—I wanted to immerse myself within the flame, to ease the pain.

In the distance, at the edge of the meadow, I saw a man striding along the trail and hope flared in me that it was Brand, come to find me—but as the hiker moved closer I knew it was Thad.

"Hey, you made it," I called, waving. I always loved seeing Thad, after all.

"Knowing you would be here today, I had no choice." He burst into song: "*Ain't no mountain hi-i-i-gh enough.* And look, I've found you—alone?"

"Yes," I said. "Quite alone."

"Tess told me you had gone off this way. And that the others had gone off *that* way—" He motioned toward the west. "I hope you didn't *want* to be alone."

"Not necessarily," I replied teasingly. "Anyway. I *have* been alone. I do like being alone, sometimes. And sometimes I like company."

We walked along together. "I, too, like being alone," he said. "With *you*. Look at that soft long grass. We could be lying in it together. Wouldn't that be heavenly?"

"Probably not. That grass is not as soft as it looks. It would be stickery and dry, and bugs would crawl into your ears and armpits, and in between your legs—"

"Enough! Enough. You are spoiling a perfectly lovely fantasy."

"I'm just adding to it."

"I don't like what you're adding."

"Well, that's just the trouble when the fantasy of one becomes the reality of two."

"You'll never convince me of that."

"I'm trying to convince *me*, I think. I have been overindulging in fantasy lately."

"Tell me everything."

"I'll leave it to your imagination. You'd probably like that better, anyhow."

"Well, I *do* have quite an imagination. But truth is stranger, right? And usually more interesting."

"I'm not so sure about that."

"Let me guess. Your fantasy . . . a deserted beach . . . a moonless night."

"Sounds good so far."

"And my good buddy Brandon Vandevere. The two of you, lying supine on the beach, all alone with the stars above . . ."

I was glad the sun had already lent a blush to my cheeks, for I was sure they were now deepening in color.

"Why would you think of that?" I asked nonchalantly.

"All the women fantasize about *him*," he said glumly. "It was a safe bet."

"Really! Am I like every other woman, then!"

He raked one black brow at me. "Let me tell you, the beach is overrated. Too much sand, gets into cracks, you know. And you're so exposed."

I laughed, thinking of Justin on the sand dunes. "I'll bet you're right," I said. "But I wouldn't know."

"Oh, so you've had no firsthand experience with that, uh, scenario?"

"Not really. With sand nor with Brand. Sorry."

"All right, all right, then . . . how about with—Saul?"

"Ah—no."

"But I've heard rumors."

"Well, whatever you've heard was wrong. What did you hear?"

He shrugged. "I don't remember, exactly."

"*Thad.*" I paused on the trail, folded my arms, and regarded him severely.

"Really, I don't," he assured me. "I never believed it anyway."

"What?"

"Nothing."

"Damn you, Thad."

We began to walk again.

"Then . . . how about Jay, the surveyor?"

"Jay is awfully cute," I said thoughtfully.

"Ah—ha! But that isn't who you were thinking of."

"It doesn't matter. I'm not going to tell you. And why do you assume it was a sexual fantasy, anyway?"

"Because that is the kind you wouldn't want to tell me about. Especially if it was about me. Was it about me?"

"No," I laughed.

He scowled. "I didn't think so."

It was late afternoon when Thad and I returned to camp. Everyone was eating already and called out when we appeared, claiming to have given us up for lost, forming search parties and all that. The food was fantastic after a hike, classic picnic food, hamburgers cooked on the grill with all the trimmings, potato salad, baked beans, deviled eggs, and watermelon. Everyone had pitched in with the food. I sat at the picnic table next to Thad and ate rapturously. He handed me a beer, which I accepted with a celebratory flourish, lifting it in tribute, and I glanced up to see Brand staring at me. He seemed startled by the eye contact and turned his head away.

As the long July sun settled behind the granite cliffs above the lake, slowly came the darkness. We all walked together in a group down to the edge of the lake where a small crowd was gathering to wait for the fireworks. Tom slipped his arm around Tess's shoulder. Alana walked between Thad and Saul, who were arguing about the history of fireworks. Thad claimed the Chinese had invented them; Saul said no, it wasn't the Chinese, but he couldn't remember who it was—Alana agreed with Thad. I lagged behind a little, watching them all, listening, feeling contentment, but also a sense of being outside, looking in. I felt Brand beside me and I glanced up at him.

"Is it safe?" I spoke quietly, and Brand drew near to hear what I was saying. "I thought fireworks were illegal in the mountains. What about the fire danger?"

"That's why they shoot 'em over the lake," he replied. "They have a special permit here. They do it every year. Since I was a kid, every year."

"And fire is never a problem?"

"It hasn't been," he answered. "Though I would never say never." He looked at me in an odd way. Intense and unreadable.

We wandered together over to the edge of the woods, where the beach sloped up into the trees. The others had gone ahead.

"Come with me," he said suddenly, decisively. Conspiratorial. "I'll show you the best place to watch these fireworks." He touched my arm and guided me through a jumble of granite boulders. We lost the group, and started up a trail around the lake between the shore and the woods. Instead of following the main trail into the forest, we pushed through a hidden passage in the wall of fern and young cedar to follow a narrow, less well-traveled path down through a small gully, and then up again on the other side, steeply. I picked my way carefully, trying to match Brand's confident pace through the darkening woods.

We came out of the trees on a cliff above the lake. Over the water we could see our friends on the beach in the distance. They were so small from this vantage that I was sure they could not see us, for we were well hidden in the trees. The air was soft and rich with the mineral scent of the lake mixed with woodsmoke and the incense smell of the forest. I felt this perfumed air against the bare skin of my arms, touching my hair. I was amazed and excited to be alone with Brand.

Then abruptly we left the path and slid down a short steep dry trail which ended at the top of a massive throne of granite thrusting high above the southeast end of the lake. He took my hand to steady me and didn't let go.

"This is where my sister and I used to come to watch the fireworks," Brand said. "It was our secret spot."

He showed me the perfect little scooped-out area on the rock where a very comfortable seat could be had for two. We had a panoramic view of the lake; beneath us the granite sheered off and gave way to more rocks below.

"Good place to commit suicide," I murmured, and I was glad when he didn't seem to have heard me.

He dropped my hand and spread his sweatshirt for us to sit upon.

"Won't you sit down?" he asked gallantly.

The last of the light went out of the sky and a chill sprang up from the water. I felt his body warm and near. I wanted to be there beside him, and the space was so small in our little hollow we couldn't help but touch, sitting so close together. But it was a teasing bliss. I longed for him to pull me against his body, I wanted to feel him heavy on me, I wanted to taste his mouth.

A ROCKET SCREAMED into the sky, burst with an explosion of color, metamorphosed into a giant golden mandala, hung brilliant over the lake for a moment, then disintegrated into a shower of light raining down into its own reflection. Dozens of smaller rockets went off, exploding and flowering and shimmering into the water. Involuntarily, I cried out, admiring, astonished. Brand laughed, delighted with my response. He seemed proud of the lake, the fireworks, the perfect cool summer night, as if it were all the essence of some special relative he was introducing to me.

The fireworks display went on and on with no pause. The explosions came furious, varied, and layered with shape and color and the sounds, screaming whistles rising in pitch until they punctured the night sky, the deep vibratory booming of the big ones slightly out of variance with the timing of the light detonation, like a film when the sound track is slightly out of sync with the picture.

I found I had to stand up—my nerves were wild. I thrust my hands into the pockets of my shorts and danced in place a little, shivering with cold or nervousness. Brand rose with me, and as we watched the grand finale fill the sky he moved behind me and slipped his arms around me. I felt his breath warm on my neck.

"So how do you like our fireworks, Stacy?" he whispered.

"Dazzling," was all I said.

His lips were in my hair. "Yes, truly dazzling . . ." he murmured. He was talking about me, not the fireworks. I thought of Nicholas Cage in *Valley Girl*. What a sweet, sexy man.

Now we swayed together without words. I felt the nearness of the sheer cliff, the nearness of him. His arms, tightening around me, his body hard against mine. The heat of his breath on my skin. There was a trembling in our bodies, a sense of hunger gaining on us, a captive wolf coming to the end of a frayed rope. But the fire had gone from the sky and we had no excuse to be there alone any longer. My doubts and worries rose, unwanted but insistent, and I suddenly felt embarrassed and awkward. I struggled to be free of his grasp. Brand let go of me abruptly and I felt myself tilting, losing my balance. Panic washed cold through me. I'd lost my footing and there was nothing between me and the rocks below.

By now it was so dark no one would see me fall to my death. He could say it was an accident—

I would have fallen if he had not suddenly grabbed my arm and pulled me hard against him. We slid back down to a sitting position in the hollow of the rock. I was shaking. He held me securely, stroking my arms, urging the trembling panic to flow away.

"Hey, it's okay," he said. "It's okay, Stacy. You're okay now. I think I knocked you off balance there. But I wouldn't let you fall. I would not let you fall—"

His voice was tender, curious, and lulling. I felt so safe in his arms. I pressed my head to his broad fragrant chest and listened to the pounding of his heart. Pounding like he'd been running.

This is where I belong, I thought.

His hands moved over my back, my arms, stroking my hair.

His fingers swept up the line of my neck. He bent over me slightly and I became aware of the smell of his skin, and the deep silence for a moment, and darkness. He lifted my face and kissed my mouth. The taste of his mouth! No light, no sound. Only smell and touch, and taste. I had wanted this for so long. The velvet touch of his mouth. The flavor of him on my tongue. The scent of him, a faint spicy trace of something, soap or aftershave, mingling with the salty, tangy, woodsy scent of his skin. His hands moved over me, pressing my body against his body, and the kiss, slowly deepening and opening and becoming one thing between us. His fingers swept my throat just where the top button of my blouse was undone.

Breathing came faster. He drew away, bared his teeth and nipped at my lips, at my neck, sending shudders through me, and then he was plunging in for another kiss, impatiently now, hungrier. I felt his hands ranging over me and I could feel the energy trembling through his fingers. The force of his eagerness was overwhelming.

I became aware of voices and the flash of a light through the trees.

They were almost upon us—a small band of hikers moving down the trail along the top of the cliff. I pulled away from Brand and rose to my feet just as they burst out of the woods above us. They shone their light down and offered to hold it there while we climbed up to the path.

"It's treacherous here when it's this dark," a deep male voice warned. "No moon tonight."

We followed the hikers down to the picnic area where our friends were packing up the truck.

Brand and I walked apart, hardly looking at one another, but I knew he must be feeling the scorch of that kiss on his mouth, the way I was feeling it on mine.

Or—had it been some kind of decoy? The thought came unbidden, unwanted. Maybe he *had* been about push me off that cliff—then heard the hikers coming down the trail and had decided against it—

No.

This man was my protector, not my enemy.

Then why can't you trust him?

Chapter Seventeen

THE NEXT MORNING I woke early, laden with dreams, deep and sensual, full of Brand. In the bedroom dim with the filtered light of dawn from the eastern windows, I lay on my back with my eyes closed, letting the images of the night mingle with my gradually waking consciousness. Something in the dream landscape had seemed oddly familiar to me. It was as if the memory of being with Brand, being in his arms, was from a time long before last night.

I got out of bed and was drawn to the window to stare out across the meadow at Brand's house. I was thinking of how I had awakened in a strange bed in these mountains months ago, the morning I had found the house, filled with a prescience that had now come to completion. The premonition that here I would fall in love.

I DRESSED CAREFULLY, wanting to look the way I felt. Simple. Female. Sensual. I thought I ought to be wearing a long, low-cut, flowing gown of sheer silk with flowers in my flowing hair. I settled for white shorts and a forest green tank top with leather sandals and my hair left loose on my shoulders. I was going into town to do a few errands, and hoped I might catch a glimpse of Brand as I came down the stone steps to my car, but the Barn was silent across the meadow.

Alana's car was parked next to Brand's International.

Well, so what? I thought. She's always over there.

And it always bothers you.

I returned a library book and picked up some blueprints, glad to be occupied, because I knew I would go crazy at home, trying to work, thinking of *him*. But I found myself wanting only to return home so that I might see him again, and I didn't stay long in town. The Barn was still quiet when I returned. Alana's car was still there, and I steeled myself not to stare at his windows when I parked my car and went into my house.

Once inside the house, I noticed immediately a strange odor, like sweet tobacco or incense. I roamed through the house, looking for something, though I didn't know what. Almost convinced that I was not, well, *seeing* things, but *smelling* things, I opened the French doors to the back patio to let the fresh air in. As I turned back into the room, I glanced at my drawing board where several of my water-color paintings were taped. Lying near them was my mat knife, and I knew something was wrong. That knife should have been in the top drawer of my desk.

I moved closer and saw the knife had been used—on my paintings. All the tentative watercolor sketches I had done of my house had each been slashed. The shock washed through me like cold blood. My work was destroyed, all except for a couple of paintings of mountains and trees, the only ones which did not include the house in their composition.

"SO YOU SAY there's no evidence of anyone breaking and entering."

"No. Though, like I said, the house isn't that secure. It

would not have been difficult to get in without actually *breaking* in."

"And nothing was stolen?"

It was the fourth time he had asked the question, and I sighed, and answered him again. "No, not that I know of. Some things were moved around, that's all."

If the law enforcement authorities in San Francisco seemed to have little time for my problems, I found the opposite situation when I called the police in the mountains after I found my paintings slashed. The officer who came to see me seemed to have plenty of time to shoot the breeze, drink coffee, and chat.

"And nothing was damaged. Except the paintings."

"Nothing was damaged, except the paintings," I repeated.

"Look," said Officer Henderson. He was a friendly, good-looking guy with most of his hair already gone, though he was only a couple years older than me. "I don't know how familiar you are with this area. But it's a lot different than what you're probably used to in the big city. We have practically no crime here. You read the police report in the local papers? Read it for laughs. The biggest thing every week is a rock through a window or a bunch of kids loitering in front of the mini-mart. We get some domestic violence. A woman throwing her drunken boyfriend out of the house, that sort of thing. The rest of it is just bored kids playing pranks."

"You think this was done by bored kids? You don't see a pattern in everything I've told you? The phone calls, the harassment, the death of my neighbor in the city—"

"You said he was an elderly gentleman in his nineties. Died of a heart attack."

"It's the accumulation of incidents," I said.

"Could be a series of coincidences. Kids playing tricks, natural occurrences."

"I've tried to convince myself of that. But I just can't anymore."

"You said there was a threatening note. May I see it?"

"I threw it into my woodpile when I got it. I know, I wish

I hadn't. I didn't realize at the time . . . I looked for it later, but . . ." I stopped, feeling stupid.

"Well," he said, holding out his cup for another refill. "You got someone in mind? You have an idea who might be behind all this?"

I took a deep breath and plunged in. I told him about Brand. I listed everything I could think of, that might implicate him. It was a horrible thing to do. I felt I was betraying a friend. But what choice did I have? If Brand was truly my friend, I would be able to trust him.

Officer Henderson listened patiently, but by the time I finished, he had a look of amusement on his face. "Brand Vandevere, huh?" he said.

"Well," I said. "What do you think?"

"I'm going to tell you exactly what I think," he said with a chuckle. "I think you're way off base. Look. I know Brand."

"You know him?"

"Since high school. He's a good friend of mine."

I didn't know whether to be indignant or relieved.

Officer Henderson finished his coffee and stood up. "I'll keep an eye on your place, but I think you're probably reading too much into things."

"What do you think I'm reading into that?" I demanded, angry now, pointing at my paintings.

"I'm thinking maybe you did this yourself."

"Did it my*self*?"

"An artist frustrated with her work, all alone late at night after perhaps a few drinks . . ."

I groaned and shook my head.

"I do have a recommendation for you. Get some better locks for your doors and windows. And you might consider getting yourself a roommate."

WHEN I LEFT the house for the second time that day, I noticed Alana's car was still parked in front of the Barn, but Brand's International was gone.

Good, he's gone, I thought, not really knowing why I felt

such a sense of relief. Gone was the fog of pure bliss through which I had been floating all morning. The sensual tones were still there, deep in me, but there was something else, fluttering in my chest, along my spine. It was fear. It was anger. I wanted answers. I wanted to know who was messing with me, and why.

As I turned the car around the meadow drive, Alana came out of the Barn, descended the steps and walked toward her beige BMW, nodding at me with the barest hint of acknowledgment.

Ha! I thought. *He's not there.* So go home.

But she was long and elegant as she slid into her car, and the knot of jealousy that suddenly tightened in my chest and slid down through my guts had the amazing power, if only for a moment, to banish all the other feelings warring inside me.

"I DIDN'T THINK you were going to come," Mrs. Shapiro said, leaning back in her chair, appraising me critically.

It was with a guilty pleasure that I shook her hand and accepted a comfortable chair near the big sliding glass doors with the view overlooking the gardens around the nursing home. I wasn't even supposed to be here. Mrs. Shapiro's daughter had all but told me not to see her mother again, afraid I would disturb the old woman with talk of the house. How would I begin to broach the difficult subject that had driven me to come here?

"I wanted to come see you, Mrs. Shapiro, but . . ." I hesitated, wondering what I should say. "I was afraid I might upset you with talk of the house."

"Upset me?" she was perplexed. "Why on earth would talking of the house upset me?" Then her brow tightened suspiciously and she said, "What have you done to it?"

I laughed at her serious expression. "Nothing. See what I mean? Already you're upset, and about nothing!"

She laughed with me. "All right. We don't even have to talk about the house if you'd rather not. I know I can be overbearing."

"Not at all—" I *wanted* to talk about the house! But I kept thinking about her daughter's serious, worried face. What if the nursing home people called her? *That strange woman has been upsetting your mother again.*

I could just see it: court injunction, restraining order—

"So what *have* you been doing with the house?" she pressed.

"Nothing," I replied gloomily.

"*Nothing?*" She was aghast. "Why *not*? There is plenty to do."

"I know, I know, but I'm broke. I lost my job and I couldn't get the loan I was counting on to do the work. I'm going to have to wait until—"

"Stop!" she held up her hand. "I don't understand any of this. What about the foundation, the allowance?"

I frowned, uncomprehending. "Well, the foundation isn't really a priority right now," I said. "My brother found that some of the supports had fallen, and he was able to straighten out some of the floors a bit, but—"

"No, no, the Historic Foundation, I'm talking about the Historic Trust Foundation!"

I shook my head, uncertain. She seemed to be losing touch with reality again.

Mrs. Shapiro looked at me with shrewd eyes. "You don't have any idea what I'm talking about, do you?"

"No ma'am," I confessed.

"So—you don't work for the Historic Trust Preservation Foundation?"

"No ma'am."

"Are you telling me you own the house? You bought it—?"

I looked at her strangely.

"I see." Her voice took on a new tone. She looked at me thoughtfully. "So you were a private buyer. You bought the house yourself? Your name is on the deed?"

"Yes, of course—" What was *this* all about? "I bought the house from Madelon Shapiro," I snapped, frightened. "That is you, isn't it? You financed the deal!"

"What did you pay for the place?"

"You know what I paid—" But I told her and she gave a little *harumph.*

"You got an awfully good deal," she said.

"But I bought it from *you.* Didn't I?"

"I suppose you did."

"You suppose? Suppose you tell me what this is all about. Why you were under the impression I was from some kind of historic trust—"

"Apparently there has been some misunderstanding," she said. "I'm afraid I'm not even surprised. But don't you fret. I am sure your claim on the house is legal and valid. What I am not certain of is . . ."

"What?" I pressed her impatiently. "What is this all about?"

"I shall have to make inquiries to find out myself. I will let you know when I have it straightened out."

"You can't just leave it at that, Mr. Shapiro. What's going on here? What are you trying to tell me?"

"I was quite ill for a while and I didn't know if I would be able to take care of things myself. My daughter did what she could, and we had an attorney helping us and I think he was trying to make the most money from the deal. He didn't approve of this idea of leaving the house to a historic trust. You know there was quite a good offer from a development company in Sacramento."

"Yes, so I was told. And I was told you had other offers as well."

"I received one rather laughable offer, if you could call it an offer (it was actually an attempt to swindle me!) from a handsome young man who must have thought I was suffering from Alzheimer's, but that's another story. I told my daughter absolutely no to the developers. They would have torn down the house and the trees and built a vacation home subdivision. I wanted the place to go to an entity who would restore the estate to its true grandeur, and preserve it for future generations. I was thinking some sort of philanthropic group, the type I ordinarily I tend to shun, but in this case it seemed just the ticket. I suppose my daughter and my lawyer got together and hatched this plan instead, to sell it

to you. Well, maybe they had the right idea. You don't need
to worry. The house is yours now, Stacy."

But that statement, far from reassuring me, only made me
feel worse. When I signed the papers for my house I had felt
it was too good to be true. I had almost expected some official-
type person to come knocking at my door and say, *Sorry
miss, it's all been an unfortunate mistake. We'll be taking
back the keys to the house now.* And was it any coincidence,
the offhanded mention of the handsome young man who . . .
the word she had used was *swindle.* He had made her a
laughable offer. Well, that wasn't so terrible, was it, making
a laughable offer? Did that make him an immoral criminal?
I just did not want to see Brand in the role of swindler. After
all, she had sold him the Barn for a lowball price. Why not
the entire estate?

Mrs. Shapiro chatted on in her deep, aristocratic voice,
wandering off the subject that interested me so intensely.
She told a long and amusing story about one of the other
"inmates" (as she called them) of the nursing home. The anecdotes she told, and her regal, slightly theatrical method of
delivery had me laughing in spite of myself, but beneath it
all I was distressed. There was a prickly apprehension growing in my blood. All the strange and menacing incidents, all
pointing toward the old white house. Was this odd encounter
more of the same? Or was Madelon Shapiro just an old
crackpot?

Before I could steer the conversation back in the direction of my concerns, a young woman dressed in official
white came in to the room. "Are you ready to go in to dinner, Mrs. Shapiro?"

"Yes, yes," the old woman said. "Stacy, would you join
me? The food isn't very good, and I didn't put in for a guest
order, but I'm sure we could manage to get you a plate."

"No, I really should be leaving," I said, resigned. "I've
got a long drive ahead of me."

She took my hand and said, "I will look into the matters
we spoke of, and get back to you, Stacy. I am glad you have
my house. So don't worry, everything will be all right,
you'll see."

She's right about one thing, I thought. Whatever problems and setbacks I encountered, I would overcome them. But my reassurance fled me when her parting words were said over me like a benediction: "Good-bye, Stacy. And please, *do* be careful . . ."

Now why did she have to say that?

As I drove away, the idea that I might have again stirred up an old woman's ramblings worried at my conscience, and yet it did not make sense. Perhaps she is a bit eccentric, I thought, but she's no more senile than I am. And yet, with all that strange talk about the house, and the lawyer, and the historic trust foundation—was she confused? Perhaps that *was* the answer. I almost hoped it was.

My thoughts ran around, dizzy and disjointed, during the long drive home. I was frustrated at the questions still unanswered. I had more doubts now than I had before seeing her. I never even got to ask the questions I had gone there to ask.

When I drove into the meadow that night, I saw Alana's car was there, parked next to Brand's International. Only one dim light shone at the Barn, and that came from Brand's rooms at the top. I struggled to make disappointment the least of the emotions that struggled within me, and I was grateful that I was so tired, so that sleep came easily, and I didn't have to think, or feel, but the feelings came even into my dreams.

I CALLED THE real estate office to talk to Iona, my real estate agent, about the house transaction, but I was told she had moved on to work for a different company. They couldn't find my file, and they gave me a number to try, and I left a message for her to call me. When she didn't call back, I called her again, and the man who answered the phone said she had gone on vacation. I checked the title to my property to make sure everything was legal, and it was, or at least it seemed to be. Still, I felt uneasy about it. I thought of contacting Mrs. Shapiro's daughter, who might have some answers, but I would have to get her phone number from Iona. Besides, Jean Maguire didn't even want me seeing her mother. I tried to convince myself the old lady was simply confused in her thinking.

And I tried to convince myself that I, too, must have been confused—thinking that what happened on the Fourth of July with Brand would change things between us. He did not come to me. In fact I thought he must be avoiding me, for I saw him even more seldom than before.

THAD LEARNED THE architect Julia Morgan was my hero, so he went around referring to himself as "Mr. Hearst," and calling me "Julia." The plans for Thad's house were nearly finished and the permit had been acquired. If I could just keep Thad satisfied with the current design! But I knew in my heart Thad would remodel as soon as the place was finished anyway, so it would never *really* be finished. But at least I would have steady work.

"This house is going to be my castle," he said to anyone who would listen. "It may not be as grand as San Simeon, but it will be more tastefully decorated. I can't wait to get my Thiebaud out of storage—!"

Thad went on talking, something about the differences between classical and primitive art, but I was hardly paying attention. I was searching the wind for the scent of Brand. We were standing on the hill above the house site. The warm wind blew against the leaning dry grasses and ruffled Thad's dark curls. He was splendid in that moment: the classical proportions of his muscular body, the lovely features of his face, like a grown-up cherub.

Funny how you can notice beauty so dispassionately and not be moved, when there is a particular desire, and all the yearning is toward the other.

And in the background, Thad's beautiful well-modulated voice, rushing along to fit in all his thoughts. And one of his words was like the snap of a hypnotist's fingers—

"Brand—"

"I'm sorry, what?" I said suddenly.

"Well, just that I don't think—" he hesitated, looking uncertain about what I had missed. "I mean, people are like art.

Like, as I said, I find an intrinsic difference between the essential nature of Brand and that of his bride—"

"His *what?*"

"His lovely bride. Alana. She is like a Mondrian, all bold colors and stark line. Pure geometry. I don't mean her look, I'm talking about her—essence, if you will. And Brand—he is a Rembrandt. Deep and spiritual, darkness edged with light."

"His *'bride?'* . . ." That was all I had heard.

"The rumors fly. Apparently the couple neither confirms nor denies it, but marriage is imminent—of course you know they've been loosely engaged for some time. You didn't know?"

"*Loosely engaged?*" I repeated, incredulous.

"Tess's term," he laughed. "Personally, I had hoped it was loose enough for Brand to wriggle out of, but—ah, well."

I struggled to keep my voice from cracking. "Why, don't you want him to marry?" I asked.

"Not her. Because I am afraid she does not meet his essential wildness with a corresponding spirit. That's what I was saying. I think one's mate either goads one toward freedom or lures one into captivity. She will not want to see him free. She will attempt to crush his spirit. But he is irrepressible, and therein lies the seed of disaster. If he were not irrepressible, they might have a chance for happiness, but he is, and I greatly fear."

I nodded agreement with Thad's analysis, but I hardly registered a word of what he was saying. I was struggling to maintain my composure. My reasons for despairing of Brand's engagement had nothing to do with how well he and Alana were suited for one another.

"Stacy, my love," Thad said, "You have become quiet and pale."

LATE ONE NIGHT I was walking through the woods, restless with apprehensions I couldn't banish, thoughts that wouldn't let me sleep in peace.

I stopped on a gentle ridge in the silent darkness. From here I could see the faint outline of the church through the trees, and to the east, a fantastic ripe full moon riding low over Yolanda's darkened cabin, casting upon its shingle roof a witchy shine. In the cover of the shadow of the trees I stood silent and curious as, unexpectedly, the door to the cabin creaked open. I was about to call out to Yolanda, but I was startled into silence to see that it was not Yolanda, but Father Daniel, who emerged from the dark cabin. He shut the door softly behind him and set off toward his own house, which was on the other side of the church property. He moved quickly, but there was no hurry in his athlete's stride.

And neither was there guilt or furtiveness in his bearing. And yet I drew back into the shadows, not wanting him to see me, certain he would not have been pleased to know I had observed him there tonight. I felt troubled by this, and it added to the disquiet in my mind.

Chapter Eighteen

BRAND WAS TO leave for Nepal in late July on a writing assignment for *Outside* magazine. He was doing a feature on trekking in the Himalayas. I hadn't seen him since the picnic at the lake, and I sometimes wondered if the Fourth of July had been nothing more than one of my overwrought fantasies. Though I longed to catch sight of him, I made no move to encounter him, nor did he approach me. But one evening I returned home to see fresh wood stacked neatly on my woodpile, and I knew he had put it there, and every now and again I saw him at dusk, standing in the dormer window on the top floor of the barn, staring through the open space in the woods left by the fallen oak, looking for me. Or so I imagined. Perhaps he was merely gazing at the sunset.

There was a party at the Barn for Brand on the night before he was to leave for Nepal, and I didn't feel like going. I'd heard rumors he and Alana were going to announce their engagement that night. All day long the air had been heavy and motionless, and at nine o'clock light still hung in the sky. Strange to think the daylight hours were gradually diminishing again. The day was so long, waiting for night. Finally the air began to move again, and long curly clouds came across the western horizon to bask in the gold and crimson of the setting sun. I took a long cool shower and brushed out my hair, leaving it long and slick down my back. With the sticky heat washed away, I started to feel alive again. I put on a sundress colored like the deep transparent aqua of the sea around an island. I could see, looking into the Enchanted Mirror, how cool and vibrant the color was against the damp darkness of my hair, the tan of my skin. On the radio U2 played from *The Joshua Tree*, "Red Hill Town." *We wait all day for night to come . . .*

I found humor in the very thing that was causing me so much pain. The irony, if you will. I would go to the party to say good-bye to him. *Good-bye, Brand, as you go off to the ends of the earth, good-bye as you go to Alana.* For my own gratification, I did not need to say good-bye to him or to congratulate him on his impending marriage. I dreaded it, in fact. But I was desperate for the chance just to see him, to be alive in his presence, maybe for the last time. That's why I went.

I walked across the drive to the Barn. I could hear voices coming from the rear of the house, so I went around back. Everyone was out on the deck. There were a lot of familiar faces, and some surprises—the beautiful blond guitarist Jeff, whom I had met at the first party at the Barn, was there, and so was Brand's sister, Stephanie, who greeted me warmly.

"Stacy, I have pining for you . . ." Someone spoke softly behind my ear. It was Thad, of course. He took me in his arms and embraced me. "God, it's been *so* long."

"Hello Thaddeus." I hugged him back with exaggerated patience and resignation.

"What?" he cried.

"I just saw you yesterday."

"And your point is?"

"You're silly."

"I know you are but what am I?" He sounded just like Russ, when Russ was about twelve.

"Conversation with you is always so eloquent."

"What are you guys talking about?" Callie popped her head between us.

"We're not sure," Thad replied.

"Thad never knows what he's talking about," said Jeff, who was passing by on his way to the food table.

"But at least *I* know how to talk," Thad said.

"If pig Latin counts as a language," Jeff threw over his shoulder.

"Hey, Callie," I said. "How are you?"

"Don't ask," she said.

"So what is it with you two?" I said to Thad, with a nod at Jeff. "Can't you leave each other alone?"

"Ah, we're old friends," Thad grinned. "Jeff just can't stand it that I got all the brains *and* the beauty, too."

Callie tilted her head and studied him. "I don't know, Thad. Jeff may be a starving musician, but he gives even *you* a run for your money in the beauty department, with that angel face and that long corn silk hair."

"Thad's got an angel face and beautiful black curls," I said. "The two of them are pretty evenly matched, if you ask me."

Thad pouted. He wanted to be the best.

"Angel face?" laughed Callie. "Thad? Devil is more like it! Speaking of the devil, have you seen Ralph? He was just here a minute ago—"

I turned my head to scan the crowd and my eyes caught on Brand as if they had snagged on a nail in the wall across the deck. He was standing by the table talking to Ralph and Tom. Alana hovered nearby, watching him carefully.

"There he is, Callie," I said. "There's Ralph."

"Good. I want to sneak a cigarette while he's not looking. Tess and I quit together, you know. She's doing great, but I'm a basket case."

"So how long you going to be away on assignment, Brand?" Tom's hearty voice carried over to us. I slowly moved closer, as if making my way to the refreshment table. I wanted to hear Brand's voice more clearly. I wanted to know how long he would be gone.

"Oh, a few weeks," Brand said. "Or longer, depending on whether I connect with the Australian Everest Expedition. That's one I'd like to cover. But I haven't got a contract yet."

"One of the leaders of that expedition is a buddy of ours," Ralph said.

"Everest . . ." Tom said with awe.

"The big one," Jeff said, popping open a beer. Standing next to Brand, Jeff might have been his brother. Similarly built, both men were tall and slender, strong through the shoulders and thighs. Both men had beautiful bone structure, a strong jaw, expressive clearwater eyes beneath fierce brows. But Jeff's hair was so blond it was almost white, while Brand's was layered darkness and gold.

Tom asked, "So if you do cover it, does it mean you'll climb the mountain yourself?"

"I'm not much of a climber anymore," Brand said.

"Bullshit modesty, Vandevere," cried Ralph. "I'll tell you what, Tom. Brand won't be back until October. Mark my words."

"That late in the year?" Tom was surprised. "I wouldn't have guessed you could climb the Himalayas that time of year."

"After the monsoon season," said Jeff, "There's this small window of opportunity to climb until sometime in October. That's when the jet stream winds drop down over the summit. Makes it virtually impossible to climb."

"So—this really *is* a going away party, isn't it?" Tom commented, impressed. He said loudly, "How are Tess and Saul ever going to get along without Brand so long? They'll starve to death."

Everyone laughed. Tess, who was tending the refreshment table, straightened up with mock dignity. "I beg your pardon. I do excellent Rice a Roni."

"We'll survive," Saul said archly. "Though I can't speak for Alana . . ."

There was a modest ripple of laughter through the crowd. Alana cast a triumphant glance my way. She moved to Brand's side and touched his arm casually with her elegant acrylic-tipped fingers. He didn't seem to notice she was there.

"So, Alana—" said Callie. "What *do* you think of Brand going away for so long?"

"I support him doing what he needs to do," Alana replied airily.

Thad served me a glass of Chardonnay with a flourish, as if he were a page, or court jester. Brand walked away.

There was no wedding announcement. But though they refused to explain themselves, it seemed they were a couple in most everyone's eyes. The only question was, why were they taking so long to acknowledge it?

Because he's for me.

How could I feel so sure of something I doubted with all my heart?

"So, STACY, HOW have you been?" Stephanie made a point of catching me alone during the party. We had just piled plates high with barbecued chicken, salad, corn on the cob, grilled peppers, and Callie's famous cornbread, and we went to sit together on the steps leading off the deck down to the woods. From inside the house we could hear the discordant sounds of instruments being tuned; Jeff and some of the others were getting ready to play.

"I'm all right," I said. "What about you?"

"Good. Listen, I wanted to thank you for your referrals. I sold two of my paintings to Carlos Garcia."

"Yeah? That's great. I'm not surprised. I always thought Carlos had good taste."

"Well, he said the same about you. He said you're a *magical architect.*"

"He said that?"

"Those were his very words."

I was touched. Clients like the Garcias were the reason I became an architect. The project I had designed for them— with them—was one of my favorites, but I had lost the opportunity to work with Carlos because of the harassing phone calls.

I tried not to dwell on regrets. "Carlos is a true gentleman," I said. "You can be sure your paintings found a good home with him."

"Yeah. I sent him some photos of my work, and he made the trip down to my studio in Pismo Beach. He bought one of the paintings from the Yosemite show—*Mirror Lake*, do you remember it?"

"Oh, yes. The one where you can see the hikers in the reflection of the water, but not on the shore."

"Right! You *do* remember." She smiled, gratified. "And, he also bought one I called *Turnpike Seven* . . ."

"*That's* the one I always wanted." Alana's voice cut in. Stephanie and I turned to see Alana standing on the deck behind us, in her short skirt and her high-heeled sandals and her sunglasses, peering down on us. "You know I would have paid whatever *he* paid."

"Oh, that's right—" Stephanie's face was all innocence. "I do remember you talking about that. I'm *sorry*, Alana, I didn't realize you were serious about wanting it."

Alana shrugged her forgiveness. "Well, I'm sure there are plenty more where that one came from."

"Yeah, I'm just a regular painting factory," said Stephanie.

Someone called to Alana, and she went off. Inside the house, the music began. Jeff had put a pickup on his acoustic guitar and the sound moved through the walls and into the woods like bells ringing.

"She wanted me to *give* the painting to her," Stephanie said to me in a low voice. "Which would have been fine. I have no problem giving my paintings to people if I know they really love them and will take care of them and hang them on the wall and enjoy them. But to *her* . . . I don't know. I couldn't let one of my *children* go to her. I had a feeling she would stick it in her shop with a thousand percent markup and sell it to the highest bidder. Not that I have anything against a dealer taking a markup. It's just—I don't know. I guess it's like—like she pretends she loves it but she just wants it for what it can do for her."

Stephanie put down her plate, her mood disturbed.

"Pretty harsh thing to say about your own sister-in-law, right?" She looked me directly in the eye.

I looked down at my food.

"Well, you know what?" Stephanie stood suddenly, a few steps down from me so she wasn't much taller.

"What?" I asked, looking up at her questioningly.

She leaned down a little, and whispered: "She's *not* my sister-in-law. Not *yet*." She straightened up and smiled. "You know, Stacy, I've suddenly lost my appetite. I'm going to get something to drink. Can I get you another glass of wine?"

"WHERE'S ALANA?" I asked. "I think these are her keys." I found Brand in the kitchen. He was washing a wineglass in the sink. It was about one in the morning. A few diehard partiers remained, sitting out under the stars, playing music and drinking. I was about to go home, having finally convinced Thad that he couldn't come with me.

"She's passed out on the sofa," Brand said. He turned off the water and set the glass on a rack. "Hang them on that hook by the door. She won't be using them tonight."

I blushed at the inference: *She* would be spending the night there. I put the keys up and was about to go out when he said, "So Stacy . . . did you enjoy yourself?"

I turned and looked at him steadily. "Which time?" I said. It was a pointed reference to the last time we'd really had anything to say to each other. The Fourth of July.

He knew it, too. He didn't try to pretend he didn't. And he didn't joke about it, which I almost hoped he would, because that would have finished it for me. He was looking at me solemnly. He took a step toward me, and for a moment I thought he was going to try to kiss me again, and I wanted him to, so much, and yet I wasn't about to let him just kiss me whenever he felt like it. I turned away from him and said: "It was a nice party, if that's what you're asking."

"Yeah." He leaned back against the counter. "It was a nice party. It's kinda embarrassing, y'know. Everyone saying good-bye, and being uncommonly nice to you, like they figure you're not going to make it back, or something. But it was swell of Tess to invite everybody. I appreciated everyone coming. I appreciated *you* coming."

"It was *swell?*"

"Yes, swell. What, don't you like that word? It's a good word."

I began to laugh.

"I love your laugh, Stacy."

"It must be something," I said dreamily, ignoring the emotion the simplest of his words could raise in me. "To think, in just a few hours you'll be flying off to the highest mountains in the world." I was resting against the counter, studying the tile, running my finger along a grout line.

"Yeah. I guess." He sounded melancholy.

"But that's nothing new for you, is it, Mr. Explorer . . . ?" I tried to tease him, but he didn't smile.

"I'm going to miss you, Stacy," he said.

He's drunk, I thought. He doesn't mean it.

"Why?" I shrugged, my voice still teasing and flippant. "I never see you anyway."

He looked at me with perplexity. "Are you saying that isn't the way you want it?"

"The way *I* want it?" I was bewildered by that.

"Well, *isn't* that the way you want it?"

This caught me off guard. "I don't know. Maybe it is." I hated the way I sounded, so detached and flippant.

"Maybe?" he said. "You're not sure?"

"I'm not sure about anything these days."

"Well, I'm sure. I *will* miss *you.*" He reached out and took my hand, gave it a squeeze. His fingers were wet. "I miss you all the time."

I drew my hand away as if afraid we might be caught touching. Or that I might get burned.

"Bring me back a piece of the Himalayas," I said blithely.

He gave me a long, significant look. "I will. That's a promise."

"Bring it home to me in your suitcase."

"I'm not bringing a suitcase. I carry my home on my back. Like a turtle."

"Better yet."

"How is business?" he asked suddenly.

"Business?" I stuttered. "Well . . . pretty good, so far, considering . . . Why do you want to know?"

"I suppose Thaddeus takes good care of you."

"Don't sound so glum about it. He's a great client."

"*Hmm.* I'll bet he is. Anyway, that's good. I'm glad things are going all right with that."

"You . . . are?" I wasn't sure what he was getting at.

"Yes, I am. You're not thinking about cashing it all in, moving back to the Bay Area, are you? That's what I'm asking."

"No." I looked at him warily. "Not at this point, anyway. Why?"

"I don't know." He shrugged. "I was just wondering if you'll be here when I get back."

"Well, that depends a lot on when—and if—you come back, I guess," I replied lightly. "They say a lot of people who climb the Himalayas never return."

For a moment he was silent.

"I'm sorry, Brand," I said quickly. "I don't know where that came from. I know you've lost friends in those mountains yourself."

"No, that's all right," he replied slowly. "You know, I think they died right where they would have wanted to die. Though maybe they would've put it off a bit longer." He flashed me a sad grin.

I took a deep breath. Oh, what a beautiful man.

"I'll come back," said Brand.

"I'll see you then."

"Can I write to you?"

"You know the address."

"I know it."

"And you know how to write," I said.

"You're punchy tonight, aren't you, girl?" He moved closer and this time I didn't turn away.

"I carry my shell on my back too," I murmured. "For protection."

"D'you think you need to protect yourself from me?"

I nodded. "Yes, I think I do."

"You do?" He was so close now I could feel the warmth of him.

"Do what?" Tess came swaying into the room. Brand and I drew apart, startled.

"Do what?" she repeated loudly. She was pretty drunk.

"Never mind," Brand said with a laugh.

"Brand, will you make me some tea?" she drawled. "I'd do it myself but I'm afraid I'll burn down your house."

"No problem." He turned away from me and went to get the kettle off the stove. He put it under the faucet and turned on the water.

I escaped from the kitchen, crazy with all the emotions he aroused in me.

In the living room, Alana slept gracefully, draped across the sofa, her long, languid limbs like a caress on the cushions. Her eyes were closed, her lashes dark against her cheeks, her hair tousled, lips full and parted. She was even more beautiful than usual because she looked so abandoned, the usual haughty expression she wore had vanished from her face and she looked as sweet as a child. I wanted to dump a pail of cold water on her. Instead, I slipped out of the house and ran home.

In the morning when I woke up, Brand was gone. There was a single long-stem red rose laying on my porch. I found myself hoping that Brand had put it there, but I figured it was probably a token from Thad.

Chapter Nineteen

WITH LATE SUMMER came the breaking of ground at Thad's place. I was nervous about starting to build so late in the year. There was no way we would have the house dried-in before the rainy weather set in. But Thad was insistent. He wanted to begin.

"God, but this is impressive," Thad said when the excavation was underway.

"Isn't it?" I agreed gaily.

"Such a pity Brand isn't here to see this."

"Yes," I said. How beautiful the house would be, emerging from its wild surroundings, a thing of the land itself, integral to the hillside as the trees and rocks, oriented to the movement of the sun. Even someone who was wary of the spoiling of nature would find it so. Brand would have enjoyed the building, if he were here, being a builder himself. He would have appreciated the creativity and work and money and time involved in such a project as this, and I imagined him watching me with admiration as I talked knowledgeably with the construction workers. These were the sort of daydreams I indulged in.

I WAS UNEASY about Mrs. Shapiro and the strange things she had said. I wrote her, but I received no response. I called several times, and finally the receptionist told me the old woman had moved to another retirement home—in Stockton, she thought; she couldn't give me any more information other than to say she had moved there to be closer to her daughter.

"If you like, I'll take your name and if we hear anything, we'll let her know you called."

"All right," I said. "Thank you."

"Don't worry. I'm sure she'll be in touch with you," the receptionist said kindly.

THE ODD, THREATENING things that had plagued me seemed to have stopped and did not resume during the months Brand was gone. No more phone calls, no more strange packages in the mail, no more threats. I tried to analyze why this might be so. I wanted to find any explanation but the obvious. If Alana was pulling the pranks, wouldn't she be less inclined to continue them with Brand gone? If it was Brand . . .

I found the idea a struggle.

If it was Brand—

No.

Face the possibility.

If it was *Brand,* he was, of course, out of the country.

ONE NIGHT I returned late from a movie with Tess. I had been hanging out with her more since Brand had been away. Alana's car was in the driveway and lights were on in the Barn.

"Looks like you have company," I said.

"Alana isn't company," Tess said.

"What is she?"

"She's—moody, lately. Brand hasn't written to her once."

We said goodnight and parted. I went into the dark, silent house and straight up to my bedroom. I opened the drawer of my writing table, took out an envelope, turned out all the

lights but the one at my bedside, climbed into bed, curled up
in the blankets, and pulled out the letter. I relished the thin
crackly delicacy of the airmail paper and the strange exotic
postmark. It had become completely familiar to me. I had
studied it thoroughly.

I lay back against the mound of pillows, staring at the
ceiling, holding the letter to my heart. I was astonished and
incredulous to think he had written to me and not to *her.* I'd
had the letter nearly a week.

Ah, well, her letter is probably lost in transit, I told myself. But I knew he had not written to her like this.

I sat up and unfolded the bundle of papers, each sheet
sheer and precious as gold leaf. What Brand had written was
a sort of journal of his travels.

> *Today we are leaving Katmandu. I don't know
> when I'll be back to the city. Last night the moon was
> full and I wondered when you would see it.*
>
> *I imagine you here with me, and I talk to you, I am
> telling you my thoughts and impressions, all the emo-
> tions this strange land evokes in me. Humility and
> wonder and gratitude. Desolation, fear. And longing.
> A sort of pain at the incredible beauty, like a piercing
> in my heart, my guts. But then I wonder—is it the
> mountains conjuring this soaring and diving and
> drumming of my spirit, or is it you? You, woman-who-
> has-stolen-into-my-life. You, elusive Raven.*

I put the paper down, unable to read more, embarrassed
with the intensity of the feeling coming through the words.
But why did he write these words to me? I thrust the letter
away as if it was on fire. But I could not stay away from it.
I grabbed it up again. I read and reread his words, which,
though never directly declarative, were full of love for the
mountains and the sky, and, it seemed, for me as well.

> *. . . Zeppelin's "The Rover" is going through my mind,
> and I think of you, on the dark side of the globe. I al-
> ways took pride in the discipline of living in the* now,

without worrying about the future. But now I find my-self wondering, conjecturing, obsessing. When will I see you again?

I studied Brand's handwriting. He had nice handwriting; hurried, yet elegant and dashing. He was a good speller.

His writing is sexy, I thought, the way certain men drive is sexy. Sometimes I ached for him physically. His writing made me ache.

But what about Alana? It bothered me. If he was promised to Alana and writing to me like this—! And what about our kiss on the Fourth of July? The memory of it lay just under the surface of my consciousness all the time and now it emerged, as it often did. The surprising softness of his mouth. Then the hardness, demanding, almost biting—then gentleness again, supplicating. Bodies trembling with the energy. The determination in his expression when he searched me out. His face, all his expressions, imperious, proud, unflinching, unguarded. He would not let me look away. His hands were like beggars, his fingers starved men. I felt them on my back, my neck, my arms. But there were voices calling at the edge of the precipice. The voices of reason, caution. Prudence. Calling down a warning, clear and unwelcome and resented. I wanted to fling myself into the abyss.

And I would have, but for the demons, or angels—

They shone their light down on me and I escaped you be-fore it was too late.

What would have happened that Fourth of July night if those hikers hadn't come down the trail?

What would his hands have done to me?

TOO AGITATED TO sleep. I decided I would talk to Alana. Her car had been parked at the Barn earlier—she might still be there, she might be awake. I didn't know what I would say to her, what questions I could ask about her and Brand, but I was crazy with not knowing how it was between them. Conventional wisdom said they were a couple, but sometimes conventional wisdom was wrong. Suddenly the question of Alana loomed foremost in my mind and I felt I couldn't rest until I had settled it, once and for all. Perhaps obsessing upon *her* made it easier to ignore the darker obstacles between Brand and me.

Her car was still sitting in front of the Barn. I felt determined and wild beneath a skyful of stars, running up the steps in my silent moccasins. The front door was open and I could hear music playing softly within. I knocked and entered the house.

There was a hush about the place. Tess was sleeping in her chair in the living room, a book on her knee. The stereo in there was silent—the music seemed to be coming from another part of the house. I went toward the den, moving silently down the hall so as not to wake anyone who might be asleep.

The music grew louder. Some of the sounds I heard weren't music, but voices, though the cries they made weren't words, but something more primitive. I thought it was the sound of the television. I peeked around the edge of the door into the den and discovered the voices weren't from actors on TV. Alana and Saul lay entwined on the sofa in violent coupling, their clothes half-torn away from their bodies, skin against skin, slick with sweat and deeply flushed, thrashing, rhythmic, furious, mouths and tongues tangled, moaning, biting, and panting for breath. They were so completely engrossed in each another they had no idea I had stumbled upon them.

I sprang back into the dark hallway and pressed against the wall as if I could make myself disappear by sheer will. But the image was already pressed into my brain—a beautiful, repulsive sight, their bodies slapping against each other, desperate and driven.

I slipped out of the house and ran down the drive, full of a guilty elation, the night wind breathing warm against my skin, lifting me like freedom. I didn't care anymore, about what Alana and Brand were supposed to be to one another. As far as I was concerned, Brandon Vandevere was fair game.

Chapter Twenty

IN THE MIDDLE of October I got a call from Mrs.
Shapiro. She told me she had moved to a retirement
home near Stockton, as the receptionist had told me, and
had been rather preoccupied with her daughter, who had
been having health problems, which was why she had been
out of touch.

"I hope your daughter is feeling better—?" I said awkwardly.

"She's been improving lately. She's out of the hospital
now, anyway. It's better now that I am living closer to her, I
think. We can take care of each other." She breathed a sigh
into the phone. She sounded tired. "Anyway. I have straightened out the situation with the house. I want to talk to you
about it, Stacy, but . . . I'd like to talk to you in person. I'll
tell you all about it when I see you, all right?"

"So what is this all about?" I asked, trying to be stern. I
pressed her, but she remained vague. She said it was nothing I needed to worry about and she would explain it all
when I visited her, which I agreed to do as soon as possible.

I hung up the phone feeling exasperated with her cagey

responses to my questions. Even on the phone, she intimidated me a little, and I didn't push her hard enough. But I was too busy to think about it much, and I resigned myself to waiting another couple of weeks before I could take the time to go see her. But I wondered. Was the old woman simply "crazy" when it came to the house, like her daughter said she was?

One night I was cleaning out one of the smaller, odd little rooms upstairs when I came across a large book, brittle with age, furred with the dust of years. It was a scrapbook, and it had belonged to Tim Shapiro, Mrs. Shapiro's son. It was something that might have come after the baby book years, filled with photos of baseball teams, track ribbons, scout awards, newspaper clippings of team winnings and notice of a spelling bee victory. I was struck anew with the impression of Mrs. Shapiro's son as a good-hearted, simple boy, perpetually young.

He was still young when the scrapbook ended abruptly, an unfinished witness to a life cut short. But perhaps the empty pages at the end of the book signified the coming of age of the young man, after which the baseball teams dropped away and certificates and ribbons became meaningless. I knew he was dead, but as far as I knew, he might have died at a rather advanced age, judging from the age of his mother and sister. Then I thought of the condolence cards I had found in Mrs. Shapiro's letters, and wondered if they were for him. He would have been very young at the time those cards were sent. I turned over the remaining empty pages, feeling bereft. It was like reading a book through to the end, only to find the last chapter missing.

Then, between the last leaves of the scrapbook, I found the announcement of Tim's death at the age of twenty, a brief, vague paragraph clipped from a newspaper long ago. The lack of detail in the obituary puzzled me. There was no mention of cause of death, which only made me more curious to know it. He had been so young when he died.

Accident? Illness? I wondered. There was no clue in any of the correspondence I had found. It was as if any trace of explanation had been deliberately eliminated.

Something nagged at my memory. Something in all the thick piles of letters that had seemed fragmented and meaningless at the time.

I went downstairs to the library. Digging through the boxes with the fervor of a detective, I finally found the sympathy notes I had discovered in the closet so many months ago when I first bought the house.

Our hearts are heavy for you . . . He was a wonderful young man . . . May God comfort you in your sorrow . . .

Yes. They were talking about Tim.

And the one that stood out in my mind, because of its eerie strangeness, written on lined paper in the now familiar, agitated, angular writing of the writer I knew only as *L:*

Now he belongs to me . . .

I began to read the *L* letters, which I had avoided previously, mostly because they tended to be tedious, disjointed, difficult to decipher. But now, as I read, I found clues, like puzzle pieces, beginning to fit together to make a picture. Often the clues would appear in the middle of an otherwise mundane bit of writing:

. . . and we had cabbage for dinner again, last night, they know how it doesn't suit me, I told them I can't digest cabbage. It wasn't my fault. I warned you. You should have heeded my warning. You should have known. You should have stopped it. Dr. Cannon said he didn't think I even belonged in here. He believes I am innocent, even if no one else will believe me. He says I will be getting out soon, if I continue to improve . . .

Am I to be locked in here for good? I tried to poison myself because I didn't want Tim to be in heaven alone. But they wouldn't even let me die. They want to punish me.

These letters had been written from prison . . . or a mental institution.

Dr. White said So, when you shot him, you simply didn't know what you were doing. But I knew it was a trick question, that he was trying to get me to pretend I didn't know how to handle a gun.

He said: Do you really believe it was suicide? And I said no. He didn't kill himself, and I know it wasn't me who killed him. It was the house. He committed suicide because the house commanded it. I tried to warn everyone, all along. I will continue to warn them, and you. When I get out of here, I will return and write the warning in my own blood on the floorboards of the house if I have to, because that is how much I care.

But you didn't use your own blood, did you? I thought. You used red paint. Did you kill the boy in the dining room of this house, my house? *But who were you?* A jealous girlfriend? A crazed neighbor? A member of the family?

And you *weren't* locked up for good, were you?

The idea that this deranged person had been freed to return and paint the letters on the floor—my dining room floor—was unnerving, though I knew it was something that had happened long ago. There were no more clues in the correspondence. I went through it all.

I was filled with a horror so immediate, I had to keep reminding myself these letters were written thirty years earlier; there was no threat to me from their author, who was probably long dead.

TESS DECIDED TO throw a big Halloween party. Everybody we knew was planning their costume, and no one would reveal what they were going to wear. There was to be live music and catered food.

"We could just potluck, you know," I said to Tess. We were sitting in the den of the barn addressing invitations to the party. It was good to spend time with her. She was always so kind to me.

"I know, but I want to make it special. Brand should be back in time for the party and I don't want him to have to worry about cooking or anything else. This time he gets to relax."

"He always seems pretty relaxed when he's cooking," I said.

"I know, and the food won't be as good if Brand doesn't do it," she said. "But in case he doesn't get back in time, I'd better have the caterer."

I could see she was sold on the idea, and I didn't argue with her. She picked up her list and frowned. "Is this everybody?"

"What about Yolanda and Father Daniel?" I asked.

"Oh—good idea. You know I never really got to know them until that day we all worked on your house after the tree fell. They were both very nice." She jotted down their names at the end of her list.

She chatted on about a recent letter she had received from Brand, and I listened with sullen interest. After the one long and strangely romantic letter, Brand had not written me again. Maybe he regretted sending me that letter.

"So . . ." I tried to sound casual. "What does Alana hear from Brand?"

"Oh, I don't know. He finally wrote her, I think."

I thought of the night I had seen Alana and Saul together on the sofa, right where we were sitting now.

"Do you think she loves him?" I blurted, immediately wishing I hadn't. What I really wanted to know was, did *he* love her?

She seemed surprised at the question. "It's difficult to know, with Alana. She's extremely private. But—it does seem as if she has finally decided to commit to Brand. Judging from the way things were going before he left."

She has a strange way of showing her commitment, I thought.

"How *were* things going?" I asked.

"Well, Stacy, all she ever did was tease him. She never

really let him get close. I think he was beginning to cool on her, and that's when she suddenly decided she would deign to accept him."

"You sound a little sarcastic, Tess."

"Well, Alana's a beautiful woman, and I think she's basically a good person, but the way she's treated Brand, it wouldn't bother me a bit if he dumped her on her butt. She would deserve it."

"So, she broke his heart, huh?"

She was thoughtful. "Oh—I don't know if I would say *that*. In the beginning she was the unattainable, gorgeous woman that Brand enjoyed pursuing. She wouldn't sleep with him, which only strengthened her position. I think he was a little disillusioned when he actually started getting to know her. To tell you the truth, now that he's finally caught her I don't think he knows what to do with her. They really don't have much in common, I don't think. Not that you always have to have that much in common. But deep down, on the soul level, I just don't think he really clicks with her. Not like he does with *you*."

Yes. A thrill of gratitude went through me at those words. I laughed, embarrassed.

"There was a time there I thought you and Brand . . ." she trailed off on that thought, then went on hurriedly: "But I guess if there was a standing offer to Alana, Alana finally accepted it."

"Standing offer?"

"The role of girlfriend. Possibly more, who knows? Brand's looking to settle down and have a family. He wants kids. He's ready. Which makes him more vulnerable, I think. Not that I'm all that worried about him. He's got a good head on his shoulders. He'll do what's right."

"So they've decided to marry?"

"Alana hinted at something like that. Brand hasn't said anything about it to me."

I was cheered by the dubious note in her voice. "I could never figure out if they were an item or not," I said.

"We were used to her, popping in all the time, but it was always on her own terms. She might or might not come to dinner, if she was invited, or to a party, if we were having one. If she felt like it, she would grace us with her presence. But she wouldn't be dependable. She refused to treat Brand special. She acted like we were all just, you know, good friends, knowing full well she was teasing him, and playing that up in a subtle way. She even brought other men she was dating over to the Barn to socialize."

"Really? And how did he react?"

"At first Brand was floored by that. Later he laughed it off. After awhile she saw it wasn't bothering him so much and she stopped doing those kinds of things. Something changed in her. I think it's because when you come to know Brand, you can't treat him with disrespect. You can get mad at him, you can be exasperated with him, but you can't not respect him."

"When did things change between them?"

"Oh, I don't know, exactly. I think maybe it was the Fourth of July. You and Brand went off alone together that night and don't think she didn't notice. I think she realized she was on the verge of losing any chance she had with him if she didn't make her move."

"So she made her move," I tried to sound ironic.

Tess put down her pen and her expression grew intense. "I'll tell you about that," she said, her voice dropping. "She came over the day after the Fourth of July picnic. Brand had to go somewhere, but she stayed around anyway. I was cleaning out the shed and she started to help me. She stayed all afternoon, helping. We were both filthy by the time Brand got home. He seemed startled to see her, but he went in and made dinner while she took a shower. She came into the kitchen wearing nothing but a tea towel.

"A tea towel!"

"I swear she must have picked out our smallest towel to wrap around herself. I was with him in the kitchen when she came out of the shower. She said, '*Brand* . . .'" Tess imitated a breathy, Marilyn Monroe kind of voice—"'Brand, can I borrow one of your *big shirts? Please?*' So he went and got her one of his shirts. She could have asked *me* for something, we're not that much different in size, but no. She took the shirt and draped it over her arm, walking around the kitchen, tasting things, giggling, brushing up against Brand, and meanwhile the towel is slipping down, falling open. Alana's a tease, but this time she wasn't just teasing. She was offering."

"I get it."

"I got out of there fast," Tess went on. "I went and took a shower myself. Alana had steamed up the bathroom real good, used up all the hot water. I went out to a movie with Tom and when I got back at midnight her car was still here. The next day Alana hinted to me that we might soon be planning a wedding. But she wouldn't say anything more. As I said, Alana is a very private person and Brand rarely talks to me about things like that. So you can draw your own conclusions."

"So. That was that," I said inanely.

"Yeah. I guess that was that." She finished the stack of invitations she had been working on and slipped a rubber band around them. She leaned back against the sofa, thinking. "But afterward I noticed Brand was—I don't know. *Subdued*. Depressed, almost. Not like a man who had finally made a conquest. Alana, on the other hand, was triumphant. She was here every evening from then on. She began to act like the lady of the manor."

She'd done that for a long time, I thought. "Did that bother you?" I asked.

"Only in that I wondered if it was what Brand really wanted. I've got my place out back, so I have my space. The house is Brand's, it's his domain, and he can share it as he pleases. Alana and I have always gotten along all right. If it had come about six months ago, I would have been happy for Brand. But now, I'm not so sure it's what he needs, or wants, anymore."

"Well, he's a big boy," I said. "He doesn't have to do what he doesn't want to do."

"You know what they say. Beware of what you ask for, you just might get it. Sometimes getting untangled from what you thought you wanted is harder than acquiring it in the first place."

"Maybe. But I can't see Brand as someone who would stay in a . . . a relationship against his will."

"He wouldn't. Not for long."

"Tess, there's something I've been wondering about for a long time. If Brand wanted my house so much, why didn't he just buy it?"

"He didn't know it was for sale."

"He didn't know it was for sale! But my real estate agent told me she thought . . . she thought he was quite interested in the property—that he was actively discouraging others from even looking at it. Implying that he *knew* it was for sale."

Tess shrugged. "I really don't remember. I do recall hearing that we had a new neighbor, how surprised we all were. We saw Iona come and put up a real estate sign on the place. It said 'sale pending' on it when they put it up. Brand was fit to be tied. He said he had asked the old woman a couple of years ago to sell him the place, if she ever wanted to sell it. But toward the end, the two of them had a bit of a falling out, weren't seeing so much of one another. Then we heard she was moving away and the house had been sold. Anyway," she added, "if Brand does end up with Alana, it's just as well he didn't get that old house. She hates the place."

"Oh really?" My voice was dry. "Well, maybe it's all for the best, then," I said falsely. I felt compelled to change the subject. It was just too hard. "So, you've been seeing quite a bit of Tom, lately, haven't you?"

She closed her eyes and smiled.

IT WAS A few days before Halloween when I smelled the odor again. It was a sweet, pungent odor, like specialty tobacco. It seemed to be coming from inside the house, but I couldn't find anything burning. I went outside and smelled nothing but the clean air and the trees. Inside again, I caught a hint of the smell, strongest near the library. I opened each cupboard, but found nothing. Gradually the burning smell dissipated and I thought something must have wafted in from outside through the open window. I decided I would have Russ look over the electrical system for me next time he came up to help me on the house.

Then I had the accident.

The day before Halloween I was driving down the mountain to pick up some things Tess needed for the party. It was a scintillating, gorgeous day. Huge jagged white clouds were moving fast across the intense cobalt blue of the sky. I had the heater on and the windows down. I was feeling high with the tangy autumn wind in my hair and the music on the stereo—Zeppelin's "Rover" was beaming up from a rock station in Modesto, and I was thinking about Brand, as always. He had mentioned this song in his letter. Another coincidence. If I had thought his absence might help me let go of him a little, I was proven wrong—it had only gotten worse. But I was feeling fatalistic. Ready to go for what I wanted and to hell with the consequences.

The vibration came on suddenly; the car began to shimmy and I lost control on the curvy, narrow mountain road. I remembered something about steering into the side of the mountain rather than going off it, if you happened to be in the unfortunate position of having to make that choice, but I didn't have much steering left. Still, it was the only thing I could think of, so I yanked the wheel and the car lurched across the oncoming lane just as a truck came around the bend, straight toward me. The truck driver's quick reflexes saved us both. He just missed me and I swerved against the mountain.

I was okay, except for some bruises around my belly, where my seat belt caught me. But the front end of my car was crumpled like an accordion. If I'd gone off the other side I would have plummeted for hundreds of feet to the granite rocks of the river below.

I made it home hours later, courtesy of AAA, without the party favors. My car was totaled. The lug nuts had been found at intervals along the mountain road. The wheel had come completely off the car. Everyone told me how lucky I was to be alive. I must have been in shock, because I could feel nothing.

HALLOWEEN. THE PARTY matured like a fast-growing organism with a personality all its own. Cars filled the drive and witches, ghosts, and vampires crossed the meadow and inhabited the Barn, the costumes so well done I hardly recognized anybody. I had planned to be Mata Hari but I had forgotten to get my costume out of the trunk of my car before it was towed away. So Tess draped me with silk scarves, fixing them on me in layers until only my eyes showed, and they didn't look like my eyes after she lined them heavily in a smoky black imitation of kohl.

"You look like you just escaped from the harem, Stacy," she said approvingly.

I felt like I had escaped, from something more immediately perilous than a harem. I had escaped my own death.

Over the past year, I had found myself continually challenged to stay sane. The constant subtle and not-so-subtle harrassments had piled up and I wondered if I would ever be able to truly relax in my skin ever again. I had fought with myself over and over to stay strong, to deal with it, not give into the fear and freak out. At the back of my mind was the knowledge that I could always jump into my Celica and run away.

But then it began to seem that no matter where I went, the Creeper was there. I wasn't even safe in my car. And now my car was destroyed; I should have been destroyed along with it. I felt trapped, somehow, and deeply lonely. I couldn't trust anyone, not even Tess, who had been nothing but kind to me since the day I'd met her, and who was smiling at me now with that sweet, benign way of hers. I couldn't trust anyone, not even the one I wanted to trust the most.

Tess had received a call from Brand that afternoon. He was still in Asia pursuing a story, she said, and wouldn't be back until next week. The disappointment made me feel heavy. Tess wasn't too happy about it, either. She was a little anxious at the thought of having to do the party herself. Saul wouldn't be much good to her. I promised her I would help.

I took a deep breath and held back the nervous tears crowding and stinging the corners of my eyes. I didn't want to cry, not in front of Tess. I looked at the mirror, tried to concentrate on the unfamiliar image shimmering there. It was me.

I felt sultry and strange, as if I were looking out at the world through a slit in a curtain.

The costume raised my mood, as did the sheer fun of seeing how everyone else had dressed up. The game of the evening was trying to figure out who everyone was. It wasn't hard to recognize Saul, even with his thick white makeup, black cape, and fangs, or Alana, a French maid in a tiny black skirt, frilly white cap and apron. And there was Tess, as Carmen Miranda, balancing a plate of fruit on her head. Others weren't so easy to fathom, like a rather debonair and bulky white refrigerator who kept bumping into people, a friendly two-headed zombie, a mysterious ghost. But the two-headed zombie *had* to be Callie and Ralph.

Tess was introducing people—those who had revealed their identities, anyway—and I helped her get drinks for everyone. I was pleased when Yolanda and Father Daniel appeared, dressed as a pair of tourists, wearing sunglasses and loud Hawaiian shirts, sporting tote bags stuffed with maps and sunscreen, and cameras slung over their shoulders.

Dracula tried to bite my neck.

"Cut it out, Saul," I said, shrugging him away. He was attempting to bite the necks of all the women at the party. I was fending off his fangs when I noticed a pirate in high leather boots with large folded cuffs, black leather trousers, a billowing white shirt, gloves, a sash, and a sword. A bandanna covered his hair and he wore a golden hoop in his ear.

I peered at him through my veils. From across the room, I saw him take note of me, too. I was sure I had met him at another party, but a black leather mask covered his face and I could only guess at his identity.

Jeff, I thought. Who else could he be? He seemed so familiar. The leather trousers accentuated his strong, lithe thighs. He reminded me of Brand—the long solid line of him, the male grace, and the height, though Brand wasn't quite as slender.

The party was going strong and things were beginning to loosen up. Conversation hummed steadily just below the music, and people started to dance. Saul did the twist with a young mermaid. Tom, in the persona of Jimmy Buffet, was playing bartender, and he was in his element. Alana was dancing in the corner with a handsome alien, a bit slower and closer than the music warranted.

Even Tess had forgotten her pre-party anxieties, and now she was laughing and swaying to the beat of the drums as she moved through the crowd, tending to her guests.

But for me there was something missing. Some*one*. I had been looking forward to this occasion as one where Brand would be in attendance, and he wasn't. I still was feeling dazed from my car accident the day before. It nagged at me, being without a car, like my wings had been clipped. Strange that I had sailed through the whole incident with hardly a scratch. Strangest, and most disturbing of all, was my sense that it had not been an accident.

But I resolved not to dwell on that now. "La Bamba" was playing on the stereo and I got up to join Father Daniel, who was demonstrating the Mexican hat dance, which really didn't go with the music, to Yolanda and a tall mummy.

The pirate made his way across the room and suddenly he was dancing with me, reaching out, taking my hand in his. I could feel the strength of his hand through the leather of his gloves. I wished I could see the expression behind that stiff leather covering over his face. I couldn't even tell the color of his eyes. He glanced at me through the slits in his black mask and looked away.

"I know you," I said. But he ignored me.

He was a passable dancer. He had no fancy moves, but he seemed to feel the rhythm of the music instinctively, as if it was coming from inside his body. He drew me closer, and encircled me with his arm. He moved so gracefully so that I moved gracefully with him, though I was startled to be led this way. His hands on me were sensitive and confident, almost arrogant, and yet shy, somehow. I loved that contradiction. He kept me centered and provided guidance for the momentum so that we moved comfortably together, and our timing was on, even when he whirled me around, let me go, and pulled me back again, we found ourselves in easy matching motion. It was exhilarating, to be with such a partner. I was a little in love with him by the time we were finished.

"I know you," I said. "But who *are* you?"

He didn't say anything, and he was careful not to let me look into his eyes. I was certain I knew the man behind that mask. He held my hand after the dance until the music started again. When I heard the strains of a slow song, I was suddenly desperately thirsty.

"Thanks for the dance," I panted. I felt the sweat in my hair, dampening the veils which had fallen away from my face. "I've got to get something to drink." I let go of his hand and escaped the dance floor as the other couples paired up, men and women slipping their arms around each other, drawing closer. Tess and Tom. Alana and the alien. The two-headed zombie. They began moving sensuously to the slower tempo. Somebody dimmed the lights.

Standing by the table, I watched the dancers, thinking about how nice it would be to have somebody hold me like that. The pirate was intriguing, but he wasn't the one I wanted. I closed my eyes, swaying slightly to the music. A strange peace descended upon me. I was thinking of Brand. Not that I ever stopped thinking about him, but I suddenly felt his presence with me, as if he had visited me in a dream.

The French maid and the alien were growing friendlier, their bodies pressed tightly together at the edge of the cluster of dancers, and from time to time she would laughingly fend off the attentions of his lips on her neck and mouth.

She wouldn't be dancing with that alien so closely if Brand were here, I thought.

"What? Not participating in the mating dance?"

I looked up at the great white refrigerator who appeared to be grinning down at me.

"Let me guess," I said. "Thad the frost-free."

"I'll not reveal myself until you dance with me."

"Slow dance with a refrigerator?" I mused. "Why not?"

So we pushed our way into the little crowd and joined

hands as gracefully as possible. I could hardly control my giggling. The crowd loved it, even though we had broken the romantic mood. The song ended, and then came "Twist and Shout," and the refrigerator did the Charleston.

"There!" The great white cardboard edifice suddenly rose up like a skyscraper in an earthquake and crashed to the floor. Thad emerged from the wreckage with his curly hair all tousled. I reached down and gave him a hand up.

"Thank you, milady," he panted, scrambling to his feet. "Whew!" He wiped sweat off his brow. "You'd think it'd be cooler inside a refrigerator."

"Whatever possessed you to be a refrigerator, Thad?"

"I'm a voyeur. I wanted to see if the mayonnaise was dressing. Sorry. I don't know. I always think of the most uncomfortable costumes."

"Well, at least you're not stuck with Ralph all night," said one of the heads of the two-headed zombie. "But did you see that *pirate*? Who *is* he?"

"I wondered who he was, too," I said.

"He was *nice*."

"Never mind that," reprimanded the other head.

"Come on," the zombies coaxed. "Let's all dance together."

Thad grabbed me and drove me across the floor in an overwrought, mocking tango.

"You realize this dancing business is only a pretext I have devised to get you into my arms," he crooned.

"I suspected as much," I said. "Though I don't think you're the first guy in history to think of it." We joined a samba train, winding around the room and into the kitchen, then back out into the big room where we continued dancing wildly until we were all exhausted.

The candles in the pumpkins were burning down. The pumpkin pie was all gone; the faint-of-heart partiers had gone. What was left of the party was a mellow companionable friendliness. I stood next to the alien at the table, poured him a glass of wine. Alana went by and he trailed after her.

"That's Lothario, Alana's *friend*. Remember I told you

about him?" Saul had appeared at my side. "They've been
working out together a lot."

"Yes, I can picture them lifting weights together," I said.
"But is his name really Lothario?" I nodded toward a ghost,
all draped in white sheets. "Do you know who that is?"

"I've no idea. She's not very friendly, I've tried to talk to
her and she won't say three words to me."

"What about that pirate who was here earlier? Who was
he?"

He shrugged. "I'm not interested in the men."

"Oh, excuse me. How do you know that ghost is a
woman?"

"It has certain womanly attributes, if you look closely.
Think about it: How do *you* know that pirate is a man?"

Well, it was obvious.

"You know, I've never been to a costume party where
people were so eager to remain incognito," I said.

"It is strange, I agree. Usually they tear their wigs and
masks off after five minutes."

"Maybe they don't want their identities revealed. Maybe
they're party crashers."

"I don't see how they could be. Tess invited everyone in
town. And quite a few from out of town."

"Why don't you go over there and cut in?" I said. Alana
and the alien, whose name was actually Jerry, alias Lothario,
had resumed their sensual dancing.

"I suppose Brand would thank me if I did," murmured
Saul. "Look at them. Vandevere better get home soon before
someone samples the goods."

That was a typical Saul way of putting things.

"Like someone already hasn't?" I couldn't resist saying.
I lifted a brow and shot him a sly look, but it went past him.
He didn't miss a beat.

"Yeah, look at them," he said, staring at Alana and the
alien.

I sighed. I was thinking again how nice it would be when
I could slip away and go home. The party had staled for me.
The dashing pirate had disappeared. And where was Thad
when you needed him? A little of Saul went a long way. But

Thad was gone too. Hadn't even said good-bye—probably got himself picked up.

"Why don't you go for it?" I followed Saul's gaze to Alana's backside and nudged him a little, feeling perverse. "Go on, cut in. I know you like her."

"I like a lot of ladies." He sounded almost insulted. "I couldn't do that to Brand."

"You couldn't, huh? But all is fair in love and war, right?"

Suddenly, into the room swept a magnificent sheik, dramatic and flowing in his long white robes. He strode directly up to me, seized me, and shouted, "Ah, my lovely Caucasian jewel. She will be an exquisite addition to my harem!" The robes were Tess's white sheets and the sheik was Thad. He had draped himself in white linen and tied a knotted scarf around his head. He looked great.

"The prospect of being owned by a sheik, or any other man, doesn't particularly appeal to me," I said through clenched teeth, struggling with his grip on my arm.

"Nonsense. You dressed this way tonight because you secretly want to be possessed by a real man."

"Well, a *real* man, maybe," I said, and got a big laugh for that one. Everyone in the room was watching us. I struggled theatrically and Thad played to perfection his role of spurned sheik, until I almost believed he would have me tortured and decapitated for resisting him.

"Enough of your nonsense, woman!" My sheik picked me up and was about to carry me off—I was laughing so hard I was almost crying—when the dashing masked pirate suddenly reappeared from nowhere. With a sweep of his arm he drew a sword from its sheath on his belt and set it across our path.

"Unhand the lady," said the pirate quietly.

Thad allowed me to slide down from his arms. I ended up on the floor while he faced his challenger indignantly. I looked up at them, the virile pirate and the flowing sheik, poised for battle. "She's mine, infidel," Thad rasped in his best sheik's voice.

But the pirate was armed, and the sheik was not. With a simple flick of his blade, the pirate separated Thad and me.

"If I had brought my scimitar with me, you would be dog meat, Christian!" shouted Thad, shaking his fist at the pirate.

The pirate reached down and I gave him my hand.

"Come, lady," he murmured. "Let us away." The fancy words were charmingly at odds with his rugged voice. The voice that pierced me like the blade of his sword. By his voice I knew his identity. I tried to stand up as gracefully as I could, but my veils had slipped and twisted around me. I stumbled and he caught me, he pulled me against him for a moment as he righted me. I reached out for his mask.

He allowed me to peel it off, and his face was revealed, at once strange and familiar.

Tess was beaming: apparently she had been in on the prank, but Alana had gone white. She exclaimed: "Well, Brand! What a dirty trick! I can't believe you didn't tell us you were home!"

"I can't believe you pulled off the deception, Brand," Tess said. "People kept asking me who the dashing pirate was. I said you were the propane delivery man."

"The bringer of gas," said Saul, who pretended he had known all along. Thad was standing off to the side in his wilted sheik costume, having had the show stolen right out from under him, which was something he wasn't used to. He was dumbfounded. Brand was usually the one who didn't even want to dress up in a costume, he said. He couldn't believe it either.

After her initial outburst Alana recovered herself and stood near Brand, her arms folded about herself, a bemused, nervous expression on her face. I almost felt sorry for her.

Now Brand was taking the welcoming he hadn't been offered before his identity was known.

"Hey, Brand—"

"Good to have you back, buddy—"

"Did you climb Everest?"

"Yes, did you?"

"Did you?"

"Nope. Well, not to the summit," he replied, and he

glanced at me. There was something in his expression, some question. Then he looked away.

"Shit," Ralph said. "You've got to go back again."

"Will you go back again?" Callie asked.

"No, I don't think so. But I never say never." Brand smiled, and looked at me again. Everyone was asking him about Nepal, the Himalayas, Mount Everest. "I love Nepal," he said. "Except for the leeches. The people are amazing. I can't even put the mountains into words."

"That's too bad, since that's what they pay you to do over there," said Ralph.

"Yes, it's a dilemma," grinned Brand. He seemed to have grown both older and younger during his months away. There was a tired wisdom about him, sketched in his body, which was leaner; and shining from his skin, which was an impossibly deep golden brown over the long muscles distinctly carved beneath his movements. When he took the bandanna off his head, his hair tumbled out, streaked platinum from the sun, and grown longer.

Alana moved to Brand's side and slipped her arm through his. "I hate to break up the party," she said in her smooth, cultivated voice, "But I have some private business with Mr. Vandevere."

Brand didn't respond to her immediately, and I noticed there was no fond embrace for her, at least not until she pointedly presented herself for one. Not that there was one for me, either, though the touch of his hand, clasped over mine when he'd helped me up from the floor, remained imprinted on my senses long after he had let go. Finally he turned to Alana, who looked up with hurt eyes and motioned toward the back rooms. "All right," he said. They went away together.

"I think Brand may not be completely satisfied with his little princess," said Callie. "Or should I say—his little French maid?"

"I don't think the little maid is terribly satisfied with her prince, either," said Saul. "Or should I say—her *pirate*?"

He's not her pirate, I thought. He's my pirate.

"She's going to clean his clock," Thad said with glee. "That was a dirty trick he pulled on her."

"She was awful tonight and she'll get what she deserves," Callie said. "Flirting with that alien!"

The alien Lothario was out on the patio smoking a cigarette.

"Oh, don't be so judgmental, Callie," scolded her husband. "That's how *you* act when I'm out of town, isn't it?"

"*I* restrict myself to earthlings, anyway."

"Hey, maybe Brand isn't so faithful to her either," Ralph said. "You know? It cuts both ways. You don't know how it is between them. I've never even heard Brand talk of her as his girlfriend."

"Alana certainly looked as though she had seen a ghost when that mask came off Brand's face," said Tess. "Speaking of ghosts—where *is* our ghost, anyway? I've been dying of curiosity to know who's beneath that sheet!" But the ghost had vanished.

I was thinking about the last time I had seen Brand, at his going-away party the night before he left for Nepal. And now he was back, and it was still a party. It seemed unreal. And Alana was still between us.

I could no longer bear the thought of Alana and Brand alone together, somewhere in the house, up in his rooms, probably. I was gripped with the urge to escape and I left without helping Tess clean up. She's got Brand and Alana to help her now, I thought bitterly.

I ran across the meadow and up the stone steps toward my house. I heard voices murmuring softly in the trees down toward the chapel and I paused, listening. I moved silently closer, feeling like a spy.

Yolanda and Father Daniel were standing together just down the slope. They were still wearing their silly costumes, strange in contrast with the intense emotional quality in their voices.

"No," she was saying. "No, Daniel. If anyone found out about us—"

He murmured something I couldn't hear.

"No," she said again, vehement. "For your sake, I couldn't—"

"Don't worry about my sake," he said curtly.

"How can I not?" she replied, stricken.

They're having an affair, I thought, awestruck, sad, and disturbed. I felt jealous of their closeness. He reached out and touched her cheek. I turned away and went silently to my house.

Later, lying in the darkness in my room, dreaming, I was still dancing in the arms of my mysterious pirate, only now his mask was gone and the strong rocky bones of his face were visible, and the expression was clear in his deep-water eyes.

I woke at dawn, and my first thought was of him. He had returned from his travels at long last. And still all I had of him were dreams. Dreams were all I would ever have of him.

Chapter Twenty-One

ALANA GAVE ME a lift to the village a few days later. She saw me walking, stopped, and offered me a ride. I accepted, too surprised to think of a reason not to.

"Bum luck about your accident," she said after she had pulled the car back onto the road. She pushed her sunglasses up on her hair like a headband. Her pale brown eyes were full of compassion. I was touched by the sincerity in her voice, but I was suspicious of her.

"I was lucky, I guess," I said.

Did you loosen the lug nuts, Alana?

It was an awful thing, this suspicion. Especially when I realized Brand had been back from Nepal by the time of my accident. I realized how happy I had been to think he had an alibi. But he had no alibi.

"You know my sister died in a car accident," she said, matter of fact.

"No, I didn't know. How old was she?"

"My age. She was my twin. It happened three years ago."

"Your twin! You must have been devastated."

"For a long time I couldn't even feel it. I was numb. I was

amazed at how easy it was to function. They say life goes on and it does, but it's never the same . . ."

For the first time I was struck with the real beauty of Alana, and I understood why Brand had been drawn to her, besides her striking good looks. She had strength and poise, so alluring a combination with her pale, seemingly fragile grace.

Her voice was smooth and rich and she spoke well. "So, no, I wasn't devastated. In fact, it's just been in the last year, I think, that I've allowed myself to start feeling again. Gradually. Little by little. Brand has helped me a lot with it."

She looked at me until I looked at her, like she wanted to read a response in my expression. She turned her eyes back to the road.

"Sometimes I'm so busy defending myself from feeling anything that I cut myself off from what I really want." There was a sound in her voice I had never heard before. In that moment she became more real to me, more dimensional than I had ever allowed her to be, and I thought about how I had shut *her* out in the same way I felt she shut me out.

Nevertheless, I felt on guard. I didn't trust her, because I didn't trust anyone.

"My mother died in a car accident," I said. "I always thought I was protected from car accidents after that. I always thought it would be too much of a coincidence if I died that way too."

"Really?" she looked at me quizzically. "How do you think you're going to die?"

"I'm going to die falling off a scaffolding on a jobsite when I'm about a hundred and fifteen!" I said quickly, picking the first image that came to mind to ward off the sudden chill her question raised in me.

She set her mouth in a grim smile. "I'm jealous of you, in a way," she said. "You're so disarming. You're like a child. Brand says you're like that little girl in . . ." she didn't finish.

"In what?"

"Never mind."

I noticed she was gripping the steering wheel so tightly

her knuckles were white. The calm smooth exterior was a mask, and it appeared to be cracking.

She said, "You know I'm going to be everything he needs."

I was at a loss.

"You can count on it," she added.

"I'm not so sure anybody is supposed to be everything someone else needs," I said slowly.

"He wants you," she snapped.

I didn't answer—what could I say to that?

"But it's too late." She laughed. Instantly she became calm and smooth again. "Because you know, we're engaged. We've been engaged a long time, before *you* were even around. We didn't tell anybody. We couldn't seem to pick a date, and put it off and put it off. After a while we stopped talking about it, but just before he left for Nepal I reminded him he was promised to me, and I intended to marry him when he got back."

"Congratulations."

"You see, I know how to play Brand. I know exactly how long to pay out the slack, and exactly when to reel it in."

"So you set the date, then? Before he left for Nepal?"

"Stacy," she said patronizingly, "You know Brand. He's not one to rush a decision. The important thing is the basic commitment is there."

"And is he committed to you?"

"There was never any doubt in my mind that when I was ready to commit, he would be there for me."

"What about you and Saul?"

"Saul?" she scoffed. She didn't even try to pretend she didn't know why I was asking. "There's nothing to compare there. It's Brand I'm going to be with. It's Brand I'm going to marry."

"Do you think you're ready for that kind of commitment?"

She pulled into the parking lot at the shopping center and turned off the engine. Slowly she turned to me and said in a quiet, gentle voice: "I am already committed. And, I will do anything I have to, to keep him." She was staring me in the eye. "Anything."

She said it conversationally, but it was a warning, pure and simple.

"Anything?" I said. "Would that include murder?"

"You're so melodramatic, Stacy."

"Well, if murder is too melodramatic for you, you might try monogamy," I said, and jumped out of the car.

Her head rose slowly above the soft roof of the convertible. She regarded me shrewdly. "You're very perceptive, Stacy. That's what I was just saying to Brand this morning. You know, in the past, we tried seeing other people. I admit it was my idea, but Brand reluctantly agreed—he said we could see how it went—so we tried it." She slipped her keys into her Italian leather bag and pulled her sunglasses down on her nose. "It was a failed experiment. An open relationship just didn't work for him. Or for me. I know that now." She began to walk away. "I'll be going back to the house in about an hour, if you'd like a lift."

"That's generous of you, Alana," I said dryly, "but I think I'll walk home."

"Suit yourself, then." She didn't look back, and she walked away across the parking lot.

"Thanks for the ride," I said, but she was already too far away to hear me.

MRS. SHAPIRO CALLED in early November, asking when I might be coming to see her. I explained I did not have a car and would have to put off the visit for awhile. She told me she would be in touch.

It was frustrating to think that the money I would have used for my house must now be used to buy a car. I'd had my old one for years and the insurance wasn't enough to re-place it with anything decent.

"Something is conspiring against me when it comes to that house, Tess," I said. We were sitting at the round oak kitchen table by the window in the barn having a cup of tea. Brand was gone. Lately I dropped by to see Tess only when

I knew he wasn't there. It was getting so that running into him was actually painful for me.

Outside, the weather hung low in the trees, thick, cold mist turning everything indistinct, muting colors.

Alana wandered into the room and sat down at the table with us. I knew that although she wasn't exactly living there, she had free run of the place. But I guess she always had. She stared out the window at the woods, not joining in the conversation.

"Every time I get ready to do something, the money has to go somewhere else," I went on, talking to Tess. "How am I going to finish paying for the paint? I'll never get new drapes or curtains, let alone rugs and furniture!"

"Well, you'll have a new car," said Tess. "That will be nice."

"Yeah. You know, Tess, maybe Tom was right."

"About what?"

"About that house. You know how he says I should sub-divide the lot, demolish the old house and put in new struc-tures, wham-bam, a tract of them, and sell the whole thing for a big profit. My brother, Russ, said the same thing the first day we saw the place. Said he'd invest in the project himself. Said we'd call it Addison Court." I stretched lan-guidly. "Maybe I'll do it! Just think. I'll be rid of that old headache of a house and I'll be a millionaire."

Tess nodded. "Sure," she said. "Mow this place down while you're at it, and we'll go in on the investment. We'll *all* be millionaires."

"Tessie, where's Brand?" Alana's voice cut in with such a contrasting tone I thought she must not have been listen-ing to us at all.

"He went down to Sonora to meet up with someone he's interviewing for a story," Tess replied. "He won't be back until later this evening."

"Oh, that's right."

Tess glanced at me with a smile. Alana was trying to pre-tend Brand had informed her of his plans, but he hadn't. Not that he talked to *me*, either. I had hardly seen him since his return from Nepal. I had taken my cues from him. He never sought me out, and I dared not go to him. I told myself it was for the best, but I was desolate. Since the moment I had lifted his mask on Halloween he had treated me with a polite coolness which I found bewildering, particularly after the impetuous heat of the letter he had sent to me. But now that seemed so long ago. Obviously he regretted sending me the letter and preferred to pretend he hadn't written it at all.

But he had. I knew every line of it by heart.

"So, Stacy," Tess said. "Are you sure you won't be having Thanksgiving with us? The Vandevere's annual Thanksgiving Feast is not to be missed."

"Somehow I believe you," I said. "But Russ and I have been planning this trip to San Diego for a long time."

"Well, next year, I guess."

Next year! That seemed a long way off. I had been looking forward to my trip with Russ but lately I had been feeling remorseful, as if I were going to miss something if I left.

Alana, at least, would be glad I wasn't around.

All three of our heads went up in surprise at the sound of the International turning into the drive.

Brand came in looking windblown and astounded at the sight of the three of us sitting at the table. As he glanced at us, the muscles in his jaw contracted.

"What are you doing back so early?" Tess asked him.

He opened the refrigerator and got out a carton of milk, took a swig straight out of the container. "Dawson canceled the interview."

"Oh, that's too bad. Use a glass, darlin'."

"I had a feeling he was going to cancel. I expected it. So I will have to try another tactic—" He strode off into the other room with the milk carton in his hand, calling behind him, "Which is fine because I have stuff to do around here."

Tess made a face. "Brand seems rather high-strung around us women, doesn't he?"

Alana shifted awkwardly in her chair. She slid off the seat and went after Brand.

"You guys are friendly!" shouted Tess.

Brand appeared at the door with a sheepish face. "Sorry." He came back into the kitchen and sat down at the table where Alana had been. "Alana's picking out a CD," he said. He looked at me as if unable to avoid it any longer. We heard the music begin: dreamy Celtic tones like the fog drifting through the woods outside.

Alana came back into the kitchen. "There. I hope you're not all sick of Enya," she said.

"It's fine with me," Brand said. There was something despondent about him. He lowered his head and stared at the floor as the lilting Irish voice sailed up on its lovely stringed wings. The melody was haunting, plaintive, and angelic. I was surprised Alana had chosen it.

Brand's eyes rolled up for a secret glance at me.

I turned away, disdainful. There was some meaning in his expression, and it sparked the turmoil he always raised in me. It seemed he was either ignoring me or giving me these strange soulful looks. It angered me. Was I some kind of trifle to him? Someone to flirt with when your main flame wasn't looking?

Suddenly, I was glad I was leaving town. The vacation I was to take with Russ was a good idea—a week away from this little mountain clique was just what I needed, and while I was thinking about it, why didn't I go ahead and sign up for that conference in Monterey after Christmas? And Yolanda had been after me to go out dancing with her. Why not? It was about time I started getting out again.

THE TRIP TO San Diego was a renewal for Russ and me. I had seen less of him since moving to the mountains, and I had missed him. I got to the source of a mystery, too—Russ finally confessed he had fallen in love. A girl he had told me about some months earlier, casually, as if she were nothing more than one of his many, had succeeded in capturing his heart. They were moving in together.

"So that's why you've been so cagey lately!" I cried.

"Cagey?" he looked baffled.

"Oh, sheesh. No wonder. No wonder you're always standing me up lately, no wonder why you're always in such a hurry to get home, why you have shown so little of your natural inclination toward random members of the opposite sex —"

"Well, let's not go *too* far with this analysis."

Katherine joined us for the last couple days of our trip and I learned why Russ had fallen in love with her.

"She'll make a great sister-in-law," I whispered to my brother, who gave me a stern look.

But now it was over, and I was glad to be home in the mountains again. As for my crush on Brand (that's what I was calling it now), the week away from the little mountain town had done more for my perspective than all the months *he* had been gone in Asia. I returned feeling connected to people I hadn't seen in a long time, friends and family, more tuned in to the integrity of myself. I had been putting too much of my mental energy into thinking about Brand, either worrying that he wanted to do me in, or mooning about him romantically, and it had to stop. I resolved to put my relationship with Brand in its proper place. We were friends, and casual friends at that. I would only regret involving myself more deeply with someone like him, anyway.

So the day I returned from my trip, I walked across the meadow to the Barn, feeling spirited, whole, independent, assured I was no longer so vulnerable to Brand. But I wasn't prepared for the reception he gave me.

He was polishing the little yellow Austin Heely Sprite, which I had once believed was Saul's. I knew now that it belonged to Tess. She let Saul borrow it, sometimes.

"Hello, Brand."

"Ah, the wayfarer returns." There was no warmth in his voice. He stood away from me stiffly, the chamois hanging from his fist. "So, what have you been up to, Stacy? Chasing foreclosure deals in San Diego?" His tone was sarcastic.

"What—?" I laughed, confused, not understanding the joke, for he must have meant it as a joke—though his manner contradicted the humor of a jest. He was cold and arrogant, much like he had been when we first met, only now it was personal.

Just friends? I reconsidered, angry. *We aren't even that.*

So he's never gotten over the fact that I snagged a prime

piece of real estate out from under him, I thought. Really, he carries things too far. I wonder why he doesn't try to con *me* out of the place like he did the old woman! I felt a snowy chill course through my blood, meltwater off a glacier. The oldest story in the book—the cad woos the lady for her estate and fortune, and then . . . Well, that was ridiculous. I certainly didn't have the fortune, and the estate—?

My temples throbbed. The property wasn't exactly an oil field, but then, Brand *did* seem rather obsessed with it. I waved the thought away; it was too preposterous. Besides, unless his tactic was to play hard to get, he wasn't exactly pursuing me with passion and ardor, feigned or not.

And yet . . . what about those long, inscrutable stares? The kiss on the Fourth of July? The letter from Nepal? Halloween, when we danced? . . .

Was it all part of some plan?

No. I can't believe that. You can't put on that trembling in the limbs, when your mouths touch and bodies ache against one another. That passion wasn't feigned. But what of it? You get the hots for somebody, you indulge yourself a bit, have a bit of fun, the feeling subsides. That's probably what happened to him. Just like it happened to me. But now it's over.

You wish.

"You *are* into land development, aren't you?" he went on in the same cruel, mocking tone of voice. He slapped the chamois against the side of the car. "I assume that was the purpose of your trip."

"Actually, the *purpose* of my trip was social. I visited my cousins."

"Stacy! You're back!" Tess hurried down the steps from the front porch and threw her arms around me. "Hey—I've missed you, lady!"

"Same here!" I said. "What a nice greeting!" I shot Brand an ironic look over Tess's shoulder. He went back to work, rubbing the car with dark energy.

I scooped a strand of freshwater pearls out of my pocket and draped them around Tess's neck.

"Oh, Stacy . . ." she gasped.

"You once told me you don't believe in presents," I said. "So I hope you don't mind."

"I guess I don't mind," she said, fingering the pearls. She was beaming like a kid. I hesitated. This was the point at which I intended to give Brand the gift I had bought him. A gift for each of them, I had thought. To signify friendship between the three of us, no more, no less.

But I couldn't bring myself to pull out the other little package in my pocket, so it stayed there, and I hardly heard Tess's exclamations.

"But you should have waited till Christmas!" she said, but from her expression I could see she was glad I hadn't waited.

"Christmas!" I said.

"It's only three weeks away."

"Wow. You're right."

"Yes. I've been after Brand to put up lights for me, but he's been stalling. He thinks it's too early."

"You two are like an old married couple!" I laughed.

"What are you doing for Christmas, Stacy?" Tess asked. "Is Russ coming up?"

"Russ's got a girlfriend now. And they're going to Mexico for the holiday."

"Mexico!"

"Yes, isn't that funny? And here I am hoping for a white Christmas."

"Well," Tess said doubtfully. "Don't get your hopes up."

"Well, what about you? What are your plans?"

"Brand is going down to his sister's in Pismo Beach, and I'm going to go with Tom to his mom's house in San Francisco."

"Oh, really?" I said teasingly. "To his *mom's*, huh?"

"Yes," she blushed. "I'm actually kind of nervous about it."

Brand finished what he was doing to the car and disappeared around the corner of the Barn. He didn't come back. Tess invited me in, but I lied and told her I had to get home. Or maybe it wasn't a lie. I had to get away from there. I didn't want her to see me cry, and the tears were fighting to be let out. I didn't cry often, but now I just felt so sad I couldn't help it. I went upstairs and climbed into my bed— ah, it felt so good after a whole week—and I buried my face in my pillow and started to sob.

"I'M GLAD YOU'VE come, finally," said Mrs. Shapiro. "I've been so preoccupied, but things are more settled now."

We were in her little room in her new home in Stockton. She was sitting in an upholstered rocking chair, her wheelchair folded against the wall. There wasn't much in the room, just a bed and a couple of chairs, a desk and a small bookshelf filled with books, on top of which stood a tiny Christmas tree.

I had driven my new car to Stockton, enjoying more luxury and power than I'd ever had before, excellent handling on the winding roads, and I was pleased with the deal I'd made. I'd found the car through Thad, who knew somebody, who knew somebody, and now the car was mine.

Mrs. Shapiro seemed happy to see me and smiled brilliantly as she accepted the foil-wrapped plate of Christmas cookies I had made for her. She took my hand briefly.

"I hope your daughter is well?" I said.

"She's better, thank you," she replied. "She has chronic health problems, and I tend to get too involved. But we all have our worries, don't we? How unfortunate about your accident. I am glad to see you look well."

"Yes, I'm fine, but I've missed my car. I wanted to visit you earlier. You have been unmerciful, Mrs. Shapiro."

"Have I? I suppose so. Well, at least now I'm closer, perhaps you'll be able to visit more often. I'm sorry it's taken so long, but it was rather important that I straighten things out completely. You see, Stacy, as I told you before, I had intended to leave the house in my will to an organization that could preserve it properly, along with a legacy for the purpose of maintaining the house. Circumstances required me to dispose of the property before my death. I had thought I had done so to my satisfaction, but it seems there were some misunderstandings in the dealings of my estate. The lawyer and the real estate agent who were handling the sale, they were—well, anyway, that's not important. I should have handled my own affairs; it doesn't matter now. What's done is done. I am actually quite satisfied with how everything has turned out. I believe you are the very person the house needs.

"When I left my house I liquidated some of my assets. I had set aside funds for the purpose of restoration and maintenance of the house. This money was diverted, but I was able to recover some of it. I want these funds to be used for the house. I know you have been struggling with finances for doing what the house needs and I would like to help. What I have done is set up a trust for the preservation of the house. When you have need for a specific project you may draw upon the money. It isn't as much as I had originally set aside for that purpose, but it will help, I think. I have had papers drawn up and you may take them and look them over, and we can talk about it some more."

She reached beneath her chair and brought out a folder, opened it and thumbed through the papers it contained, as if to assure herself that everything was in order. She closed the folder and thrust it into my hand.

"Mrs. Shapiro—I don't know how to respond to this."

"I hope the possibilities excite you."

"Well, yes, but—"

"I suppose you mistrust the deal. You might attribute it to the ravings of a senile old woman." She gave me a mocking smile. "But I hope to make you see it is all very straightforward. What I would like in return is a verbal commitment to the house and property, to preserve it as best you can. I realize, Stacy, that I have no right to ask you anything in this regard. I am only going on what you have told me of your own intents and values. I understand that someday you may wish to sell the property, subdivide, or otherwise use the building and land. And that is your right, of course. That won't change, legally or otherwise. But I am hoping the financial support for the house will help make an unfortunate choice unnecessary. You've got the paperwork. Read it over.

Have your lawyer look at it. Think about it and give me a call."

"All right. It's going to take me some time to digest all this."

"I should think so."

I was dumbfounded. Life truly was an adventure unfolding, I thought, and anything could happen, anytime.

"Mrs. Shapiro, there is something else I wanted to ask you about. It's important to me, or I wouldn't—"

"Yes?" she said irritably. "What is it?"

"You know I've become friends with the neighbors. And you know Brand—"

"Are you seeing Brand, Stacy?"

I was stopped short by that. "No."

"Well, then. What you do with your neighbors has nothing to do with me."

"No, but . . ."

"But what?" she demanded.

Damn, I thought. She got me every time. I was as tongue-tied and intimidated as a teenager. "About Brand . . ."

"What about him?"

"He takes quite an interest in the house."

"Don't tell me nothing has changed around White Pine Court. Is Father Daniel still skulking about in the woods? And that darling fairy Yolanda. She does have potential, doesn't she? But I worry about the her. And Tess. I *did* like her . . ."

"I suppose you know Alana," I said.

"Alana, no . . . can't recall the name."

"Mrs. Shapiro, I wanted to know if Brand—"

"And Saul? He's still strutting around like he owns the place?"

"Yes," I laughed distractedly. "But Mrs. Shapiro, please. I need to ask you. What I want to know is, did he really try to con you out of your property?"

Mrs. Shapiro smiled. "It was nothing. The young man must have thought I was foolish or senile, or both. But of course, I am neither. Well, I'm not *senile* anyway. I told him I intended to leave my property to a trust, and that was that!"

She lapsed into thought, and some of her fire died away. "Of course, that did not turn out to be that, did it? I suppose I *am* foolish after all. But not you. You're too smart for that fellow. He's a swindler, Stacy. I know he can be charming when he wants to be, and he's not bad looking—but once you get past that, there is something rather sinister there . . . and I see from your expression that you already know this. I don't need to convince you to keep your distance from him."

"How do you mean, a swindler?" I asked her. We had come this far. I needed to know the truth.

"I mean, as in forging documents and falsifying contracts, that's what I mean," she replied. "He was lucky I didn't have him arrested. I probably should have. It wasn't the first time he was involved in something like that."

"Do you think he is . . . dangerous?"

"You mean, would he actually harm you, physically, to get what he wanted?" she considered the question carefully. "With people like that, you can never be sure. I certainly wouldn't want to be alone with him in a dark alley. Not if I had something he wanted."

I couldn't speak. So, I thought. There it is. It went beyond ingratiating oneself to vulnerable elderly women and making a lowball offer on choice real estate. It was real criminal stuff. She had confirmed everything I feared about Brand.

Mrs. Shapiro called to a nurse's aide who had passed by in the hallway, and asked for her medication. "My hip has been bothering me quite a bit, today," she said.

She seemed tired, and I did not stay much longer.

As I drove home a bewildering mixture of feelings churned in me. I should have been thrilled about this offer of help on my house—but I felt uneasy and suspicious. I thought about Mrs. Shapiro's daughter and what she had told me about her mother obsessing over the house. Was this the sort of thing where an old person dies and leaves her entire fortune to her cats? Was I in danger of getting involved in a lawsuit from her unhappy family? I must definitely seek legal advice. I decided that until I had checked it out thoroughly I would tell no one about the proposal but my lawyer.

But what really mixed me up were her words about Brand. I should be *glad* of it, I told myself. I finally knew the truth, but I wished I had never heard it.

When I got home I went into the house and I caught the strange familiar scent, sweet-flavored tobacco. I searched for the source of it, aimlessly, agitated, and found myself in the library, where I had noticed the odor before. And, as before, it soon dissipated. I opened all the cabinets, but I found nothing.

Chapter Twenty-Two

CHRISTMAS EVE.
There was nothing of snow in the atmosphere, but it was cold, and it felt like Christmas. The sky was clear and stars punctured the darkness over the trees as I crunched over the glistening floor of the woods, my boots sinking through the crystal crust frosting on the mat of dead leaves. Yolanda's cabin was blinking and glittery with Christmas lights. Despite the cold, the doors of the chapel were open to the night and a small knot of people huddled on the threshold because there was no room for them inside. As I came nearer, I could hear voices raised in song, the choir singing "O Holy Night." Mounting the steps, I peered through the crowd, but the only thing I could see was the big stained glass window portrait of the Madonna and child above the altar, illuminated from behind, spears of colored light radiating into the darkness.

A powerful feminine voice lifted from the choir in a solo.

A thrill of hope
The weary world rejoices—

The crowd parted and a man emerged from the church. I stepped back to let him pass. For a moment I didn't recognize him. I had never seen Brand dressed up in a suit and tie. I looked up and we locked eyes for a moment. He seemed reluctant to let go of his fix upon me, and as he went by he turned his head so as not to drop his gaze from mine but the moment was gone in an instant. I watched him take the steps and move across the yard with his long mountaineer's stride. He glanced back at me again before disappearing around the corner of the building.

I felt strangely elated at the encounter. Those intense, serious eyes. Why did he leave the church? I wondered. The music was so stirring. Why didn't he stay?

Forget it! Forget him.

When the song ended I thrust my hands into my pockets and walked on, watching my breath form ghosts on the night air. When I reached the road I turned around. I had planned to walk up to the village square to look at the decorations but now I just wanted to go home and sit by the fire.

There was a message on my machine when I got in. I recognized Mrs. Shapiro's elegant voice, and I expected a Christmas greeting, but I realized immediately it was something very different.

"Stacy, it is imperative that I speak with you. I will be out tonight, but I will be back the day after Christmas. I will try to call you again. There is someone I must caution you against. You are in danger and I blame myself—"

There was a click and a buzz and the machine rewound itself. The tape was full.

I WAS KNEELING by the hearth in the front parlor, kindling the fire, when I heard the soft knock on the front door. It was almost midnight. I knew it was him. The character of his step, the soft firm rhythm of his knuckles on the door. Or was it through some more subtle faculty of instinct that I knew him? Was he the one I was cautioned against? Was he my danger?

Oh yes. He was my danger.

I went into the entry hall and saw him through the beveled window. My hand was shaking as I opened the door.

"Hi, Brand."

"Merry Christmas, Stacy." His breath came out in a cloud. He looked at me expectantly.

"Merry Christmas to you." I waited a beat. "Come on in," I said, trying to sound casual, as if I was used to him dropping in all the time. We went into the parlor, and I went back to tend my fire. He took off his jacket and threw it over a chair. He had already taken off his tie, and his white shirt was opened slightly at his throat. His cuffs were dazzling white against the brown skin of his wrists.

I felt nervous and the match trembled in my hands as I struck it into flame, but my fire flared up nicely. I turned to him with a sigh.

"Christmas Eve," I said.

"Yes."

"Why did you leave the chapel?" I asked him.

"I wanted to find you."

I felt my face grow hot from the flames, from his words. I looked back toward the fire to avoid his eyes.

"I thought maybe you would be there tonight," he said. "When I didn't see you, I got restless. I couldn't sit anymore. I got up to go, and then—there you were at the door. I was so surprised to see you, I'd given you up. I forgot what I wanted to say and I bolted."

"What did you want to say?"

"Well, now that I have you here all alone, maybe I can put off saying it for a little while." He smiled, teasing me. I was unsure how I should take him.

"Oh, come on," I said. "What?"

"Stacy, I was wrong about you. I owe you an apology. I owe you lots of apologies."

"You'd better explain that, Brand."

"It's Christmas Eve, and I don't wish to speak ill of . . . the dead."

"Who is dead?"

"Not a who, really—more of a what. But it died a long time ago, if it ever lived in the first place. I'll explain it another time, if you want, but tonight, I just . . . here. I brought you a present."

He put something in my hand and I felt the touch of his fingers as they swept my palm.

My heart was in my throat as I unwrapped the small, heavy object from glitter-sparkled tissue paper. It was one of those glass balls with a little scene inside. A white house like mine, surrounded by evergreens. Snow swirled all around the tiny house.

"Oh—" I laughed with pleasure and looked up at him. "Brand! It's my white Christmas!"

He was watching me intently.

I held the glass ball in my hand, tenderly, and turned it over, and stared at it. "I *love* this."

He smiled shyly. "You knew what it was."

"It's the white Christmas I was hoping for."

He nodded. "If I could I would have conjured up a real white Christmas for you."

"This is even better. I'll always have it. I have something for you, too." I got up quickly and went out, carrying his gift along with me, into the dark entry hall and up the stairs to my room. I opened the top drawer of my dresser and drew out the little package. I glanced at myself in the Enchanted Mirror and was astonished. I felt like a stranger to myself, as if I had never seen myself before. My hair fell across my brow, half-hiding and half-framing my eyes, which glowed moist and dark, harboring a fugitive passion, an expression of hunger. The mirror saw me as beautiful—did *he* see me that way?

He was waiting by the fire, leaning toward it, sitting on a footstool with his arms resting on his spread thighs, his long hair swept away from his broad forehead, gleaming gold and bronze in the firelight. I could see the flames in his eyes when he lifted them to look at me.

"Here's yours," I said.

He straightened up, accepted the small, soft pouch. I knelt beside him and watched as he drew out the little velvet case and opened it. On the tiny satin pillow sat a large pearl.

"A gray pearl." And for a moment I thought he was angry, but it was another kind of emotion. He held the pearl at different angles to watch the firelight dance on its skin. I could see he was entranced with it, and this made me feel absurdly happy.

"I picked an oyster out, for you," I explained. "When I was in San Diego. And this is the pearl that was in your oyster. I meant to give it to you when I got back, but then—" I stopped, thinking about how cold he had been to me the day I'd returned.

"But then I was a total jerk."

I smiled at that.

"Stacy, I thought you—" He stopped, shook his head. "Nobody ever gave me anything like this before," he said. He stared at me, and shook his head again, only this time it meant something different, and he murmured something I didn't quite catch. Finally, he carefully put the pearl back into its pouch, back in its box.

He reached for my hand and braided his fingers through mine. He leaned close, and he kissed me on the mouth.

The clock on the mantel was striking twelve. His lips were warm. I thought, my lips must be cool for his lips to feel so warm against mine. This is a Christmas kiss; he'll say I wish you a merry Christmas and then he'll put on his jacket and go home. This fantasy will turn into a pumpkin.

But he didn't stop. He was gathering me in his arms, kissing me and kissing me. The glass ball tumbled out of my hands and fell onto the sheepskin rug. Brand slid off the stool and we knelt together on the soft white fur. His touch was excruciating pleasure, driving out thought, argument, analysis, leaving only the desperation of bliss. He moved his mouth softly, insistently against my lips, parting them slowly. I felt his tongue on my tongue. Slowly, he drew away, yet returned again, kissing me again, tentatively, opening his eyes a moment to see if it was all right. We closed our eyes and moved more deeply into one another, mouths exploring, searching for messages, opening. For a long time we kissed, suspended between rapture and pain, the exquisite longing.

He pressed me down on the sheepskin next to the hearth, lowering himself over me, slowly descending as he kissed me, until at last he was pressing the length of his body hard against mine, his breath coming on faster, ragged, his mouth becoming greedy on me. He kissed me continuously, even when he pulled away and moved his mouth down over my neck to the hollow of my throat, licking the salt off my skin. It was rapture.

But it was too much. Too fast. When our mouths parted, it was as if I could suddenly think again. I mistrusted myself because I did not trust him. My mind was reeling with the contradictions, how much I wanted him in spite of all the reasons why I shouldn't, despite my fears that he was some-how connected with the strange pattern of threatening, sin-ister incidents, and the odd message of warning from Mrs. Shapiro on my machine just that evening . . . coincidence? Just what *was* his motivation for being with me tonight? Half the time he ignored me—and what about Alana?

The confusion I felt turned my blood cold. My body stiff-ened. He sensed it immediately and his hands faltered. He raised himself up above me on an elbow and stroked my hair.

"What's wrong, girl?" he asked softly.

I slid out from under from him and sat up. I picked up the glass ball and shook it, watching the snowflakes swirling around the house in slow motion. I cast about for a way to put into words what I was feeling, but it was no use. If I could have been open with him about what I was feeling, I wouldn't be feeling it.

"I'm just not sure this is something either one of us really wants." My voice was strained.

The snow slowly settled. He stared away from me, silent. I longed for him to challenge me, to argue about it, tell me I was wrong—but he said nothing. He got up slowly, grabbed up his jacket. He touched my hair with the tips of his fingers and walked to the door.

He turned and looked at me through the arched doorway, his face half shining in the pale golden light from the parlor, half shadowed in darkness. "I know what *I* want," he said. And he went out.

I didn't know if I had just made the biggest mistake of my life, or if I had just narrowly escaped *with* my life. Through the window I watched him disappear into the night. The glass ball lay heavy in my hands. I turned it over and let the snow fall.

I WENT TO Christmas dinner at Callie and Ralph's, whose house was decorated with blue and gold garlands for Hanukkah (for Ralph) and a Christmas tree (for Callie). Saul was invited too; grudgingly, I think, because Callie and Ralph didn't like him much. But after all it was Christmas, and Tess had probably suggested it. I gave him a ride to Callie and Ralph's and he told me that Brand had left for Pismo Beach before sunrise.

Ralph's Australian friend Pete Clark was at dinner that evening. He was the leader of the expedition Brand had climbed with when he was on Everest. And Iona, the real estate agent who had handled my house, was there, with her husband, who was a friend of Ralph's from the Chamber of Commerce.

"Small world, isn't it?" Iona said, flashing her big white teeth. She gave me a hug and sat down beside me in Callie and Ralph's newly done living room. Now that the wall was gone, there was a gracious flow to the home, and the kitchen and dining area were not so isolated. And yet a sense of individual space remained, privacy and comfort within each area.

"I haven't seen *you* in a long time," I said. "I tried to call you. I hear you changed companies."

"You tried to call me? I don't recall getting any messages. What's up?"

"Oh, nothing we can't talk about later," I said. This wasn't the right time to get into it.

"So how's business?" I asked her.

"Not bad. How you doing with the old Apple Ranch?"

"Well, it's a beast," I said, "but I do love it."

"It was quite the fixer-upper. I wasn't sure the house could be salvaged."

"So you're the girl who bought the house Brand Vandevere wanted?" Pete spoke up, looking at me in a new way.

"Yep, this is her," said Ralph.

"What a claim to fame," I said.

"Well, you *are* famous for it—all over the world," said Peter in his charming Australian accent. "Guys from Australia, New Zealand, Britain, Canada—even New Jersey—know about you."

"I don't think he's joking," said Ralph.

"Hell, I'm not even exaggerating. You were the talk of the Everest expedition."

"Why—what did Brand *say*?" Callie wanted to know.

"Not much. You know how he is. But it doesn't take much for the rumors to fly. All he said was, there was this girl who stole his . . ." he stopped, looked at me long and hard.

"What?" I said.

"*Oh* no you don't," Pete said, laughing. "I'm not touching *that* one."

"I think you already did," I said. "Stole his—? His what? His house?"

He just grinned at me.

"So what the hell was the deal with that expedition, anyway?" Ralph asked. "Brand never did talk much about it. I got the sense things kinda fell apart."

"We put two guys on the summit," said Peter. "And everyone got down healthy. I'd call that a success."

"I thought for sure Brand would nail that mother this time."

"Actually," said Pete, "so did I. He was strong, well acclimated, healthy. What happened was, he got involved in helping a couple of boneheads from another expedition who were having some problems. He got diverted, which was too bad. He lost valuable time. But one of their guys probably wouldn't have made it back alive if Brand hadn't sacrificed his own climb."

"Sounds like Brand," Callie murmured.

"Anyway," said Pete. "What it came down to was, he lost some crucial hours. It was getting late, and he was only a couple hundred feet from the summit, and it was a judgment call, you know? The weather was looking dubious. There was a point where a decision had to be made—to continue up and risk an exposed bivouac, or to go back down. He went down. Turns out, it was the correct decision. A storm came in fast and it was a bad one. He very well might not have got back down at all if he'd chanced it.

"The funny thing is," Pete went on, "I've known Vandevere for years, and there was a time when I don't think he would have made that particular decision, to turn around at that point."

Callie was nodding.

"I talked about it with him afterwards. He told me that maybe for the first time in his life, he had a better reason to get home than he did to reach the top of the mountain." Pete finished with a level gaze directed at me.

"So what was his reason?" Iona wanted to know. "Was he talking about that girl he was seeing—Alana?"

"He didn't say her name." Pete gave me a wink. "But he did mention a girl who had stolen his house."

I felt a strange thrill pass through me, and wondered if I was trying to find significance and meaning where none existed. After all, I reminded myself, Brand certainly hadn't rushed into *my* arms when he returned from Everest. But then I remembered how he had come to me that night, disguised as a pirate, and he had claimed me, and brought me out to dance, and he had pulled me close to him, and he had taken me in his arms.

Why had he drawn away again?

He had come to me, but only in disguise. Once the mask was gone, so was the connection.

But then he came again last night. Christmas Eve. And with a word, he was gone again. I could have either laughed or cried, thinking about it. Thinking about him.

"Well, Ralph," said Callie. "I hope you're satisfied."

"I hope Brand is satisfied," Ralph said with a sigh. "That might have been his last chance."

Pete said thoughtfully, "I think that remains to be seen."

I WENT INTO the kitchen with Callie to help her wrestle a huge turkey out of the oven. She got it to the counter and stepped back from it as if she had just vanquished a monster. "Hand me that bowl, Stacy," she said. "I'm gonna take the stuffing out of this big old bird."

"Do you want me to help?"

"Yeah, can you make gravy?"

"Sure. Have you got drippings—? Oh good, there's lots— Is this your famous cornbread in the stuffing?"

"You know it."

Iona came into the kitchen. "Mmm. Smells good, Callie. Listen, Ralph wants to know where the Mitch Miller Christmas album is."

"Tell him it's right with all the other Christmas music!" Callie said. "Oh, never mind, *I'll* get it for him. He'll never find it himself." She went to help Ralph.

"So, Stacy," Iona said when we were alone together. "You and your neighbor appear to be getting along pretty well." She was looking across the passage into the dining room at Saul, who was standing by the buffet eating the olives.

"Saul?"

"I noticed you two came in together. You're not—*involved* with him, are you?"

"No, nothing like that. Trust me."

"I was so surprised to see you together."

"Me too, actually. I'm doing a favor for a friend."

Her voice dropped low. "He's not pressuring *you*, now, is he?"

"Pressuring me about what?"

"Well, I can see you know how to handle him, but I've gotta tell you, he's just a sleazy guy. He tried to get Madelon Shapiro to sign over the papers for that house for some crazy low amount of money—did I ever tell you about that? He tried to scam her."

I was confused. I had thought she was referring to Saul. "Yes, I remember you told me about that," I said.

"But as I hear it, he's always trying to scam somebody."

She was almost whispering now. "He lives rent free, has his meals cooked for him—"

"Saul?" I repeated stupidly.

"The *Creeper*, I call him." She gave a wicked giggle. "But you've been there nearly a year, haven't you? You must know by now what he's like."

"Yes. I know Saul, but . . . I didn't realize *he* was the one who tried to get the property. I thought it was Brand Vandevere—"

"Oh, Brand wanted it too, I think. In fact, I was surprised he didn't buy it. But it was Saul who tried to do this dirty deal with the old lady, tried to get her to sign a bogus contract giving him all the rights to the place."

"Saul!" I was stunned.

"I'm sorry. I hope I haven't said something I shouldn't."

"No. Not at all. But I thought . . ." My mind raced furiously, and I tried to recall my recent conversation with Mrs. Shapiro. Was it possible I had misunderstood her? We had been talking about Brand, and then she mentioned Saul, but I was fixated on Brand . . . had I misunderstood?

"So why *didn't* Brand buy the place?" I asked.

"I don't know."

"Did he know it was for sale, then?"

"Well, it hadn't been listed, as you know, but I did call and let him know about it. I think it was probably the day before you came into my office."

"So—you *did* tell him about the house being for sale?"

She hesitated, remembering. "Well, yes, I—" She frowned. "Actually, what I recall is that I talked to Alana— you know Alana?"

"Yes, I know Alana."

"When I called to tell him about it, she answered the phone and said Brand was out. So I asked her to let him know the place was up for sale. I remember the conversation because she said he had gone to Yosemite that morning, to interview some nut who had just climbed El Capitan with no hands, or something. She said she would be sure to tell him. So I assumed he was informed. Then you came in with an offer on the place, so I never followed it up with him."

So Alana had kept the information about the house going on the market from Brand! But why would she do that? Tess once told me Alana hated the place, so maybe that explained it. I didn't know, but the darkness in my heart was lifting and I was beginning to feel utterly free and joyful. What was it he had said last night—? *I was wrong about you, Stacy.* I didn't know what he had meant by that, but I was beginning to understand I had been wrong about *him.*

He wasn't the kind of man who would try to swindle an elderly lady. He was, rather, the kind of man who would give up a chance for his own glory to help someone in trouble. And it made sense. It made sense with everything I knew about him.

I had been so busy doubting my own instincts that I hadn't been letting my instincts work for me.

I wanted desperately to see him again.

"SO, MRS. SHAPIRO. What was this warning you left on my message machine? The tape ended before you had a chance to finish." I settled into the chair she offered me. It was Boxing Day, the day after Christmas. I had wasted no time in coming to see her. I was going to get the whole story about her and Brand if I had to drag it out of her. And I wanted to know what she had tried to warn me about on Christmas eve.

"I am relieved you are safe and sound, Stacy. I have ordered tea, and after tea we will talk about it."

"You are a tease, Mrs. Shapiro. Always leading me on. Leaving me in suspense."

"Perhaps it is my own weakness—I suppose I have a tendency to put off disagreeable tasks . . . and topics."

I was exasperated with her. "All right, Mrs. Shapiro, then I'm going to ask you about something else. You might think this is none of my business, but I want you to tell me what happened between you and Brand, about the house. I need to know."

"*Ah . . .*" she balked. "Yet another disagreeable topic of conversation."

"*Please.* I have to know."

"All right," she said at last. "If it is so important to you."

"It is," I said firmly.

Mrs. Shapiro sat with a thoughtful expression and began to speak slowly. I heard genuine fondness in her voice when she talked about Brand.

"I watched him grow up, you know. It seemed he was always underfoot! He used to come for the apples, when he was little. I used to laugh and say he didn't know my house wasn't his. He had a perfectly nice family of his own, but he loved the Apple Ranch. And it was odd for me to allow someone else to feel at home like that in my place. I admit, I preferred my solitude, that's the way I wanted it. That's why this damn nursing home is going to drive me into an early grave. Too many old people. But I didn't mind Brand. I used to think we must be kindred spirits.

"Anyway, I told you about how Brand used to come with his father to do the repairs and such around the old place. And after his father went out to the coast, Brand took over. He would come over and fix the porch railing, or patch a wall, put in an outlet or some such thing. Anything I asked, he'd know how to do it or he'd figure it out.

"Of course, I always paid him, always insisted upon it. It was that way since he was a little fellow, picking apples for me, and when he got older he needed the money even more. But when he began to make his career, there came a time he didn't need the money I paid him. Still, he would come. He started being difficult about taking the money. I'd write him out a check and he'd refuse it, but I was more stubborn than he was and I'd insist. Then I'd find it lying on the table, left behind. At the same time, things were getting worse for me. My health was failing and the house was needing more and more attention I couldn't give it. I guess I grew more and more stubborn. I decided Brand was patronizing me, and I didn't want charity. I stopped asking him to do things for me. But he kept coming, even when I told him not to.

"Finally one day he was over at the house, and he'd gotten it into his head that the porch roof needed some repair and he was busy doing it and I decided enough was enough.

I took his tools and dumped them all in the fountain, including several expensive power tools which weren't supposed to get wet."

"Oh no!" I said, trying not to laugh.

"I told him to get the hell off my roof. I told him if he set foot back on my property again, I would slap a restraining order on him. And I meant it."

"I'll bet you did."

"I can see you think I was wrong."

"Yes—I think you were wrong." I was filled with joy.

"Well." She was loath to admit she might have been at fault. "Perhaps so."

"Mrs. Shapiro, did Brand ever try to get you to sell him your house?"

"He certainly let it be known that he'd be interested if I ever decided to sell it. And I entertained the possibility of offering it to him one day. But then we had our falling out, and I was too stubborn to tell him I was being forced to leave. So I came up with the idea of the Historic Trust. I thought perhaps the place might become a museum. You know it has a bit of history—"

"And what about Saul? Is it true he tried to get the house, too? . . ."

"Oh, *that*—" She waved off the mention of Saul with irritation. "He's the one I told you about. He paid me a visit once or twice when he first came to stay with Tess. He talked about buying the place from me, mentioned some rather ridiculous figures, apparently assuming I was some sort of senile idiot, and when that didn't work he tried to get me to sign some papers—"

I felt capable of flight.

"Stacy . . ."

"Yes? . . ."

"I do regret what happened with Brand. The way I left it with him. I suppose I always thought I would make things right with him again, someday. Would you tell him I'm . . ." It was hard for her to come out with it. ". . . sorry?"

"Sure I will. But maybe you can tell him yourself."

She stared out the window. "Perhaps."

We sat in silence for a moment, then she looked up at me as if she had just thought of something. "Did you get snow for Christmas?" she asked hopefully.

"A little," I said, thinking of Brand's gift, and I was washed with all the crazy conflicted feelings of Christmas Eve. *If I had known then what I know now . . .*

I wanted to groan out loud.

When we had finished our tea, she said, "No more stalling. There is something I must tell you."

I nodded, ready to hear it.

"I abandoned my family, Stacy. That's the long and short of the matter. That's not how I thought of it, at the time. But that's how they looked at it. My daughter was a teenager, my son a little younger. He would have been all right. Tim was very resilient. And Jean, well, I think we would have had problems with her anyway, but there's no question she was very disturbed by the divorce. My husband, he was a decent man, I think, but he just didn't understand. He couldn't see that I needed to get away, or simply explode. I felt trapped in the marriage, trapped by the conventions he insisted upon upholding at every turn. He asked me repeatedly what he could do to make things right, so that I might have a change of heart, come home. But the very things that would have had to change, he was constitutionally incapable of doing. He was very frustrated, and that was my fault, I suppose. He might have taken it out on the children. I don't really know. My daughter accuses him . . . of some horrible things. At the same time she says it's my fault. Anyway. I don't know how much of what she says was true, how much was simply confusion and hurt. I'm telling you all this, so you'll understand why . . ."

"Mother—" We looked up toward the sound of the low, resonant voice. Mrs. Shapiro's daughter Jean appeared in the doorway. She was wearing a denim skirt with cowboy boots and a yellow sweater set. Her auburn hair fell to her shoulders in a soft wave. She was pale and looked even older than I remembered, especially about the mouth and eyes, which made her beautiful thick rich hair all the more incongruous. I was certain it must be a wig.

"Jean! I thought you were feeling too poorly to come."

"I'm feeling better."

"Are you, love?" Mrs. Shapiro's voice was tender. She reached out for her daughter's hand and clasped it firmly. I was touched to see the maternal side of her.

"I'm perfectly fine, Mother." Jean looked at me and seemed startled to recognize me. "Well! Hello, Miss—" she hesitated. "Addison, isn't it?"

"Stacy," I said. I blushed and felt shameful, as though I been caught in a criminal act, or a lie.

"Stacy. Yes. How are you?"

"I'm fine . . ." I hesitated.

"So . . . of course you two have met." Mrs. Shapiro seemed at a loss. She didn't seem to be aware of the tension between her daughter and me, but neither did she seem to know how to handle the social niceties. She looked about the room; we needed another chair. There was a moment of awkwardness then, whether between them or because of my presence, I wasn't sure.

I rose and said: "I was just about to leave—I've got a long drive home. So I will leave you two alone, but first—?" I looked at Mrs. Shapiro pointedly. The sudden appearance of her daughter made things awkward, but I wasn't leaving until she told me why she had made that call. "You were going to tell me something?" I prompted her.

"Yes," Mrs. Shapiro said. "It's very important, Stacy. These mortgage companies. You know, the ones who pester you with cards and phone calls and those phony twenty-five thousand-dollar checks you can cash if you're willing to put up the equity in your home. You know some of their terms amount to highway robbery. It may sound like they are offering a decent mortgage rate, but if you read the fine print . . ."

I was incredulous. *That* was what she wanted to warn me about? That couldn't be it. I had the feeling she didn't want to say whatever it was in front of her daughter.

Mrs. Shapiro could read my thoughts on my face. "Well, Stacy," she said softly, her eyes innocent. "Such offers are tempting, are they not? Look. I've got something for you.

She got out of her chair with some difficulty and went to her bookcase. I could see that just standing up sent her into pain, and I couldn't help but notice Jean's expression of rancor toward me. I couldn't blame her for feeling protective of her mother. But I wasn't sorry I had come. Besides learning the real story of what happened between her and Brand, I felt she and I were developing a true friendship.

It was a shame she had lost her friendship with Brand. Someday, I thought, Brand and I will come and visit her, together. All will be forgiven . . .

Mrs. Shapiro fumbled about at the bookshelf until she found the book she was looking for, which she handed over to me, while her daughter helped her back into her chair. It was an old hardcover novel with a beautiful cover illustration of windswept moors above a dark sea, a young woman running through the night, her long dark hair ravaged by the elements, her pale gown twisting sensuously on her lissome body. The suggestion of castle ruins emerged from swirling mists in the distance behind her, and poised on the cliff above was the vague cloaked silhouette of an enigmatic young nobleman astride a rearing horse.

"*The Secret in the Schoolroom*," I read the title out loud.

"Are you familiar with the author?" the old woman asked me.

"No, I don't think so. But I love these old gothic romances."

"Take it home with you, and read it. You do read?"

"Yes!"

"That is—you appreciate books? That's what I mean. I don't question your literacy."

"Yes, I understood your meaning, and yes, I do read. In fact, I've already read a few books from your library."

"Is that so? Well, that's excellent." This seemed to please her more than anything else I could have said. "But I do especially want you to read this one."

"Well, sure I will—"

"Ah, I must have read this thing dozens of times," she mused. "I don't need the book anymore, I can call up any paragraph in it at will. I don't know why I feel the way I do about it. God knows it's nothing like my life. Perhaps that's the point. Anyway. It's not what some would call great literature, but a good story is a good story, to my mind. And this is one of my favorites. I suppose you remind me of the heroine, in a way, alone and in peril in that old house."

I laughed, alarmed. "In 'peril'?" I said.

She shrugged off the word. "I know it's an old fashioned notion, and probably chauvinist, but I can just picture a valiant knight breaking down doors to rescue you from harm."

"Well, I wouldn't appreciate him breaking down my door," I said. "I've got enough to take care of around that old place without adding a door repair to the list."

Mrs. Shapiro started to laugh, but the laughter broke into weak coughing.

"Really, Mother, you're tiring yourself," Jean said. "I think it's time you rested."

"Please don't fuss about me, Jean," sighed the old woman.

"I guess I'd better go," I said. I gave Mrs. Shapiro a hug, and it was the first time I had done that. She accepted my embrace stiffly, as if she wasn't used to physical contact, but I knew she was moved. "You have a happy new year," I said to her. "And I'll see you soon." I looked defiantly at her daughter, who merely shook her head slightly, and looked a little sad.

WHEN I GOT home that evening, I went down to Yolanda's cabin to return a CD I had borrowed. I found her outside in the church parking lot, packing her few belongings into her VW.

"I'm moving away," she explained.

"But . . . where are you going?" I asked, astonished.

"I've got an aunt in Santa Monica. She said I could stay with her a while. I'm thinking about trying to get a job in the film industry. Building sets, and stuff. I did some of that in high school. I'm going to check out Hollywood," she added with a dramatic flourish.

"But the caretaker's job—I thought you said it was so right for you—"

"It was. It was right for me, Stacy. But now it's right for me to do something else. Be somewhere else." She smiled. "An' I got good references."

I helped her put the last of the bags into the cramped back seat of the Volkswagen. I felt bewildered, disturbed at her going. I had come to like her very much.

"But, why?"

"But, but, but," she scolded me. "Is that all you can say?"

"I don't know. Yolanda, is this *your* decision?"

"Oh, do you mean, was I *fired?*" she laughed at the idea. "No. Well, not really." She reached out and hugged me. Then, as she straightened up, she glanced over my shoulder, and I could tell by the way her face went through a dozen simultaneous expressions that Father Daniel was behind me.

"Let's keep in touch," she said to me. And whispered: "Someday I'll tell ya the whole sordid story." She went to Father Daniel and they embraced. He kissed her on the top of her head and she pulled away from him with her last bag slung over her arm. She tossed it into the window of the car, and went around to the driver's side. With one smooth movement, she slid into the seat, slammed the door, started the car and stepped on the accelerator. The little car moved off with its pinging, steady engine.

When we couldn't hear it anymore, I turned to Father Daniel, reluctant to face him. He was already looking at me. He was smiling.

"I know what you think," he said.

"What do I think?"

"You think I slept with her."

I didn't answer.

"Well?" he pressed.

"I can see what's between you is way beyond *sleeping* with her, Daniel," I said, for once dropping the "Father."

"You're right, Stacy." He smiled gravely. "Ah, Yolanda! She is a beauty, isn't she? And because of her, I might have lost everything. Gladly too. But she isn't my lover. She's my daughter."

His daughter! I was completely blindsided by that one.

"It is true," he said, "as you have speculated, that I once broke my vow of celibacy. But it wasn't with Yolanda, it was with her mother. And it was almost twenty-three years ago."

"So why is she going to Santa Monica?" I asked.

"Because she wants to be in Santa Monica," he replied enigmatically, shining a smile on me, full of charm, so that I wouldn't be angry with him.

THAT NIGHT I went to bed early with the book Mrs. Shapiro had given me. There were so many old books of hers downstairs in the library, I wondered why she had been so particular about me reading *this* one, which appeared to be a fairly run-of-the-mill romantic suspense novel. But I was in the mood for just such a read. Anything, I thought, to distract me from thoughts of Brand. Though to tell the truth, I really didn't want to be distracted from thoughts of Brand. It was just so maddening, not knowing when I would see him again. I opened the book and turned to the first page.

When Daphna saw the mansion for the first time, she felt an inexplicable urge to command the driver to turn the coach around. The huge stone edifice was imposing, with its high towers and battlements on its lonely height above the sea, but ordinarily that would have only intrigued her. She was a sensible Yorkshire girl. She was not one who tended toward flights of fancy. But the icy touch of fear had seemed to rise from within her own soul and it was so unusual a feeling for her that she could not help but wonder at it. And yet there was something else in that moment, equally inexplicable, and perhaps stronger—a curiosity, a pull toward the mystery there in that fortress of stone. One day she would look back on that hour with the perspective that is the gift of time, and she would ponder the question: if she could have foreseen the future in all its length and breadth of tragedy and glory, would *she have run away? Or would she have stayed?*

And at last, she thought, the answer would be no, she would not have run away. In spite of everything, she would have stayed. Because if she had not, she would never have found him.

Oh boy, I thought, nestling deeper into the blankets with my book. Cheap thrills! Sometimes they were the best kind.

TESS AND TOM returned shortly after Christmas. Tess was full of stories about Tom's family—I had never seen her so bright. After a while, I casually turned the conversation to what was most burning in my mind.

"Brand came to see me on Christmas Eve," I said.

She nodded, waiting to hear what else I would say.

"He told me he had been wrong about me," I said. But he wouldn't say about what."

I could see from her expression she knew. It was also clear she was hesitant to speak. "He wouldn't say?"

"Maybe I didn't give him a chance," I said, agitated. "It all ended kind of strangely. But Tess, it's really important to me, to know."

"I suppose you have business to know," she said. "Since it involved you."

"Tess, you've *got* to tell me."

"Well . . ." she thought for a moment. "Just before he was to leave on his trip, Brand and Alana had words."

"Had words? You mean, a fight?"

"Not a fight, really. You would never hear breaking glass and tantrums with them. But Brand was angry. I don't think I've ever seen him so angry. Still, there was a calm about him. A deathly calm," she added drolly. "They were arguing about you, Stacy. This is funny. Do you know that conversation you and I had a few weeks ago about you tearing down your house and building a tract of new houses on the property—you know how we were joking about that? Well, you know Alana was there in the room, listening. So she goes and tells Brand what you said, verbatim, as she put it. She quoted you as saying you had decided to make big money out of subdividing the land and tearing down the house—but she didn't mention to him you were joking when you said it."

I mulled this over. So *that* was why he had been so cold to me that day I returned from my trip with Russ. *So, what have you been up to, Stacy? Chasing foreclosure deals in San Diego?* He had thought I was planning to demolish the old house to make a buck, which would mean I had deceived him on top of everything else.

"He happened to mention it to me," Tess said. "On Christmas Eve. He told me how disturbed he was by what you meant to do. I laughed and asked him where he got such an idea, and he told me what Alana had told him. Well, I set him straight. We talked, and one thing led to another—he told me about some other things she had told him about you—apparently she had her own little campaign of misinformation going. I guess she sensed his attraction to you and tried to sabotage it. Like on my birthday last year, when she found out I had invited you to dinner, she revealed to Brand her inside knowledge that you were having an affair with Saul."

"And he believed her—?" That was so absurd I had to laugh.

"Well, you know, it was earlier on, before he knew you very well, and he didn't have any reason to think she would be lying. And there were other lies along the way. Little stories, here and there, told to make him wary of you. He began to feel really confused, he said, because the things he thought he knew about you didn't fit with the *you* he was getting to know."

"Funny. That's how it was for me, about *him*."

"It didn't take him long to figure out you weren't involved with Saul, but he thought the lies were coming from Saul, not Alana. And he was just confused enough by what she was telling him to be suspicious of you."

It explained so much: why he stayed away from me when I sensed he was as drawn to me as I was to him.

Tess said, "So after Brand and I talked on Christmas Eve, I was getting ready to go out of town with Tom, and Alana shows up. Brand says to her, 'Alana, we have to talk.' They go into the living room, and I don't know what all was said between them, but I think he forced her to admit to what she'd been doing. He was furious, and he didn't care who knew it. He got up and slammed out of the house. She went after him, and was she a mess, crying and begging him to stay with her, saying anything she did was only because she was afraid of losing him. Completely out of character for her. My jaw was on the floor. But he was gone.

"I've never seen Brand so angry, and I never saw Alana so dejected. So she comes back into the house, looks at me, and for a moment it's like she's trying to decide whether to lash out at me or break down completely. She's muttering to herself, 'I could do better anyway. I *deserve* better. He won't even have sex with me, for godsakes. What do I need this shit for? I can do a *lot* better.' So she collects up all her CDs, and her scarves, and the special oil she keeps in the refrigerator, and just as she's about to leave, she says to me, 'You know what, Tess? Brand was always way too much of a hick for me, anyway!'"

Tess and I both had a good laugh at that. "So later," she said, "Brand came back to the house before Tom and I left for San Francisco. He didn't seem particularly disturbed. In fact, it was as if a huge weight had been lifted off him. He showered and got dressed up. He asked me to tie his tie for him—he didn't know how to do it. He seemed nervous, like a teenager getting ready for the prom. He says to me at one point, real casual, "So, Tess, do you think Stacy will be at the Christmas Eve service tonight? and I just said, "I'm not sure *what* Stacy's up to tonight! I was going to tell him you had a date or something, just to rib him a little, but his face just got so worried and intense I couldn't bring myself to do it." She smiled, remembering.

I thought of how beautiful he had looked that night. If only I'd known.

"I've been suspicious of Brand, too," I said. I was on the verge of telling her of my deeper fears, that Brand, or someone, was trying to drive me out of the old house, maybe even trying to kill me. But something held me back, or maybe I just let it go. I did tell her about Christmas day, when I discovered that Saul was Iona's *Creeper*, the neighbor who had tried to "steal" Mrs. Shapiro's property, and how Alana had kept the information of the house being for sale from Brand. Tess said she had known nothing about any of that.

"I'm not surprised about Saul," she said with a sigh. "Though I'm sorry to learn it. It's not the first time he's tried to pull a stunt like that, but I had hoped he had learned his lesson. I thought if we were patient with him, he would get himself together and make something of his life."

"So I take it Saul is no investment banker."

"He's made some investments, but nothing that ever panned out. Nothing ever does, for Saul. He's been disowned by his own family. My brother-in-law George is just the nicest guy you would ever want to meet. He tried so hard to help Saul, but that ended badly, and he gave up on him. It just broke my heart to see the family splintered up. So of course I got involved in something that was none of my business. Brand helped me bail Saul out of some trouble he got into in Phoenix, and he let me take Saul in, but Brand said it was against his better judgment. In fact, for a while there Brand was really concerned that Saul might try to hurt *you*, and at one point I was afraid he was going to do something drastic about it. Brand would have liked to run him out on a rail, but I think that had as much to do with jealousy for your affections as anything else!

"As for Alana, I've never liked her very much," Tess went on. "But I'm rather surprised by all this. I feel sorry for her. Or do I? I guess I can't help feeling she got what she deserved. Lately she'd been clinging to this notion that she and Brand were a couple, but it wasn't true. It never was. When he wanted to be a couple, she refused it, and when *she* decided it was time, it was too late."

"I hope it's not too late for me," I said.

"Why, Stacy? . . ." Tess said gently, curious. "Why would it be?"

"Tess," I said. "I have been so stupid."

I told her about Christmas Eve. How Brand had come, and the gifts we had given each other, and how I thrown up a wall between us, because I didn't trust him.

"I always had a feeling about you and Brand," Tess said thoughtfully. "Since day one. I thought it would be lucky, if . . ." She hesitated, shy. "Anyhow, it does look like you've both had to battle some misconceptions about each other. But now you can put all that behind you."

"When is he coming home, Tess?"

"Well, he had planned on being home today, but there was a message on the machine saying he might have a project down south, and he'd be gone indefinitely."

"*Indefinitely*—?" I groaned. "This isn't another one of your tricks, is it, Tess? You don't have him hidden upstairs, dressed as a pirate or something?"

She smiled kindly. "Afraid not."

Gone indefinitely? How could that be? How could he stay away? Didn't he need to be with me?

But I had turned him away. Deep in the night, in front of the fire, on Christmas Eve. I had turned him away.

Chapter Twenty-Three

LISTLESSLY I PREPARED for my trip to the architecture and design conference in Monterey. The only motivation I had for going was that in Monterey I would be closer, geographically, to Pismo Beach. Closer to Brand. Any other time I would be excited and eager to go to this conference, but now I felt despondent and frustrated, not knowing when I would see him again.

I wanted to let him know that *I* had been wrong about *him*. Never had I been so pleased to be wrong about anything, but I was scared I might have found out too late.

I obsessed.

I thought about asking Tess where I might reach him. I could probably track him down. But what if I was throwing myself at a man who didn't really want me? Perhaps the reason he gave up without a fight on Christmas Eve was that he wasn't all that interested anyway. He had finished it once and for all with Alana because of her lies . . . her lies about *me*. But maybe that didn't mean anything. Maybe he had other reasons to end it with her. The fact that she had lied to him at all would be enough. And yet he had come to me directly after learning the truth. Finally, for him, there was no hesitation. And I had pushed him away.

Did he believe I was truly not interested? He must have sensed the struggle in me when he came to me that night. He *must* know how I had wanted him. Just as I knew he had wanted me.

But did he still?

I drove out to the coast and turned south on Highway 1. I imagined continuing on past Monterey and driving all the way down to Pismo Beach, as if I could find him there in a crowd. But I turned off at Monterey as planned, and my mood brightened when I got to Abby and Ed's cottage overlooking the ocean. They were gone for the weekend, vacationing in the wine country while I stayed at their place and attended the conference. The little beach house was perfect, with its wooden deck overlooking the water, the ocean breezes blowing in through the funky old windows, rattling the bamboo windchimes. It had a fireplace with a cast iron woodstove, and the iron bedstead that took up practically the whole bedroom.

Saturday morning I took in a workshop on feng shui and architecture, a topic I found intriguing, and in the afternoon I caught a lecture about seismic engineering, which didn't intrigue me at all. During the earthquake talk, someone passed beside me in the aisle and whispered, "Psst! Look alive. This is important stuff."

I looked up and saw Janine, my ex-boss. She winked at me and I had to stifle a laugh.

Coming out of the auditorium an hour later I ran into— almost literally—Janine, who was waiting outside the door.

"You left before they got to the good part," I said.

"Yeah? What'd I miss?"

"Just the part about how to make sure the building doesn't collapse in an earthquake."

"Oh, well, then. If there is an earthquake, remind me to stay out of any building I've designed. Hey, I was hoping to catch you, Stacy. How the hell have you been?" She studied me unapologetically. It was just like her to have no sense of lasting remorse about firing me. But that was okay. I couldn't hold it against her. She was obviously happy to see me, and curious about what I'd been doing.

"Come on," she commanded, as if she was still my boss. "Let's go get something to eat. I know just the place. There actually are good restaurants around here in this tourist trap, but you have to know where they are."

We sat in a curved booth in a small cafe and we could see the ocean through the windows. We ordered wine and I told her about how I had started my own business in a new area.

I picked up the menu. "This town makes me hungry for clam chowder," I said.

"The chowder here is all right," Janine said. She glanced down and saw the novel Mrs. Shapiro had given me sticking out of my bag.

"*The Secret in the Schoolroom* . . . lord, what are you reading? Nancy Drew?"

"Oh—it's this great old gothic romance novel—"

"Misty moors? Stone mansions?"

"Exactly."

"This isn't the one where the heroine's old nurse locks her in the dungeon that fills with water when the tide comes in?"

"Uh—no. I don't think so."

"Or is it the one where someone is trying to make the girl think she is going insane so she will lose the child she is carrying, who is the rightful heir, since the heroine's first husband mysteriously died?"

"No," I laughed. "In this one, the heroine comes to the mansion because a tutor is needed for a mysterious pupil who will take lessons only from behind a curtain. She never sees her pupil, only the guardian, who is this young lord, and he's very handsome, but he's also very dark and secretive. Well, it turns out the pupil and the lord are one and the same, only the heroine doesn't know that, because he disguises his voice when he is with her, and the voice he uses behind the curtain is his real voice. The guy is able to pull off this deception because of a secret room in the library, which is accessible both from a tunnel outside the house and a hidden door in the library."

"Oh, of course. The old secret room scenario."

"Yeah. She finds herself falling in love with the man be-hind the curtain—because of his kindness and humor, his interest in learning, the little presents he leaves for her, and things like that. But at the same time, she finds herself phys-ically attracted to the young lord, who is very sexy, who speaks but little and treats her gruffly."

"This is good. So what happens?"

"Well, one night she lets the lord of the manor kiss her and she is overcome with the incredible sensuality of the whole thing, but also she feels horrible, because she has be-trayed the other."

"Don't tell me any more. I want to read it. Are you fin-ished with it?"

"No, not yet."

We ordered chowder and salad, and the waitress brought baskets of warm sourdough bread.

"So, Stacy. How are you *really?*" Janine asked me fi-nally, leaning back against her upholstered seat, studying me critically. "Did that wacko ever stop harassing you?"

I shrugged. "It's weird, you know. You start getting para-noid. You start thinking everything that goes wrong is part of some sort of conspiracy."

She set down the forkful of salad she had been about to eat, shoved her plate aside. "Well, it's a damn shame," she said. "I have to tell you, you left a big hole in my business when you left. I hadn't realized how much I'd come to de-pend on you."

I thought about how things had worked out after I was fired. I had moved to the mountains to live full-time and started my own business. In spite of the circumstances, the outcome, for me, had been positive. But I decided that might not be the most tactful thing to say to her at that moment.

We parted with social promises to keep in touch, and I knew it had been a good thing for me to see her again. I felt a sense of finality about a certain part of my life that I had been reluctant to entrust to the past. I realized I was glad I had been forced to move on.

LATE THAT NIGHT, alone in the cottage, I sat in front of the fireplace and opened my book.

Daphna threw up the sash of her window to the sea and leaned out to breathe deep of the chill night air. Fanny had always warned about the evil humors in the night air, but the young woman found an obstinate pleasure in ignoring Fanny's warnings. How could something that felt so wonderful be harmful?

She sighed with pleasure at the caress of the breeze on her skin. And she blushed, for this made her think of Lord Grenville, and the way he had touched her that evening as he had passed behind her chair, his fingers lingering on her bare shoulder the way the light lingered on his hair. She had tried to possess herself, so that the shudder which ran through her body would not be discernible to the others, but she knew he had noticed it. He paused a moment at the door, and their eyes met. In his face she saw all the suffering between them, as if it had come from her own heart to rest in his expression. Though days and weeks had passed since the night of their kiss in the minstrel's gallery, the memory of it was as strong as if it had happened only moments before. She thought of the kiss with longing, and a sort of blissful shame.

How could something that felt so right be so wrong?

But it was wrong, and there was no use defending it! She did not wish to defend it!

She reached for the shutters suddenly and slammed them shut, her breast heaving, her mind torn and wild. She ran to the bed and threw herself down upon it, burying herself in the cool white softness, trying not to think, trying not to feel, but it was impossible. For the first time, she thought she understood why the Lady Anne might have felt compelled to throw herself off the tower balcony onto the cruel teeth of the rocks grinning out of the sea below.

*Suddenly, she heard a click. And slowly the door
began to open.*

DURING THOSE THREE days by the ocean I began to feel
more centered, more serene in myself. What is meant to be
with Brand will be, I told myself, finally almost believing it.
If we were to be together, we would be together when it was
right.

It was Sunday evening, my last night in Monterey. I
leaned over the wooden railing of the deck, watching the sun
setting over the Pacific. The waves seemed to hold their
breath in the instant before they fell, crashing and spilling
with massive force into themselves and the shore, inhaling
again, drawing back, curling hesitantly, crashing again.

I went down to the water in the gathering darkness. The
beach was deserted. The tide was low, withdrawn in some
places over pitted, greasy rocks. Long strands of kelp draped
across the damp curve of the shore. The sky, full of wheel-
ing gulls earlier, was empty now in the twilight. I walked
down the beach, my senses drinking in the salt smell of the
water, the roaring of the waves. I had walked about a half a
mile when suddenly I felt a strong urge to go back to the cottage.

I ran most of the way to the little curve of sand just down
from the beach house. It was dark now, and secluded in the
dunes. I climbed a crest of sand and watched the waves
moving into the land. The stars came out and stood vividly
against the moonless sky.

I became aware of him, like a bell ringing against the
roaring night. I didn't see him, because I was facing the
ocean. It couldn't have been a physical sound I heard—
he was too far away and I was too close to the crash of
the breakers. But I sensed him there, on some deep elemental level, maybe because he was always with me. I turned,
and I saw him standing on the cliff, his hair blown by the
wind above the plane of his broad shoulders. I had no trouble recognizing him, in spite of the darkness, which obscured all but his silhouette, and the distance between us,

which was like the distance between yesterday and tomorrow, and reason, which told me he couldn't be there.

I took a few steps toward him, but he was moving faster than me, striding over the humps of dune with his long mountaineer's stride. I closed my eyes and breathed a prayer of thanks, and a request. For courage. When I opened my eyes he was nearly upon me and he came at me with an expression of imperious determination. A few feet away from me, he hesitated for a moment. It was almost imperceptible, but a look of anguish passed over his face.

So he knows it, too, I thought.

Right here, right now, taking another step meant passing into another world. No way back. Not stepping across the line was another choice, another kind of last chance. Or maybe it wasn't a choice at all.

These thoughts came in a synapse of nerves, rather than words, and the decision was made in a split-second. He came straight to me and caught me in his arms. There was so much I wanted to tell him, but not now. At first we simply held each other. I buried my face in his neck, breathing in his scent, amazed and overcome, feeling him, his big, hard body against mine, his arms pulling me so tight to him. He lifted my face, and he was staring down at me, looking for me. Our eyes met, and then our mouths, crushing kisses, dozens of them, mad and drunken and frenzied.

We stumbled together down onto the sand, all alone on the beach in the darkness, kneeling, face to face. He was holding both my hands in his. His hands were shaking.

"You're not going to run away from me again, are you?" he asked in his deep soft voice, with its new note of emotion.

"I've never run from you, Brand."

"Haven't you—?"

He came at me with his whole body, his whole being, caging me with his body as if to test my words, to see if I would try to escape. I reached up and gathered his head in my hands. I felt his long hair silky between my fingers.

"You're so beautiful," he said, echoing my own thoughts

about him. "I can never stop looking at you. God, I can't believe I've finally got you in my arms."

We were laughing together, giddy, like the kids in Zefferelli's *Romeo and Juliet*, we were so high on one another.

"It's where I've wanted to be," I whispered. Then: "I love your laugh, Brand."

"I love *your* laugh. And I love your eyes. And I love your—I love you. I love *you*."

"But you don't know me well enough to love me."

"But I do. Yes, I do. I have. I've loved you all along.

He crushed me to the ground as he kissed me, his body heavy, deepening into me.

"I'm not too heavy on you—?"

"No! You're not hurting me."

"I want you so bad. I've got to hold myself back."

"No you don't."

His arms tightened my body against his, his hands and mouth moving over me eagerly, greedily. It was incendiary between us—an intensity of pleasure and longing so acute I thought it would shatter me.

He was kissing my mouth again; he nuzzled my ear and I felt his tongue there, and his hot breath, and I heard him groan. "From the moment I saw you, standing in the woods last autumn, it's been *you*, Stacy . . . only you—" He was breathless, gasping, lust and emotion entangled in the soft and urgent tone of his voice. I was practically clawing at him, and if we were not still clothed he would have been in me already.

"I thought you were a wild animal," I whispered against his mouth.

"Wild about *you*."

Laughter spilled over me like water, my head thrown back, ecstatic, magnificent laughter, cut short with a gasp as he suddenly tore aside the clothing that separated us, like he was yanking shackles off a prisoner. I felt the naked hardness of him, poised like an arrow in the invisible moment before it connects.

I clasped him desperately, frantic to bury him inside me. The alchemy of joining; it was a primal insistence. I cried out, and I noticed, as if I were floating above us, that he cried out, too; instantly I was back down in my body and I found him there, and there was no more thought, only deep, throttling sensation, the pounding, taking my body to his will in the tremendous, repeating thrust, shattering and fertile. I gasped at the volume and power of him. He filled me, deeply, such piercing sweetness, groaning helplessly and crying out my name—

Against my back was the cold grainy shore and above us, the immensity of night and the universe. It was thunderous.

HE STAYED INSIDE me for a long time, his mouth against my neck, our bodies still heaving, trying to catch back our breathing. I explored him with the tips of my fingers. At last my hands had free reign of him. So surprisingly soft, his skin, except along the edge of his jaw where he had shaved hours ago. And the calluses on his hands. It was so easy with him. After so long struggling.

"Did Thad put you up to this?" I teased him, thinking of a conversation I'd had with Thad, months ago —he'd accused me of fantasizing about laying with Brand on a deserted beach.

"Thad?" Brand said darkly. "What do you mean? Tess told me where to find you. But what about Thad? Put me up to what?"

"Never mind."

"Never mind! Humph."

"Brand!"

"He's my best friend. But he's also my rival. Isn't he?"

"Thad has let it be known he'd be happy to sleep with me anytime, if that's what you're asking."

"You think that's all?" Brand shook his head.

"But you threw us together! There were times I thought you *wanted* . . ."

"I wanted you to have a clear choice."

"Brand, you don't have to worry about Thad."

"No?"

"No. Not Thad—or anyone."

He propped himself up on his elbow, and brushed the hair away from my eyes.

"Your eyes are the color of the heading on my word processor," he said.

"The color of *what?*" I laughed.

"My word processing program. There's a little strip of blue along the top and when I run it in sixteen-bit it's this deep indigo blue."

"I don't know how you can see the color of my eyes in this darkness," I said.

"I can't. But I know the color of your eyes by heart."

WE STUMBLED TOGETHER up the steps to the beach house, arms entwined, stopping every few feet to kiss, and when we got to the top, he picked me up, booted open the door, and carried me over the threshold. Once inside, he let me slide down against him, but he did not let go of me. He held me in his arms as he glanced around the beach house.

"Yes," he said with satisfaction. "A perfect honeymoon cottage."

"Yikes," I said. *Honeymoon.* But I was grinning like a fool.

His gaze returned to rest in mine, long and deep, searching. I reached up to kiss him, felt him shudder against me. I felt dizzy and powerful and full of bliss. Then it was as if he lost control. He pushed me through the door of the little bedroom, backed me up to the bed, and pushed me down with the bulk of his body. I closed my eyes. His mouth on mine, his body and mine like candlewax, two flames melting into one pool, sent me swirling into another consciousness, and we were warm whales swimming through a tropical sea.

When I opened my eyes he raised himself above me, panting, gathering command of himself. He dipped back down for a gentle, tantalizing, full body kiss. He was pacing it slowly this time. This time was different. On the beach, it was the sheer need for physical union—fast, urgent, essential. Pleasure was secondary.

This time, pleasure was everything.

WE LAY TOGETHER on the thick rug next to the fire, and he said, "You know, Stacy, I used to call you sometimes. When you were living in San Francisco. I'd call you just to hear your voice, either on your machine, or if I got lucky, in real time. I felt like an idiot, but I could never bring myself to say anything to you."

One more sinister mystery explained.

He slipped something from his pocket and pressed it into my hand.

"What's this?" I said.

It was a small smooth white stone.

"It's the piece of Everest you asked me for," he answered shyly. "I have been carrying it around with me, wanting to give it to you . . . but the time never seemed right. I think now the time is finally right."

I was dazed with emotion. This plain white stone in my hand held more significance for me than a diamond in a ring of gold.

Chapter Twenty-Four

I N THE LATE morning we came to the eastern edge of the Central Valley. The air was clear and we could see the mountains, snow-frosted peaks crisp against the eastern sky. Along the side of the road next to an orchard we stopped. He came up beside me and we slid our hands together, entwining fingers.

He pulled me against his body and held me tight in his arms. "I wish you were sitting next to me as we drive so I could keep touching you," he said.

I felt the flare of arousal. He made me catch my breath.

But I liked watching him in my rearview mirror, or ahead of me on the road. I liked the silent communication between us when he went by with a wave, or when I raced past him, laughing, taking the lead. I liked the space flying between us. I needed to distance myself from the night. The night we had spent together, and the night that was sure to come. After-shocks ran up and down and through my body, tremors that swept through me, thrilling and tormenting me with images of the ascension we had shared, exploding, incendiary memories. It was so intense I needed relief from it.

And so we returned to our separate vehicles and continued on toward the mountains, leaving the valley behind, moving on up into the rolling foothills.

I was reluctant to go back to the people and places where so much had come before. On the beach and all night long in the cottage on the cliff, Brand and I had been isolated and new, the only two beings in the universe. But in the mountains, we were part of a community. I didn't want to deal with the specter of Alana or the commentary of Saul. I wanted us to be alone with this new love.

But I had to get back. I had work to do. Not only that, but I had the papers from Mrs. Shapiro to get to my lawyer. I wanted to talk to Brand about her proposal but there had been so little time, and what time we'd had we'd spent making love. And that was all I had wanted to think about anyway. Maybe I was reluctant to talk with him about the house for other reasons. I still wondered how much of Brand's passion for me had to do with the house. I realized I was grateful we had come together somewhere else.

When we pulled up into the meadow drive, Tess came out to greet us. She asked me to come in; Callie and Ralph were there, and so was Tom. There was something she wanted to tell us.

It seemed odd to be with Brand in the same room and not be touching him. We were like two rivers rushing to fill the same watercourse and being back in society felt like a dam erected between us. But here with our friends I was reluctant to announce our sea change. He grabbed for my hand, but I eluded him. He gave me a fierce look, questioning, amused. He understood me. Part of it was that I just felt shy. But another part of me was terrified of the magnitude of the intimacy we had unleashed, and I needed a retreat. I had spent so many months fighting my feelings for this man that it was strange, at last, to surrender. Being *together* with our friends was another step, and I wasn't ready to take it just yet.

But my taste of Brand left me craving more. Sitting in his softly lit home with our friends, I pretended I wasn't enflamed by his presence. I could feel his eyes go through me: *All right, you. I'll honor our truce. For the moment.*

Tess plopped down beside Brand on the loveseat. Ralph and Callie were on the sofa.

When Tom came into the room, Tess said, "We have an announcement to make."

"What is it?" Brand asked.

"We already know, we already know," taunted Callie.

Tom went to stand beside Tess, took her hand. "Tess has agreed to be my wife," he said with obvious pride.

"Tess!" Brand leaned over and embraced her enthusiastically. "Way to go, lady!"

"He proposed to me last night," she grinned.

"Well, congratulations," Brand said. "You got a good woman, here, Tom."

"Don't I know it."

"I think he does," I said. "I'm so glad. You two are really good together." I got up from my seat and gave Tess a hug.

She whispered in my ear, "And I'm glad it's you and Brand . . ."

Brand went to get a bottle of champagne from the kitchen.

As we toasted the happy couple, I was brimming with feelings; joy and gratitude and nervousness, and longing, to be back against his body—

I would hold him to me again. Tonight.

It must be tonight.

I desperately wanted to outlast the other visitors so that I might meet Brand discreetly, but Tom and Ralph were telling stories and seemed little inclined to be finished soon. It was getting late and I needed to get home and get some sleep—we had slept so little the night before—so I said goodnight to everyone, and congratulations again to Tess and Tom, and I went home.

I hoped Brand would follow me—all my resolutions of discretion be damned. But in the time it took me to cross the drive there was no sound of the porch door banging shut behind me. I unlocked the door and went into my house alone.

It was a few minutes before I noticed the odor was in the air tonight. The pungent, sweet smell of specialty tobacco. And suddenly, into the lonely dark silence of the big old house, a strange and plaintive strain of melody, scratchy and unclear and distant, as if from a Victrola played in the depths of some hidden wardrobe.

I tried to ignore my senses as I unpacked and undressed, but the fear I had been able to ignore lately crept over me once again. I went to bed with my book, the one Mrs. Shapiro had given me. The strains of music and the smell of smoke dissipated and I questioned my perceptions yet again.

Against my naked skin, the worn sheets felt incredibly soft. Deep in the warmth of the blankets I began to feel safe again. I was about to finish the book. The heroine was about to discover the secret room and find that the two men she loved were really one and the same.

Daphna wondered how her heart would ever withstand the violence of its pounding. Her hands paused on the smoothly polished wood of the panel, and began tracing the pattern. In a moment, she heard the click, and the little door opened into the wall . . .

My own heart began to pound harder. *Secret doorways, passages, and chambers.* Was it possible there was something like that in *this* house?

I remembered Mrs. Shapiro's words. She had told me the heroine reminded her of me. And she had held something back, too. I was sure of it.

Ha! I thought. I've got you. I set the book down and reached for the phone on the bedside table and my planner. It was late, but something compelled me to call.

I dialed the number.

Several minutes later I hung up the phone, dazed. The woman who answered the phone had apologized and told me Mrs. Shapiro had died early that morning. She couldn't give any details.

I slipped on my robe, ran downstairs to the kitchen and

put on the kettle. I felt so sad. It seemed so unbelievable. I
was shocked, frustrated, bone-achingly tired, and no longer
sleepy. I leaned against the counter as the water heated, and
picked up the book again, reading on. I was trying hard not
to allow the grief in, though I knew it was inevitable.

There was a clue in the book; I was certain of it now. And
it suddenly seemed vital to find it.

I almost didn't notice the knock.

It had to be Brand—it was too late to be anyone else. My
impulse was to fling the book down and run to the door, but
instead I breathed deeply, put the book down on the counter,
spread open to the page I had been studying, and walked se-
dately out to the entry hall.

Mrs. Shapiro's daughter was standing on my porch. It
didn't seem strange that she would be there. The unreal
quality of her presence fit with the hallucinatory reality of
the news of her mother's death. She was neatly dressed in a
quilted black leather jacket and black slacks, black cowboy
boots. Her thick auburn hair was pulled back and tied with
a black bow. Her hair, in its rich abundance, seemed so at
odds with the drawn tiredness of her skin, the skull-like
fragility of her face.

"Come in!" I said breathlessly. "I just heard about your
mother! I'm so sorry."

"Yes. It was so sudden. And yet, it was only a matter of
time. It was obvious she didn't have much time left."

Obvious? I thought. Well, perhaps to her it was. She must
have known her mother much better than I did.

"So . . ." I waited to see if she would explain herself, but
she merely looked at me mildly.

"What brings you here so late on such a night?" I asked
at last.

"*You* do," she said. "Don't you know?" Her calm, deep
voice held a note of resignation.

Oh, God, I thought, here it comes. Mrs. Shapiro's proposal . . . of course her daughter would not be happy about
it. Probably has an army of lawyers to contest it. Well, it was
sweet while it lasted. But it was all happening so fast—

"It's about the house, isn't it?" I said.

"I knew you'd understand." She came in and looked around as if she was planning to move in. "Finally, things can be set right."

"Would you like some—tea?" I asked her. "Or—?"

"No, thank you."

"Let's sit down." We went into the parlor and she sat on the edge of the sofa, looking uncomfortable. I switched on a lamp.

"First let me say," she began slowly, "That I have nothing personal against you. My mother is, as you know—I should say, *was*—an unusual person. She had certain ideas and she was extremely strong-willed. We disagreed on certain things. I tried to protect her from her own willfulness. I believe I succeeded, to a certain degree. Do you have any idea what I would like to ask of you?"

"I think I have a pretty good idea. You think your mother's estate should go to you. Not in trust for an old house somebody else owns."

She nodded solemnly.

"I can understand your position," I said. "But I'm not sure exactly what we're talking about here. I haven't thoroughly read the paperwork your mother gave me, so I can't discuss the matter intelligently. And given the circumstances, I think we would do best to wait on it for a few days, at least."

"That sounds reasonable," Jean said. "I suppose I can't ask for more than that." She stood.

"I'm really sorry about your mom," I said. "I liked her very much."

"Thank you." Jean started slowly out of the room. She paused in the entry hall. "There's something she would have wanted for you," she said. "Something she intended for you to have. I'd like to give it to you, for her, if I may. It's a little secret about your house. May I show you?"

"Of course," I said.

I followed her down the hallway beneath the staircase, past the kitchen and dining room, around the corner and through a small vestibule to the library. She went directly to the paneling near the place the makeshift closet had once stood. She pressed something, and waited, but nothing happened.

"It would be a bit stiff on this side," she said pleasantly. "The opening at the end of tunnel on the outside of the house is much nicer. Ingenious, really. You'd never know it was a doorway—" She worked with it some more, and her expression darkened a little when nothing happened. Then suddenly one of the cherry panels clicked away from the molding around it and a small door popped open.

"See? You're not surprised. That's too bad, I'd hoped to surprise you. You like it, though, don't you? That's why Mother gave you that book, you know. She had a thing about that book. Just like she had a thing about this house. She was intrigued with that whole business of secret rooms and such. And so naturally she had a secret room built into this house, being the eccentric she was. Come, I'll show you."

This was all very strange, I was thinking. I'm reading a novel, flash on the idea of a secret room, make a call to ask Mrs. Shapiro about such a possibility and learn she is dead—as of this morning. The next thing I know her daughter is on my doorstep, presenting herself to me like a tour guide, ready to show me the way, the way into a secret room in my own house.

I crouched down and peered inside.

"It's roomier than it looks," she said. "Come on, it's a marvelous little hideout. She dropped to her knees and scrambled through the opening. Her black leather cowboy boots were polished to a shine. I hesitated, then followed behind her, unable to resist. We were close together in a narrow passage; ahead of Jean I could see there was another door, outlined in light. The outer door latched itself behind us. I hesitated again, suddenly claustrophobic. I reached behind me and pulled at the latch. With a bit of a struggle, it opened, so I relaxed a little, and crept after Jean deeper into the passage, letting the hidden panel door shut behind me again. We climbed through the small door at the end of the passage, one at a time, into a diminutive, softly lit parlor.

I was stunned to find this hidden place. There was a large comfortable chair with a lamp for reading, a small table, and lots of books piled around the tiny windowless room. Here the odor of specialty tobacco was fresh and especially strong. A book lay open beside the glowing lamp, facedown on the table beside the chair, as if someone had just set it down and stepped out.

All this, inside my house? It was eerie.

"This is too strange," I said. I should have been terrified at that point, and part of me was. This whole scene just wasn't right. I should be beating a quick retreat. But the architect in me was thrilled with this discovery, and I wanted to examine it.

"I can't believe this room existed, all this time, right in the middle of my house, and I had no idea," I said, thinking hard. Perhaps the lamp had been burning since I bought the place—it wasn't inconceivable. I was lucky the place hadn't caught fire. And this would explain the smell of specialty tobacco—it must have wafted through into the library, a faint reminder of a long-ago smoker.

"I guess it's the way the additions fit together, you don't even notice there is this space missing in the floorplan—I always thought there was something strange about it. Something that didn't quite fit." I walked along the edge of the room, checking out the construction. Persian rugs covered floors made of old stone. "You say your mother had this room built for her?"

"She had these." Jean pulled a large leather folder from a shelf and spread it open on the table. At first I thought it was an old manuscript, then I saw it was a drawing, a plan. I studied it a moment.

"It's my house," I said. "Only it's not. This must be the way it once was."

"This is the way it was when the house was built over the site of the old tavern. A very wealthy family was deeded this land and hundreds of acres around it. Very devout Catholics, built their own chapel. Had a passageway built from chapel to the cellars."

"Cellars?" I knew of no cellars. But then the exterior of

that part of the house was almost impassable with blackberry vines. If there was any access from the outside of the
house, it was possible I hadn't found it yet. "Here it is," I
said, pointing at the plan, careful to touch the old paper as
little as possible. "This is where we would be now, I think.
There was already something here—"

"Yes, that's right. The passage led down here, to the cellars. It was nothing but a dank stone hidey hole. But she had
it all fixed up."

Why? I asked myself. Why would anyone go to the trouble? But I understood. She said the house was her sculpture.
Her sculpture and her escape. She had sculpted an escape
into the sculpture. A hidden room, accessible from the
house, with its own escape route. And it wasn't so odd, really. Lots of people build hideouts into their houses, for various reasons.

"Wow," I said. "This is really amazing."

"Mother was right. You do love this house."

"I want to see the tunnel leading down to the chapel. Is it
this little paneled doorway here?"

"So it would be all the more satisfying to me if I were to
destroy it."

"What?"

"With you in it."

At this point I wasn't even that scared. I figured I could
handle Bonnie Jean.

"I have dreamed of burning it down. That's what I would
really like to do. But it's so valuable. I'm not sure what to
do. I have certain resentments built up around the subject of
this house, you know," she went on calmly.

"All right. Let's talk about it."

Jean laughed. "Talk! I *tried* to talk . . . but she would
never listen to me."

"Who?" I asked gently.

"Oh, I know you probably think she's perfectly nice."
She pouted. "But what kind of mother does such a thing?
What kind of mother leaves her children for a *house?* She
belonged with her children. Do you know, she loved this
house more than she loved us. My brother Timmy and me.

My father. My poor father. But Tim! Tim would have been able to forgive her. That wasn't right."

"From what I saw, your mother loved you very much."

"Loved me?" she repeated, incredulous. "What do you know about it? Love! Love, do this, Love, do that. Love, take your medication. Love, don't wear so much lipstick. Love, you're better off living with your father . . . as if it mattered to *her* where I was better off!"

Love, I thought. The way she kept saying it, so sarcastically, struck me as odd. Struck me as familiar. *Love.*

L . . .

A shudder swept through me.

L was Love.

Jean was *L.*

It fit. She was old enough. She could have written those strange letters years ago and she could have written the more recent ones, too.

"Better off!" The calm had suddenly left her voice. "Better *off.* With him! Maybe so. I loved my daddy." She smiled tenderly, remembering. "He taught me many things. Some things a father should never teach his daughter. He broke the rules. That's probably why he died so young. He loved me more than he should have. After my mother broke his heart, he loved me more than he loved anyone, even my brother. But *I* loved my brother. I loved him most of all. It was a suicide, you know. But everyone thought I did it. It was a suicide . . ."

"Of course it was a suicide." I tried to sound soothing, edging my way to the passage. It was time to get the hell out of there. Way past time.

"*Of course?*" She smirked. "Like you would have *any* idea. Where do you think you're going?"

"It's getting stuffy in here," I said, trying to sound natural. But my teeth were chattering.

"You'd better get used to it." I heard the click and then I saw the gun. I didn't know anything about guns, but I could see it was the real thing, though with its long shiny barrel and its pearl handle it looked like a fancy toy. Jean drew it slowly out from under her jacket and held it up, directed at my face, point-blank. I could actually see the bullet in the chamber. And I wondered how I could have been so stupid as to walk, or crawl, rather—straight into this trap.

"Because," she continued, "You aren't leaving this room for a long, long time. After you die this house becomes mine. In spite of all your meddling, Mother's money will never go into this house. I managed to forestall Mother's plan to give this old place to some charity. I needed the money, so I decided Mother would have to sell the property. But I had no intention of letting anyone else have it, not for long. I had no idea *you* would make things so complicated."

"Did you murder your own mother, Jean?"

"I thought you would be an easy foreclosure. But you turned out to be so intrepid! Who would have thought a young girl like you could be so stubborn. And, I must say, you don't scare easily."

Well, I'm scared now.

"I left the kettle boiling on the stove," I said, suddenly remembering it.

"Good try," she smiled. "You *are* good. I'm very impressed with you. God knows how I tried to frighten you away."

So she had infiltrated my life from the inside out. She had easy access to my personal belongings, my personal papers, my clients' phone numbers. It was all beginning to make an absurd kind of sense. Even the absence of the strange persecutions during the months Brand was in Nepal—that would have coincided with her stay in the hospital. And now I knew it was a mental hospital.

"If anything happens to me, the house goes to my brother," I said. "Next of kin. Not you."

She ignored that. "I thought it would be easier for both of us if I didn't have to put you out of your misery. But you wouldn't take a *hint*—would you? And then you became friendly with mother. You just wouldn't mind your own business."

All the while she spoke she was tending to me: pushing me down on a chair, stuffing a gag into my mouth and tying me up, awkwardly, since she was holding a gun on me at the same time, the hard steel mouth of the gun touching my skin with its coldness. She used duct tape. I calculated our relative strengths. She was smaller than me, and older. She seemed to be a rather capable woman, but I didn't think she could be all that strong. It wouldn't take much to overpower her. But the fact that she had a gun in her hand and seemed quite comfortable using it gave her a distinct and paralyzing advantage.

She stepped back and tilted her head, studying me critically as if she had just given me a haircut.

"I think that will do. I'm going to wait until the middle of the night. That way there is less of a chance somebody will hear the shot. Not that it matters, really. They'll never find you, not in time. And they won't find me. Nobody knows I came here. It's the perfect crime." She laughed, making her fingers of her free hand into quotation marks around the words *perfect crime*.

"Not that I'm a criminal. I'm not. I have no desire to hurt anyone. I would have made you see, eventually, that you don't belong here. But now that she's gone, it's too risky for me to wait. Sometimes I felt like I was her. Sometimes I felt like I was you. I *was* you, *for* you. Do you understand? But I'm not as crazy as they think I am. I know both of us can't be her. Both of us can't be you. Not for long, not for long. Still, when I was you I thought, maybe I shouldn't destroy the house. Maybe I should just destroy *her*. First my mother, then you. But would that be destroying myself, if I am you? Because I am. Like when I got your mail. I thought—why shouldn't I read her mail if I *am* her? Oh, don't bother trying to figure it out. Nobody understands me."

She took a letter from her pocket and dangled it in front of me. It was addressed to me, with Yolanda's name above the return address. It was already sliced open. "Yolanda," said Jean. "Do you know I knew her mother? Yes, indeed. I spent the summer here, one summer years ago. The summer that priest was strutting around like the cock of the walk. He could have had either of us. He picked her. That was his mistake."

Jean took the letter out, unfolded it, and read it out loud.

She read it in a strange, droning sing-song, which was a
strange contrast to Yolanda's casual phrasing:

Dear Stacy,

*I didn't realize I'd miss you so much. I miss the
mountains too, living here with my aunt in Santa Monica until I get a job and my own place. At least the
ocean is nearby. Anyway, since I've been gone, I've
been thinking about what I said when I left, and I feel
like maybe I was avoiding the issue. I think you deserve to know what's going on. Not only that, but I'm
worried about you. I think you might be in trouble.*

*I don't remember if I ever told you about how my
mom died when I was seventeen. I was on my own,
with no money, no education. I knew who my daddy
was—my mama never kept it from me—and I went to
him for help, after my mom died. Simple as that. I
showed up and said, I'm looking for Father Daniel.
He said, I'm Father Daniel, how can I help you?*

*Well, Father is an appropriate title for me to use
with you, I said, (sort of a smart-ass seventeen-year-
old) because it happens that I'm your daughter.*

*He just looked at me, for a long time, stared into
my eyes. I think he was looking for my mother. When
he didn't respond I said, in my nervousness, I haven't
got money and I've got nowhere to go.*

*I hadn't planned to ask him for anything. I told my-
self I just wanted to get a look at him. But he took me
at my word and figured he better come up with something. He offered me the job of caretaker. He never
asked me to lie, but it didn't take a genius to figure the
only way it could work was if no one had a clue who I
was, that I was his daughter. It made sense to me. And
it didn't feel like lying, at first, because he was no father to me. He was just some friend of the family who
happened to be a priest.*

*It seemed like an ideal situation. I loved having my
own little cabin in the woods. The work suited me, taking care of the church grounds, doing light repairs on*

*the buildings, keeping them painted, stuff like that. I
didn't go to mass, usually, not having been raised a
Catholic, but I enjoyed having Daniel around to talk
to. We acted just like we'd agreed—even between the
two of us, there was never anything said about our
real relationship. Then one day I ran into Mrs.
Shapiro and she looked me over good. I think she
could tell who I was just by looking at me. I guess I
look like my mother. She didn't say anything, but I told
Daniel about it, and he told me that when my mother
had become pregnant with me it was Mrs. Shapiro
who had helped her out, helped her to find a new situation in another town, but there had been some kind
of rivalry between my mother and Mrs. Shapiro's
daughter. It was the first time I got the feeling this situation might be too good to be true. The old lady next
door could blow our whole scene if she wanted to.*

*But Daniel said just chill and see what happens.
And the old lady went about her business, and we went
about ours, and I realized she was going to leave us
alone. And everything went fine until the last couple
months before she left for the nursing home. I went
over to see if I could help out, which I did every now
and then. Mrs. Shapiro's daughter answered the door.
She took one look at me and boom. I knew she knew.
She stared at me as if she wanted to kill me. She said
it right out, "You're that priest's bastard, aren't you?"*

*After you bought the old Shapiro place, I caught
her one day, sneaking around the back of your house.
I thought it was strange of her to be there when you
weren't home, but I really wasn't that alarmed about it
or anything until she told me that if I said anything to
you about her, she would make sure everybody knew
about me and my father.*

*And that's when you two met up, because you came
home right then. I have to admit I was glad to leave
her to you. She seemed to calm down and you two
seemed to be getting along, so I thought, okay, everything's cool. But it bothered me. I didn't know what*

she was so afraid of, why she would threaten me. I went to Daniel and asked him about it. He said she was psychotic and that she had shot and killed her little brother in the dining room of the old house the summer I was conceived.

I told him about her threats to expose our relationship. He shrugged her off, saying she probably wasn't a danger to anybody but herself. He thought the killing of her brother was probably accidental, as it had been explained at the time, though there was some question as to whether it was an accident or murder. He didn't think there was any need to run out and tell you anything. He thought it would just disturb you unnecessarily.

So, at first it was like, okay, we'll leave it alone, which was a relief. I didn't want my nice situation to end. But since then I saw her on other occasions. I saw her the night of the Halloween party—it was so weird, she was just sneaking around. I think she even came into the Barn that night, disguised as a ghost. Creepy. That night Daniel and I had an argument about it—he said he'd changed his mind, it was time we warned you about her, and he didn't care if she let out that he was my father. But I talked him into not saying anything. I was afraid I'd be out of a good situation, and that it could wreck his career. And so I never told you about it. But it made me realize it all was bound to end someday, and so I started making other plans. Because it wasn't fair to Daniel, and it wasn't fair to you. And that is why I'm writing to you. Because I think you have a right to know. I wanted to warn you, Stacy. I mean, maybe she's harmless, but you never know what might happen, right?

Jean didn't bother to read the rest of the letter. She folded it up, gave me a smile. "You never know what might happen," she repeated. "*Right?* I think we've heard enough of that. It's funny they don't realize the tunnel ends right behind the chapel. They don't even know about the door there, down the steps by the laundry. They think it's just part of the wall."

She put the gun on her lap a moment and lit a cigarette, a long, slender, brown cigarette that filled the room with the thick, pungent smell I would forever after associate with her and the nightmare hours of that night.

I could be dead by morning, I thought, astonished. But I felt a perverse relief to know, at last, who my tormentor was.

She hoisted the gun again, blew out a breath of smoke. "You're probably wondering how I even knew she was that priest's bastard?" Jean said conversationally, as if we were sitting at the kitchen table having coffee together. "My mother doesn't exactly keep me filled in on the news."

I could be dead in any moment.

"But I make it my business to know things my mother would rather keep to herself."

She laughed quietly to herself. And then she began to sob.

"Oh, Mother," she cried softly. "Oh, Mother." She said that over and over again. Finally she stopped and the room was silent and the cigarette smoke slowly settled.

I became confused by time. Hours passed.

Or was it only minutes?

I thought about something Brand had once said, when he talked about the avalanche he had survived, how he thought he had thirty seconds to live, and so he had to make those thirty seconds the most fulfilling thirty seconds of his entire life. But in the avalanche, he had been rushing toward death. Here, in this secret room with a killer, I had to sit and wait for death to come to me.

Chapter Twenty-Five

W E BOTH HEARD the sound at the same time and our heads jerked in unison toward it—the vibration of a door closing somewhere in the house, a voice calling.

Brand! I screamed into the handkerchief stuffed in my mouth, knowing he would never hear me; but I was able to kick my foot out a few inches and knock over a pile of books next to my chair. She merely held the gun closer to my head and checked my bonds.

"Don't waste your last moments struggling," she said to me. "He can't hear you. You could be screaming without that gag and he wouldn't hear you. I know. I've tested it. You've never heard *me*, have you? And I've done it all—screamed, yelled, cussed you out. Just a few yards away from you from within your *own home*. And you never knew it, did you? I even played music, sometimes."

After a while there was another vibration of a door shutting somewhere in the distance of the house.

No God please don't let him leave.

"I can be patient," she was saying. "Though I think he's

gone now . . . you know, even if they find your body, they won't ever find me. You'll be dead, and the house will be mine. If they have to find you, they'll find you. But they'll see you killed yourself. They won't blame me. If I burn down the house, they won't even find your body."

There it was again. The sound of Brand's voice, calling out my name. And another voice, higher . . . Tess?

The vibrations of people in the house were unmistakable, and they didn't fade. Jean began to look nervous. Things weren't going quite as she had planned. They were already looking for me.

But how would they ever find me in here? They wouldn't even think to look.

THE NIGHT MUST have nearly turned to day, but it was impossible to tell. Every moment was interminable. The voices had finally gone away and I was unable to keep sleep from descending upon me like another level of hell. I jerked awake every few minutes, the horror washing over me. Every time I opened my eyes she was still sitting there, smiling at me.

"Patience," she said pleasantly.

I dreamed. I dreamed of Russ, and our parents, playing in the water. Floating down the river in Yosemite Valley on a blow-up raft. Playing softball in the cul-de-sac. I dreamed of Asilomar, where, as a young girl, I had first seen the work of Julia Morgan and knew I would become an architect. I dreamed of the mountains and the ocean. And I dreamed of the waves pounding on the beach as the man I loved arched above me, the contraction of his muscles curving him into me, hips cleaving, the bracing muscles of his shoulders and arms tight and hard above me, the strength of his body a primal force, earthquake or hurricane . . .

Another vibration from somewhere in the house alerted me awake from my twilight doze, and Jean too, I noticed, for she jerked her head and her gun up—for a moment it wavered crazily in the air until she steadied it, aiming at my heart.

There was a scratching sound and a thump on the wall behind me.

"He doesn't give up easily, does he?" she grumbled, and suddenly her passive expression widened into shock as there came the metallic rattling sound of a lock mechanism and the door opened behind me. Someone was entering from the passage.

I felt his presence like warmth. The barrel of the gun swung away from me and pointed behind me, at him. I couldn't see him, but I knew it was Brand she was aiming at now.

"Put the gun down, Jean . . ."

I felt the caress of his hand on my shoulder, and I heard his voice softly chanting, "Give me the gun, Bonnie Jean. Give me the gun."

She looked as forlorn as a child, and the gun wavered.

We heard more voices from outside the room and she knew her plan had failed. Her whole body was shaking violently, and in desperation she pulled the trigger aimlessly and the gun went off, a blinding, deafening, explosion.

Brand let out a grunt; he stumbled and fell against me, knocking me to the floor still tied to the chair.

That moment was the worst of them all: the everlasting moment before I knew he was all right.

He pulled himself up beside me and tore the gag from my mouth in one motion. His shoulder was torn and bloody.

"Brand—" I gasped, and then I saw her, standing above us, raising the gun again, steadier now. She was aiming at Brand point-blank and her finger was pulling back the trigger. Aided by a giant surge of adrenaline, I lifted and swung my legs around, clubbing her legs with my legs and the chair still strapped to them. She went down and the gun spun out of her hands. Brand lunged for it and in an instant he had it trained on her.

He stripped the duct tape off me with the help of his Swiss army knife, and managed to free me while holding the gun on Jean. His wound must have hurt like hell but he didn't seem to notice it. "Get out of here, Stacy," he said quietly.

"But—"

"Get out! I'll deal with her—you get help!"

I reached out for him before I slipped out the little door into the passage, my hands shaking, careful of his bloody shoulder, desperate just to touch him once again.

Tess met me outside the room. Father Daniel was there, too. Tess put her arms around me protectively and held me. She had called the police when she'd heard the shots and already I could hear the sirens in the distance.

"God, Tess, he's in there with a madwoman!" I heard my voice high and trembling.

The sirens grew louder until they stopped right outside the house. The flashing lights lit up the woods with a weird throbbing effect. I ran outside to meet the officers, breathlessly explaining the situation. One of them was Brand's friend Officer Henderson. It turned out they knew something about Jean. It wasn't the first time the police had occasion to deal with her.

I led them into the library, and they went into serious police mode, guns drawn. Officer Henderson called out into the passage, exchanged words with Brand, and disappeared within.

More police arrived with their wailing sirens. Never had there been so many people in the old house. Another officer went into the secret room. One took me aside for more questioning. Another was talking to Tess and Daniel.

But where was Brand? I was so worried I could hardly think to answer the questions I was being asked.

At last he emerged from the passage, no longer holding a gun. He gave me a smile, full of love. His jacket was torn and drenched with blood, and he was drawn and exhausted-looking, but never had he looked so beautiful to me. I had to hold myself back from dashing up to him and flinging myself upon him while was talking to the officer on guard outside the room.

It seemed the sirens would never stop. More and more officials were arriving. When they finally brought Jean out of the hidden room, she had degenerated into hysteria. As they led her through the house to the patrol car waiting outside, she caught sight of Brand and began screaming: "How did you find it? How did you *know?* No one knew about that room—*I* wasn't even supposed to know about it—only my mother knew about that room!"

"Only your mother," Brand said with a sigh. "And me. I built it for her."

And they took her away, looking so lost and forsaken I could almost pity her.

"We'd better take a look at that arm, sir," said one of the paramedics who had appeared on the scene. "Looks like you've lost some blood."

"Yeah, okay," Brand said, and he did look pale. "But first I'm gonna kiss my girl."

He started toward me and I ran to him. And I didn't care who saw that we were together—by now a rather large crowd had formed—I was so utterly grateful to be alive and to have him alive, both of us alive, at the same time in history, on the same planet, in the same place—it seemed such an amazing and miraculous thing.

He shrugged off his injury as nothing, but of course I was happy to make a big deal of it, coddling him and nursing him and touching him, every chance I got.

Chapter Twenty-Six

YEARS PASSED BEFORE I spent another night in the old house. I never stopped loving the place, but now it was tainted with associations that would take a long time to dissolve or mellow. Jean was put back into the hospital, and it wasn't long before we heard of her death. Mrs. Shapiro's wishes were granted; a modest trust was established for the care of the house. But still I didn't think of moving back in. It was the birth of our second son that convinced me it was time to give up my superstitions and do the practical thing. We needed the space.

We had outgrown the Barn, but I would always be grateful for it. Brand brought me home with him that night, and from then on the Barn was home to me, too. Tess moved in with Tom, and Saul found himself another woman willing to support him—we didn't see much of him after that. So Brand and I had the Barn to ourselves until Ian was born.

Our boys, of course, have no problem with the sinister, secret room. They love showing their friends the hidden door and the little passageway. They relish telling the story of the night their mother was trapped in the secret room with a homicidal maniac until their father came to the rescue.

Brand told me later he had decided he wouldn't bother me that night, to give me some space. But that resolution had lasted about twenty minutes. To hell with *space*, he had said to himself. *I want her now.* And he had come looking for me.

The front door had swung open when he knocked, and he came in to the house, calling my name, perplexed to see the place empty and the tea kettle rocking away on the stove, empty of water. He turned off the burner and waited around for a while, but when I didn't appear, he went home. He came back later, and still I was gone. He went through the house, searching for me, and this time he noticed the book lying open, the gothic romance novel Mrs. Shapiro had given me.

He thought it was strange, that I had disappeared, that I had left the tea kettle boiling, and that I happened to be reading the book Mrs. Shapiro had shown him years earlier to describe the room she wanted built. Brand went back out into the night, and he paced up and down the porch, thinking. He was beginning to put it together. He went and got Tess, asked her to come with him, to watch his back.

At first he thought I had entered the room alone and locked myself in. But when he got into the chamber and saw Jean, he wasn't entirely surprised. Daniel had mentioned to him that Yolanda had seen Jean sneaking around my house. They were both aware of Jean's past, and both were suspicious of her motives. Later, both Brand and Father Daniel confessed they felt terribly guilty for not having warned me about Jean. They thought they were protecting me from having to worry about her.

Brand and I were married a year later, surrounded by family and friends, on the patio in the woods, joining our lives—and our properties—at last. By then I no longer worried that he desired me only for my house. Tess had told me that when Brand began to suspect what had happened to me, he had exclaimed, in his frustration and impatience to get the panel door open: "I'll find her, Tess, if I have to tear down this fucking house to do it!"

I secretly prized those words.

When Brand brought me home to the Barn that night—actually, it was morning by then—he hardly let his arms fall away from me, so eager was he to help me feel secure and safe again. He settled me down on the sofa with a cup of hot tea. He wrapped my legs in a blanket. He was the injured one, his shoulder done up in white bandages, yet he was still tending to me. He started out of the room and I called to him.

"Brand . . ."

"What is it?" he laughed softly, and returned to me, took the cup from my hands, set it down on the table. He slid beneath the blanket next to me and gathered me in his arms. "What's wrong?"

"I don't know," I said, embarrassed. "I just didn't want you to leave me."

"Stacy, as long as you will have me, I will never leave you."

"Never? But Brand, you *never* say never."

He slowly drew the tip of his finger over my lips, curious and sensual, his eyes candid, fixed on me intently, and he smiled. "My love," he said softly, "I'm saying it now."